SHE BURNED WITH A FIRE THAT SEEMED TO CONSUME HIM...

With all the skill of a practiced torturer, she enjoyed her conquest, sitting between his legs, holding him in both hands, her mouth opening and shutting, her teeth gleaming and disappearing behind the licking red tongue, until he thought he would burst. But with the certainty of knowledge, she timed his thrust, turning on her hands and knees, away from him, yet still reaching behind herself to guide him, to feel his belly pressed against her buttocks.

> And still she laughed. She was a savage, bloodthirsty cannibal, and she delighted in destroying. She taught him to use his mouth and teeth on every part of her body, and she cared not where he made his entry so long as she felt him in her and against her.

But how would he know where pleasure ended and sin began? Or did sin belong here at all, in this enchanted, heathen place? Could he sin with a girl who had torn a living man to pieces with her teeth . . . ?

CARIBEE

CARIBEE

by

Christopher Nicole

Library of Congress Catalog Card Number: 73-78130

Published by arrangement with St. Martin's Press, Inc.

SIGNET TRADEMARK REG. U.S. PAT. OFF. AND FOREIGN COUNTRIES
REGISTERED TRADEMARK—MARCA REGISTRADA
HECHO EN CHICAGO, U.S.A.

SIGNET, SIGNET CLASSICS, MENTOR, PLUME AND MERIDIAN BOOKS
are published by The New American Library, Inc.,
1301 Avenue of the Americas, New York, New York 10019

FIRST SIGNET PRINTING, JULY, 1975

. 11 12 13 14 15 16 17 18

PRINTED IN THE UNITED STATES OF AMERICA

Contents

CARIBEE

1

The Tower

Rebecca stirred, sighed, and raised herself on her elbow. "It is dawn, Mr. Warner."

Thomas Warner rolled on his back, glad of the company, at last. After ten years of marriage she still called him "Mister," still considered herself the fortunate, dutiful bride. Sarah had never been so. But then, Sarah had married a boy, a soldier in all the glory of a recent campaign; she had loved and laughed as an equal. Especially laughed. And she had died before the boy could reach manhood, still laughing. Her smile was the last thing he remembered of her.

And on days like this he remembered Sarah's smile above all else. "It has been dawn for three hours, woman," he grumbled. "The month is June." June, in the year of Our Lord 1618. Fifteen years since the death of the queen, as it was twelve since the death of Sarah. An eternity, reaching back to when the world had been young, for it also meant that for fifteen years the country had endured the whims of the Scotchman.

Rebecca was not abashed. She had anticipated ill humor this morning. Now the bed creaked as she moved across it. No bed had ever creaked for Sarah; she had been light as a feather, a wisp of a girl. Rebecca would have made two of her; she very nearly made two of her husband.

"I did not know you were already awake, sir," she said. "I, too, have watched the light grow." She lay against him. Heat welled from her body into his. Her legs, long and strong, trembled, eager to cross his. Her hands, dry and aided by powerful fingers, slid on to his belly, awaiting only the invitation to move lower. Her lips were close to his ear; they would be full and red, and backed by a questioning tongue; her hair, thick and straight, not dark enough to be brown and not pale enough to be gold, clung sweat-wet to her head and shoulders; her surprisingly small nose nuzzled his neck. What more could a man want from his wife? What more had he sought?

He turned his head, and her lips caught his for a moment. Still she was not distressed by his disinterest. After ten years, she knew she had but to be patient, and stay close to him in the naked warmth of the bed, and her day would yet begin as she wished.

What more, save fire in her eyes as well as her belly. He had been introduced to her by Rich. They had been friends as boys, when their fathers had been plain William Warner and Robert Rich. The Warners had remained gentleman farmers; Rich had gone to court to serve his queen and be rewarded, but his son, however important a man the Earl of Warwick might have to be, had never forgotten his childhood playmate. He had rescued Tom Warner from the wreckage of Leicester's army and secured for him the most coveted position open to a penniless soldier, the captaincy of the King's Guard. And then he watched the young captain lose his confidence, at once in himself and in his future, with Sarah's death, and had pronounced judgment, as he was so fond of doing. "You must marry again, Tom," he had declared. "And I know the very girl. You'll have met Payne, the Dorchester merchant? His daughter. She'll make you a good wife, Tom. She'll bear you strong sons."

The future Earl of Warwick was never wrong, at least according to his lights.

Tom moved her hands, rolled out of the tent bed in the same movement, and shivered as his feet touched the stone floor. Only rushes, throughout the Tower of London. He would not have his chamber any different from those of the prisoners.

"Mr. Warner?" Her voice was anxious.

"I could no more enter you this morning than I could fly, sweet." He crossed the room, his nightshirt tickling his ankles; he was shorter than the average, but with thick shoulders and muscular legs; if he had given up active soldiering close on a decade ago he had made sure that he remained, at forty-one, physically able to embark upon a campaign at a moment's notice. His features were rounded, and at first sight even soft, but there was stubbornness in the flat mouth, and vigor in the blue eyes. Both hair and beard were worn short; the dark brown remained untouched by gray. He stood at the window to look down at the courtyard. His empire. The window itself was hardly more than an arrow slit, yet through it he could see the green where so many noble men and women had lost their heads, and behind, the bulk of the Beauchamp Tower. Already the sun was high in a cloudless sky, giving promise of a splendid summer's day. But there was no summer inside those bleak walls, not for prisoner, and not for jailer. Another of Rich's pronunciamentos. To solve a situation he had not properly understood.

"I see you, Tom Warner," he had said, "captain of the King's Guard. Can there be a higher summit to the ambition of any gentleman? Why, man, think of your predecessors. Your own grandfather, Tom Jerningham; Walter Raleigh . . ."

"Who now languishes in the Tower," Tom had protested. "And they guarded women with the hearts of men. I . . ."

Rich's finger had crept to his lips. "You'll be speaking treason before you know it, Tom."

"My lord, it will be forced upon me. To hear his Majesty gargle, to be sprayed with a spit at a range of twelve feet, to watch his tongue ballooning, is an exercise in disgust. And by God, sir, should he ever seek to slip his hand inside *my* breeches . . ."

" 'Tis a fact you will never make a courtier, Tom, and that's a pity." Robert Rich had commenced to pull his lip, a characteristic which some supposed had contributed to the narrow, conspiratorial cast of his features. "Was there ever a monarch who lacked some fault? And I do not only speak of men, now. You worship her late Majesty because you only knew her from afar. Ask Master Raleigh, indeed, what she was like at close range."

"I am not likely to have that opportunity, my lord," Tom had replied. "As I am in Whitehall and he is in the Tower."

"The Tower," Rich had said, frowning, as he invariably did when there was some deep scheme boiling in his mind. "Aye, Walter is in the Tower, to be sure. You'll have heard of the troubles there?"

"The Overbury murder? They say it will even bring down his Grace of Somerset."

"*Her* Grace, certainly, Tom. There have been many awaiting *that* day. But Elwes is involved. Make no mistake about that. There will be a vacant lieutenantship, soon enough.

What say you, Tom? There is a world you can make your own. No dandies, no penis-pulling monarchs, no damsels who would tease you to distraction, no banal pronouncements given the accolade of genius because they happen to echo some long-forgotten sentiment. There *you* would be king, Tom, forced to acknowledge only that there is a superior in Whitehall, much as you are forced to acknowledge that there is always a superior in heaven."

For Robert Rich, if no friend to Raleigh, had certainly imbibed too many of the atheistical opinions expressed by that wayward genius.

Rebecca stood at his shoulder, at twenty-eight a perfect statue of naked femininity, perhaps lifted from the very studio of Michelangelo. "You make too much of it, Mr. Warner. Mr. Walkden is a traitor. Traitors must die."

"To bed, woman," Tom snapped. Even an arrow slit could allow a peeping gaze. In any event, he could hear feet on the corridor outside.

Rebecca heard them too, and scrambled back beneath the blanket, at the same time reaching for the shawl which lay across the foot of the bed and wrapping it around her shoulders. Thus the greater part of her breasts were left bare, but this was no more than was sported by Queen Anne herself.

And it was only Mother Elizabeth, with the boys, already dressed, and Berwicke.

"Mama," Edward shouted. "There's to be an execution." Nine years old, he was her son in every respect, already almost as tall as his father, with the promise of similarly broad shoulders and clear blue eyes, in his case well set off by the fair hair and big friendly features of the Paynes.

"Who told you that, boy?" Tom Warner demanded from the window.

Edward checked, and flushed, and glanced at Mother Elizabeth, to whose skirts little Philip, only four, clung with both hands.

"It was my fault, Captain," Berwicke said. But then, Berwicke could take the blame, knowing that Tom Warner would never hold a fault against him. Berwicke was almost an old man now, with iron-gray hair and the plainest of dress, not a ruffle nor a tie, not a trace of silk, nor even a sword, for all that he had soldiered with his master through Ireland and Holland when they had both been young men. "I gossiped before Mother Elizabeth."

"Death is not a matter for children, Ralph. You'll attend me."

"Will you not breakfast, Mr. Warner?" Rebecca asked.

The lieutenant shook his head. "I doubt I'd keep it down, madam. I'll take a glass of wine before I go."

The oaken door closed, to shut out the whisper of the awakening prison. Mother Elizabeth freed herself from Philip's embrace and set the boy on the bed; immediately he crawled toward Rebecca.

"Captain Warner is too good a man to play the jailer." Having delivered both these lads, and the three stillbirths as well, Mother Elizabeth was as intimate with her mistress as Berwicke was with his master.

"He has hardly been himself since he came here, and there's the truth." Rebecca closed her arms around Philip's head, pulled his face into her breasts. She loved to feel him gnaw at the teats. By now there should have been another toothless mouth to give her comfort. She craved it. But Tom was not the man he had been. And surely this gloomy pile of stone was to blame.

"Traitors, traitors, traitors," Edward shouted, jumping up and down at the window. "Mama, is it true that when they took down Mr. Trevalyan and attended to his privies, he spurted juice on them?"

"God's mercy, boy, but hush your mouth," Rebecca cried. "Were your father to hear you I doubt not he'd take his whip to us both. Begone with you and your foul tongue." But as her gaze shifted from his face to Mother Elizabeth's, it was all she could do to prevent herself bursting out in laughter.

Edward scuttled through the door, banged it shut behind him, and paused for breath. He stood in a wide, deep stone corridor which ended in a flight of steps leading down to the guardroom. From the window on this side he looked out at the Thames itself, brown and impatient, rushing toward the sea. Not fifty feet away he could see the steps at Traitors' Gate; often Berwicke would take him there to cast their lines, and wait for a careless bream, confused by the speed of the water and the increasing saltness. Once, indeed, they had been there when a boat had arrived with a prisoner, the Duchess of Somerset, wife of the king's own favorite, and condemned for murder. "Will her head be cut off?" Edward had whispered to Berwicke, as they had bowed low and doffed their hats.

Berwicke had chuckled. "Not hers, lad. But it would make a pretty sight."

The duchess had not given them a glance. She had arrived in a towering rage, and she had remained in a towering rage ever since; her apartments were the only part of the huge prison barred to the boy. But elsewhere he was permitted to roam as he wished, to march the walls and pretend he was defending the castle against a horde of rebellious barons, to finger the weapons in the armory, to talk with the prisoners when they were exercised, famous men and women, lords and ladies, who knew his father as Tom because of his years as captain of the King's Guard, and who all had a word for the lieutenant's son.

And he had explored the green, where stood the block. He had examined it the day after an execution, and found it hardly changed, save for the trampling of so many feet. But he had not been permitted to witness the deed itself. On those dreadful days, when Father was never less than angry and often wild as a bull, the children were confined to their rooms, and the windows were shuttered. Edward could not understand why. To chop off people's heads, or to see that it was properly done, was the lieutenant's responsibility. In the name of the king. And surely, as the reverend said so solemnly, it was no more than a temporary inconvenience, as head and body would be mysteriously restored only seconds after the ax had fallen, up there in the vault of heaven. It had occurred to Edward Warner more than once that heaven must be scarcely less than an enormous workshop.

Nor had he ever been allowed downstairs into the chamber where lay the Duke of Exeter's daughter. This was one of his great ambitions. Indeed, up to but a year ago he had supposed that mysterious dungeon to contain a real woman, although as the duke in question had died more than a hundred years ago she must by now be a pretty hag. But now he knew better. Down there were the instruments which procured the truth from the villainous traitors who were imprisoned here. And the rack was given the name of a woman because on it a man was placed as Father lay on Mama—Edward had watched them through the keyhole in their bedroom door.

But today there was no confinement, and as yet Berwicke had not gone to the schoolroom; he would be standing at the upper windows. Cautiously Edward tiptoed down the broad stone stairs, listening to the growing hubbub. Mr. Walkden had no noble blood, and therefore was not to have his head chopped off, at least, not until sundry other things had been done to him. Things Edward had overheard Berwicke discussing with Mother Elizabeth. Horrible things, which made his juice fly. And thus Father was in more of a rage than ever.

Perhaps with reason, this time. Mr. Walkden was a pleasant fellow. He was learned, had followed the profession of schoolmaster, could converse in brilliant style, and was, indeed, now paying the penalty for having conversed a shade too brilliantly, with his noble Majesty as the butt of his remarks.

Edward reached the iron-bound door to the lieutenant's quarters. It stood ajar, and beyond, the gate to Tower Hill also stood open. There were people out there, an immense crowd of merchants and apprentices, and their women, come to watch the show. For it was time. The guard was mounted, Captain Warner at their head. As the day was already warm, and promised to become even hot, he wore no cloak, but his best crimson braided doublet and breeches, with its falling ruff settled neatlv on his shoulders. His stockings were lost in the brown leather boots which were all the rage, and his hat was a brown felt. His gloves were leather too, and Berwicke had polished the faded and well-used hilt of his sword. Of all his father's possessions, Edward most worshiped the sword. It had killed wild Irishmen in the bogs of Killarney, and it had slashed at haughty Spaniards among the sand dunes of Walcheren. Not anymore; nowadays there were no wars. King James did not believe in them. Soldiers were nothing more than fops, strutting their way through life, their effeminacy revealed by the thin, useless Spanish blades which were all they wore.

The cavalcade moved through the gate, raising a spray of dust from their hooves. Behind came the foot guard in their brilliant red uniforms, carrying their halberds on their shoulders, their flat hats uniformly horizontal. If Father had accomplished little else, he had brought discipline to the Tower Guards, and the beefeaters had sorely needed that. According to Mama.

In the midst of the guards, there walked another horse, drawing the hurdle to which Mr. Walkden's wrists were tied, not too tightly, to permit him to squirm without getting free, for this humiliation was but a part of the entire humiliating punishment. He had been stripped to his shirt, and was in this regard fortunate that there was scarcely any breeze, yet as his feet and legs and buttocks banged and scraped on the ground he could not help but twist and turn and writhe to give himself some comfort, and thus for the most part remain exposed to the gaze and the jeers of the crowd.

Behind him walked the reverend, his book open in front of him, praying. And now, as the procession moved down the hill, the crowd fell in behind, setting up a loud chant. They surely had no cause to love Scotch James, who had proved himself but a shadow of what they had come to expect in a monarch, and a mean, timorous, and vicious shadow at that. But here was spectacle, and a challenge to speculation. Would Mr. Walkden die like a man, or a shivering cur? Many a wager passed on this point, and on other, less savory aspects of the coming execution. Even the guards remaining on the gate had forgotten their duty, and were inquiring the odds and calling their bets to the eager touts outside. Edward gazed at them, at the dusty street down which the procession had gone, and felt excitement and a distinct nausea. Neither would be abated by roaming the walls this day. Out there was the world, and the terrors of the world, too. He was allowed out only twice a year, to the Midsummer Fair and for the Christmas Eve drive through the snow to Uncle Edward's farm at Framlingham. But today . . . he sucked breath into his lungs until they swelled, and darted through the gate.

"Hey," shouted one of the guards.

" 'Tis Master Edward," shouted another, and started forward. "Come back here, Master Edward."

But Edward was already into the last of the crowd, swallowing dust, dodging around feet and breeches and skirts. The guards had no chance, now. The crowd might taunt Mr. Walkden to his death, but they would brook no interference with *their* pleasures from the king's men. Cudgels and fists were waved, and rather than risk a riot the discomfited beefeaters retired to the gates of the Tower.

The procession went down the Strand, contained now by the two steep walls of houses, while dust and heat and noise rose into the still morning air, and hung there, a blanket of obscenity over an obscene occasion. Edward felt choked by the stenches of unwashed bodies and uncleared refuse, of belching breaths and dripping horse manure. True, the Tower often smelt as bad, but never in such volume, such concentration. He wondered how Mr. Walkden, virtually at ground level, breathed at all. Perhaps it would be better did he not.

Perhaps he would wish to be taken off immediately, to be spared the humiliation of the gallows. But Mr. Walkden was lost to sight behind the forest of people. And soon enough the procession, gaining numbers every moment, reached Charing Cross, and could there explode into the fields beyond, swelling out on either side, to converge on Hyde Park, like an advancing army. Here they were joined by the ale sellers and the sweetmeat distributors, and the day took on the aspect of a gigantic picnic. The citizens of London Town, *en fête*, to see Mr. Walkden taken off.

Now there was more room, to see and to be seen. Glances began to be thrown in Edward's direction. Not on account of his age; there were sufficient children in this mob, and sufficient babes even at breast. But his clothes were a shade too fine. He belonged on one of the horses which were beginning to appear in the lane close by the park, mounted by brilliantly clad ladies and their equally gorgeous husbands or lovers, hurrying ahead of the procession to be sure of a good place once Tyburn was reached. Because there it was already, the waters of the stream trampled and muddied by hoof and foot, the sweat and the stench and the noise slowly settling as the crowd waited for the fun to begin.

Edward saw his father, sitting rigidly on his horse, flanked by his guardsmen, immediately before the raised platform on which stood the gallows. To the right, up wind of the mob, the ladies and gentlemen had also gathered to enjoy their pre-breakfast sport. The mob itself was all around him now no longer pushing and heaving, but anxious to listen and watch.

Mr. Walkden was released from his hurdle, and escorted up the steps to the gallows. Out of town a slight breeze had come up, and it ruffled his shirt, revealing his legs, long and spindly, too white, and appearing to tremble. Undoubtedly he was afraid; his face was pale and his hands shook. He stood between the executioner and his assistants, and when the sentence was read he broke out into a violent shivering, while tears rolled down his face. The crowd booed and whistled, and Edward found himself shouting with them. But now his throat was dry, and he had the queerest feeling in his belly.

The reverend did his talking, and then stepped aside. The crowd stopped its noise, and waited for Mr. Walkden to speak. Mr. Walkden took a step forward, and stood on the edge of the gallows. His mouth opened and closed, opened and closed, and someone shouted, "He's lost his tongue," the remark being drowned in a howl of contempt.

Mr. Walkden turned, shuddering, and the executioner stepped forward, to drop the noose around his neck and adjust the knot, for there could be no mistake here. Many a man had cheated justice and the spectators by managing to break his neck or suffocate before he could be let down. Mr. Walkden stared into the crowd, his shoulders heaving now as he sobbed; he seemed to be staring directly at Edward, but surely he was crying too hard to see. Edward had the strangest desire to wave, but he wished Mr. Walkden would show more courage.

The executioner gave the signal, and his two assistants heaved on the rope. It ran smoothly through the pulley, and the slack was taken up. Mr. Walkden stood on tiptoe, and seemed to be sucking air into his lungs, and then his body stretched, and his feet left the boards, and he swung a good six inches clear, his shirt now flying freely in the breeze, his privies hanging for the last time, his face turning purple as his eyeballs bulged. But the executioner was signaling again, and the rope was being slackened. Mr. Walkden's feet touched the boards, and his ankles and then his knees gave way; he sank forward onto his face. But then his head jerked. He had not even been rendered unconscious for a moment; no more than a few bright lights had blazed in front of his face.

The crowd roared in anticipation. They too could see how alive he was, how responsive. They jostled each other and cackled happily as the executioner's assistants came forward, one to seize the condemned man's shoulders and the other to control his legs.

Mr. Walkden's shirt was around his neck, and his body was naked from the chest down. But there was no life down there, not even when the executioner laid hands upon him. Not even a twitch. And no juice. Berwicke had been wrong about that. Or perhaps some men were more virile than others. But there was life in the brain. Mr. Walkden began to scream, in a high, thin voice, and his body awoke and arched itself this way and that, so that the executioner's assistants had to use all their force to hold him steady while the sharp-bladed knife was drawn across his groin and the triangle of lifeless flesh was raised on high, to be greeted with cheers from the crowd. Edward's stomach swelled, and continued to swell as Mr. Walkden's screams grew louder, for following the castration must come the disembowelment. And suddenly he hated everyone in the crowd, everyone in London, even Father, sitting his horse so stoically. How he wished he possessed a sword, and the strength of a hundred men, so that he could charge to the rescue. Except that it was too late.

The people around him began to laugh, as the boy vomited, while still staring at the horror in front of him. Almost he seemed to hear the rush of air from the punctured belly, and then he could stand no more, and he turned, to burst his way through the clapping hands and the stamping feet, to run from the throng, to return, breath pounding, Mr. Walkden's screams still ringing in his ears, all the way across the park, along the Strand, homeward, to collapse, panting, at the top of Tower Hill.

"You'll enter, boy." Berwicke looked unusually grave; his round cheeks had lost their gleam, and his chin for once appeared from the middle of the rolls of flesh which surrounded it. He had served Tom Warner too long and knew too well his rages. Now he feared for the child.

Edward sidled through the door, and Berwicke closed it, taking his place behind his charge. Edward stood on one side of the huge, bare schoolroom, his father on the other, by the desk and the blackboard, gazing at the Latin phrase left from the previous day.

"You not only played truant, but you left the premises without permission," Tom said, without glancing at his son.

Edward saw the stick in his hands; his stomach started to roll once again. "Yes, sir."

Tom Warner turned. "To follow the mob?"

"Yes, sir."

"Why, boy?"

"I had never seen an execution, sir."

"There's reason enough, by God. And you've seen one now. Did you cheer and howl and whistle with the rest?"

Edward flushed. "No, sir. I . . . I vomited, sir."

Tom frowned. "Vomited? By God. Now there's a hopeful sign."

"Sir?"

Tom came across the room, ran his fingers through his son's hair. "I said hopeful. You'll have been the only weak-bellied lad there. Or female, I suspect. And that's to the good." His frown deepened as he saw the boy's bewilderment. "I have often enough felt like spewing the ground myself, on these occasions."

"But, sir, Mr. Walkden was a . . ."

"Traitor. And traitors must die. Oh, I do not quarrel with the law on that score, Edward. Traitors, felons . . . a man must serve his king and country, or there can be no room for him on earth. But to deprive him of his life is sufficient. To make a spectacle of it, to deprive him first of all of his manhood and then to butcher him before his own eyes, that is surely not fitting for a civilized nation."

Edward stared at his father, eyes wide.

Tom turned away once more. "You'll not understand. I scarcely do myself. I stand here, governor of this prison, determined to do my duty, while . . . I tell you this, boy, were there a campaign and a command to which I could attend, I'd be off tomorrow. And once I had thought a campaign the least pleasant of all earthly ills."

"And I'd accompany you, sir," Edward said eagerly.

Tom almost smiled. "Why, so you should, were such a thing possible. It could never be worse than remaining in this . . ." He changed his mind about what he would have said, and sighed. "So you vomited. No doubt you have been punished enough, on that score. But leaving the Tower without permission is the more serious offense, Master Edward. A man must learn discipline when he is yet a boy, or he will never be able to impart it when he is a man. And where would my future captain of the guard be then? You'll not leave these quarters for a month. You understand me, boy? Even that courtyard is beyond your reach, for thirty days."

"Yes, Father." He was not sure whether he wanted to weep from relief or from misery. Certainly he was happy to have escaped a whipping. But within this keep there was a sore absence of company. Philip was just a babe, and Berwicke was always too much the schoolmaster. And it was June, the best month of the year.

He walked the brief area of battlement every day after his lessons, and brooded at the city. But the city had lost its charm. When he looked out there, he saw less of the great lords and their fine ladies, their magnificent horses and their long Spanish blades, now, than of the grinning, odorous mob which had followed Mr. Walkden to the end. If he had been relieved to discover that his father felt much as himself, he was nonetheless frightened. His feeling had been a weakness. Was not Father's also a weakness? The more so, in a man.

Father had been a soldier of some fame. He was still, strictly speaking, a soldier. And indeed, when they had visited Uncle Edward last Christmas, there had been enough contempt in Father's voice and manner, at least on the journey there, for farmers and their pigs. Yet at the same time he quarreled with the sentences for treason, and perhaps even with the definition of the word. And at the same time preached discipline to his own son. It was a sorry world, confused and becoming more so. For if criticism of the king and his ministers was treason, then a deal of it was spoken. Again, after Christmas, when Mr. Merrifield and Uncle John Winthrop had ridden over to finish off the roasted sow, and the men had gathered in the parlor afterward to smoke their pipes and talk politics, the conversation had inevitably turned to the ruination the king had brought upon the country, and not even by unsuccessful wars, but by the extravagance of his court and his unseemly gifts to his many favorites, and by his high-handed treatment of Parliament. There had been the most tremendous quarrel, Edward remembered, with Uncle John saying that he no longer considered England the country it had been in Queen Bess's time, but rather a conquered nation, quite overtaken by the rapacious Scots, and that for his money he'd as soon remove himself and settle in the Virginias or elsewhere in the Americas; and Mr. Merrifield, to the horror of them all, declaring that the fault lay in the whole institution of kingship, and pointing out that in Holland they made do without a king at all, and could not be considered the worse for it.

Sentiments which had all but brought them to blows. Father had sprung to his feet in a rage. "The king is the king, and there's an end to it," he had declared. "There may be some kings who are better than others, but without a king England would no longer be my country, nor could I contemplate living in any country where such a state of affairs obtains. I'll trouble you to speak no more treason in my brother's house."

Mr. Merrifield had apologized, and the matter had been smoothed over. But whatever the truth of the matter, Edward preferred the dreams of Uncle John, of lands across the sea, of great forests populated with Indians with red skins, of acres of gold, of endless plantations of corn. Father scoffed, and pointed to the miserable fate of Mr. Raleigh's Virginia colony. But Mr. Winthrop had maintained that there would be others, and that the Virginias had suffered by bad organization and careless selection of the colonists.

Endless quarrels. Endless differences. It was hard to believe, listening to the men talking, that England was not in a perilous state. But England would always be great, because of the sea. Even the solutions offered by Uncle John Winthrop depended on the sea. By walking around a corner of the battlements, Edward could look down on the river, hurrying under London Bridge, racing for the estuary and the North Sea, and beyond, the world. He was going to be a sea captain. He had long decided this, privately. Father might grumble that there were no men nowadays like Drake and Frobisher and Hawkins of his own youth, that indeed there were no opportunities for men like those. But the opportunities would come again, and meanwhile there was the sea itself, and its highways.

Even the river was a highway. He looked toward the upper reaches, where lay Hampton Court, and watched the barge coming downstream. No ducal barge, this, but a plain affair, although it contained soldiers; he could see the June sunlight glinting on their helmets and from their halberds. A prison barge, bringing someone to take up residence in the Tower. Then there might well be a noble lord or his lady aboard, having fallen foul of his Majesty or my lord Villiers.

Edward leaned through the embrasure to watch the boat as it came alongside the steps below. Traitors' Gate, for those the king would condemn without the knowledge of the citizens of London Town. Father was down there, dressed in his best, with a guard of honor to receive the new arrival.

The prisoner stood in the stern. He wore a broad-brimmed hat, and beneath it a dark blue velvet cloak over a similarly blue doublet and breeches. And boots. But no sword, and Edward realized that his dress was quite lacking in jewelry, as his fingers lacked rings. And now he removed his hat, as he stepped ashore, and filled his lungs, and looked up at the forbidding gray walls, and seemed to smile. His face was long and a trifle thin, and his beard had speckles of gray, although it remained carefully trimmed into a fashionable point. His skin was burned by tropical sun and endless wind, and lined with years of misfortune and endeavor. And yet he smiled, and with his smile the morning came alive.

Edward left the embrasure and raced toward the staircase leading down to the family's apartments. He panted, missed a step, and landed on his hands and knees, regained his feet, and burst open the door to his mother's withdrawing room. "Mama," he shouted. "Mama. Mr. Raleigh is back."

The door to the huge, vaulted chamber stood open; Tom Warner and Walter Raleigh had been friends for many years. And the chamber gave an echo. Thus by kneeling at the nearest corner in the passageway, hard by the stone staircase, Edward could hear every word that was spoken, and more, he could watch Raleigh himself, standing by the barred window as he lit his pipe, although his father was out of sight around the buttress.

"I should say welcome back," Tom said. "But I doubt it would be well received."

Raleigh sucked on the stem. "There are worse places than this tower, Tom, although you may not believe it."

"We had heard, of course, that you were sighted off the Lizard. After Whitney's calumnies, and the rumor that the court believed much of them, we had expected you'd stay at sea."

"And become a pirate? Not my way, Tom. In any event, if Whitney is to be faulted for deserting me, I doubt he related much save the truth. 'Tis my fortune to attract an evil fame."

"And yet, as I remember, you sought no fame at all. Was it not a city you looked for, and not even Spanish, but inhabited by Indians of such ignorance they use gold for their every need because they lack any other metal, and yet are quite unaware of the wealth they squander?"

Raleigh smiled, a humorless widening of his lips. "The storytellers have been at it again, I see, Tom. No, no, nothing so fabulous. But there *is* a people beyond the Orinoco, who indeed know the value of gold, and possess it in abundance. Thus they suppose it is a gift from the gods, and who knows, they may well be right."

"No blasphemy, Wat. I beg of you."

"No blasphemy, Tom. I had forgot I was home. These people, then, in honor of their heathen god, make a sacrifice to him once in every year. The sacrifice is at once human and rich. For they take a sacred youth, and after paying him due ceremony throughout the year, they gild him from head to foot in the marvelous metal, and on the appointed day they row out into the center of the lake which is near their city, and cast this man of gold, *El Dorado*, into the waters, where the weight of his metal suit very rapidly takes him to the bottom, and the god is made happy, and so their harvests are made good."

"Fanciful, Wat."

"Oh, indeed. But it is their belief. And has been their belief for untold ages. So, once in every year, some unfortunate boy has been cast into the waters of that lake, clad from head to toe in gold. Now, imagine, if you can, dear Tom, what the bottom of that lake must be like. A solid carpet of gold-clad skeletons. An expanse of wealth to pay the debts of even Scotch Jim and his friends. And their friends as well."

"If this wealth can be recovered."

"A simple matter, I do assure you. This is a lake, not a Scottish loch. It is not deep. Indeed, on a fine day, with the sun high at noon—and on what days in that magnificent climate are there not blue skies and a hot sun?—it is said you can see the metal, gleaming twenty feet beneath the surface. Now, it is probable that these people will resist the removal of their offerings, but if Cortez and a few dons could take Mexico, are Englishmen to be stopped by a handful of naked savages?"

"If the place and the people do exist."

"They do, Tom. I have heard this tale corroborated by too many men, Spaniards and Dutchmen, priests and soldiers, even the coastal Indians of the Guyanas themselves. Why, this city of golden people is even named on the maps. Manaos. It is there, all right, Tom."

Edward listened to his father knocking out his pipe on the wall of the chamber. "But you did not find it."

"I did not get within a measurable distance of it, Tom. I will not bore you with my misfortunes. Suffice it to say that I must be the most unfortunate of human beings. No sooner had we reached the Orinoco than I was laid low with fever, of a virulence I had never known. Indeed, I thought that I would die. And surely it would have been better so. I placed Keymis in command. You remember Lawrence Keymis, Tom?"

"Very well. You could hardly have made a better choice."

"I had forgot his impulsiveness. I sent him up the Orinoco with five ships, while I stayed and suffered with the other. He was to find Manaos, Tom. Nothing more. This I swear to you as lieutenant of this tower. But he came across a Spanish settlement, was challenged, and attacked them. Men were killed, Tom. My promise to the king was broken. When Keymis returned, I was finished."

"You, Wat? It seems but a slight misfortune, so to affect a character like yours."

"Slight? You have not asked me what sort of a lad young Walter has become?"

"I had heard a rumor, which I do not believe. . . ."

"He is sunk deep in the Orinoco mud, Tom."

The chair scraped as Tom Warner got up. "Walter?"

"He died with Keymis. No doubt I was more ill than I had supposed. God knows he was hardly less impulsive and hot-blooded. But when I heard he was killed, I lost my head for a while, and said things I do heartily regret. And thus I lack the assistance of Lawrence as well."

"But you said he came back to you?"

"And went again, when I railed at him, and took his own life. There was nothing left for me there, Tom. Whitney had already left. I followed his example and sailed home."

"Knowing that you would be returned here?"

Raleigh shrugged. "It seemed likely. After all, there was a fight with the Spaniards. Depend upon it, Gondomar will complain. 'Tis another misfortune that his own brother was in the Spanish force on that occasion, and was killed. You'd not suppose this world small enough to admit such a coincidence. But it happened, and so Scotch James must keep me locked away for a spell. But God knows, and he must know, that I am past conspiring or antagonizing the court of Madrid. It will only be for a season."

Tom Warner strode the room, to and fro, pulling at his lip. "And your wife and other son?"

"I have seen neither Lizzie nor Carew since my return to town. I was whisked down here with some speed. And to say truth, I wish a day or two to compose myself. I have spent the entire voyage home endeavoring to compose myself, and yet I find it hard. Wat was ever her favorite."

"Aye," Tom said. "Well, be sure that you have but to ask and it shall be yours. And when you wish a message conveyed to Lizzie, you have but to say that too. And I will endeavor to discover what is the mood at court concerning you."

"You worry yourself needlessly, but as a good friend, Tom. I do not know what I should do without you. It seems to me that in these days I have too few friends."

"Now, that is a consideration you should bear always in mind," Tom recommended, and turned toward the door, so sharply that Edward had no time to withdraw. "Holloa," he shouted. "A spy, by God." He ran down the corridor, whipping his sword from its scabbard.

Raleigh came at his heels. "From the court, you think? Villiers?"

Edward stood his ground, but his knees trembled against each other.

Tom put up his sword. "No," he said. "Our local vagabond."

Raleigh stooped before the boy. "Can this be Edward? When I left . . ."

"He was a babe of seven. Now he is a boy of nine and considers himself a man. Did I not confine you to the lieutenant's quarters, boy?"

"Yes, sir." Edward licked his lips. "But to see Sir Walter again . . ."

Raleigh burst into laughter. "He flatters like any courtier."

"And I shall whip him like any Scotch James out for pleasure," Tom growled.

"Please, sir," Edward said. To his surprise, his voice was steady. "I did but wish to hear of the Guyanas, sir, of the Orinoco and Manaos and the man of gold, sir. I am sorry."

"By God," Raleigh said. "He has a memory. And an interest I would wish had been shown by my own. I shall intercede for him, Tom, as I am sure you shall intercede for me at court. God knows, I will be lonely here, as you have your duties to attend. Spare the boy for my company."

Tom frowned, glanced from Raleigh to Edward, plucking at his lip. "You'll speak of your adventures. Of Guyana and the man of gold, Wat. Nothing more."

Raleigh flushed, and seemed about to protest, then thought better of it. "I shall be the most circumspect of men, Captain Warner." But the humor was gone from his eyes.

"Ten miles from the Guyanese shore, lad. Well, out of sight, anyway, it is that low lying, and the water turns from blue to brown. You think it is a heat haze, at first, for by now you are but eight degrees north of the equator. Then you suppose it must be shoal, and your vessel doomed to be stranded. But it retains several fathoms. You'll take a pipe?"

Edward fingered the long, thin stem. Father had never offered him a pipe. "But what is the reason, sir?"

"Why, 'tis mud, to be sure. You'll have no conception of the rivers, Ned. You see the Thames beyond that window? A great river, would you say?"

"Oh, yes, sir. There is none greater in the world."

"There speaks your Englishman. Here, let me fill that for you." Raleigh took the pipe, crammed the bowl with the folded leaf, turning it over and over again, yet making sure there was room for the air to pass between each fold. Edward stood at his shoulder, watching and wondering. It seemed a lot of trouble to go to for a few minutes of pleasure.

But whatever Walter Raleigh did had to have purpose. To be alone with him was to possess purpose. This day, as usual, the door was closed, and they were isolated by the window in the huge, empty chamber. There was a tent bed in the far corner, and Tom Warner had added a desk and a chair, and a stand for some books, but that apart the room was bare. Yet Raleigh filled it, with the immensity of his personality, with the glow of his dreams.

"But the Thames, lad, is nothing more than a stream, compared with the rivers of Guyana. The Orinoco, the Essequibo, the Demerara, the Berbice, the Courantyne, the Oyapoc, and then, farthest south of them all, and greatest of them all, so it is said, the Amazon. The word 'Guyana' itself means 'Land of Many Waters.' "

"What strange names, sir."

"Indian names, in the main. Not the Amazon, of course. It seems that the Spaniards discovered some warlike females in those parts, or so they claim. But those rivers, lad, are upward of several miles and more from bank to bank, sometimes lost to sight in the morning mist. So imagine, if you can, those great waters, all rushing toward the sea in unison, carrying their silt with them. 'Tis no wonder they turn the ocean itself brown."

"It must be a marvelous sight, Sir Walter." Edward took the pipe back, and cautiously sniffed the tobacco.

"Now you need tinder and flint. And I happen to have them here." There was a flash of flame and a puff of smoke, rising from the folded leaf. "There you are, lad, draw on that, and forget the misfortunes of this world."

Edward sucked smoke into his mouth, and promptly spat it out again.

"It takes time. As it takes time to traverse that country. Because the brown ocean is only the first of its wonders. On the shore you'll find forests such as you can never have dreamed. Trees taller than any castle in the world, packed so close together it is often impossible to make your way between, and where there *is* sufficient room for a man to walk, there nature has laid an endless snare of roots and indeed ropes, spread like a trap, to catch at your feet and send you sprawling. Nor is that the least. In the midst of these ropes and bushes there lurk a variety of horrendous creatures. Spiders, Edward; none of your fingernail-type insects, but bigger than a man's hand. They leap, feet at a time, and when they land, they kill. And snakes. None of your puny adders. Some no larger, to be sure, but where *they* strike, the victim is dead before a count of ten can be accomplished. Yet are these nothing compared with their larger brethren. Now, these, Edward—these can measure fifty feet in length."

Edward was so bemused by the suggestion, he swallowed smoke, and commenced to cough violently.

Raleigh smiled. " 'Tis a mishap you'll become accustomed to. Fifty feet, lad. You'd not get one end to end in this chamber. And these do not bite or sting; they wrap themselves around a man and crush him to a pulp, and then swallow him alive."

Edward stared at him, eyes wide.

"And there are cats, boy, bigger than anything you'll have seen, springing from tree to tree, and vicious as they come. And the waters of those rivers, why, for a man to fall into those brown depths is the same as if he were to put a loaded pistol to his ear. There are fish, no larger than my hand, truly, but with teeth like razors, and they swim in shoals of a hundred, a thousand at a time. They can strip a man to his skeleton in a matter of seconds. And there is another fish with a paralyzing quality; but touch it and your muscles solidify, so that you drown." He lowered his voice. "And there are dragons, lad. Water dragons, huge beasts, thirty, forty feet and more, wearing armored skins. You see them sometimes, swimming in the rivers, or more likely basking on the mud banks by the shore. Woe betide any unfortunate creature who comes within *their* reach."

"And do they breathe fire, sir?"

Raleigh chuckled. "Hardly, lad, as they live in the water. Perchance they have land cousins, but these I have not seen."

"But all these other creatures you have seen, sir?"

"Think you I would report on rumor? Yet I would not have you suppose this land is too dangerous for living man. To be sure, there are men there already, Indians, the sweetest and most gentle of creatures, and comely, too . . . but you are too young for that. I would tell you of the land. These forests, these animals, these fish, and these dragons are but the guardians of its wealth. For beyond the forest, where the rivers dwindle to streams themselves, there is a paradise, Edward. The land is somewhat high, and uniformly so, except where it rises into mountain ranges. Thus the heat of the sun is a trifle mitigated. And of such a fertility as you never saw or could imagine, because there is a deal of rainfall, and the earth is already soft and receptive. There is heaven indeed, and there you feel close to heaven, Ned."

"And there is Manaos, Sir Walter?"

"Now, look, you have allowed your pipe to go out. You must keep drawing, lad. That is the secret. Manaos? Why, no, Manaos lies beyond even the great plains and the high mountains. Now, here I am forced to speak with hearsay. But if the forests are so tremendous, and the plains are so splendid, and Manaos is superior to all of that, why, boy, allow your imagination to roam, and think what Manaos must be like."

The boy sucked air into his nostrils. "And shall I ever see it, Sir Walter?"

"You can, provided you have the courage to brave the ocean and the forest and the jealousy of your fellow men. The Spaniards claim a monopoly there, given them by the pope. I would count myself neither a good Englishman nor a good Protestant did I accept *that* ruling."

"But the king would have peace with the Spaniards."

Raleigh left the window to pace the room, and then checked. "We'll not discuss his Majesty. I promised your father."

"But, sir . . ."

"Enough, boy. You'll to your dinner." He went to the door and opened it. And then smiled. "But visit me again tomorrow, sweet Ned. Without your company life would be scarce bearable. And leave the pipe. Your father would not approve of such modern habits in a child."

This day he was disconsolate, and lay on his bed, fully dressed, watching the smoke curl from his pipe toward the ceiling. The paper lay beside him. "Hard," he said. "I am forbidden the company of my wife and son until after my trial. Trial, bah. I have been tried before. This king carries his dissembling to extremes, to suit the papists, and he the champion of all the protesting nations. But then, he has ever been my enemy, and through no fault of mine."

Edward knelt beside the bed. "Tell me of it, sir. Of the king. Of yourself."

Raleigh glanced at him. "I promised your father, no politics and no religion."

"How can it be unseemly, sir, to discuss religion?"

"There's a point. And truly, I no longer wish to change heaven and earth. I have lived too long, and seen too much. But because, unlike so many of the time-servers that hold office, I have occasionally given myself the time to think, so have I dared, from time to time, to question, and to wonder, and when standing amidst the forests of Guyana, I wondered most of all. . . ." he smiled. "You have no concept of what I am speaking?"

"No, sir," Edward said. "Is it true that you knew the queen, sir? Mama has said so."

Raleigh swung his legs off the bed. "I was by way of being intimate with her on occasion. To my sorrow. Oh, mistake me not, Edward. I sought her love, because the love of that queen was the only road to preferment, and I was always anxious for that. But it was hard."

"Was she not as beautiful and as magnificent as they say, sir? Father will hear nothing but praise of her."

"Your father, Edward, is a good and faithful man. On occasion, perhaps, he allows his sense of duty, his awareness of his own reliability, to cloud his judgment. Indeed, I fear this tendency grows within him as he himself grows older. And yet, who is to say he is not right? He is at least a happier man than I. No, Edward, if you will swear not to repeat it, I will say that good Queen Bess was not the paragon she is remembered. She was a mean and vicious and spiteful little woman, and worse than that, she was old when I knew her. Yet vain. One had constantly to reassure her as to her beauty, and I would estimate that even as a girl she had little enough of that. Presence, aye. Willpower, aye. She could not be in a room but everyone was aware of it. And in a girl, or a young woman, this power can take a plain face and make it shine with beauty. But it cannot displace wrinkles, replace thin, ugly hair when there is none, or remove hair where there is too much."

"But it is said you loved her."

"Love is no more than a game, boy. Yet was she better than her successor?"

"Why does everyone hate King James, Sir Walter?"

Raleigh looked down at the boy. "They hate him, Edward,

because he too is mean and vicious and spiteful, but he, poor fool, lacks in addition the presence and the power. Oh, I am prejudiced. As I have told you, he has been my enemy from the start. I would not have had it so, but Cecil hated me, and Cecil had the king's ear. Thus have I languished here for fourteen years."

"But he let you out two years ago, sir. He will let you out again."

Raleigh sighed, his whole body seeming to swell and then sag. "That I doubt. Had Prince Hal lived, now . . . but I think I will remain within these walls until Scotch James is buried. Then I must look to my succor from Prince Charles. I know little of him, and I find it difficult to believe he can be the man his brother was. On the other hand, I find it impossible to believe he can be so small-minded as his father."

"It is treason to wish for the death of the king," Edward whispered.

"Why, so it is. But you'll not repeat it, Edward. And when you are grown somewhat, take the advice of an old man and seek not your fortune at court."

"How else may fortune be achieved, sir? My father's benefactor, the Earl of Warwick, has already promised me a page's place, whenever I am right for it."

"And your father approves of this?"

"I do not know, sir. I sometimes think my father approves of very little in me."

"You have an old head on those shoulders, Master Edward. It only lacks experience. Your father disapproves, as I know him. Even if he dare not show it. For this James is hated for another vice. All kings have vices. All men have vices, for that matter, but in kings they are more easily gratified. So many a man has lost his wife, or at least his possession of her, for a while, to a king. The Scotch James has not even that portion of manhood. Rather than slip his hand beneath a woman's skirts, he would prefer to delve in your breeches. Yours more than any, Master Ned; you are that handsome a child."

"Sir?"

"You have no conception of what I am speaking. Yet you are of an age to understand. Do you never feel a fullness in there? When close to your mother? When a pretty woman bends toward you? Aye, you do; I see it in your flush. And of course you count it sinful. Who knows? Yet it is all the pleasure, and all the beauty, a man may know. You tempt me yourself."

"Sir?"

Raleigh's head jerked. Almost he had been speaking to himself. "Aye. There is the small matter of my promise to your father. I tell you this, Edward, and remember well my words. Kings are but ordinary human beings, blessed with what virtues we all possess, and cursed with what vicious passions we all suffer. And when they die, Edward, like us they wither into dust, and smell most disagreeably while doing so. Only by virtue of their births, they are enabled to influence better men than themselves, to bring some down, and to elevate others high. Yet after all, there is no man who ever lived and got the better of his king. So give them a wide berth, Edward. Now put away your pipe; I hear footsteps."

Edward scrambled to his feet and faced the door as it swung inward to admit his father. Tom Warner looked unnaturally grave and carried a paper in his hand.

"You'll leave us, boy."

"Now, why drive him away, Tom?" Raleigh asked. "He is all the comfort I possess, or am likely to, while Scotch James dispossesses me of my family."

"He will dispossess you of more than that, Wat. This is a grave matter." He handed Raleigh the paper.

"You wish me to read this, Tom? It is addressed to the lieutenant of the Tower, and marked secret."

"Read it," Tom said.

Raleigh sat on the bed to peruse the document, at first with only a faint frown, but then with a slowly increasing gathering of his brows, while the color began to drain from his face, leaving only the yellow stain of the suntanned skin behind. "Is this some royal humor, Tom?"

"Not so. Think you Scotch James knows humor, Wat? Oh, no, regardless of the outcome of your trial, he orders me to prepare for your execution. And on a sentence fourteen years remitted."

2
El Dorado

Tom could not spy the stag, but the hunt itself was easily found, from the baying of the hounds, the cries of the beaters, and the halloos of the horsemen. He sat his horse on a low hill and watched the cavalcade straggling across a brook which formed a tributary of the Thames, forcing their horses through the shallow water and over the boggy land, using whip and spur to bring them out onto the firmer earth of the meadow beyond. Mud flew with water, splashing velvet doublets and lace frills at collar and cuff; hats were askew and scabbards slapped thigh and haunch; booted feet jerked in the stirrups, and then the leaders debouched from the swamp and came galloping toward the thicket below him.

Tom picked up his own reins and urged his horse down the gentle slope. No need for him to hurry; he would arrive at the foot long before the rout which approached him. And indeed, from the edge of the meadow it was a sight to make all but the stoutest heart quail, as the multicolored huntsmen spread their ranks, waving whips and fists at the sight of this intruder who seemed to be placing himself between them and their prey.

He drew the back of his glove across his forehead to remove a layer of sweat; he was under no misapprehension as to the risk he was running. But the bulk of the chase he could ignore. He was concerned with those in the middle, and more especially with the two who rode at the head of this center group, not faster than their fellows, certainly, but nonetheless permitted to lead. They made a peculiar contrast. On the left the rider was young, tall, and well built, bareheaded and with long dark hair flowing behind him in the wind. His clothes were velvet, crimson slashed with gold, so that he created a blaze of color amid the blues and greens which surrounded him; the diamond clasps on his doublet winked like miniature lanterns. He sat his horse like a Charon, viewed the morning's proceedings with a contemptuous smile, only now beginning to fade into a frown of disapproval as he saw his way barred.

His companion slouched in the saddle and swayed, giving the impression of being tied into place, as indeed he was. His clothes were a muddy brown, on which the dirt kicked up by the horses around him had made but little impression, and he wore a tall hat firmly secured under his chin. His beard straggled and his mouth flopped open, and his arms seemed to lack strength as he vainly pulled on the reins to stop himself charging full tilt into his lieutenant of the Tower.

Fortunately, there were aides on either side to seize his bridle and bring him to the halt. His horse dug its hooves into the soft earth, and the muscles rippled up its legs and into its belly, as it commenced to pant, while the whole mighty army around it also came reluctantly to a halt, gasping and steaming.

"Whoa," my lord of Buckingham remarked. "A messenger from the grave."

The king shuddered and all but dislodged himself. Although it was only the middle of the morning, his face was already suffused with wine, or perhaps the flush remained from the previous night. If so, it was a lack he seemed determined to correct. He waved his hand, and a page rode forward with a flagon. "Warrrner?" his Majesty inquired, and drank deeply. "Ye'll no say the folk are rrioting?"

Tom replaced his hat. "London Tower is as quiet as any man could wish, sire. Indeed, I left it before it had even awaked."

James drank some more. "To come out here and do awa' wi' me sport? Och, ye're a daftie, Warrrner. Steenie, he's a daftie."

Buckingham was smiling again, but this time there was more venom than contempt. "You'll seek to be an inmate of your own cell, Captain Warner?"

"I came out here, sire," Tom said, choosing to ignore the duke, "because I have waited three days for an audience, and been granted none. From Whitehall I rode to Windsor, to be informed your Majesty will conduct no business this week."

"And ye'd break in on me few hours of sport?" James

cried. "Awa' wi' ye, man, awa'. The beastie will ha'e gone to ground."

Tom drew a slow breath. The older this man got, the more incredible was it to believe that his mother had been known as the most beautiful and accomplished woman in Christendom. That being so, it was too easy to believe all that had been said of his father. But Darnley had also been handsome; that was acknowledged even by his enemies. And when James had been a young man, there had been a certain nobility to his features, which disappeared only when he attempted to speak, and the raw Scottish brogue fought the overenlarged tongue to escape the loosely thick lips. Now the nobility was gone, sunk to the bottom of endless barrels of wine, untold midnight debauches with his favorites. Only the fool remained, in brain as well as appearance. But the fool held so many lives in the palm of his hands.

"Sire, believe me, this is a matter of great importance. Sir Walter Raleigh . . ."

"Wha'? Wha'? Ye'd mention that man's name to me? A traitor, who'd see us at war wi' Spain? Ye've sons, Tommy, man, would ye watch them dying to gratify Raleigh's ambition?"

"Sire, it was no doing of Sir Walter's. He lay sick abed at the time."

"He's no daid? Dinna tell me he's daid, Tom. I maun ha'e his haid. I promised Gondomar. God's blood. I'll ha'e it off if he's in his grave."

"I spoke of the battle on the Orinoco, sire. Sir Walter is in perfect health at this moment. I but sought to intercede with your Majesty for his life. To kill such a man, sire, and purely for the gratification of the Spaniards . . ."

"Ye'll preach to me, Tom? God's blood, ye'll be asking for a place in the kirk, soon enough. Be off wi' ye, man. Back to your duties. There's a stag out there."

"Sire . . ."

"Steenie, ha'e him moved. Ye've nae right, Tom, nae right, to interfere wi' a man's pleasure."

"Get away, you fool," Villiers hissed.

James made to urge his mount forward, and Tom laid his hand on the bridle.

"Wha'? Wha'?" cried the king. "Ye'd stop me, ye rascal?"

"Sir Walter can come to no harm in the Tower, sire. He'll not escape."

"He dies, and there's an end to it. Ye'll not trouble me again. Tom. I'll not ha'e it."

"Then you'll have another lieutenant to do your bidding, sire," Tom shouted. "I resign my post." He pulled his horse aside. "Now, get to your stag."

"You're a fool, Tim Warner. A good friend. The best a man could ever dream of possessing. But a fool." Raleigh filled his pipe with great care, and Edward stood on one leg. He had not expected to hear any man call his father a fool and survive.

But Tom was nodding. "Perhaps, Wat. And yet I'd be a criminal were I to stay here another day. I have not the stomach for it. I only grieve for you."

Raleigh sucked, expelled smoke, sucked again. "I'd better enjoy my pleasures while I may, eh? But look at it this way, old friend. I have lived a full life. Fuller than most. Fuller than Scotch Jim, by God. There's more to it than licking a royal arse, male or female. I'd not have anything change, except maybe . . ." He smiled. "I'd have liked to have seen El Dorado. Even if I'd yet failed to bring him away with me. I'd have liked to have seen him. But you . . . what will you do?"

Warner shrugged. "I'll join my brother in the farming business. There's land enough."

"And think you that Suffolk will be sufficiently removed from Jamie's anger? Or if not his, for I doubt he will remember much of this morning, then from Villiers'? That young man has a vicious streak."

"Favorites come and go. I'll be out of sight and out of mind for a while."

"I hope you're right." He held out his hand. "Godspeed in whatever you attempt, Tom. You've the character for greatness, should you be given the chance."

"And you've a courtier's tongue, even in your old age, Wat. I can offer you nothing in return."

Raleigh smiled. "Leave the boy, for a minute."

Tom hesitated, then nodded. "You'll join your mother before the hour strikes, Edward."

"Yes, sir." He wanted to weep. But now was not the time. He listened to his father's boots hitting the stone floor, slowly receding, all the while gazing at his friend, who was again attending to his pipe.

"So, we must say good-bye. And this time forever, I think, Ned."

"Sir . . ." Edward licked his lips. "We'll meet in heaven, sir." The reverend was always saying things like that.

Raleigh glanced at him. "I should not count on it, lad. Better to forget me. Or at least, the man. I'd not have you forget what we've talked about these few weeks. You'll go to sea, Ned?"

"Oh, yes, sir. My resolution is made."

"Keep it from your father for the while. Tom has no use for the briny. And when you do take ship, sail west. There's where a man can make not only his fortune, but his life. Be sure of that, Ned."

"I'll find your man of gold, sir."

Raleigh chuckled and clapped him on the shoulder. "You do that, lad." He held the boy by the shoulders for a moment, and kissed him on the mouth. "Now you'd best be off. We both have a distance to travel."

No crowds in Suffolk. No buildings either, and even the low hills lay hidden beneath the drifting snow in this winter of 1621. It had blown for three days and nights, an easterly gale which had gathered all the cold of the North Sea and laid it evenly along the eastern coast, obliterating farm and copse, river and village. But now the wind had dropped, and instead of the constant howl there was a silence as if the very world had come to an end.

It was a time to do. Not all of the cattle had been brought in before the onset of the blizzard, and even those got to shelter had all but perished in their barns. The men were out in groups, each commanded by a Warner, hunting for any strays who might conceivably have found shelter and survived the disaster. The children were forbidden to do more than wander the garden, where Mother Elizabeth and Berwicke were hastily compiling a snowman for their amusement. But this was, truly, children's entertainment. Suitable for Philip.

Edward climbed the stile at the back of the garden, and walked. He had a long stick with him, with which he prodded the ground, for he had no wish to fall into an unsuspected hole or to find himself plunging through the ice into the pond where Berwicke had last summer taught him to swim. He wished *he* were leading a search party; his two cousins were only a few years older, but they were treated as men, whereas he . . . At least this was one way to keep warm. Sweat poured down his face, and he could feel it gathering between his shoulder blades, beneath his layers of warm clothing. Although the sun was out, it contained little heat; it was the exercise, the energy required to lift his foot from one drift and place it in another.

And it was exhausting. He had walked better than a mile, he thought, and was out of sight of the farm itself, hidden as it was behind the snow hump which was the orchard. A mile. He doubted he would get back so quickly. But he had to keep moving; to stop to rest would be to freeze.

And out here, alone, he could think. There was so much to be thought of. Father. He was no farmer. His boredom was plain to see. He had brought no happiness to Uncle Edward, despite the apparent joy with which he had been received. He brooded, and remembered. Sir Walter? They had cut off his head, three years gone. Nothing more than that, at the least. Edward wished he could get Mr. Walkden out of his mind. But he also wished he had looked more closely. Then he would have had more to remember. But Sir Walter had been spared the ultimate humiliation, and he had died with the support of the crowd, calling down damnation on the head of Scotch James. And how many others had died since, or would die in the future? It seemed an odd way to rule a country, to execute every man who would think for himself. But the king would have it so. To think for oneself was treason.

Edward found himself stopped, and staring at the next shallow rise. Then, was he also guilty of treason? For thinking? Father, certainly. Father had quarreled with the king himself. When Uncle Edward had heard of that he had been aghast. But that was also some time in the past, and no doubt the king had forgotten about it. Besides, perhaps he knew Tom Warner well enough to be sure that the greatest punishment he could invent would be to leave that active spirit to stagnate in the marshes of East Anglia.

And at least Mama was happy. Recently she had been happier than Edward had ever known her, for all the lowering clouds of winter outside. Now she kept much to her bed, and yet she smiled, and laughed, almost as if she were nothing more than a girl. And her laugh held a great secret, which was undoubtedly shared by Father, if by no one else. Only when Father looked on her did his face soften.

Still he watched the ridge in front of him. There was movement on that near horizon. And now he saw the men, rising and falling in their saddles. The pair kept to the bridle path, where the snow was no more than a few inches thick.

"Holloa," he shouted. "Holloa."

They reined, and turned their heads this way and that. The leader wore a tall hat and a long cloak, in dark brown, and his boots were of a similar color. As no doubt would be his doublet beneath, for Edward had recognized him.

"Uncle John," he shouted, floundering through the snow. "Uncle John."

John Winthrop smiled. He had uncommonly tight lips, and wore his beard longer than was fashionable, so that the lower half of his face seemed to drop away when his features relaxed. "Edward." The smile faded into a frown. "You're too far from the house in this weather."

"It is so good to be out of doors, sir. But I'd beg a ride home."

Winthrop extended his arm. "Get up here, then. You'll have met my godson, my lord?"

The other man nodded. "When he was a babe, Mr. Winthrop. I doubt he remembers me."

Edward gaped. Now that the stranger's cloak had swung open, it was easy enough to tell that he belonged to the nobility; there was a great deal of velvet and lace under there.

"The Earl of Warwick, Edward."

"My lord." Edward hastily raised his hat.

"You're a fine lad, Edward," Rich said. "We seek your father."

"He is out for strays," Edward said. "But if you'll visit the house, I'm sure Aunt Jane will make you welcome."

"We'll do that, Mr. Winthrop," Rich decided. "Jane Warner's mulled wine is the best I've tasted. Just the thing for a day like this. And God knows we need some cheer."

He kicked his horse and sent it ahead, wisps of snow flying from its hooves.

"A grim man, Uncle John," Edward whispered.

"'Tis the title, not the man, Ned," Winthrop remarked. "Only grim men can survive the overheated air in Whitehall these days."

•

The fire blazed in the hearth and gave a tremendous glow to the huge room; its heat even managed to reach the far corners, and although it was only the middle of the afternoon, the flickering flames sent shadows crawling up the walls and racing across the ceiling. After all, the farm was that much more comfortable than the Tower.

Philip rode his cock horse to and fro before the blaze, singing to himself in a high-pitched voice. The men seemed not to mind. At the back of the room Mama and Aunt Jane and Mother Elizabeth sewed industriously, every now and again raising their eyes to smile at each other, for all the gravity of the men's talk. The table had been cleared of the remains of the side of mutton, of the capons and the tarts, of the ale, and in their places Berwicke poured the wine, and saw that it remained at a suitable temperature, while the scent of the spices filled the room. Edward chose to stay close to the table, for he had been allowed but a single mug and hoped for more; the entire day had become warm and friendly. And besides, from here, sitting next to the carved oaken legs, he could watch and listen to the men, without their apparently being aware of it.

Certainly they seemed to have much to discuss. The Earl of Warwick might pretend that as he was in any event on a visit to his Suffolk estates he had thought the moment opportune to visit his old friends, but no one could doubt that he had more on his mind than the festive season. Even Uncle Edward, who had grown uncommonly stout and seldom allowed much to disturb him—it had been his cattle gone astray during the blizzard, but it had been Father who had spent the sleepless nights—was looking grave as he sipped his wine. On this occasion, remarkably, Father looked the most calm, although he remained standing, an empty pipe in his hand; he used it more for punctuating his sentences than for smoking. Mr. Winthrop, seated by the table, his long legs thrust out toward the fire, to cause the steam still to rise from his boots, also looked tranquil enough; but then, this was his manner and his character. Not so the earl, who moved, restlessly, to and fro, stopping only to allow Philip to navigate between and around his legs.

"I but spoke my mind," Tom Warner said. "There's no treason when done to his face. He'd not find a witness against me for any other matter in this entire country."

"As if needs witnesses," Rich said. "Tom, you're a trusting man. You know your own honor, and you assume all others possess the same. 'Tis remembered your mother was a Jerningham."

"Better quality than the Warners, and ever faithful to the throne," Uncle Edward declared.

"Too faithful, Mr. Warner. Did not old Tom Jerningham raise these parts in support of Bloody Mary?"

"In support of his rightful queen, my lord."

"Undoubtedly. But she was a papist. As was he."

"All of seventy years ago, my lord. Since then all loyal men have changed their opinions."

"Which were a worthless statement to his Majesty. I beseech you, Tom, take heed of my words. I know not why I trouble myself, and here I speak the truth. You have ever been a wayward soul. Had you but conducted yourself as a courtier when I gave you the chance, you might have had a title by now."

"My lord . . ."

Warwick held up his hand. "I criticize in a carping spirit, Tom. The man in me honors your recalcitrance. The friend in me bemoans it. Shall I tell you why you are yet at liberty? It is just because you have nothing worth taking. Buckingham and his family have little interest in any criminal, even, be he not possessed of a thousand a year. Yet your name crops up at court, too often."

"Then you risk yourself, my lord, in coming out here," Edward Warner observed.

"Saving that no one outside this rooms knows that I *am* here, Mr. Warner, which is exactly why I made my visit in this manner. But I care little for myself, in this matter. For good or ill, Tom has been my friend for twenty years. I would he thought enough of me to take my advice."

"Which would be?" Tom demanded.

Warwick sighed, and shuffled his feet once again, and glanced at Winthrop.

"You'll remember John Carver, Tom?"

"I remember his name. Did he not flee to Holland to avoid the hangman?"

Winthrop nodded. "Leyden. With many others of his belief."

"Puritans," Edward Warner muttered.

"Their numbers grow daily. And not all take themselves to Holland."

"I do believe you're one yourself, at heart, John." Tom smiled.

"I believe in liberty of conscience, Tom. And so do you. As for the other, the worship of God is too precious a possession to be submerged beneath acres of incense and stained glass, to be managed by men who think more of the burden of their own table than the burden of their souls."

"Mr. Winthrop," Warwick said. "I did not come this distance for a religious dissertation, sir. Indeed, I shall pretend I heard not one of your words, and will be obliged if you would start again. But if I may give you a word of advice, as a friend, even Christ prescribed that a man should render unto Caesar what is his. So do you attend the church on a Sunday, and for the rest of the week believe what you will."

Winthrop's turn to sigh. "Yes, my lord. I did not mean to embarrass you. The fact is, Tom, Carver and his associates would leave Holland. They fear that they will become Hollanders themselves, and all appearances to the contrary, he is as loyal an Englishman as yourself. And besides, this dreadful war in Germany comes too close, with Spinola on the march. Carver has obtained a grant of lands in North America."

"Virginia," Tom said, with a contempt to equal his brother's.

"Not so. Farther north."

"The man's a fool. If Raleigh with all his experience could not make a success of the Virginia colony, where will Carver make a success of less hospitable clime? And there is not the slightest chance of his discovering gold there."

"He does not seek gold," Winthrop observed patiently. "Nor even wealth. He seeks a place a man may live, and be healthy, and worship God as he chooses, begging your pardon, my lord."

"And you'd invite me to ship with a Puritan? John, did I not know you so well, I'd take offense."

"He has need of fighting men," Winthrop observed mildly. "You'll have met John Smith?"

"An adventurer."

"A good man to have at your side, in a set-to. But Smith has none of your experience, Tom. Now, hear me out. My lord of Warwick feels that it would be a wise thing for you to leave England. Carver's band is the best available means at this moment, and it is a settled matter. They have even procured a ship. They will not turn back now. But Carver is not your future, Tom. I will let you into a secret. I also seek a grant, and it will not long be delayed now. There will have to be money spent on it, but it shall be done."

"You, John? You'd give up all this?"

"All what? A few farms? A certain solidity which all but

stifles me?" He raised his hand. "I'll say no more, my lord. Suffice it is that I see my future home in America. But it will take me a few years yet to prepare, and I doubt you have that long, Tom. Go with Carver, but be ready to join me when I call for you. You'll have experience of the terrain, of the conditions, of the aboriginals. You'll be my right arm, Tom."

"You have the devil's own tongue," Tom muttered, and glanced at Warwick.

The nobleman shrugged. "Mr. Winthrop and I agree that it would be best for you to leave England, certainly, Tom, and I further agreed to allow him first application for your services. But you are right in your estimation of the northern part of the Americas. A barren, bitter place. I have talked with those who came back from Jamestown. Yet is that vast continent the place of the future. I have also obtained a grant."

"You, my lord?" Even Winthrop seemed surprised.

"And why not? My colonists will at least not lack financial support. And my grant is for the lands surrounding the Oyapoc."

" 'Tis in Guyana," Edward cried, before he could stop himself.

The men turned to look under the table. Then Warwick burst out laughing. "Why, so it is, boy. You know your geography. But yet far removed from the Orinoco and the Spanish sphere. You'll remember Harcourt? He planted a colony there a few years back."

"And it died also," Winthrop observed.

"For lack of support. Now, Tom, my men shall do nothing of that nature. Roger North will command. He may be young, but he is ambitious and I have confidence in him. The fleet fits down in Plymouth, and will load for the better part of this coming year. There you have the only reason I'd not go down on my knees and beg you to accompany them. A year may prove too long for you."

"But in any event, Guyana is an unlucky place," Winthrop said. "You'd do better in the north, Tom."

Tom Warner looked from one to the other, and then at his wife in the corner, and smiled, which nowadays was sufficiently rare. "Gentlemen, you flatter me. What, two such brilliant men bidding for my services? To carry your swords for you? Mistake me not, I *am* flattered. Indeed, I thank you for your concern on my behalf, from the bottom of my heart. But, sir, whatever the faults of my ancestors, whatever the faults of my own quick tongue, I have served this king too long and too truly for me ever to believe that he would wish me harm. With due respect, my lord, I was quite unfitted for the lieutenancy of the Tower. I knew it ere I had been in residence a year, and yet I would not give it up, partly out of gratitude for your own great interest, and partly out of my own stubbornness."

"Tom . . ." Warwick began.

"You'll pardon me, my lord. There is another reason why I shall remain here, and hope to find better employment before long. 'Tis a secret *we* now reveal to *you*. I shall be a father this year, for the third time."

There was a moment's silence, and heads turned to regard Rebecca, who bent low over her sewing.

"My most hearty congratulations, Tom," Winthrop said.

"You'll accept mine as well," Warwick said. "And I would beg your forgiveness, and yours, Rebecca, for all this careless talk which would seek to deprive you of your husband at such a time. Then I will redouble my efforts on your behalf at court, Tom. As you say, his Majesty will not forget one of his most faithful servants, when it is put to him properly. We'll have you a regiment of foot before the spring. Now I will take my leave."

"You'll not spend the night, my lord?"

"It would be my pleasure, Tom, but I must be at court by noon tomorrow, which means that I must travel at least part of the distance tonight. You'll accompany me for a while, Mr. Winthrop?"

"Of course," Winthrop agreed, with some regret. "Again, my congratulations, Tom. Perhaps you'll ride over to visit me before too long."

Edward Warner heaved himself from his chair. "I'll see you to the door, gentlemen. 'Tis truly sorry I am not to have the pleasure of your company for a trifle longer."

The men left the room, save for Tom and Berwicke. Tom remained by the fire, shifting from foot to foot. "It had to be done," he muttered.

"And I have no grudge on that score, Mr. Warner," Rebecca said softly. "I would also say that my lord of Warwick and Mr. Winthrop spoke a deal of good sense. There is no future for you here. Were you to decide to join Mr. Carver's expedition, I would be more than happy."

"But . . ."

"Your brother and Jane will see that I do not want, and I could join you, with the children, whenever the babe is strong enough to travel. Depend upon it, there will be more ships traveling west should the colony prove to be a success, and should it prove a failure, why, then, will you not be back in short order, in any event?"

Tom smiled and held out his hand for another glass of the mulled wine. "You are a true wife, Rebecca, and would, I have no doubt, make a good pioneer. Nor did I for one moment suppose that you would oppose my departure. But truth to say, my sweet, I have no faith in these colonizing expeditions. God knows I value and trust John Winthrop above any other man, but he seeks room to practice his own religion and his own views on government, which are more than a little republican, although he would never admit it. He is himself the most tolerant of men, but you may be sure he will populate his colony with those of a like mind to himself, and these will lack his toleration. So we shall exchange the rule of king and bishop for that of elder and pulpit-thumper; the first pair is at least ordained and encouraged by God. As for Mr. North and his patron, they too play a false game. 'Tis well known that Harcourt's colony failed because the place is not suitable for tobacco on any scale. Warwick dreams of El Dorado, although he has more sense than to admit it."

"It is there, Father," Edward said. "Mr. Raleigh was convinced of it."

Tom glanced at his son. "Eavesdropper. No doubt it is there. But gold brings a man no more happiness than does tyranny. Indeed, they are but different sides of the same coin. Now, were someone to propose an expedition to a place where there would be no religious persecution, no grasping after wealth, no political adventures, no laws, perhaps, but the sheer good of all, well, then I might be tempted."

Rebecca smiled. "Then should you not apply for your own letters patent, Mr. Warner, and lead your own expedition?"

"Aye," Tom said. "Had I the slightest notion where to go. But every colony ever launched has seemed to depend upon the climate, the necessity to fight for existence, and more, to fight their fellow man, be he Indian or Spaniard, for survival. To begin with injustice were no way to found a paradise. I'll stick to my profession, and do the best I can with a regiment of foot." He raised his finger, as his wife would have spoken again. "And there's an end to it, woman."

But with the spring, and no news from town, he became restless. Rebecca was now beginning to swell, and some of her good humor had departed. The best of mothers and of wives, she needed the stimulus of sex to be also the best of women; Tom now avoided her bedroom, and she was left to Mother Elizabeth, who was inclined to fuss. With spring, as well, Edward Warner and his sons were hard at work from dawn until dusk.

"Farming," Tom said with a snort. " 'Tis downright slavery. I've a mind . . ."

"You'll not go to town, Mr. Warner," Rebecca said. "You'll not beg George Villiers."

Tom sighed and nodded. "I'll not. But you'll agree that in this imperfect world a man is nothing without patronage."

"And you have the *best* in the world, Mr. Warner, if you would be patient."

"Now that is not a characteristic of the Warners, my sweet. If I stay here I'll be fit for nothing. Would you spare me for a week?"

She picked up her sewing. "If I knew where you'd gone."

"To Plymouth. I know Rich is down there, fussing over his fleet. I have no doubt at all 'tis his preoccupation with this venture that prevents him giving thought to my problems, nor do I in the least blame him for that. But perhaps were I to be more in his sight . . ."

"A splendid conception, Mr. Warner." Rebecca put down her needlework and raised her head. "I'd have you know that you have not changed my mind, sir. Should my lord of Warwick have no cheer for you, or indeed, should he paint a more gloomy picture than when he visited here in the New Year, and should you in those circumstances decide to seek your fortune in a new land, be sure that you will have my blessing."

Tom laughed and kissed her on the forehead. "I am neither seafarer nor colonist, sweetheart. My roots delve deep into this muddy soil, much as I despise it. I'll prove my point. I'll take Edward with me. He is as restless as I am, and the journey will do him good. With that millstone around my neck, be sure that I will return."

Here was adventure. Edward was supplied with a horse—true, hardly more than a pony; but nonetheless, for the first time he would not have to ride in the wagon with Mama and Philip. And they were going a very long way, from Suffolk and the fens up into the low hills of Hertfordshire, then across the great Chilterns on to the chalk downs of the south coast, on, ever on, soon leaving even civilization behind them as they rode across the moorland of the southwest. The journey took upward of a week, nearly all day spent in the saddle, and through a variety of showers of rain and sleet and hail, for the month was only April and it remained chilly, and stopping for the night at the roadside inns, where Father and Berwicke would gulp their ale and smoke their pipes, and Edward, granted the dignity of a full tankard, would quietly drink himself to sleep, and dream of tomorrow.

He thought little of the country through which they traveled, for all that the land, just awakening from its winter sleep, was at its most beautiful. Green grass and green leaf sprouted everywhere, punctuated with brilliant wildflowers and occasionally a rose garden, all white and crimson and purple, adjoining inn and posting house; the copses were loud with birdsong, and the farms with the lowing of cattle. "What, leave this blessed land?" Tom shouted. "A man must be criminal to envisage such a fate." But Edward thought only of the sea, and there it was, six days after leaving home, a sight to drive the aches from his buttocks and bring him up in his stirrups with joy. The channel, and beyond, the Atlantic, seething whitecaps before a westerly breeze, pounding on the great white cliffs toward which they rode. For all his short life he had waited for this moment.

And of the ships. Never had he seen ships like these; three-masters seldom got up above London Bridge. But Plymouth seemed not houses built to accommodate a few vessels, but a town of vessels built to accommodate a few houses. Here was that seat of history of which he had dreamed for so long. Here Sir Francis Drake and his other heroes had played at bowls on the day the Armada had commenced its sweep up channel. Here . . .

"There is the boy in you," Berwicke declared. "There is more history in one stone of the Tower than in any ship ever built. And you did no more than scuff your shoes on those."

"I am going to be a sea captain," Edward insisted.

My lord of Warwick's fleet, five stout little ships, was moored alongside one of the innumerable docks which thrust their timbers into the calm water. The travelers stood on the quay and stared at the flagship, the *Great St. George,* in wonder, while Mr. North came ashore to greet them and explain the hustle and bustle which went on all around them.

" 'Tis amazing, Captain Warner, what a list of necessaries there is, for we must not only be fitted with the requirements of war, cannon and cutlass, pistol and ball, but with everything that we may need for daily life as well, tools and nails, food and clothing, for a considerable period. We have no idea how long a time may elapse between our departure from here and the reaping of our first crop. Why, before we leave, we'll have a full cargo of goats on board each ship."

He was a handsome fellow, surprisingly young, to Tom's eyes, tall and straight, and affecting plain clothes, although he was brother to Lord North.

"I'd no idea a colonizing expedition was such a venture," Tom confessed. "How long have you been at it now?"

"Four months," North replied. "And it will be at least two more before we are ready. But come, we'll take a glass of wine and I'll show you our maps."

"I had hoped to find my lord of Warwick here," Tom said.

"He was, but he was recalled to London on urgent matters. I expect to see him back again any moment, though, so perhaps your journey will not be wasted. You'll accompany us, Mr. Berwicke?"

Edward stood on one leg.

North smiled. "You too, lad. But you'll find us men uncommon tiresome, I have no doubt." He raised his voice. "Mr. Hilton."

The boy was not a great many years older than Edward himself, tall, with narrow shoulders, lank black hair, and a rawboned, rakish face, pitted with pox, and dominated by a thrusting nose and chin. It was not a handsome face, but there was strength in it, left the more obvious as he had not yet begun to sprout a beard. "Aye, aye, Mr. North."

"This is Master Anthony Hilton," North explained. "Captain Thomas Warner, Mr. Ralph Berwicke."

"Captain Warner, sir," Anthony Hilton saluted. "I have heard much of you, sir."

"He's a flatterer," Tom said, but he was obviously delighted.

"Indeed not, sir," Hilton declared. "I do wish you were accompanying us. 'Tis a fact we shall have need of fighting men."

"You've a large tongue in your head, Tony," North observed. "This is a peaceful venture, and there's an end to it. Now, here is your charge. Master Edward Warner. You'll show him the vessel."

"Aye, aye, Mr. North." The gash of a mouth split into a smile. "Welcome aboard, Master Warner."

"It is my pleasure, Mr. Hilton."

The young man gazed at him for a moment and then led the way up the gangplank and jumped down onto the deck. "Here we stand in the waist. 'Tis the main deck of the ship. Back there is the quarter deck, and farther aft, highest of all, the poop. Up there belongs to the admiral alone. Forward there's the forecastle, where the men have their quarters."

"She's so much bigger from here." Edward gazed at the brass cannon which peered at the closed ports.

"Oh, we've teeth," Hilton said. "Five pieces to a broadside, and a couple of sakers aft, with a falconer on the poop to discourage boarders. We'll not fall tamely to any Spaniard, you may be sure of that. But where we really have our strength is up there. Speed, lad. That's our secret."

They stood at the foot of the mainmast, and Edward gazed aloft into the forest of rigging and furled sails.

"Think you'd make the main top?" Hilton asked.

"It looks hardly higher than a stout oak," Edward said.

"And stout oaks mean nothing to your worship," Hilton observed. "Except that should you have to climb that one at sea, she'll be hanging sideways over the waves, and you'll be food for the sharks."

"Have you ever fallen overboard?" Edward asked.

Hilton glanced at him and flushed. "I'm to show you the ship," he said, and opened a door in the after bulkhead. Here was a large cabin, although so low that Hilton had to stoop and Edward's head all but brushed the deck beams. There was a table, bolted to the floor, and berths along each bulkhead. "The lads sleep here," Hilton said. "Gentlemen, you'll understand. We'd be ship's officers, in a normal crew. But we're colonists first."

"I thought you were the mate," Edward said.

Another quick glance. "Colonists first." Hilton went farther aft and down a short ladder. "Now, here's the tiller."

But the huge piece of timber leading to the rudder interested Edward less than the even bigger saker, protruding through the open port. And then the nearness of the water. Down here it was not six feet away. "Do the waves ever come in?"

"Often enough. 'Tis like a dark hole at sea, with the ports shut. You'll smell the tar?"

"It is pleasant enough."

"We're alongside. She'll take on a different aroma when we're at sea. We've a driving admiral, Master Warner. What thought you of him?"

"He looks like a sound man," Edward said.

"God's blood," Hilton remarked. "How old did you say you were?"

"I am all but twelve years old," Edward said. "And I have seen a deal of life. I knew Sir Walter Raleigh."

"Did you, now?" Hilton led him forward from the tiller, bending low to avoid the deck beams, and down another ladder into the bowels of the ship. Here there was a single lantern, and the smell of tar, added to the stench from a coal fire, welled around them, while they could hear the lapping of the water above their heads. "The orlop deck," Hilton said. "Where we store our food. You'll see those barrels? Salted beef, to last us the voyage. And biscuits. 'Tis bad enough now, but it will be far worse ere we have been a week at sea, when the weevils come crawling out of every mouthful."

"You'll not disgust me, Mr. Hilton," Edward said. "I have seen a man taken apart at Tyburn."

"Have you, now?" Hilton descended the ladder into the hold. "Yet I would say there is some difference between watching an event and participating in it. I doubt you'd do so well at sea, Master Warner."

"I'd do as well as you, sir," Edward insisted, following him down the ladder. Now he stood on an open grating, beneath which black water slurped to and fro in the bilges, while the stored casks of food and water rose around him on every side; but at least they could stand upright.

"You think so?" Hilton inquired. "Well, 'tis easily decided, if you have the nerve."

"You'll not find me lacking, sir," Edward declared, keeping a guard on his temper with difficulty.

"We'll see," Hilton decided. "Holloa, Ben. Dicky. Come and see our new mate."

They emerged from behind the barrels, where, Edward had to suppose, they had been lurking all the while. Thus Hilton had known they were there, both when guiding him in this direction and when beginning this conversation. Edward cast a glance toward the ladder, but Dick had already taken up his position there. And this pair he liked even less than Hilton; they were no older, but scarcely had so prepossessing features.

"He don't look the type to me, Mr. Hilton," Ben observed. "A regular mother's boy, he looks to me."

Edward licked his lips. Suddenly he was afraid. But his very fear gave him a desperate courage. "Tell me what I must do," he said.

"Oh, we shall do that," Hilton said, leaning against a barrel and folding his arms. "The secret of success at sea is comradeship, and determination, and silent courage. 'Tis a hard, uncomfortable life, but if you'd be a mate of ours you'd have to prove to us you can stand up to anything."

"I can," Edward declared.

"We'll see," Hilton said again. "You've that pot of tar handy, Ben?"

"Right here, Mr. Hilton." Benjamin produced the large pot out of the darkness. The liquid in it looked more like treacle, and was black and sinister, giving off a strong smell; it still smoked from the heat which had melted it.

"Now, we'll have your breeches down," Hilton said.

"What for?" Edward demanded, his voice trembling.

"Because, if you'd be a seaman, Master Warner, you have to learn to live with tar. We'll give you a coat, from your navel to your knee, and all the in-betweens, Master Warner, and we'll see how you react to that for an hour or two."

"It burns," Benjamin whispered in Edward's ear. "Oh, mighty unpleasant it is, Master Warner. But if you can stand it without crying for your mum, well, then, you'll be one of us."

The tears were already there, lurking at the back of his eyes, threatening to make the horrible day worse. "How'll I get it off, after?"

"Now, there's a problem," Hilton agreed. "You'll not be riding again this day, I hope? That'll be uncomfortable, for certain."

Edward stared at his grinning face, and turned to look at Benjamin, stirring the pot of tar, and Dick, leaning against the ladder. Now he could no longer control the tears which rolled down his cheeks. But they were tears of anger and indignation more than fear. He had so wanted to enjoy this journey. He *had* been enjoying this journey so much, until now. And he was Edward Warner, son of Captain Thomas Warner. Why, Hilton had been glad enough to bow and scrape before Father.

"You'll not touch me," he said. "Stand aside, please. I wish to rejoin my father."

"There," Hilton said. "What did I tell you, lads? He's not really cut out to be a sailor, after all."

"You let me pass," Edward demanded.

Benjamin looked at Hilton.

"But as he's here," Hilton said, "we may as well have a little sport with him. Tell you what, Master Warner, we'll just put a little tar on, in one or two places, so's you get the feel."

"You'll not," Edward shouted. "You'll not."

"Hold his arms, Benjamin," Hilton commanded. "Dicky, come grab his legs while I get those breeches off. He'll be a sight for sore eyes, I'll wager."

"You'll not," Edward screamed, and kicked Benjamin on the ankle.

"Ow," Benjamin roared, and dropped the tar pot. "Ow, me God."

"You'll not," Edward screamed again, and kicked him again, this time in the stomach as he bent over. Suddenly all of the vicious anger he had known at Tyburn welled into his stomach, but this time he did not feel sick; he wanted to hurt them, all of them, wanted to kill them, in his hate.

Benjamin howled and rolled against the barrels.

"By Christ, you little beast," Hilton shouted, reaching for him. But Edward ducked under his arms, scooped up the tar pot—it lay on its side, and the evil liquid was already running across the grating and dripping through into the bilges—and swung it around before letting it go. Hilton received the full contents on the chest. He tumbled backward, and Edward made for the ladder, but checked as he saw Dick waiting for him.

"By Christ," Hilton said again, getting to his feet. "You gutter rat. By Christ, I'll have the skin off your arse, before I stuff tar up it, by Christ. Benjamin, fetch that rope's end."

Benjamin was struggling to his knees, still muttering and cursing.

Edward looked right and left and saw the rope lying across a barrel. It was about five feet long and ended in a series of nasty-looking knots, tight and hard, to break the skin where they bruised. He sucked air into his lungs, leaped across the hold, and seized it.

"Get him," Hilton bawled, attempting to claw tar from his clothes.

Benjamin came toward Edward, and Edward took hold of the rope in both hands and swung it as hard as he could. The knots took Benjamin across the face, and he gave a howl of real pain and fell back, while blood spurted from a cut on his cheek.

"Don't just stand there, Dicky," Hilton bellowed. "Go get him."

Dick chuckled and came forward. Edward swung the rope to and fro again, and Dick hesitated, beginning to crouch.

"I'll kill you," Edward said in a low voice. "You come a step nearer and I'll kill you, by God."

Dick glanced at Hilton, who removed another lump of hardening tar and threw it on the deck before raising his head in a frown.

"And you," Edward said.

"By Christ," Hilton said, half to himself, "I believe you would if you could. His name is Warner, lads, remember that. His father is a famous soldier. Seems the cub has all that spirit, too."

"You'll help me, Mr. Hilton," Dick said, weaving to and fro and watching the rope's end. Behind him Benjamin sat against the barrels and moaned.

"I'll not, Dicky," Hilton said. "Who'd have thought it, a lad of twelve taking on three strapping louts like us? So you won't have tar on your tool, Mr. Warner. That's a fair decision, and a bold one. So let's call it a halt. Put down your rope, and here's my hand on it."

Edward hesitated. Of course, if the three boys really wanted to capture him, they could do so without the slightest trouble. Slowly he lowered the rope.

"You're an honest fellow, Master Warner." Hilton came across the hold, hand outstretched, and Edward dropped the rope and extended his own.

"Got you," Dick shouted, and threw both arms around Edward's waist.

"Dishonest wretch," Edward exclaimed.

"He is that," Hilton agreed, and fetched Dick such a buffet across the ear he cannoned into the barrels and joined Benjamin on the deck. "I gave my word, and Tony Hilton's word sticks." He squeezed Edward's hand. "Master Warner, I'll tell you straight, when I clapped eyes on you I put you down for a right dandy with ideas above his age. Now, sir, I'd be proud to have you along. Let's go on deck and leave these two rascals to themselves."

"Willingly, sir," Edward agreed. "And I am happy to have made your acquaintance."

That night Edward and his father were given a berth in one of the tiny cabins opening off the wardroom, for there was scarce a bed to be had in the town. This was after dinner in the great cabin, at which Master Hilton attended, together with Mr. North's officers, while a variety of wines and toasts were indulged, and the deck beams rang with song and laughter. Edward was overwhelmed, and now he had a friend. Hilton kept winking at him and making faces behind his glass as he mimicked his betters.

But even Father seemed to be impressed with the preparations and the spirit of the crews. "Tell me, boy," he asked as they climbed into their bunks. "What do you make of the ship?"

"It is magnificent, Father," Edward cried, hopping up and down in his nightshirt. "It is so much larger than I imagined, and so . . . so magnificent."

"You'll not have forgotten that we are still moored alongside a dock, I hope. But I like adventure in the air. And I like this North. The venture will do well. Almost I wish I had accepted my lord of Warwick's invitation to sail with them."

"And I, Father," Edward said. "You promised you'd take me on your next campaign."

"Then I'd be daft indeed." Tom Warner pulled the blanket to his neck. "Ah, well, we'll tarry tomorrow, and then begin our journey home."

A moment later he snored, and Edward had to blow out the candle. He had little chance of sleep himself, he imagined. But then, he had no wish to sleep. He did not wish to miss a single moment on board the ship. He lay in his narrow bunk, and felt the vessel move, for a slight breeze had sprung up; now the warps creaked, and the timbers too, and he could hear the whisper of water past the sides, and there were twanging noises from the rigging, and scurrying noises from within the hull, sounds which would at home have had him sitting up in bed with fear, but which seemed the most natural in the world. While from above there was the steady tap-tap of the boots of the night watchmen patrolling the deck.

He wondered if Tony Hilton slept. He had made a friend of a man who was going out into the world to seek his fortune, and he could hardly be older than eighteen. Perhaps less. But *he* had proved himself. He sweated with excitement when he thought of it.

He slept before he realized how tired he was, and dreamed

he was standing on the poop deck of a tall ship, conning her through a narrow passage between jagged rocks and raging seas, with Walter Raleigh on one side of him and Tony Hilton on the other; he wore a sword, and there were loaded brass cannon on the deck; for at any moment a great Spaniard might appear out of the night, ports open and blazing flame.

He awoke to the crashing of feet, and sat up so suddenly he banged his head on the deck beams.

"What in God's name . . . ?" Father was also awake, and pulling on his breeches. Edward hurried behind him into the main cabin, where Mr. North and his sailing master faced a messenger whose cloak and boots scattered mud onto the clean deck.

"What a devil of a noise," Tom said. "Is daybreak always like this at sea?"

"Would that we were at sea," said the master, a little bluff man named Henry Ashton, with short hair and short features, too, the whole made pleasant by his ready smile. "But the admiral has received ill news."

North had finished reading the paper. "The Spaniards have got word of our expedition, and Gondomar is to protest to his Majesty."

"But the grant is given," Ashton protested.

"Grants can be revoked, Hal."

"I'd trust my lord of Warwick to fight for his property, Mr. North," Tom said. "And he has the king's ear."

"He would fight, Captain Warner, had he that precious possession. But this message is from him. He has quarreled with Villiers, and is confined."

"My God," Tom said. "The Tower?"

"His house, for the moment. Who can say about later?"

"And what would he have us do, sir?" Ashton asked.

North scratched his chin. "As we think best," he said slowly. "His words. Words he seldom uses. I wonder what . . . ?" He raised his head, gazed at Tom. But Tom was also frowning.

"Warwick confined," he said, half to himself. "This affair touches us all, Mr. North."

"Aye," North agreed. His forehead slowly cleared, and his mouth set in a firm line. "I have a copy of the grant here on board this ship. It says that we are to proceed whenever we are provisioned."

"Which will take not less than another month to accomplish, sir," Ashton protested.

"To accomplish to our satisfaction, Mr. Ashton. Life is ever an unsatisfactory affair. It will take only a few hours to fill our water casks. When is tide full?"

Ashton's turn to frown. "At dusk, sir."

"Then pass the word quietly to my other captains to make ready for sea. We shall leave this night."

"But, sir . . ."

"Or we shall be forced to seek fresh employment, Mr. Ashton. And I for one have invested too much in this venture for it not to succeed. But let us put to sea, and Gondomar will waste his words on the empty ocean. Now, see to it, man." He clapped Ashton on the shoulder, pushed him toward the companion ladder, and turned back to Tom. "Captain Warner, it truly grieves me that our acquaintance has had to be of such short order. But you'll understand the circumstances."

"Warwick imprisoned," Tom muttered. "This is a serious blow, Mr. North. I am in none too good an odor at court myself, save through the intercession of the earl."

"Then you had best look to yourself, sir. I have observed that heavy weights, in falling, invariably bring down with them any and all to which they may be attached."

Tom was pulling his nose. "While you sail away to freedom. I tell you, man . . . You'll know it was the earl's wish that I accompany you?"

"Indeed I do, sir. And were you to decide on that, I would be the happiest of men."

"With no money contributed to the venture?"

"I'll accept your experience of warfare in lieu of money, Captain Warner. We may seek peace, but 'tis likely some sort of defense will be forced upon us. You'll have command of my military."

"I will have to make arrangements for the boy; Berwicke will certainly accompany me."

"You'll wish him returned to Framlingham," North said thoughtfully. "Now, there will be a problem. But we shall certainly find him a room here in Plymouth until a suitable companion can be found to take him home. I'll speak with my factor."

"Father," Edward cried.

"Boy, there are times when a man must act. This is destiny."

"I do not quarrel with that, sir," Edward said desperately. "But why send me back? There are boys on this ship not greatly my elders. And Mama is well cared for by Uncle Edward. Be sure that I shall only be a nuisance to her. And will you not be sending for her within the year?"

"Take an eleven-year-old to Guyana?" Tom asked at large.

"You would leave me in Plymouth, sir, a prey to heaven knows what temptations."

North was grinning. "He seems a likely lad, to be sure, Mr. Warner. And if we are to found a nation, there will have to be other eleven-year-olds, and less."

"And you promised, Father," Edward begged. "Be sure that if left behind I shall dwindle into a skeleton, and a vagabond besides."

"And would Mrs. Warner ever forgive me?"

"She gave you her blessing, Father," Edward pointed out. "Please, Father. I'll not disgrace you. This I swear."

Tom chewed his lip and pulled his nose, and then smiled. "It goes against my nature to send you back. You've the spirit of Wat Raleigh tucked away in there, Edward. You'll find me paper, Mr. North, if you will. I've a letter I must write. Edward, locate Berwicke and tell him there's been a change of plan. We'll go and see if we can find this El Dorado."

3

The Enchanted Isle

"Handed over to the Inquisition, they was." Niles, the boatswain, settled himself in front of his scanty meal with a sigh of pleasure. "Careless, see, lads. They was making down this river by pinnace to regain the ship they'd left snug at anchor, and they killed birds for food, and dropped the feathers over the side, so the dons figured which way they'd gone. Burned, they was, Oxenham and all his men. Oh, savage, the dons."

Edward leaned back and allowed the sun to beat on his face. Although he had already finished the tiny chunk of salted meat and the single tooth-cracking biscuit which had been his share, and felt as hungry as when he had taken his first mouthful, noon was still the pleasantest part of the day. However poor the food, it was best at midday, and at midday, too, they could listen to Niles reminiscing, while now the sun was at its hottest, far warmer than he would ever have supposed possible; beating on his face and through his shirt, it almost made him forget the gnawing ache in his belly.

"At least they died fed, I'll wager," Hilton said. "Tell the truth, now, Niles, have you ever been this hungry?"

"Or ever been this long at sea without sight of land?" Benjamin suggested.

Niles considered. He was the only one of the watch below with food still in front of him, because he had carefully chopped his meat ration into tiny cubes, each one of which he masticated slowly and with great enjoyment. "But once," he said. "Then I sailed with Johnny Painton. Now, there's a sly one to be sure. He'd trade with the devil, if he had to. But if the devil wasn't armed, why, Johnny would change his tune in a moment and send a shot across his bows."

"And once he took on more than he could handle?" Hilton asked.

Niles chuckled. "Not Johnny. But we was hit by this storm, north of Hispaniola, oh, ten years back it was. Took all the masts out of her, it did, and so we drifted, for days. Oh, we rigged a jury at last and got her home to Plymouth. Johnny Painton's a proper seaman. But there wasn't so much as a piece of leather left unchewed by then. Oh, aye, you lads ain't seen anything yet."

"Boys to the quarter deck," came the shout from aft, and Hilton and Edward scrambled up the ladders to attend Mr. Ashton at the noon reckoning.

"Hold it steady, lad. Hold it steady." Ashton stooped to peer through the eyehole of the astrolabe. It was difficult even to approximate the aperture, so unsteady was Hilton's hand, much less to line it up with the sun. "Easy now. Easy. Write these down," he snapped at Edward. "Six . . . six . . . why, 'tis neither more nor less. Write that down, Mr. Warner. Six degrees of north latitude. Now, fetch me up that log board. Quickly."

The boy lurched toward the ladder, passed his father without a glance, and Tom sighed. It was necessary for Ashton to drive them constantly, for all that he felt no stronger than they, and more than sorry for them; left alone, they would do nothing but bask in the sun at the foot of the mast. They moved like ghosts, and their bones showed wherever their clothes allowed. Tom leaned on the taffrail. But at least they could be occupied from dawn to dusk. Two months at sea. Two months on this cursed, empty ocean, which Walter Raleigh had described in such glowing terms. Two months of storm and tempest and invariably contrary winds. Even now it blew half against his face, although today at least it was no more than gentle.

He climbed the ladder to the poop, stood at the after gunwale, and surveyed the four ships plowing along in their wake. No doubt it was, despite all, a beautiful sight. The sea had a blueness in these equatorial climes he had never suspected; and the splashes of white, as the occasional crest broke, but added to the intensity of the color. The ships themselves, seen from a distance might just have navigated the channel. He would need a glass to tell how scarred were the hulls, how much weed trailed from their bottoms. Even without the glass he could make out the strange rigging of the *Goliath,* for she sailed under jury mast, having lost her main in that tempest of a week ago. That had been their worst storm. So far. And it had all but done for the *Goliath.* He supposed they should be grateful that all the ships had survived. But he grieved for Edward, for the hunger in the boy's face. He had borne up magnificently, had taken his place under young Hilton and performed his duty splendidly. Clearly he loved the sea, even with its discomfort and danger. And he was fortunate in having such a good friend to help him and protect him when, as happened with increasing regularity, tempers became frayed in the wardroom. But the eagerness with which he snatched at his dwindling rations was hard for a father to bear. And what Rebecca would say, was already saying, indeed, hardly bore contemplating. She would now be at the point of delivery, and he was four thousand miles away, and more, had carried with him her eldest son. He dreamed of her every night, and awoke in a sweat of desire and frustration. At least, he dreamed of women every night. But less, perhaps, of Rebecca, tall and strong, than of Sarah, small and light and laughing. It was six months since he had known any such reality.

Roger North stamped onto the quarter deck below him. The admiral had not stood up well to the rigors of the voyage. He had lost weight, where he had little to spare, and had become ill-tempered and discouraged as day had succeeded day. Now he regarded Ashton with contempt, as the sailing master laid off the distance they had run during the night, allowing for the leeway and the increasing sluggishness of the hulls, watched as ever by the attentive Hilton and Edward.

"At your endless calculations, Mr. Ashton?" the admiral remarked. "Truly, I have no doubt at all that you are as lost as any of us. And pray, sir, show me where we are today?"

Ashton made his cross on the chart. "By my reckoning, Mr. North."

"By your reckoning, Mr. Ashton. Then where is the land I see beyond your thumb? The mainland, by God. How far is that? Scarce half an inch."

"An inch is yet thirty miles, Mr. North. There is no man alive can see thirty miles, unless there be mountains at the horizon, and this land, so I am told by my books, is flat and low-lying. And we may be closer or farther off than that. It is difficult to be sure on a voyage of such duration. But we are near, sir; I promise you that."

"And the land *is* low-lying, Mr. North," Edward said. "I was told so by Sir Walter Raleigh."

"Hold your impudent tongue, sir," North shouted. "By God, Master Warner, you'll address me when I address you, and not before. Understand that? As for your calculations, Mr. Ashton, I'll allow you one more day, then I'll up helm and run for the Caribee Islands. They too are there, just over the horizon." He mounted the ladder to the poop. "You'll take your stick to that lad of yours, Captain Warner, or I'll be forced to consider him a member of the crew and use a rope's end."

"I'll speak with the lad," Tom promised. "To make for the islands would be to break the king's patent. Or would you go a-pirating?"

North glanced at him. "I have men's lives on my mind, Captain Warner. Do you know what was reported to me this morning? The crew are so famished they are eating the calf skins from around the halliards. Now, sir, I have no right to inflict such suffering on my followers."

Tom sighed. He had entirely misjudged this man. There was no resolution here, nor firmness of purpose. But now was a sorry time to discover that.

"Ahoy the deck," came the call from the main top. "I see shoal water on the larboard bow."

"Shoal water?" Ashton called. "Breakers, you mean?"

"No, sir, Mr. Ashton," the seaman called. " 'Tis the whole ocean turning brown, with the appearance of sand."

"By Christ," North muttered. "Here were no place to go aground." He ran to the rail. "You'll wear ship, Mr. Ashton. And signal the fleet to follow."

"Shoal water?" Ashton said again. "Beyond sight of land? It cannot be."

"It is not shallow, sir," Edward said. "You may sail with confidence through it."

"What? What?" North bellowed. "By Christ, Master Warner, you go too far. Boatswain. Boatswain. Trice me that boy up. Ten lashes, sir."

"You'll not flog my son," Tom said.

"You'd argue with me? Beware, Captain Warner, that I do not hang you beside him. I am in command of this fleet, sir, and you are nothing but a passenger. An unpaying passenger, by God. Boatswain, do your duty."

The boatswain climbed onto the quarter deck, seized Edward by the shoulder.

"But, sir," Edward cried.

"Be quiet," Hilton whispered. "It will but increase your punishment."

"Sir," Edward screamed, "it is not shoal. It is the mud brought down by the great rivers. Sir Walter told me so."

"By God, sir," North shouted.

"The lad is right, Mr. North," Ashton said. "I have recalled the tale myself. With your permission, sir, we will stand on. Take in sail, by all means, but we can easily test the depths by sounding, and risk little."

North hesitated, glared from Edward to his father, and then turned back to the gunwale. His indecision was pitiful to see. "Do as you see fit, Mr. Ashton," he muttered. "Do as you see fit."

A low, seemingly solid wall of green, appearing to grow out of the brown water. The wind had dropped entirely now, and the boats were out, towing the ships toward the shore. And still they remained in three fathoms of water, as announced every few minutes by the leadsman in the bows. Edward had crawled forward to watch the boats, and the approaching land, and Hilton standing in the stern of the pinnace, urging his men on. Land, and calm water, after all these weeks. And it was Raleigh's land. There was no mistaking that endless forest.

Time now to forget the voyage. But he had little wish to do that. Time certainly to forget the cold, stormy nights they had suffered immediately after leaving Plymouth, and his consequent seasickness, to forget the hungry ache in his belly, if he only could, the growing misery on Father's face, if he could. But Father would become cheerful when he got back to land. And it was time to remember the good things, the long days in the sun, as testified by his brown skin, the hours spent aloft with Tony, as testified by his muscles which welled in his arms, their long, intimate chats about intimate things, which had allowed him to understand more of Mr. Walkden and the reasons for his screams of shame more than pain, and to grow more than ever afraid of his own insistent manhood. It had been a good voyage, he thought. But for the lack of food and the tempers of the admiral. But even those were behind them now.

"I see the break, Captain," shouted the main top. "A point to larboard."

Ashton scrambled onto the bowsprit beside Edward and

put his telescope to his eye. "It is there, all right. Where it should be. The Oyapoc, Mr. North. Do we stand in?"

"Aye," came the call from the poop. "You're to be congratulated on your navigation, Mr. Ashton."

"And you're to be congratulated on your memory, and your courage, Master Warner," Ashton said. "Or we'd have been making west, for the gallows, I have no doubt." He looked down at the boy. "You'll sail with me again, Mr. Warner. You can have an apprentice's birth on my ship for the asking."

"Then I accept, sir," Edward said. "Here and now."

Ashton scratched his head, and then laughed. "Twelve years old. Now, let me give you a word of advice, Master Warner. You're growing too fast. No doubt it is the circumstances. But without care you'll be an old man at twenty. And that would be a shame. For the meanwhile, if you'd be my apprentice, take this glass and watch that river and the banks. We don't want to stumble on any Spaniards, like Mr. Raleigh. And by God, boy, drop my telescope overboard and I'll have the skin from your arse."

He returned to the deck, and Edward took the heavy telescopes carefully in both hands, legs wrapped around the hot wood of the bowsprit. But by now he was as at home out here as on his bunk, and this sea was calm as a lake. Yet his hands trembled as he gazed at the shore; through the glass he could separate the trees, and now he could pick out the mouth of the river, and the swirl in the water. "There's a bar," he called.

"I see it," came the answer from aft.

The boats edged closer, the oars dripping into the brown sea, the bare backs of the men sweating brown as well, as they swayed and heaved. Now each blade came up in the center of a mass of discolored ooze, and a moment later the *Great St. George* seemed to shudder, very gently, and quite without noise.

"By Christ," North shouted. "We're aground."

Ashton was peering over the side. The boats were still floating and pulling. "Just," he said. "And it's soft mud. Nothing more. Give way," he bawled. "Put your backs into it. Give way."

The men strained, the boats surged forward, and the *Great St. George* continued to move through the turbulence caused by the mud bar and into the deeper, calmer waters of the river beyond.

"Through, by God," Ashton called. "Quartermaster, you'll signal the fleet to follow."

Edward stared at the banks of the river, the telescope forgotten. Trees. As Sir Walter had promised. It was midmorning now, and the sun blazed down from a cloudless sky, yet there was no light in there, save for the occasional shaft, startling in its suddenness, piercing leafy crown and reflecting from huge, rounded trunk. A silent, empty forest. But if the trees were there, and the brown ocean, as Raleigh had said, then the dragons would be there, too.

"*This* is El Dorado?" Tom muttered from the deck.

Edward slid back to stand beside him. "It is as we expected, sir."

"Aye. But somehow . . . I dislike the silence. Walter never mentioned the silence. This place has no life in it."

"There is life there, sir. Surely. Look." In front of the boats a fish had jumped.

" 'Tis that unused they are to the splash of oars."

"But there, sir." Edward pointed again. "Look, there."

The *Great St. George* slowly came around a bend in the river, which seemed to widen before them. Still the trees clung to the right-hand bank and filled the left-hand bank too, at a distance; but immediately in front of them there was a clearing of some size carried back from the water; here there were wooden huts, and beyond, an expanse of pasture, covered with weed and growth, but nonetheless cleared, once, and not too long ago.

The admiral and Ashton had seen it too. "Houses, by God," North shouted. " 'Tis the Harcourt settlement. We'll anchor, if you please, Mr. Ashton, and make a signal to the fleet to do likewise. We've arrived, man, arrived."

Tom Warner stood up and shaded his eyes. "At a dead colony," he muttered. "In a dead land. May God have mercy on our souls."

The pinnace nosed into the shore, pushing its prow through reed and sand, to come to rest against the more solid bulk of the bank. The sailors backed their oars, and the boat remained still, clasped in a green-and-brown vice. Now that the splashes and the grunts were ended, there was complete silence. Edward, seated beside his father in the stern, pressed against Mr. North, wanted to hold his breath. Behind him the five ships waited at anchor, so still as to seem grown out of the mud-brown water which swirled gently around their anchor chains. Astern of the pinnace the other boats waited to come ashore once their admiral gave the signal. And before them, behind them, on either side of them, wherever the river meandered, the green forest also waited.

But the huts were closer at hand. Now they were actually at the shore they could see that the roofs had in many cases fallen in, and the windows gaped, and vines and bushes lay curled over the ground. Yet this had been an English settlement. The houses were arranged in two rows, enclosing a would-be village street, leading up to a larger building at the inner end. The town hall, no doubt. It had been very neat, once.

Mr. North rose and made his way forward. He had donned his best blue doublet and wore lace at collar and cuffs, although in common with the other gentlemen of the fleet he had discarded his ruff; it was simply too hot. His hat was a broad-brimmed felt, with a peacock feather, and his sword was a Spanish rapier. His beard had been combed and trimmed, and he wore long leather boots. The perfect picture of an Englishman taking possession of a piece of the world for his king. He hesitated for a moment in the bows, gazing at the village and obviously enjoying this moment to the full, and then jumped onto the bank. The ground squelched beneath his feet, but he sank only an inch. He turned, took off his hat, and waved it above his head.

A ripple of cheering broke out from the ships and drifted across the silent river, immediately accompanied by the roar of the cannon as they fired their salute, and a *feu de joie* of musketry rang through the trees. Smoke clouded into the still air, and the birds rose in profusion at this strange sound.

"By Christ," Tom growled, "we'll awaken every Spaniard or savage within miles."

"You'll come ashore, Captain Warner. And bring your musketeers with you."

"Stay close by me, Edward." Tom climbed out of the boat. He also had saved his best suit of clothes for this occasion, and they had found a morion to suit him, but no breastplate. Edward scrambled behind him—his clothes were by now sadly threadbare—and felt the mud give under his shoes. Behind them came a file of musketeers, wearing helmets and breastplates and carrying their staffs and heavy firepieces across their shoulders. Now the other boats came into the bank and also unloaded their crews, until Tom had command of two score armored men. The sailors remained by the boats, but several of the other gentlemen, and the boys from the flagship—Tony Hilton, Benjamin, and Dick—also came ashore.

"A fair place," North declared. "Hot, by God, but fair. There'll have been tobacco in that field over there. We'll gather the seeds first thing, as soon as we have put these houses in repair. Mr. Ashton, you'll take a file and find us fresh water; I suspect this river will prove brackish, but there will be streams entering it. And see what you can locate in the way of fresh food; there will be much of that. Captain Warner, you'll accompany me with your men, if you please."

"We'll have skirmishers, Mr. North," Tom decided, and gave the orders. Four of the musketeers went in advance, two on either side of the street, kicking their way through the long grass, while the main body followed Tom and Edward and Mr. North up the center, and the sailors remained in a huddle by the boats.

"By God, 'tis close," Hilton remarked, taking off his hat to fan himself. " 'Tis to be hoped there *is* fresh water close at hand."

"There will be, Mr. Hilton," North assured him.

The skirmishers were throwing open the rotting doors of the cottages, peering into the interiors and then returning to the street, when without warning the sun went in. The men stopped, to stare at the heavens and the huge black cloud which was coming up out of the forest.

"Now, there's a relief," North said, still speaking loudly. "Some rain will just cool the air. Well, Captain Warner? No savages, eh? Not a thing. We shall to work. We'll make this place our headquarters, as it is the most imposing."

They stood before the large building. This had been raised a little higher than the others, and needed four steps. It had also been more stoutly built, and seemed in better repair.

Tom looked up as the first drop of rain fell. "Then we'd best to shelter. Mr. Williams?"

The lieutenant nodded and ran up the steps, drawing his sword as he did so. He put his boot to the door and thrust it in, while the rain became heavier, dampening the dust of the street, crashing downward with amazing force, bouncing off helmet and breastplate.

"Well, Mr. Williams?" North demanded.

"The roof is in good repair," Williams called. "It will afford shelter. I will just test the flooring." He stepped into the darkness. But scarcely had he gone when he uttered a shriek, which came booming out of the doorway in a long echo.

"By Christ," North shouted.

"Musketeers, draw your swords," Tom ordered, realizing that the matches would be useless in this downpour. "Stay here, Edward." His own weapon thrust forward, he ran at the steps, and stopped as the door moved. It had been no more than brushed by the monster which emerged, orange and brown in great splotches, fully six inches thick, a whipping eight-foot-length of deadly horror with a vicious flat head dominated by the thrusting split tongue. It slid across the little porch and down the steps, paused to glance at the terrified men, and disappeared into the long grass fringing the village. For a moment they stood as if petrified, then Tom regained his courage and hurled the door open, sword ready. The men made to follow, and North checked them with a shout. "Wait. There may be others."

"Others," Edward cried, and ran up the steps behind his father. Tom Warner knelt in the darkened room beyond, beside Mr. Williams. But the young Welshman was dead, his face black and his body stiff.

It rained. It had rained now for nearly a week, and no English drizzle, this. It teemed down. They could see it moving along the river toward the shops, and the ships themselves swayed at their anchors under the impact of the rain. There was no wind.

The clouds seemed to have settled immediately above the village, or perhaps there was only one cloud, and this stretched forever, encompassing the entire continent, perhaps the entire world, setting itself with the utmost determination to drown this upstart land. Certainly this was easy to imagine. The overgrown village street dissolved from soft earth into liquid mud beneath the pounding water. The very trees seemed to bend.

The Europeans bent too. The rain had refilled their water casks. There was relief. Now it sought to crush them. Their spirits still sagged beneath the shocking death of Mr. Williams. It was the speed and the silence with which it had happened. Now they expected poisonous snakes under every root, posted a guard on the doors of every house all night to keep away intruders. They were afraid. The bushmaster had been nothing more than a symbol of the hell into which they had so hopefully sailed. They felt that the very jungle was dead, but a living dead, which sought only to bring them to a similar state. And the rain kept them pinned down, waiting, unable to get out and seek food, unable to plant their tobacco, unable to do more than survive, and that was becoming difficult.

"It will stop," North said. No doubt he sought to convince himself, for he spoke in a low voice. "By Christ, it was not raining when we came. It had not been raining for several days, then; the ground was dry."

He stood in the doorway of the large building, the driest of the houses, the one taken for their own by the gentlemen. Here there were three separate rooms, and once they had cleared out the dust and weeds which in places threatened to come through the rotting floorboards, it was quite habitable. Certainly there was no need for heat, for the very rain was warm, and it only seemed to make the atmosphere more oppressive. And they had enough to do to repel those who would share the house with them. Tony and Benjamin and Dick and Edward were busy the whole day long, for if it was not columns of ants, large and voracious, sliding up the piles on which the house stood, seeking to consume any and everything that lay in their path, it was spiders, not so huge as those described by Raleigh, certainly, and apparently unable to jump, but nonetheless hairy, sinister-looking things which lurked in dark corners. And there were other creatures, such as one which rose up on its legs and thrust a deadly sting forth to challenge the intruders, and more, seemed to relish attacking the white men rather than scuttle away into the corners. Dick rapidly fell foul of this one. He sought to pick it up and hurl it into the yard, and the scorpion had struck before dying. Dick lay in a corner, wrapped in two blankets, shivering and shuddering. His right hand was twice the size of his right foot.

"The rain will stop," Tom Warner agreed. "For a season, and then it will start again. Walter Raleigh spoke nothing of this."

North nodded. "And yet, fools that we were, we wondered why all expeditions to the Guyanas are plagued with disaster. I feel beseiged. We *are* besieged, Tom. The rain will keep us here to die of starvation. 'Tis no longer merely an inconvenience. Ashton tells me there is not a slice of rotten meat left aboard. And those fish they catch will not make up the difference. And without a wind, we have not even the power to leave."

"You'd do that?" Tom demanded. "Is this not your future? By God, man, if I am to believe your account of what you have invested here, 'tis your past as well."

"To redeem which I must drown on dry land?"

They spoke like this every time they came together. North lacked the determination which breeds success. But then, Edward wondered, did Father not merely possess the determination which arises from desperation? Failure here would affect him more than most, because he was too conscious that he was here *as* a failure, a penniless exile who had deserted wife and family. He could only redeem all of those pawns by returning with a cargo of prime tobacco and the solid achievement of a successful venture behind him. There was none to be obtained in this rain.

Edward stood at the rear door of the house and watched the trees. The rain fell like a screen between himself and the forest, but the green wall was not so very far away. He wondered why he thought that. To gain the forest—would that help the colony? The trees were not edible. They were merely filled with dangers. Sir Walter had outlined those clearly enough, and the bushmaster had given substance to his imagination.

Suddenly he wondered if he was going to die here, at twelve years old. Dick was dying. Every hour he grew weaker, and his skin grew hotter. They had tried bleeding him, without success. Benjamin sat by him whenever he had the time. They had been friends. And Tony Hilton? Tony also knelt by the corner in which his mate lay, or stood in the doorways and glowered at the forest. Tony's high spirits had deserted him.

As had his own. To die of starvation or snakebite in the rain and the heat and the silence. He had now seen two men die, and both violently. What would it be like to die peacefully? Only it would not be peaceful to die of starvation. The grinding, wind-producing pain in his belly reminded him of that.

He stared at the forest, and the forest stared back. How despairing it was to be this helpless. Better, surely, to be doing. If this weather had greeted Lawrence Keymis when he had attempted to make his way inland, no blame could be attached to him for attacking the first Spanish post he came across. But might it not be an idea, to tow the ships higher up the river? They might find a more hospitable clime. After all, there was the highway to Manaos and El Dorado. They were here because Harcourt had been here, and Harcourt had failed.

Still the forest stared at him, not moving its head. He realized that he had been gazing at the face for some minutes without even properly seeing it. A small face, thin, with prominent cheek and jaw bones, eyes hardly more than slits in the tight brown flesh. There, and then gone. It had seen the understanding in his own face.

"Wait," Edward shouted, and ran down the steps. The rain leaped on him like a playful giant, seized his clothes and his head, and reduced them to sopping rags in a matter of seconds. Water splashed out of the ground and into his boots, and he staggered and almost fell. Behind him someone shouted. But they would only be calling him back. They would not have seen the face, nor would they believe that he had not been deluded.

He reached the trees, hesitated for only a moment, and then burst into the semidarkness of the forest. He tripped, and landed on his hands and knees, rose to his feet again, and ran on. "Wait," he shouted. "Wait. I must speak with you. Please wait."

He panted, fell again, rose, staggered on, and fell again. He found himself on his hands and knees, while little puddles of water rose around his thighs. Surprisingly, in here the rain hardly seemed to reach him. It gathered on branches and in giant leaves above his head and occasionally cascaded downward. It crashed into the crowns fifty feet above him with a monotonous roar. But it no longer constantly pounded on his face and shoulders.

In here. Slowly he dragged himself to his feet. The trees stood all around him, shutting out the light, shutting out all conception of place and time. These trees had stood here since the creation of the world. They would stand here until God reclaimed His own. He was aware of a sense of helplessness which made nonsense of his earlier feelings. He turned, looked back the way he had come. But which way had he come? The trees waited, gathering around to regard this inquisitive stranger from another world. Now they had him here they would not let him go. But . . . he had come *that* way, surely. He took a few steps, and checked. No, he recognized nothing of this. It looked the same as any other, but there was no imprint of his feet. As if his feet could leave any imprint on the endless soft-packed fallen leaves. Better to return to where he had first stopped. But where had he first stopped?

He panted, and looked up at the trees, and fought the wild desire to run and run and run until he dropped from exhaustion. The village, the river, could not be very far away. But for the teeming rain, in fact, he would be able to hear the rushing water and use it as a guide. Oh, God damn the teeming rain.

"Help," he shouted. "Please, I need help."

He panted, and now fought against the tears which welled up behind his eyes, and gazed at the face again. Perhaps it was, after all, only a face, disembodied and floating around the jungle, the ghost of some long-dead savage.

"Help," he whispered. "Will you help me?"

The leaves parted slowly, and a man came out. Or perhaps he was a boy. He was no taller than Edward, certainly, although more heavily built. This was easy to see because he was naked. Nor did the rain seem to affect his skin; it struck the flesh and skidded away again, to leave him almost as dry as before. His hair was wet, however; it lay in a damp black mat on his head, uniformly cropped just below the ears. And he carried a long spear, made of thin wood, but nonetheless sharply pointed and quite capable, Edward did not doubt, of killing a man. His eyes were black, and suspicious. His body was somewhat ill-proportioned, seeming to be short in the legs; but the strength was there, even if his feet, splashed with mud and with spread toes, were ugly. Edward, now becoming preoccupied with his own growing manhood, was struck by the absence of body hair. But then. the little man did not wear a beard, either.

"Will you help me?" Edward asked. "I have lost my way."

The man's eyes moved very slightly and then returned to Edward's face. Edward started to turn, and checked himself. There were little men all around him, all naked, all equipped with wooden spears. Yet he did not feel afraid. They mistrusted him, that was all. But already there was less mistrust than in the beginning. They could see that he was unarmed.

"Will you show me the way back to the village?" Edward asked. "And come with me? The admiral would like to make your acquaintance."

Someone spoke, and now Edward did turn. This man was no different in appearance from his companions, except that he wore a thin band of rawhide around his forehead, holding his hair close to his head; stuck in the center of the band was a single feather, very bright and long, although drooping sadly in the wet. But most surprising of all was his voice. It was deep and guttural, and it spoke a foreign tongue. But the language was Spanish. He was sure of that.

Edward shook his head. "I do not understand you," he said. "I am English. Not Spanish. Enemy of the Spanish. English. If you will show me the way back to the village, my father will speak with you." Father had learned Spanish during the Dutch wars.

The man spoke to his companions, and now his language was quite different, and seemed nothing more than a series of grunts. Then he came forward as noiselessly as ever and extended one hand to touch Edward on the chest. "Inglese," he said. "Har-court."

"That's right," Edward cried. "We are like Mr. Harcourt. We are living at his village. I am Edward Warner." He checked, for the Indian was frowning uncertainly. "Edward," he said. "English."

The Indian almost smiled. He tapped himself on the chest. "Tuloa," he said. "Arawak." He pointed, and without waiting set off into the trees, in the opposite direction, Edward was sure, to that in which he had come. But the other Indians were also heading that way, and he had no intention of being left behind. He hurried with them, tripping and stumbling, where they seemed to glide through the trees, and then checking as he heard the explosion. Someone had managed to keep his powder dry.

"My father," he said instinctively, and looked around him in horror. The Arawaks had disappeared. "No, wait," he shouted. "We are friends."

"Edward." The undergrowth crackled, and half a dozen men came through the trees, led by Tom Warner and Tony Hilton. "Where have you been? You know you are not supposed to leave the village."

"I saw a man, Father," Edward explained. "And there were others."

The Englishmen insensibly accumulated into a huddle, gazing around them at the forest, their swords looking punily useless when directed against the silence of the great trees. For the men were back, standing amid the ferns and leaves, their spears thrust forward, staring at them.

"That one, Father," Edward whispered. "The one with the feather. His name is Tuloa, and he speaks Spanish."

Tom hesitated, and then sheathed his sword and stepped

forward. "We are friends," he said in Spanish. "Englishmen come only to farm tobacco."

"We know the English," Tuloa said. "We remember Harcourt. The Spanish are evil men. The English are good men. Welcome."

"Our thanks to your people," Tom said. "We would trade with you. We have no food, but many goods. You have food?"

Tuloa nodded. "We have food. We will come to the river."

"Good men," Tom Warner muttered. "And how long, do you think, will they consider us good men?"

As if to celebrate the coming of the Indians, the rain had stopped. Or perhaps the Indians ventured forth only when they knew the rain was about to stop. In any event, the sun had come out, and from the endless gloom the afternoon had become startlingly bright. Only an hour's burning sun had been necessary to end the damp; they had watched it disappear in clouds of steam, rising from every bush and every tree, from the very river. Even the ships had steamed, and the men with them. And the Indians had brought dry wood, unbelievable after a week's downpour, and had lit a fire in the middle of the village. Now it blazed, and smoked, and sent showers of sparks in every direction, without risk, for the huts still remained too soaked to burn. And now they ate.

The Indians had come in strength, men and women and children, near a hundred of them, carrying fish and various root vegetables. Strange fish, with names like queriman and haussa, and even stranger vegetables, eddoe and cassava. But all good to taste when smoke-roasted on an open fire.

And they drank, not the last of the moldy beer and stale wine, but piwarrie, a clear liquid made from the cassava, which burned the bellies of the seamen and had them roaring with song and laughter.

And lust. For the women and the children were as naked as the men, nor did they find in embraces or even fornication anything more than a natural end to an evening's amusement. Tom sat somewhat apart, next to the chieftain, Tuloa, with Edward on his left, and watched the men, rolling about in their drunkenness, discarding their clothing, reaching for pouting breast and widespread crotch, to the accompaniment of shouts of laughter and high-pitched giggles from the girls, while their menfolk similarly enjoyed themselves with each other, with homosexually inclined white men, or with their own women, as the mood took them. The forest had suddenly become a place of pointed genitals and slobbering mouths, of semen and saliva.

On which Tuloa looked with benevolent pleasure. Unlike the others, he had drunk the last of North's wine, and now swayed to and fro, eyes half-shut, humming to himself.

" 'Tis a scene from hell itself," Tom said. "And God will not help us when these savages awake and remember what happened here tonight."

"God's blood, Tom Warner, but you are very nearly a Puritan," North complained from the other side of the chieftain. He still sat, at the least, and his clothes were still intact, but he eyed the women with much attention. "Can you not see that these Arawaks are but children, to whom every natural act is no more *than* a natural act? I see us living here happily, man, in a very Eden. And they spoke to us of savages."

"You could hardly describe them as civilized," Berwicke observed. He sat on the other side of Edward, and had also refrained from joining in the festivities, perhaps out of loyalty to Tom Warner, perhaps because he was one of the older men present, and therefore felt less of the sexual urge.

The urge to . . . to do what? Edward wondered. He gazed at Tony Hilton on the far side of the huge fire. Tony had drunk a great deal of piwarrie, and lay on his back. His breeches were off, and a brown leg was entwined with his, while brown hands searched his body with gentle insistence, and a black head of hair nuzzled his shoulder. The Indians did not appear to kiss, but this was the only physical contact they rejected. And Tony's hands were also busy, sliding from pointed, high-nippled breast, down rounded belly, to seek the damp warmth which lay between the girl's thighs. Edward's throat was dry. Manhood had grown upon him during this voyage. But to lie naked with an Indian girl in front of all these people—and these girls were no more handsome than their menfolk, really. In England they would not be spared a glance. But they were women, and it had been upward of two months since any of the colonists had seen a female, much less been granted access to their bodies.

Edward glanced at his father. Tom Warner was flushed as anyone, and his bad temper was growing. Because he was not old. And he would know what it was like to hold a soft body in his arms and find a soft receptacle for his anxious manhood. That he refrained was a conscious act of will, a decision made because he was a leader and a gentleman. Was Tony Hilton, then, not truly a gentleman?

Tuloa was swaying across, his arm thrown around Tom's shoulders, muttering in slurred Spanish. His face seemed to rest on Tom's back, and he gazed at Edward, mouth drooping, saliva dribbling out of each corner. Truly he was an unprepossessing sight; the idea that this man could on occasion glide with silent ease through the forbidding forest was ridiculous at this moment.

Tom replied brusquely, more brusquely, indeed, than Edward had ever heard, a combination of outrage and anger, accompanied by a push which sent Tuloa rolling over onto North. Not that the Indian seemed disturbed. His mouth continued to loll open, and he nuzzled the admiral's chest, while there could be no doubt about *his* erection; he sought to sustain it with his own fingers.

"Easy, Tom," North whispered. "We cannot afford to antogonize him."

"You heard what he wanted? The boy? Why, by God . . ."

Edward gazed at the chieftain in horror. Or was it excitement? He had a peculiar lightness in his chest. He too had sampled the piwarrie. Why not? he thought. How can it be wrong, if we both wish to enjoy it?

The forest echoed. The noise went up the river and struck the tree wall, to go bouncing around the village, an endless boom, slowly dwindling into a mammoth silence, as men dropped cup and woman and stared at each other, at the sky, at the very ground, in stupefaction.

North was first to recover. "Cannon, by Christ," he shouted, scrambling to his feet in such haste he upset the Arawak chieftain. "We are attacked. To arms. Man the ships. Quickly, now."

Tom had also regained his wits, and ran around the circle of drunken lovers, kicking and slapping. "Get your armor. Man the ships."

The men got up slowly, reluctantly. Naked girls were laid on the grass, trodden on as the seamen searched for their weapons. The Indians were themselves alarmed, and the men gathered by the water's edge, looking past the anchored vessels toward the bar, pointing and muttering among themselves. Edward ran down to join them, and stared at the ship which felt its way into the river, propelled by a faint breeze.

" 'Tis only one ship," he shouted.

"Nonetheless, she is afloat and we are ashore," Berwicke said. "She could sink our fleet."

"But she won't." Tony Hilton jumped up and down, and waved, holding his breeches up with one hand. "She flies the cross of St. George."

"John Painton, at your service, Mr. North. Captain Warner, I am happy to make your acquaintance." Painton was the very picture of the seadog Niles the boatswain had described, a short, thickset man with a heavy black beard and tremendous eyebrows; they seemed to protrude like windows. He was clearly a seaman pure and simple, affected no fine clothes, and carried a cutlass rather than a rapier; he kept his hand on the hilt as he eyed the Arawaks, and his followers were careful to prime their pistols most ostentatiously and remain close to their pinnace.

"Oh, fear them not, Mr. Painton," North said. "They are the most friendly people conceivable, if entirely lacking in manners. But what brings you to this desolate place? No accident, I would wager."

"No accident, Mr. North. I have urgent dispatches from the Court of St. James."

"Dispatches?" North took the sealed wallet, glanced uneasily at Tom. "Dispatches. Hm. You'll take some of our refreshment, sir? And your crew?"

"Willingly, Mr. North." Painton raised the cup of piwarrie brought to him by an Indian girl, tasted it, the while eyeing the naked body in front of him. "By God, gentlemen, but you have very much of a paradise here, I do declare. You'll be sorry to abandon it."

"Abandon it?" North turned the wallet over once again. "You have read these documents, sir?"

"You'll observe that the seal is unbroken, Mr. North," Painton pointed out. "But there is sufficient rumor in Plymouth."

"You'd best open them," Tom recommended, "and put us out of our doubt. What news of England, Mr. Painton?"

"None, sir. You'll realize that I left but a few days after yourselves. I was delayed on the way by a storm which set me some distance off course, or I would have been here sooner."

"Would that you had," North muttered. He gazed at Tom, his face pale. "The grant is revoked."

"It is no more than you anticipated, sir," Ashton said.

"Revoked," North said. "Revoked," he shouted. "Gondomar's doing." He looked at the men, who had formed a vast circle, in many cases still attached to their Indian friends; these had not been sobered by the arrival of the English ship, and seemed entirely bemused by the incident. "Would to God you had come sooner, Mr. Painton. While we yet despaired."

"I carried out my duty to the best of my ability, sir," Painton said.

"Why so sad, Mr. North?" demanded Tony Hilton. He had accumulated a second girl, and held one in each arm. "Scotch James is no less than four thousand miles away from us. So is Gondomar. As for the dons, would it make any difference to them whether you held the king's patent or not, should they discover us here? I'd say nothing has changed."

"By God, sir," North declared. "You are nothing less than a pirate at heart. A drunken, debauched buccaneer. By God, sir, I've a mind to hang you from that tree. What you said was nothing less than treason."

"Yet the lad is right," someone muttered.

"Aye," said another voice. "To what should we return, Mr. North? All our wealth is sunk in this venture."

"By God," North said. "That I should unknowingly have associated myself with such a pack of mutinous traitors. The king bids us return. There can be no answer to that, other than obedience. What, would you set yourselves up greater than the king?"

He is a man, as we, and he dies, as we, Edward wanted to say. But he dared not. And yet, to abandon everything and go crawling back home, because of a Spanish don. He gazed at his father, and to his surprise found that his father was staring at him.

"Disobey," North said, "and you think nothing will change? We'll be men without a country. I see you already, after one evening's debauch, men without religion, without concept of good or evil. I would not interfere. You have suffered long and hard. But has life nothing more to offer you than a brown belly? What of your wives and families at home? Your mothers and fathers, your sisters and brothers? And what of your tobacco? Suppose we raise a fine crop? Where'll we sell it? Or shall we degenerate into white Indians here in this swamp?"

"Knowing his Majesty," Tom Warner observed, "he'll forgive you anything, should you bring back something of value. That were the sum of Raleigh's crime."

"Tom," North cried, "I'd not have expected to hear *you* uttering treason. No, no. This was an ill-fated venture, from the very start. It is my fault. I admit it freely. It was my decision to go rushing off before waiting for the king's final decision. I take the blame. But now we must return, as we are true-born Englishmen."

There was a moment's silence. But the crew's decisions were evidenced by the way they slowly released their Indian girls, the manner in which they straightened their clothing. No, Edward wanted to shout. No. I do not want to abandon the venture. I want to stay here.

"I think the men, having suffered so much, both in getting here and in staying here this while, deserve to have a free choice in the matter," Tom said.

"Am I not admiral of this expedition? And governor of this colony?" North demanded, going very red in the face.

"You have just elected to abandon your responsibility, sir," Tom said.

"Do you seek to impugn my judgment?"

"I would impugn your very courage, Mr. North. Certainly your fitness for so arduous a post. And you may take offense if you will, sir. This good right arm of mine is disposed to give you satisfaction."

North hesitated, but there could be no question of his opposing his inexperienced blade to such a man as Tom Warner. He turned away, arms outstretched. "Captain Warner wishes the matter to be settled by a popular vote," he cried. "Very well. I show you the king's command." He waved the paper. "And as the ships are mine, I show you an empty river, an empty coast, once I have left. I show you the lad Dick, sweating his life away in that hut. And be sure, too, that I will make a full report of these events to his Majesty, as I am in duty bound to do. Now, make your decision, and quickly."

The men shuffled their feet and cast glances at Tom.

"And I say, as we are here, so let us stay, and do what we came for," Tom declared. "We have found a settlement. And we have found friends in these good savages. Provided we remember always to treat them as friends, we have naught to fear. There will be other ships. Failing that, we shall build our own. And as for his Majesty's displeasure, I promise you that he acts now under pressure from Spain. Did not her

Majesty in days gone by disavow Drake and Hawkins, and issue orders for their recall from more than one expedition, never meaning them to be obeyed? Are we less men than they?" He walked away from North's side, stood close to Tuloa. "Let those who would look to the future rather than the past join me here."

Edward ran to stand beside his father, panting, watching the other men with growing apprehension as they shuffled their feet, glancing from the Arawak girls to the ships to Painton, standing by with an amused expression.

"I will stay, of course, Captain Warner," Ralph Berwicke said, joining them.

"And I'll not desert my friend Edward," Tony Hilton said. "Faith, there's more life in one of these charmers than in all London's whores added together."

Which raised a laugh but did nothing to dispel the tension in the atmosphere.

North smiled. "Well, Captain Warner, I'll wish you good fortune with your colony. You've all of a nation there, two men and a boy. No doubt you'll be sending for your wife and family."

"I'll stay with Captain Warner." Ashton declared himself from among the crew of the *Great St. George*. "Because he's right. There's more future for us here than ever in England, with Scotch James and his favorite lads breathing down our necks."

"And good riddance to you, Mr. Ashton," North declared. "You were ever a revolutionary. Well, who else? You have my leave. Anyone? What, no one? Well, then, man those boats and let's get back to the ships. Captain Warner, you'll do us the courtesy of asking the chief to supply us for the voyage."

Tom Warner hesitated and then addressed Tuloa in Spanish. The chieftain listened, frowning, and seemed to expostulate. But Tom insisted, and finally the Indian shrugged and agreed.

"He will see to it," Tom said. "When his folk have recovered from their debauch. But it will take some days."

"This is reasonable enough," North agreed. "It will give me time to change your mind."

"I'll not return to England like a whipped dog with my tail between my legs."

"And how will you stay here, with but five of you all told? That would be to commit suicide."

"We'll manage," Tom said stoutly. But instinctively he cast a glance at the silent forest.

"Aye, 'tis a grim place, this Guyana," Painton said, for he had come across to overhear their conversation. "They say a man lives but a short while here, and then contracts a kind of shaking sickness which rapidly brings him to his grave."

"Sir, you seek to alarm my companions and myself," Tom said angrily. "You'll not succeed, so you had best take yourselves off."

"I intend to, Captain Warner," Painton said. "The moment I have filled my water casks and obtained some fresh food. If I sought to discourage your impression of this place, it was mainly in the hope that you and your men, and the boy, would sail with me."

"What?" North demanded. "You are not returning with my fleet?"

"No, Mr. North," Painton said. "I am with messages as well for the Virginia colony, and will take myself thither."

"The Virginia colony," Tom said. "Well, then, if that is to be our destiny, so be it. Gladly will we accept your offer, Mr. Painton, as all other avenues seem closed to us." He glanced past North to where Ashton was shaking his head and going red in the face. "What is troubling you, Mr. Ashton? 'Tis a fact we cannot remain here by ourselves; Mr. North is right about that."

Ashton opened his mouth and then closed it again. "It is of no account, Captain Warner. I shall be happy to accompany you wherever you choose."

El Dorado. It was, then, no more than a dream. But he would return. Edward swore this as he tossed in his narrow bunk. Where Walter Raleigh and Thomas Warner had failed, he would succeed, the moment he was grown to manhood. It was not so very far from Virginia to Guyana. Meanwhile, it was good to be at sea again, and in so fine a ship as the *Plymouth Belle*, manned by seamen, rather than would-be colonists, well found and equipped, and more heavily armed than any of Mr. North's vessels. Edward found this out the first day, and hastened aft next morning to ask Father if there was any chance of a set-to with the dons.

He found Tom staring at the empty horizon, for the low coastline of Guyana, and even the brown water off the coast, had dropped from sight during the night; there had been a land breeze to blow them along.

"Aye, boy," he said. "You have told me nothing I did not suspect, after a word or two with Mr. Ashton. It appears that he was trying to warn me against this step, before we embarked. Well, gentlemen?"

Their three companions had also come on deck.

"She's a strong ship, all right, Captain Warner," Tony said. "She'd make a meal out of any Spaniard."

"But strays are not so common in these waters," Berwicke said. "I hope this Painton is not a rash man."

"Rash man or not," Tom growled, "he will end his life on the gallows, and those who sail with him."

"But, sir," Edward said, "he is but a seadog who wars on the dons. Niles, the boatswain, told us of him on the voyage. 'Tis said he is a first-rate seaman."

"Hush, boy. See him there. We must face this thing out now. There'll be no backsliding, gentlemen. You'll stand by me to the end. Ralph?"

"You know me well enough for that, Captain."

"So I do. Mr. Ashton?"

"To the death, Captain."

"Mr. Hilton?"

Tony hesitated. "And should he offer to put us in a way to making our fortunes?"

"By God, boy, you're all of a buccaneer, as Mr. North suggested. Those days are finished, Mr. Hilton, at least with any justice on the pirate's side. This Painton will break every law of man as well as God. And as I said, he'll dangle before long. Believe me, boy, I regret having placed you, and ourselves, in this position, but as we are here, we shall only escape the consequences by staying close together."

"But Father . . ." Edward began again.

"Hush, lad. Here, take this, and if necessary, use it."

A pistol was pressed into his hand, and he turned, his back against the rail, to watch Painton approach.

"By God, Captain Warner," he cried, gazing at their swords and pistols with mock alarm. "But you're expecting to be attacked by the dons at this early hour? We'll not encounter them much before the Bahama Passage, and that's a good week away, even with the benefit of the Florida current."

"And do you, sir, not expect to be assailed by the Spaniards?" Tom demanded. "As you sail their waters."

"God made these waters for all, Captain Warner," Painton insisted. "Besides, it is the most direct route to the Virginias."

"And is it your intention to go to the Virginias, Mr. Painton?"

Painton glanced from Tom to Berwicke, and then to Ashton.

"Aye," Tom said. "It seems I was rash in accepting your invitation. Some of my companions have heard of you before."

"And you thought I'd force a man? Especially one of your reputation, Captain Warner?" Painton guffawed. "Come, now, man, I'm no pirate. But it seems to me, sir, that should we encounter a don in the Bahama Passage, and it is more than likely that we shall do so, we'd be fools not to take what we can and send him to the bottom."

"And you'd not call that piracy?" Berwicke inquired. "Our two countries are at peace."

"Because Scotch James says so," Tony cried. "The queen would never have it."

"Hold your impertinent tongue," Tom shouted. "If you are to follow me. Sir, I came on Mr. North's expedition to make a new home for myself, to which, in the fullness of time and by the grace of God, I had hoped to invite my wife and remaining children."

"And you'd expect to do that in Virginia?" Painton was contemptuous. "If your people do not starve to death within a six-month, it's sure the savages will have them. Would you see your wife on her back before a red-skinned devil?"

"We had no difficulty with the Arawaks."

"The Arawaks don't live farther north than the Guyana coast, Captain Warner. For a very good reason. They used to inhabit all the Caribee Islands, once upon a time. But they were destroyed by other, more warlike redskins."

"We are straying from the subject, sir," Tom insisted. "We mean to be no pirates."

Painton looked at their weapons. "And the four of you, and this boy here, would seek to challenge me and my men? You'd be a madman, Captain Warner."

"You'd take arms against Englishmen, villain?" Ashton asked.

"By God," Painton demanded of the sky at large, "and were you not just proposing to do that against me?" Then he laughed again. "But I like your style, Captain Warner, and that of your men. Now, I'll tell you what is the custom of the sea for those who would go against the will of the captain. 'Tis to place the offenders on some deserted isle, with but a single musket and a single cutlass, a barrel of water and a side of beef, and leave them there to make the best of it."

"You'd maroon us?"

Painton was suddenly serious. "It would be best. These men of mine are hand-picked, and there's not a colonist among them. They'd give you short shrift if they thought you'd stand between their hands and a don treasure chest. And we don't mean that any word of what we do should ever get back to Whitehall. But I say again, I like your courage. Listen. I told you, before we left Guyana, that we had departed Plymouth Sound only a day or two behind your fleet. Yet it took us near a month longer to gain the river coast."

"You were delayed by bad weather," Tom said.

"True. A gale blew us off course, and so we found ourselves among the islands of the Caribees. We were low on water by then, so we put in to one of them. There was no harbor, so we dropped our hook and went ashore. Oh, well armed, to be sure. Shall I tell you what we found?"

"We're anticipating you'll do that," Tom said.

"Well, this island is green as a berry. Except where the great mountain peak sticks up amidships. But the soil is so fertile you'd grow a man overnight, I do swear. There's rainfall regular as you'd want a clock to be. Two hours at noon. Neither sooner nor later. That keeps it watered, you'll understand, and yet never lets you in for a downpour such as you experienced at Guyana. There's a breeze all the time, a brisk easterly, sometimes with a shade of south in it, sweeping across the hills. So you'd settle on the leeward side, see, where the mountain acts as a natural windbreak, and you'd just get the gentle zephyrs filtering down the passes. And tobacco? Why, it grows there wild, yet in such profusion you'd think God Himself planted it. As no doubt He did."

"You're sure this paradise didn't happen in a dream?" Tom inquired with some sarcasm.

"It's on the chart. I'll show you."

"And it has a name?"

"The Spaniards call it St. Christopher. You'll know the tale of the saint, with the boy Jesus on his shoulder? Well, this island has another, smaller island, hardly more than a rock, projecting to the southward and connected to the main island by a narrow isthmus. So, seen from afar, to the Spaniards it suggested the picture of the saint and the boy. Thus the name."

"And if it is this splendid, why did the Spaniards not settle it?"

"Because there is no gold to be found there, and that is all they seek. But you gentlemen are not after gold, I'd have thought."

Tom pulled his lip, glanced at his companions. "And you'd put us ashore there, Mr. Painton, with a single musket and a single cutlass?"

"It's certain you'll need nothing more. But I'm not that kind of a man, Captain Warner. I'll put you ashore with every one of your possessions. You have my word on it."

"As you yourself went ashore armed," Ashton observed. "You have not told us the outcome of your adventure, Mr. Painton. Is this island uninhabited?"

"By no means, Mr. Ashton. It belongs to the Carib Indians, as do all the islands in this sea, except where they have been exterminated by the Spaniards."

"And has not the very word 'Carib' been corrupted into 'cannibal,' meaning 'man-eater,' and with good reason?"

"So I have heard," Painton agreed. "And 'tis certain that these Indians are a sight more warlike than their brethren on the mainland. But their enemies are the dons. As we also hate the dons, they were our friends, and will be yours. Why, they welcomed us with open arms, and would have had us stay. And these are *men,* Captain Warner. And women. By God." He glanced at Hilton. "They are of the same race as the Arawaks, but far superior. Taller, and more straight, and more comely, and more proud. Savages, to be sure, but noble, fit to set alongside a white man. They'll be happy to see you, Captain Warner, can they but be convinced you mean them no harm."

Tom Warner leaned on the rail and gazed at the empty ocean. A tumult of thoughts chased themselves through his mind. Painton had indeed described what he had hoped to find in Guyana, where a man might after all make a home for himself and his family. But there was the problem. "And yet would we be marooned," he said. "Without hope of succor, or of seeing our families again. Every argument raised by Mr. North against our remaining in Guyana is valid also for your St. Christopher."

"Except that on St. Christopher a man might very well live forever," Painton pointed out. "But if you've no taste for that, Captain Warner, why, I but sought to save you from participation in my crimes, supposing I commit any. Why not try the place, man? I promise you in a six-month you'll have a crop of tobacco, and then, why, it is on my route home, and I shall need water in any event. You'll see the *Plymouth Belle* again before Easter. But I'll make a small wager that by then you'll refuse a passage home."

Tom smiled. "You make this place sound a paradise, Mr. Painton. The kind of place of which I have ever dreamed. I find it hard to believe that such an enchanted land can exist."

"It exists," Painton vowed. "I have seen it, and so will you, for it lies just over the horizon, not two days' sail from our present position, by my reckoning, if this wind holds. And you have put your word to it, Captain Warner. It is enchanted. Aye, to the very Indians it is known as the Enchanted Isle."

4

The King's Lieutenant

"They're peaceable, you say," Tom Warner observed, as the longboat approached the shore. For the people gathered there carried spears and bows and arrows, although they were not actually making a noise or hurling their missiles.

"They are," Painton said. "Or I'd not have come with you." He pointed. "And you'll admit, Captain, that it's a fair sight."

Tom nodded. He could not deny that. The island, and several others, had been peeping above the horizon at dawn, purple clouds clinging to the eastern sky. The Leeward Islands, so called because they were downwind of the outward bulge of the Caribees, which were known, appropriately enough, as the Windwards.

They were volcanic, reputedly, although he was relieved to see that there were no patches of smoke to suggest that there was anything active in the neighborhood. And certainly they were beautiful. Deep blue water gave way to pale green, and the pale green to the dark sanded beaches; behind lay the lush green forest, which in turn dwindled into the purple of the mountains, and in St. Christopher the mountain seemed higher than most, thrusting its peak toward the heavens, a time-hardened lava finger. But the central mass, if easily the highest point on the island, was not the most distinguished. There was another hill, lower and closer at hand, protruding over the sea a few miles to the left. "Now, there is a natural fortress," he muttered. "It would require fire and brimstone from heaven itself to reduce that rock, properly defended."

Then there was the peninsula to the right, which ended in another mountain. The Christ Child. Perhaps there was no water there. In any event, there was little vegetation, and no promise of tobacco.

His only worry was that the island was not so isolated as he had been led to believe. To the south there were the peaks of another island, which Painton said was called Nevis, and they had seen other peaks earlier in the day. They were venturing deep into the heartland of the Carib nation, and there could be no doubt that the people on the beach belonged to this most vicious of savage tribes.

"You'll observe that I spoke the truth." Painton's hand closed more tightly on the tiller as they entered the gentle surf leading to the beach. "These people are far superior to the Arawaks."

Tom nodded again, and was relieved that he had left the boy on board. Time enough for Edward to land later, when they were assured of a welcome.

"They are that." Tony Hilton wore a sword and carried two pistols in his belt. A dangerous man. But dangerous, at this moment, only to the savages, whatever problems his lusts might cause later.

Tom frowned. "You'll observe, gentlemen, that they truly are different."

"By God," Berwicke said. "The women wear skirts."

"If you can call them that," Ashton pointed out.

" 'Tis to be sure they cover their privies," Hilton said in disgust. "And the men . . ."

"It is a sort of pouch, in which they hang their genitals," Painton explained. " 'Tis but a device, you'll understand, dictated not by modesty, but by their warlike characteristics. 'Tis difficult for a man to carry himself well in battle with his all waving in the wind."

"But surely the women take no part in warfare," Berwicke said.

"Do not suppose that these are ordinary females. They will fight shoulder to shoulder with their men, and hurl a spear with as much power and accuracy. You'll do well to present a peaceable front, and a confident one. They regard courage as the only virtue, in either man or woman. Follow my example."

The longboat rushed at the beach, carried on the last of the waves. The sailors backed their oars, and then shipped them, and the keel grated. Two men leaped over the bow to hold the boat steady, while the gentlemen disembarked. Painton went first, followed by Tom Warner, Ashton, Berwicke, and Hilton. The Indians remained in a group where the sand faded into grass, perhaps a hundred feet away; they fingered their spears and bows, men and women, but made no move toward the white men.

Behind them, amid the trees, could be seen the houses of the village, if they could be so called. For each hut was nothing more than four uprights sheltering beneath a palm-frond roof, leaving the interior exposed to every careless glance and every quirk of the weather. But it was easy to suppose, looking at the clear blue sky and feeling the steady gentle breeze, that there *were* no quirks of the weather in these surroundings.

Sanitation and fresh water were provided by a stream which rushed through the bushes before dissipating itself in the sand. The atmosphere was entirely different to the oppressive stillness of Guyana. The very air smelled cleaner.

"Wait here," Painton said, and walked up the beach, his boots leaving deep prints in the sand. Certainly he was a brave man, or he had complete confidence in his relations with these people. After fifty feet he stopped. "Pain-ton," he said. "Pain-ton." He pointed at the sun, then stooped and with his finger drew several lines on the sand, before sweeping them away with a flick of his hand. He stood straight again. "Tegramond."

There was a moment's hesitation, and then one of the Caribs came slowly down the beach. Undoubtedly he was a chieftain, although now he was isolated from his fellows it was possible to observe several differences between himself and Tuloa. He wore his hair long; it lay on his shoulders in a straight black shawl. His features were not quite so flat, although his cheek and jaw bones were as pronounced; the firmness of his lips, no less than the height of his forehead and the intelligence in his eyes, all suggested a nobility which had been lacking in the Arawak. His body, too, if less heavily muscled, was far more agreeable to European eyes, for he possessed long legs, suited for running and walking rather than penetrating thick forest, and he stood very straight. He wore nothing on his head, but rather indicated his authority by a necklace of what appeared to be shells, and like his fellows he wore the breechclout, although, this apart, he was naked.

He stood in front of Painton, and extended his arms to

place a hand on each shoulder of the white man. "Pain-ton," he said, and pointed to the sun.

"He bids us welcome, gentlemen," Painton said, without turning his head. "You'll advance, slowly, if you please."

Tom glanced at Berwicke and then set out. The other three men followed in a row; Hilton rested his hand on the hilt of his sword, but a shake of the head from Berwicke had him marching like the others, hands swinging at his sides.

"War-nah," Painton said. "Tegramond. He is the cacique of this tribe."

The Carib chieftain stared into Tom's eyes, and Tom felt a sensation of weakness, and although he was not prepared to admit it even to himself, almost of humility.

Painton walked along the row. "Tegramond, Ash-ton, Tegramond, Hil-ton. Tegramond, Ber-wicke."

Tegramond looked from one face to the next, without moving.

"By Christ," Ashton whispered, "I had thought they were shells."

For now they could see that the necklace was composed of human teeth.

"You'll keep your opinions to yourselves," Painton recommended, for the cacique was frowning. "War-nah," he said, throwing his arms wide, to encircle the entire island. "Ashton. Hil-ton. Ber-wicke." He put his hands together, rested them against his cheek, and closed his eyes.

Tegramond gazed at Tom.

Painton opened his eyes and drew his sword, being careful to hold it in both hands. He thrust the point into the sand and turned over the soil.

Tegramond continued to gaze at Tom.

Painton cleaned his blade and restored it to his scabbard. Then he knelt beside the small hole and pantomimed planting, before covering up the hole again. Next he stood up, put his hand to his lips, inhaled, and gave a great sigh of pleasure.

"Tobacco," Tegramond said. His voice was deep but entirely lacking in the guttural intonations of the mainland Indians.

"He knows the word," Tom said in wonder.

"It is *his* word, Captain Warner," Painton pointed out. "War-nah. Ash-ton, Hil-ton, Ber-wicke, friends. Place your swords on the sand, as gifts, gentlemen."

"What?" Tom demanded. "Leave ourselves unarmed?"

"That I shall never do," Hilton declared.

"If you would live here," Painton said, "you will depend upon this man's goodwill. Not your strength, which, when pitted against that of these savages, is worthless. And you'll still have your pistols, in the last resort."

Tom hesitated, stared at Tegramond for a moment, and then took off his sword belt and laid it on the sand. Reluctantly his companions followed his example. Tegramond picked up Tom's weapon, and his followers crowded around to examine the wonder.

"Now," Painton said, "give him your hand, Captain."

Tom stepped forward, hand outstretched. Tegramond looked at it for a moment, and then grasped it. His grip was firm and dry. Then he handed the sword to one of his people and placed both hands on Tom's shoulders. His fingers ate into the flesh, and his eyes gleamed. "Tegramond, hammock, War-nah hammock."

"What does he mean?" Tom asked, still gazing at the chief.

"He offers you the sharing of his bed," Painton said. "It is symbolic. You have naught to fear from these people, Captain Warner, so long as you treat them right."

They marched, following the beach. Tegramond went first, following by one of his men; the cacique wore the sword belt Tom had given him; the blade slapped his bare thigh. Tom Warner came next, Edward by his side, Painton walking immediately behind. Then came Berwicke, Ashton, and Hilton, carrying the belongings of the white party. Behind them were four Indian women laden with plaited straw baskets containing fish and fruit.

The sun was high, and the white men sweated. Behind them the *Plymouth Belle* rode at anchor, dwindling in size with every step. On their right hand the sand gave way to forest, above which the huge central mountain peak loomed toward the sky. Ahead of them the hills swerved toward the sea, ending in the massive seven-hundred-foot-high outcrop which had attracted Tom from the first.

"It is a fair land, don't you agree, Edward?" he asked.

"Oh, beautiful, sir. Exactly as Mr. Painton described."

"Aye. I wonder if we shall at last find our El Dorado in this place, in this warmth and this health, this vigor, these charming people. Do you think your mother and Philip would be happy here?"

"Oh, yes, sir. Why, it is so . . . so beautiful."

"And more than that," Hilton observed. "A man could truly be content here. These girls could walk anywhere and bring a coach and four to a halt. I say, my pretty, why don't we exchange loads? I'm sure that would be more fitting."

The young woman gazed at him in surprise. She was certainly far more attractive than any of the Arawak females. Her black hair was even longer than Tegramond's; it brushed her thighs. Her pointed, big-boned features were handsome rather than pretty, but there could be no argument about the beauty of her body, unless it was merely that the white men were quite unused to seeing blooming womanhood walking around wearing nothing but an undersized apron. Here were narrow shoulders giving way to full and high but curiously pointed breasts, with dark nipples which seemed less teats than extensions of the paler flesh supporting them. Here were wide thighs containing the disturbingly pouted belly—but then, these girls had never been taught posture or worn a corset—so scantily endowed with pubic hair which but attracted the men's attention the more. And here were strong, muscular legs; too muscular, perhaps, for beauty, with feet and toes flattened by endless shoeless walking, but suggesting endless pleasure when separated. And above all, here were smiling black eyes and the purest of white teeth.

He attempted to relieve her of her basket, using his opportunity to pass his hand over her breasts, which seemed to offend her not a whit. She continued to smile.

But Tegramond had stopped and was watching. Tom Warner stopped also. "Mr. Hilton," he said. "You'll cease that. And mark me well. We shall exist in this place only by continued friendly relations with these people. I say here and now that we must all swear, by everything we hold holy, that we shall forever treat Chief Tegramond and his people with respect and friendship, acknowledging them as our equals, using their women as we should use our own, granting them all the honor that we should extend to our closest friends."

"Well said, Tom Warner," Painton declared.

"I willing swear to that," Berwicke agreed.

"And I," Ashton said.

Hilton glanced at them, and then at the girl as he released her. His face was flushed with a combination of embarrassment and unsatisfied desire. "I swear," he muttered.

"Then let us hurry behind the chief," Tom said. For Tegramond had resumed his march.

Edward opened his mouth and closed it again. But he was

nonetheless angry. Father had quite excluded him from the ranks of the men. No doubt unwittingly. He was very preoccupied. For now Tegramond had rounded the bluff formed by the protruding hill, and stopped, and with the shaft of his spear drew a line across the sand, from the bushes down to the rippling surf. This done, he turned and beckoned Tom to come closer, and indeed, made him stand astride the line, and then pointed inland from it, to the mountain in the center of the island. Next he pointed at the sun and made a wheeling motion with his arm, right down and back up again, pausing when his hand was horizontal. He gazed anxiously into Tom's eyes.

"I understand you, Tegramond," Tom said. "This line is drawn where the sun will be hidden by the mountain as it rises. But does not the sun change its place in the heavens with the seasons?"

"In these latitudes, very little," Painton said. "Show the cacique that you understand him."

Tom stooped and placed his hand on the line, then he pointed at the mountain, at the sun, and back beyond the mountain again.

Tegramond nodded and smiled.

"He is giving you the use of this land," Painton said.

"And how much more, I wonder?" Tom peered along the beach, shading his eyes.

Tegramond nodded and pointed to the next outcrop of rock, perhaps a mile away, and then inland again. He made a swinging motion with his hand, from side to side. "Tobacco."

"He's right, there," Painton agreed. "'Tis a good soil. Well, Captain Warner, are you pleased?"

"I am overwhelmed," Tom confessed. "It is far more than I had hoped." He held out his hand, and Tegramond took it. Then he placed his right forefinger on Tom's chest, next on his own, and then took away both his hands together before pointing at the sky.

"You are friends forevermore, Captain Warner," Painton said. "And I count my wager safe. Yet we shall return in a six-month, as I promised."

"By then we shall have a crop to be shipped, so we shall be right pleased to see you. And my thanks, John. You truly were an angel in disguise, with your Enchanted Isle."

"It was my pleasure. Now you'll come back on board and take a glass of wine before we part. You too, Tegramond."

He rested his left hand on the chief's shoulder, and with his right hand made the gesture of raising a cup to his lips.

Tegramond smiled, and then laughed, and clapped his hands together, almost like a child.

"For depend upon it," Painton said, "if these savages have a weakness, it is for strong drink. You'll understand, Captain Warner, that this land is rather rented than given to you. He will expect his share of European goods, and especially European liquor, from time to time."

"Indeed, he is welcome to all I can procure," Tom said.

"Then there should be no fear as to your future prosperity. Now, come, gentlemen. Edward?"

But Edward was gazing at the forest, where two more Indians had just appeared, although they remained half-hidden by the bushes.

Tegramond made a grunted remark, and the pair came closer. The cacique rested his hand on Edward's shoulder, and then pointed at Tom's belly.

"Well, yes, in a manner of speaking," Tom acknowledged.

Tegramond nodded and indicated the boy. He was not so tall as Edward, although it was impossible to gauge his age. He resembled the chieftain quite closely, but Tegramond pointed at his own belly and shook his head. Then he embraced the boy and said, "Wapisiane." He pointed at the sun, opened and closed his hands several times, and laid his forefinger, most expressively, across his own eyes. Then he touched the tooth necklace he wore, and with the same fingers touched Wapisiane's neck. The boy smiled.

"His successor," Painton said. "Already designated."

"But not his son?"

"Oh, he will be a relative of some sort."

"And the other?" Tom asked. "What a splendid child."

Tegramond could see the admiration on the white man's face. He gestured the girl forward, and at the same time seized his genitals and moved them to and fro, before pointing, to indicate that she was his daughter. When she came close, he took her hands and said, "Yarico."

"Maybe you'd do better to stay ashore, Edward," Tom suggested. "If this is to be our home, the sooner you make friends among the Caribs, the better, and these look a likely pair. If the chief has no objection."

He touched Edward on the shoulder, gestured toward Wapisiane, and then at Yarico, and found himself still staring. Because here was no mere savage female, considered as a creature capable of conceiving and bearing children in contrast to her male counterparts. Yarico could hardly have been Edward's age, he supposed; her hips were slender, between which the small cloth square seemed an unnecessary extravagance, and her breasts were no more than pointed mounds on her chest, but she already possessed more height than her companion, and her face, far from being a gaunt, pointed accumulation of bones and tightly drawn skin, had sufficient flesh for beauty, and there was beauty in the black eyes, too, which flickered up and down the white man in response to his obvious admiration. While the whole—face, shoulders, hips, even thighs—was shrouded in the straight, coarse midnight hair, which fluttered in the breeze. Christ, how long had it been since he had touched a woman's hair, felt the softness of a woman's flesh, allowed his fingers to wander through the damp splendor of a woman's crotch. Oh, Rebecca, Rebecca.

"You'll bear in mind that she's the cacique's daughter," Painton whispered.

Tom started, and flushed. "I'll bear my own oath in mind, Mr. Painton. And the child's youth. And my own marriage. But there's no harm in admiring beauty. What does the chief say?"

Tegramond smiled and waved his hand, and then turned and walked back along the beach. The white men followed, with the Carib women. Hilton was last to go. "I never thought I'd want to be your age again, Ned," he said. "Now I wonder what's the good of being a man, after all."

Edward stared after them in some anxiety. He had not been afraid of the Arawaks. He had been terrified of the forest, but the Indians had never been other than gentle. He could not imagine them being otherwise. But he could feel no gentleness here, although both Wapisiane and Yarico were gazing at him in a perfectly friendly fashion.

He licked his lips. "Good day to you, Master Wapisiane," he said. "And to you, Miss Yarico."

Yarico stared at him, frowning slightly. Wapisiane reached forward and plucked the pistol from his belt.

"Hey," Edward said. "Just hold on a moment. . . ."

Wapisiane was sighting the pistol at a tree, and now he released the lever. And then lowered the weapon and examined it. He glanced at Edward. "Bang?"

"It is not primed." Edward rolled the match with his fingers, made the movement of pouring powder into the touch-hole.

Wapisiane gave a grunt and looked up expectantly.

"Here." Edward touched the pouch which hung from his belt. "But we'll not fire it," he insisted, shaking his hand as Wapisiane reached for the belt.

The Indian boy scowled and made a gesture with the pistol, but was checked by the girl, who said something, removed the weapon from his grasp, and handed it back to Edward. She did not immediately release it, however, but left it as a bridge between their hands for a moment. When she did let go of the weapon, it was to touch the cloth of his shirt, allowing her fingers to stroke up to his neck.

"Would you like a shirt?" he asked. "It would be more fitting."

Her fingers released the ties, and her hand slipped inside before he could stop her, to squeeze the flesh of his breast.

Edward thrust the pistol back into his belt, yet was strangely reluctant to try to pull her hand out. But she was withdrawing it, smiling and making a remark to Wapisiane.

He merely turned, to walk off down the beach.

"I did not mean to offend him," Edward said.

To his dismay, Yarico also turned, not toward the beach, but to begin walking into the trees.

"Oh, don't go," Edward cried.

Yarico paused at the edge of the grass and looked over her shoulder. It was a strange look, and yet familiar; he had seen it on other girls' faces, perhaps even on his mother's face—but never directed at him.

He glanced from left to right. The white men and Tegramond had disappeared around the corner of the beach; Wapisiane stood on the edge of the sea, gazing at the horizon. Edward ran up the sand, his feet scuffling the soft surface, his breath quickly beginning to pant. For Yarico had disappeared also. Yet she was there; he could hear her moving in front of him, and after a moment he caught up with her. This was no Guyanese jungle, but dry, and with far less undergrowth. He wondered if there were any snakes and poisonous spiders in St. Christopher's forest, but he would not have liked to ask her, even had he known how; he did not wish her to suppose him afraid.

In any event, he was too occupied with watching her, moving in front of him. For now they climbed, and the grass was giving way to pebbles and loose rock, and occasional firm outcrops. Over which Yarico passed with indifference, although some of the coral heads hurt *his* feet right through his shoes.

He had never observed someone so closely before. Her hair swayed from side to side. Little balls of warm muscle moved up her calf whenever she rose onto her toes; longer slivers of hardening muscle drifted up and down her thighs and her buttocks moved in separate spasms, seeming to tighten and then relax, to spread apart and then come back together, almost like gigantic lips opening and closing. He realized that he had never in his life actually watched a girl's buttocks moving before, or a man's, for that matter. He sweated, and had the discomfort of an erection while he walked, together with a peculiar lightness in his stomach. It was a feeling he had not known since he had watched Mr. Walkden lying on his back staring at the knife which was about to destroy him.

But Yarico sweated too. This was as fascinating as her movement. Great beads of sweat trickled out from her hair and rolled down her legs, and when, without warning, she stopped and turned, he saw that there was sweat on her stomach and rolling over her small breasts, and incredibly, sweat on her upper lip. He wanted to wipe it off, but he was afraid to touch her.

Yarico wiped away her own sweat with a flick of her finger and tossed her hair to dislodge more liquid and send it scattering into the bushes. Suddenly he was obsessed by her scent, at once fresh and stale, repulsive and compellingly attractive. He had the most amazing wonder as to what she would taste like.

She pointed. They had reached the top of the first slope, although the tree-clad mountain rose ever before them. But in the dip which lay at their feet was a pool of water. Yarico stretched out her arm once more, and with her finger stroked down his shirt and across his breeches, before he could stop her. She laughed, the most delicious sound he had ever heard, and shook her head. Her fingers moved back to her own waist, and she untied the rawhide holding her cloth in place. Edward found himself licking his lips in a mixture of fascination and admiration. Like the Arawak girls, she had no body hair, only the faintest darkening of her crotch. He thought she was the most beautiful thing he had ever seen, but he hoped she wasn't going to stand there while he also undressed. This whole business was distinctly indecent, and if

Father were ever to find out about it . . . Yet it had not really crossed his mind to refuse to join her.

Yarico laughed again and dived into the water. Edward scrabbled at his breeches, but before he could get them off she had surfaced on the far side of the pool, which seemed to be deeper than he had supposed, for he could see her legs moving to and fro as she trod water. He turned his back to finish removing his clothes, and then jumped into the water without looking at her. He went down, down, into the clear, fresh, and unexpectedly cold water, sinking far into the depths, and yet, looking down, it seemed to stretch away forever. He had never been in water this deep before, and suddenly he was afraid. He thrashed his arms, kicked his legs, and saw the brown body in front of him, black hair now rising away from her head and toward the surface as she sank beside him. Her presence restored his confidence, and a moment later he had regained the air and the warmth of the afternoon sun. But he felt too tired to remain in the water, and so swam to the edge and climbed out onto the smoothest of the rocks, to sit there panting.

Yarico leaned on the rock immediately below him. Her gaze was anxious, and tentatively she put out her hand and stroked the palm down his thighs, where the weary muscles still jumped beneath the wet flesh. He felt a sudden necessity for conversation, placed the edge of his hand on the earth, and wriggled the whole arm through the dust, hissing and spitting. Yarico gazed at him in wonder, and then placed a finger on her lips, while her eyes darted to and fro. Now he could hear a faint rustling, and fear sweat stood out on his neck. Yet he remained still, watching the girl; she moved with startling speed, whipped her hand into the bushes, and brought out a lizard, green, clammy, and terrified, its tongue a wisp of shuddering flesh. Yarico held it up before him, laughed, and tossed it back into the bushes. That done, she cast him a quick glance, and he smiled his congratulations. Her confidence grew, and her smile widened. He watched her hand, mesmerized by its gentle and yet quick movements. It slid across his thigh once again, reminding him of the slither of the bushmaster, and then moved between his legs to seize his flaccid penis and draw it once more into erection.

For a moment he sat still, gazing down at her, his body filling with warmth and belly lightness, his mind crying out for so many things, most of which he did not even understand, and then the complete wrongness of what he was allowing, especially after Father's instructions, overwhelmed him. Before he could stop himself, he had seized her wrist and thrown it away from him.

Yarico stared at him for a moment, in surprise and, perhaps, he thought, even fear. Then the expression on her face became more certainly one of anger. Her head tossed, to scatter hair and clouds of water, and she released the rock and sank back into the pool.

"Don't go," he begged. "Let me explain."

But Yarico was already swimming away from him, if swimming was the right word for a body which seemed merely to flick and be out of his reach. On the far side she crawled out, stooped, and picked up her cloth from the bush where it had lain, and disappeared into the trees. It had all happened so quickly Edward was left with only the impression of her, and the desire in his belly.

"By Christ, the heat," Henry Aston complained, dropping to his knees and fanning himself with a wide palm leaf. For the month was April; it had been November when they had arrived. "Without that damnable sun, this would be a paradise."

"It *is* a paradise, Hal," Tom Warner insisted. "I bless the day that John Painton's path crossed mine. Ours. The heat is but an aspect of paradise. Has any of us known a day's illness since we arrived? Are there any pests on this blessed island? Snakes, spiders? Even the rain is as moderate as we had hoped. El Dorado. We have no need to look further."

Tony Hilton lay on his back, his hat over his face. "A complete heaven, Tom. Maybe just a shade too much like heaven, in truth. It completely lacks female companionship. At least . . ."

He sat up, watched Yarico walk by, at the water's edge. She did this every day. No doubt she had somewhere to visit, and the English village lay on her route. They could not be sure of this. They had explored little of the island, Tom not wanting in any way to offend Tegramond.

And meanwhile, he thought, they had done well. He leaned against a good wooden wall, with the roof of the porch over his head. Inside there were two rooms, furnished only with one or two wooden utensils, and the inevitable hammocks, made of plaited coconut fibers, which had been Tegramond's presents to the white men. He had never slept in so comfortable a bed, swaying gently to and fro, cooled at once above and below. Rebecca would look magnificent in a hammock.

She would feel magnificent in a hammock. But to dream of Rebecca was to drive himself mad. Tony had a point. And to Tony, young and never married, the difficulty must be greater than for most. Berwicke was also unmarried, but in Berwicke the urges of manhood no longer made themselves felt. Or so he pretended. As for Ashton, his wife was the sea. He had but to look at the ocean, as he was doing now, and he was content.

Yarico disappeared up the beach. She never looked at the white men, never appeared to notice them. She just passed, no doubt well aware that they were noticing her.

"By Christ," Tony muttered. "To think that I shall have to watch that child grow. . . . Tom, you'd have no objection to a proper marriage, now, would you?"

Tom sat up. This was delicate ground, now risked for the first time, although he had known it must come. He looked around him. They had christened the settlement Sandy Point, appropriately enough. Theirs was a world of sand, and sea, and sun, and utter peace, which only internal discontent could ever disrupt. Berwicke was on kitchen duty today, and thus scraped away at the luncheon platters. Ashton remained lying on the hot sand in front of his house. Edward sat not far from his father, also gazing after the girl. But Edward scarcely mattered at this point, for all that he was growing fast, not upwards but outward; muscles filled his arms and his chest, and as he never wore a shirt, his flesh was almost as brown as Hilton's or indeed the Indians'. He would make a fine figure of a man; he was already a fine figure of a man. But he was still only thirteen. Hilton was the problem here.

But Hilton also lounged on the porch of his own house. There was a suitable starting place.

Tom got up. "You'll be married, Tony. Soon. But not to one of these girls." He pointed at the cross of St. George fluttering above the village. "We're Englishmen, and we'll stay English."

"You're a dreamer, Tom. We made our decision when we refused to sail home with Roger North."

"We made *a* decision, Tony. The right one. Listen to me." He stepped on to the sand, turned to face the four houses which formed a half-moon just inside the cleared jungle. "You'll agree this island beats any part of England you've ever seen?" He glared at them. "You'll agree that these Caribs are as friendly and pleasant a lot as we've ever known. There's the first part of my dream, come true. You tell me where are the laws, the burnings and hangings, you show me our star chamber, our high churchmen, our covenanters. We pray to God every Sunday morning, because we are Christians. That's all a man needs to be Christian. And God has been good to us. Look around you. Every man of us has a house of his own. Modest, maybe, but it's a house, and nobody is going to take it away from you. Come out here." He stamped aside, to gaze inland, and and feel his heart swell with pride. Five months' work, and it was all done now. Tegramond had played his part there. No men had come; the Carib males considered it unmanly to work in the fields, and indeed they had gathered in groups to watch the white men. But their women had worked as hard as anyone. They had cleared the ground, burning it to destroy the last tree stumps, and then they had dug trenches three feet apart, as Tom wished; he had not wasted his time on the voyage from England, and had studied every book on tobacco farming that North had possessed.

While the women had been clearing and plowing, the white men had been gathering the seed, for tobacco grew wild in many parts of the island. Tom had himself prepared the seed beds, which remained close behind the houses, ready for the germination of the next crop. According to North's books, one ounce of seed might produce forty thousand plants.

The beds had been carefully sited; the village had been built facing the south, with the huge bulk of the mountain acting as a natural windbreak; here they got the maximum sun and warmth, and here they could be easily watered—in the course of clearing the forest the colonists had come across a deep pool formed by a spring of water as sweet as any of them had ever tasted.

For eight weeks they had tended the seeds, while building their houses and continuing their work on the fields. Next had come the transplanting, a splendid occasion on which the whole Carib nation, over a hundred men, women, and children, had gathered to enjoy, had made their own encampment down by the water, had celebrated while they watched the white men work.

Then it had been done, and for two months now they had been required to do no more than weed, and occasionally water, although there was sufficient rainfall to care for this, and in recent days, to "top" the plants, to cut off the flowering crests as Tom had been taught by North, so as to allow the leaves beneath to grow larger and more luxuriant. And now . . .

"Look at it," he cried. "Look at it." Between them and the forest, looming some four hundred yards away, there were endless rows of graceful plants, huge leaves drooping, each leaf worth . . . he had no idea. "Within a week, now," he shouted, "we'll be reaping. There's a fortune in that soil. And it's ours. Think on it, Tony. There's sufficient wealth to make each of us a rich man, and that's but one crop. There'll be another by the end of this year, and then another, and another . . . and not a tithe, not a penny of ship money to be paid to anyone."

"Aye," Henry Ashton said. "But who's to buy it, Tom? The Caribs?"

Tom stared at him, chewing his lip. Painton should have returned over a month ago. But they had only his word that he was coming back at all. And even if he was a man to be trusted, he had gone off pirating. His ship might be at the bottom of the sea by now, and he and his men either dead or imprisoned by the Spaniards; the dons did not regard Englishmen caught in the Americas as being worthy of lawful treatment.

"Painton will be here," he asserted confidently. "He gave me his word, and he'll be here. I give you *my* word on that. Why . . ." he looked up the beach, watched the girl running toward them. No, not toward them, past them, and on this occasion there was no studied movement, no planned coquetry. She ran excitedly, her cloud of black hair rising behind her, wisps of sand flying from her heels.

"By Christ, what a picture," Hilton said. "And when her breasts begin to jounce . . ."

"Avast there," Ashton growled. "She's seen something."

"A ship," Tom said. "It'll have to be a ship. Edward, lad, get up that mountain. Your eyes are as good as hers. See what she saw."

"Yes, Father," Edward got up slowly, as he had to adjust his clothes so that none of the men could see. By Christ, as Tony would say, what she did to him. What she knew she did to him. Only he knew why she walked past the village every day. She tortured him with all the angry memory of a white woman.

He ran across the sand as she had done, his bare feet digging into the hot white, no longer concerned with large shell or stray coral outcrop; his flesh was as hard as leather. He wore only breeches, and these were sadly tattered. Indeed, but for Father's insistence that they preserve their identity as Europeans, he would as soon have tied up his privies in a cloth like the Caribs and left it at that.

"Hold on there. Not so fast," Tony panted at his shoulders. "Think your father can be right?"

"She must have seen something," Edward gasped. They climbed the rocky slopes of the hill. Father called it Brimstone Hill, and dreamed of planting his fortress here, one day, to command with its cannon the roadstead and the village, no, the town, perhaps the city below. One day, perhaps. But it had to begin with the ship.

He staggered up the slopes, now some four hundred feet from the beach, with Father and Ashton and Berwicke no more than specks beneath him, and the houses like toy huts. There were still another four hundred feet to the summit. He paused for breath, gazing down at the empty ocean. Not entirely empty. From here he could see the peak of the island of Nevis, no more than a few miles distant. Farther off there were other peaks, rising above the horizon, other islands, other Carib tribes, perhaps even other European settlements. But they might as well have been on the moon, or on one of the stars which at night seemed so close he thought he could pluck them out of the sky.

"Nothing," Hilton said, having got his wind back. "It was another of her tricks. Oh, she's a cunning one, that Yarico. But Christ, Ned, I'd not confess this to your father, but I'll not wait any longer. I'm going to climb aboard if I die for it."

"Yarico?" Edward asked, and wondered why he suddenly hated his friend.

Hilton winked. "I'm not that stupid, Ned. A chief's daughter? Why, by God, she's all of a princess, by her own reckoning, I'd say. Anyway, I'd like to get my fingers on to more than what she has, right this minute. I'll settle for one of those dark-haired beauties that helped us with the planting."

Wrong. And dangerous. But how could he say anything to Tony, save the obvious, that it would anger Father. What would happen then? Would Father and Tony fight? Experience and ability, backed by age, against youth and determination? The question would be, how much age; when did age cease to be an asset and become a weakness? And how could he stand by and watch his friend fighting his father, and not take sides? Oh, God damn John Painton.

But there had to be something out there. When he looked down at the beach he saw a large crowd of Caribs, gathered on the shore where the neck of land joined the main island to the offshoot mountain; the current, such as it was in these parts, maintained a set into the bay, and he watched one of the large canoes used by the Indians for offshore fishing being carried down the beach from the village.

"*They've* seen something," he said.

"Well, they must have better eyesight than us," Tony grumbled, shading his eyes as he stared at the shimmering blue water. "Hold on, though. What's that?"

Edward followed his pointing finger, frowning as he thought he saw a dark speck bobbing on the waves, perhaps half a mile from the shore. A log of wood. No, it was a canoe. A small one, to be sure, but drifting.

"Another Indian," Tony said in disgust. "So much for our hopes of rescue from this place."

"I wonder why they are so excited," Edward said.

"Maybe they recognize the boat," Tony said. "Anyway, there's nothing to be gained from staying here, if that's all that alarmed the girl."

They climbed down. Tom and the others were waiting for them.

"Just a canoe. Fishing, I'd say, and lost his paddles," Tony said. "All that climb for nothing."

"But the Caribs seem greatly agitated, Father," Edward said.

Tom frowned. "He may have brought news of some event. I'll go along the beach and see if I can learn anything."

"May I come too?" Edward asked.

"Of course." Tom looked at the other men, but they shook their heads.

" 'Tis too hot, Tom," Berwicke said. "If there is news, I'll be glad to learn it. But walking on this sand gives me the palpitations."

"Aye," Tom said. " 'Tis a fact that the only thing any of us is likely to die of in this enchanted place, saving old age, is heat stroke. Well, come on, Edward, lad."

He strode along the beach, pausing every now and then to wipe his brow. His shirt clung to his back, and he insisted on still wearing shoes, although his were sadly scuffed, and his stockings were full of holes. His beard was untrimmed, and his hair was longer than he had worn it in England, still thick and dark. He was a fine figure of a man, Edward thought, keeping up without difficulty, for he was now several inches taller than his father. How would he fare against Tony? And supposing he lost, what then? But that was too terrible a possibility to contemplate.

They rounded the outcrop of sand and coral, and looked along the beach toward the Carib village. By now the large canoe had reached the derelict and gone alongside. Men swarmed across into the drifting vessel, and it seemed they had found someone alive, for they gave a great shout, which even reached the beach, and carried him on board their own vessel. The smaller canoe was left to drift.

"What spendthrifts they are," Tom complained. "But at least they have a care for human life."

The Indians on the beach were crowding into the water to greet the returning canoe, while Tegramond came toward the white men.

"Greetings, Tegramond," Tom said. "Where do you suppose that fellow came from?" He pointed at the canoe, and then at Nevis.

Tegramond shook his head and stooped to draw on the sand. Quickly he sketched the unmistakable outline of St. Christopher, and next to him drew the outline of a man. He pointed to himself, and drew in weapons, all somewhat small. Then he drew another, large loaf-shaped island, to the south of St. Christopher, and separated by a number of smaller islets. Once again, next to the large island, he drew a man, but this man was twice the size of himself, and the weapons he added were also large.

"A race of giants?" Tom frowned. "That man did not look so different to me. At least from a distance."

"I think he means they are a much fiercer people, Father," Edward said. He made a grimace and shook his fist at the approaching canoe.

Tegramond smiled and nodded. He pointed at Tom and said, "Dominica."

"Now, that makes sense," Tom agreed. "I had heard that the savages in the island so named by Columbus were an uncommonly fierce lot. But you seem pleased to see this fellow." He pointed at the canoe again, now well into the shallows, and smiled, and held out his hand.

Which seemed to amuse Tegramond. The chief burst into laughter and then drew the back of his hand across his mouth, before hurrying down the beach to greet his returning seamen.

"Now, what did he mean by that?" Tom asked, looking at his son.

But Edward was too busy watching the Indians; he had no doubt that Yarico was somewhere in the crowd, could he but discover her. And why should he want to do that? He had resisted her advances, and there was nothing more to be gained in that direction.

The Indians parted, to allow four men to bring the rescued man up the beach. Bring? Or rather drag, for the Dominican did not seem pleased to be ashore. Yet clearly he had suffered much from thirst. And indeed a woman now came forward with a gourd of water. The man shrank from it, while his eyes rolled and became white, and his muscles strained, quite unavailingly, as he was securely held by four men every bit as strong as himself. Now two more women came forward, one to hold his head and the other to dig her fingers into the base of his jaw and force his teeth apart, whereupon the woman with the gourd emptied the water down his throat, to the accompaniment of much laughter from her fellows.

"Rough medicine," Tom muttered. "Perhaps we should be away, Edward. I doubt that we are welcome here."

But Tegramond had returned, and had taken him by the hand, to lead him into the village, Here, in the center of the houses, a large stake had been driven into the ground, a stake which had obviously been carefully selected, and used often in the past; it had little bark left upon it, while it possessed two forks, one at the top and the other about halfway up its length, both of which were well scored as if a rope had been passed to and fro around them on several occasions. To this stake the rescued man was taken, and now he was fighting with the utmost desperation, and making a peculiar calling sound, hideous to hear, which Edward had to suppose was an appeal for help or mercy. The whole scene reminded him horribly of that dreadful day at Tyburn, mingled with so many other occasions when his belly had become light and his genitals had reared into life.

"By Christ," Tom said. "By Christ. You'll leave, Edward. Quickly."

But he could not, hemmed in as he was by the exultant Caribs, who had gathered in a huge circle around the stake, men, women, and children, setting up now some kind of a chant, and moving their bodies, although not their feet, so that the entire afternoon seemed to be swaying. In the center the rescued man was secured by a rawhide thong passed around his wrists, binding them securely, following which they were tied to the lower of the two forks. Then another rope was passed around his neck and made fast to the upper fork, so that try as he might he could not bend or fall, although he continued to struggle and stamp his feet, to roll his eyes and utter his high-pitched cry. But now his captors stepped away and joined their companions, and for some seconds they gazed at the twisting, howling man, who knew the worst that was to befall him, obviously, from his terror.

Edward's throat was dry. He was to watch another man die. Now. Because suddenly everyone around him possessed a knife, or at the very least a sharp-edged shell, and the chanting had stopped.

Tegramond stepped forward, slowly walking up to the man. He said something, which the prisoner answered with a tumultuous shake which all but displaced the stake. Then Tegramond grasped one quivering buttock, and with a sweep of his knife sliced through the flesh.

"By Christ," Tom Warner shouted. "Alive? By Christ." He fell to his knees and vomited in the sand.

But he was ignored by the Caribs, who swarmed forward, shouting and screaming, all eager to seize a piece of flesh and tear or cut it free, while the women stretched their hands through the forest of legs and arms, holding gourds to catch the spurting blood, licking fingers and smacking lips where the liquid splashed or overflowed. Edward stared at them in horror, at his father in amazement. He wondered why he was not vomiting himself, why he felt so detached; this scene was far more nauseating than the execution of Mr. Walkden. Or was it? It was more bestial, more sexual. There was naked emotion in front of him, where before there had been enjoyment but not participation. But here . . . He saw Yarico. She had secured the penis, and sucked it with the enjoyment of a child with a sweet. Blood dribbled from the corners of her mouth and down to her chin, hanging there as the water had done that day at the pool. It trickled down her neck and between her breasts, made patterns against the sweat of her belly.

"Oh, Christ," Tom Warner muttered, wiping his mouth and retching. "Oh, Christ. . . ."

But the Dominica Carib was dead; the onslaught had been too vigorous. Indeed, he could have known only a few seconds of pain. And now he no longer existed. Bare bones drooped against the stake where his feet and legs had been; bare ribs gleamed white amid the red-brown rags which hung from his shoulders. Only his head and face were untouched by knives or hands. But the contorted features were almost the most horrible event of the whole terrible afternoon.

And now the Caribs danced.

"Taken from a don, by God." John Painton poured wine and smiled at the ragged colonists. He wore a huge brocaded coat, in red velvet, quite unfitted for the climate, although as splendid as anything ever seen at court; underneath there was no doublet, but an open-necked shirt. Yet the shirt itself was of cambric, and his shoes sported golden buckles. Behind him his men were similarly clad, and armed, too, with a variety of new weapons, gleaming rapiers, shiny-hilted pistols, and endless bottles of wine, which they were pouring for Tegramond and his eager people.

"You've done well," Tom said. "Would you'd come a week sooner."

"And was that your first Carib feast?" Painton demanded. "Tom, you've led a sheltered life. To these people, to eat a savage from Dominica, why, 'tis like taking the sacrament."

"You blaspheme, sir," Berwicke growled.

"I deny that," Painton said. "This is their religion. That of animal spirits, physical courage, and physical harm. This man was a famous warrior, no doubt. By partaking in his living flesh, all this tribe benefits, and grows stronger and bolder. Oh, it is a brutal, unchristian point of view, to be sure, but none the less valid for that. You'd do well not to brook on it, Mr. Berwicke. Nor you, Tom. Nor any of you. You're to be congratulated. I spied your houses, and your tobacco, through my glass when we were standing in. You've a handsome crop, there, Tom. Worth as much as my Spaniard, I'll be bound. And I've the men to help you reap. For a ten-percent share, it's that and its transport home."

"Done," Tom said. "We'll start tomorrow, and then we'll turn our backs on this cursed place."

"Man, you are difficult to please, and that's a fact. Can you not see the future? With that crop, that profit, you'll have men flocking to join you. 'Tis something to think of, Tom. With a colony of three or four hundred men and women settled here, and the tobacco to attend to your needs, you'd not have to fear the Indians."

"Fear them?"

"Oh, man, be honest with me, as I have ever been with you. You are suffering less at this moment from watching a man torn to pieces than from the supposition that one day it might be you and yours."

"And think you I could bring any other white people to so savage a place, and expose them to such a fate?"

"There'd be nothing at risk in it, Tom, had you only sufficient numbers. Man, half a dozen crops like this one and you'll be able to snap your fingers at the king himself. It's money that buys strength, Tom. And you've the money now. Not that I truly feel you have a thing to worry about. Tegramond gave you his word, and he is a man of his word. Why, look at the fellow. Could you imagine a more harmless tippler?"

Tegramond sat with his back against a tree, his legs spread wide, while he drank wine from the bottle; as ever, Tom's sword was strapped to his waist. At least a score of his men were similarly inebriated, and their women were gathered in a cluster close by, as eagerly snatching what remnants of the precious liquid as rolled their way in the discarded bottles as they had snatched the dying man's blood a few days earlier; indeed, the red liquid spurting down their cheeks seemed little different.

Edward watched his father anxiously. No matter what had happened, he did not want to go home. He wanted to stay here, in the heat and the sun and the savagry. He wanted to see Yarico again. He had to see her again soon, for the memory of her with bloodstained mouth and teeth, chewing at the lifeless piece of human flesh which was so precious to all mankind, hung before his face like an angry cloud; he had not slept soundly since the feast.

But he did not want to leave.

Tom was sighing, and glancing at the other men. "What say you?"

"Mr. Painton is right," Tony said. "There is nothing for us in England now. Be sure that Mr. North will have told no flattering account of our decision to remain behind. And Mr. Painton is right on the other score, too. But let us recruit some reinforcements, and some women as wives. By God, Tom, you were promising us no more than that only a while ago."

"The lad is right, Tom," Ashton sàid. "Yet with due respect to Mr. Painton, I feel that one of us ought to take the tobacco home and attend to these other matters. 'Tis no business for agents. Although be sure that I do not seek to carp about your share, Mr. Painton."

"I agree with Hal," Berwicke said. "And indeed, it is the more dangerous task, if Mr. North has really spread rumors concerning us. I would willingly volunteer . . ."

"No," Tom said. "I will go. I know best what we have achieved, what we can still achieve. And I will have the king's ear, especially if my lord of Warwick survives and prospers. Will you three remain and hold the colony for me?"

"Against all, Captain," Tony promised.

"Then it shall be so. We'll reap tomorrow, and be away the day after. If that is satisfactory, John."

"That will be splendid," Painton said. "But if you gentlemen will excuse my interfering with your affairs, you should appoint a deputy, Tom. Every society, no matter how limited, requires a leader to cope with whatever emergency may arise. A leader who is acknowledged, and whom the others will obey."

Tom glanced at his friends.

"Again, Mr. Painton is right," Tony said. "Else shall we fall to quarreling. And be sure that I have no interest in the post."

"Hal?"

The sailing master shrugged. "The decision is yours, Tom. I am easy in the matter."

"Then it shall be Ralph. You have no objection, old friend?"

"I am flattered, sir."

"You had agreed to call me Tom. I appoint Mr. Berwicke, gentlemen, deputy governor of this colony, before you all, and before Mr. Painton, as my witness, until my return. He is a good man and my oldest friend, and will shirk neither duty nor execution. Now, there, it is done. And it was uncommonly solemn." He filled his glass and held it up. "I drink a toast to Mr. Ralph Berwicke and his colony of three."

"Four, Father," Edward said.

"Eh?"

"With your permission, sir, I would also remain here. You will return with Mama and Philip. I can wait until then. And St. Christopher is more my home than England."

Tom stared at his son.

"The lad is right," Berwicke said. "And we shall be happy to care for him, Tom."

"I know he's right," Tom said. "Then he shall stay. Truly,

he's safer here than chancing his life upon the ocean, there and back. By God, I feel a perfect woman at the thought of leaving. Tell me what you would have me bring for you, as a reward for your labors here. Ralph?"

Berwicke took off his battered hat. "I'd be grateful for a new one, Tom."

"You shall have it. Best beaver. Hal?"

"A keg of English beer, Tom. God, my mouth waters at the thought."

"Then your thirst shall be quenched. Tony?"

"Just bring me a woman, Tom."

"I have promised you all one of those. Edward?"

"A sword, Father. A sword of my own."

"Spoken like a soldier's son. Well, then, be sure that I shall return before Christmas, with your requirements, with money, and with men. With women, Tony, lad, and with your mother and brother, Edward. Aye, and the new babe, too."

Edward stood on Brimstone Hill long after the *Plymouth Belle* had disappeared over the horizon, her dirt-gray sails merging into the haze. Up here he could weep, if he wished. If he discovered it to be unavoidable.

There was no reason for it. Father was going, to return with Mama and Philip. How they would be surprised to see the man into which he had grown. How they would be surprised at the island. Delighted. Until the next Carib feast? But the Carib feast was no worse than an execution at Tyburn. They would breed a different type of man here, perhaps, and woman. In time.

And meanwhile there was the tobacco to be cared for. How bare the field looked with the huge brown leaves departed. But the seed beds were full, and long before Father returned they would have to be planted out; he must return to a better crop than even that he carried with him. Because there was no question that it would grow. He could not imagine anything not growing here.

But it was no longer paradise. No longer, perhaps, even the Enchanted Isle. Although enchanted did not always mean nothing but happiness. The enchanted forests and enchanted castles of legend invariably contained snares and dangers which had to be overcome. So perhaps St. Christopher was, after all, an enchanted place.

He turned at the sound. Yarico pointed at the sea, held her

hands together in the shape of a boat and rocked them gently, and then put a forefinger to the corner of each eye and slowly traced them down her cheek.

"Don't be ridiculous," he said angrily. "I but wished to be sure they were safe away. Ah, what's the use? You don't understand me. And I don't understand you, to be sure. Anything about you. You'd do best to leave me alone."

He walked on the path leading down, and felt her fingers on his arm. Lightly. Not the way she had torn the penis from the dying Indian. And now there was no blood on her teeth as she smiled, and none dribbling from the corners of her lips. But Christ, one day her mouth could be full of him, should he ever fall out with her father's people. The lightness began to fill his belly, but it was a surging feeling, an awareness of himself as a man. The feeling he knew whenever he thought of this girl; certainly whenever he saw her.

As she knew. She smiled and moved her head toward the inland path. He had never been there. The north end of the island was nothing more than rocks and forest. Not even the Indians visited there, as a rule. But Yarico went everywhere, a spirit of the forest, of the pools, and of the mountain. A bloodstained, bloodthirsty spirit.

Here was madness. Because when she released him, he followed her, where he should have taken to his heels. But Father had gone, across the ocean. As she knew, too. Here was no childlike savage, merely because she spoke a different tongue. And perhaps, no vicious monster, either, merely because she drank human blood. It occurred to him that she was a woman, much older than himself, although surely younger in years, moving through life with the single-mindedness of any woman. A life in which he was included. His whole being became thrilled at the conception. Because this island was his life now. This island, and Yarico. His gaze was once again held by the undulating buttocks.

Which ceased movement as she turned and gazed at him, allowing her delighted smile to travel from his ankles to his eyes. She could not see inside his breeches, but she knew she had obtained what she wanted. She pointed to the mountain, shrugged her shoulders, and gave a delightful little shriek of laughter as she released her cloth. Edward could not resist a glance at the ground, at the leaves and the coral outcrops and the endless creatures which would surely inhabit this world. Or did creatures matter at a time like this?

Nothing mattered. He was back at school, and the school

was at Tyburn. He lay on his back, and his breeches were being removed by a fiendish executioner whose fingers were light as snowflakes and whose smile continued to shroud him. He was helpless, and deliberately made himself more so, arms spread and legs spread, huge manhood launched at the sky, quivering and begging. Only this time he did not hate.

And with all the skill of a practiced torturer, she enjoyed her conquest, sitting between his legs, holding him in both hands, and flicking him gently with her thumbs, her mouth opening and shutting, her teeth gleaming and disappearing behind the licking red tongue, until he thought he would burst. But with the certainty of knowledge, she timed his thrust, turning onto her hands and knees, away from him, yet still reaching behind herself to guide him, to feel his belly pressed against her buttocks. And still she laughed.

While she burned. With a fire which seemed to consume him as well.

Then she was content to be the victim. She sat against the trunk of a tree, and smiled, mouth sagging. He knelt beside her and dragged his fingers through her hair. How long had he wanted to do that. And kiss her eyes and her nose. This mystified her, but she liked it, judging by her expression, as she liked him to stroke her breasts. Small breasts, but throbbing mounds of womanhood, with strangely flaccid nipples, even when aroused. Or perhaps he had not yet fully aroused her. But she preferred him to explore her belly, moved it and thrust it in his face, and exploded into more delighted laughter when he allowed himself a gentle bite.

And then the laughter died, and he straightened in some haste, gazed at Wapisiane, felt fear rising from his own belly to meet the strength coming down. The Indian boy was unarmed, but he had his hands and his teeth, and he too had tasted blood at the feast.

He asked a question of Yarico, and the girl tossed her head and answered him vigorously and angrily. Wapisiane gazed at Edward for several seconds, seeming to be drinking him in with his eyes, and then turned and disappeared as silently as he had come.

Yarico laughed, touched Edward with her forefinger, and then thrust it between her legs, before cupping her hands and encircling her belly.

"You mean he would have you mother his children?" Edward asked in horror. "But then ..."

She shook her head gently, from side to side, and an expression of utter contempt crossed her face.

"But he is angry," Edward said. "He will tell your father." He pointed at the village, waved his arms above his head, fists clenched.

Yarico gave another of her unforgettable shrieks, and again her head was shaking, from side to side, slowly. But now her arms were reaching for him once again.

The sun, Yarico, rose at dawn and declined at dusk. The moon, Yarico, was already high in the sky on most nights, and remained there, bathing St. Christopher in its unforgettable light. The tobacco, Yarico, took to the fields and grew like weeds, sprouting forth in unimaginable profusion. The yams, the fish, the coconuts which were their staple diet, all contained Yarico. Every dream, every waking moment, was but an aspect of Yarico.

Even the men contained Yarico. But with them he must be careful. They saw his contentedness, and were pleasantly surprised. But then, they were content themselves, and put his obvious happiness down to the withdrawal of the stern command and criticism of his father. Certainly Berwicke was more easy. Or perhaps life itself was more easy. There were some hours' work needed on the tobacco every day, and there was some cooking and laundry to be done. But now they could smoke their own crop, and Painton had left them delicacies like cheese and even a few bottles of wine. They dreamed of Tom's return with ships and men. And women. Tony Hilton might spend hours watching the Indian girls going about their various tasks, but he remembered too well the blood rolling down their chins to wish more than that. He too was content to wait. And so they assumed that Edward also dreamed, whatever boys dream about. They had forgotten, as they had forgotten snow and hail, market days and storms at sea, King James and Steenie Villiers, and all the ills of life. There were none here.

But they were also a reminder that one day Father would return, and with him, Mama. There was onrushing cataclysm. Which made him the more anxious. He spent his leisure hours climbing Brimstone Hill, where he would be sure to find her, and his nights escaping the solitude of his house and seeking her behind the tobacco field, for she was always there. They sought love and found it with a passionate intensity which frightened him, when he thought about it, but which could not be resisted when he was in her presence. He endeavored to introduce some aspect of rationality into their relationship by teaching her English while they were both regaining their strengths, and indeed she proved an apt pupil, for she was intelligent and anxious to please him in every way. Yet he could not escape the overwhelming feeling that to her he was no more than a large toy, fascinating in the color of his skin, the texture of his face and hair and flesh, the innocence which she delighted in destroying, for she taught him to use his mouth and teeth on every part of her body, and she cared not where he made his entry so long as she felt him in her and against her. But how to know where pleasure ended and sin began? Or did sin belong here at all, in this enchanted, heathen place? Could he sin with a girl who had torn a living man to pieces with her teeth? Was she not, equally, his plaything, to be done with as he chose? There was a satisfying thought, and when he remembered the law laid down by Father on their first day here, he could not convince himself that sin had come into that at all. Father had been afraid of antagonizing the natives. He was just as afraid of that, and lived for some weeks in terror of what Wapisiane might do or say, but Yarico was reassuring, and certainly it seemed that she knew her people, and her designated husband, for Tegramond was as unfailingly good-humored as ever, and every day his women made the trek along the beach with their fish for the white men, and stood and giggled together and pointed at whatever took their fancy, and seemed amazed that the men should choose to keep to themselves.

Surely, no sin in paradise. Nothing in paradise, save unchanging sun and heat, daylight and darkness, a dawn breeze and a midday rain shower, the rumble of the surf and the desire of Yarico. Until the day that she was not on the hilltop when he got there, toward dusk, as was usual. For a moment he was too surprised to think. It had been an unnaturally hot day, even for St. Christopher, and so they had done less work than usual, and now he was surprised to discover that it was as hot at dusk as it had been at noon. The breeze was absent, yet the clouds still moved, and when he looked at them from this vantage point he saw that they were far more numerous than usual, and thickly clustered, and in many places dark gray and even black, instead of fleecy white. And strange, now his interest was aroused, there were no Indian children bathing off the village, usually clearly to be seen from up here. The island gave the appearance of having been deserted, save for the three Englishmen below him, lying on the sand and smoking their rolled leaves and dreaming aloud to each other.

The breeze puffed against his cheek, returning without warning, and he looked up in surprise. There was no twilight in these latitudes, but this transition from light to darkness was too sudden. It was caused by the cloud. It was huge and black, and it spread and spread and spread to the eastern horizon, and the breeze was suddenly filled with rain, moving along, stinging his face and hands, filling his belly with fear.

But Yarico was here. She stood amid the trees, arms outstretched. "Hurricane," she said, and pointed. "Wind." And waved her hand.

He ran to her, and they ducked into the trees. But this was Guyana again, as the huge raindrops crashed downward, only here there was wind, stinging and sending branches thrashing to and fro. And then there was a louder sound, a noise he had never heard before, a growing whine as if every bird in the world was gathered together and rushing at St. Christopher, crying and beating their wings in unison.

Yarico threw herself to the ground, and he dropped with her. He watched her digging her toes and fingers into the earth, hands scrabbling to find some solidity, and wondered if this was a new means of self-satisfaction. Then she was gone, and he was gone. He did not know how or where. He felt no pain, just an enormous dizziness, and looked up. But he saw nothing, although his instincts told him he had been rolled off the path and down into the jungle below. How long he lay there he had no idea. The howling of the wind became one continuous roaring in his ears, shutting out all possibility of thought. The rain pounded on his face and body, hurting him, but not suggesting that he move. And then, sometimes, it would stop, and leave only the wind, before returning again with incessant power. The night grew ever darker, and the noise around him, when he could hear it above the wind, the crashes and the thuds, the huge booms of the breakers on the beach far below, the rumble of the thunder and the crackle of the lightning which cut vivid slashes through the darkness, grew ever more terrifying.

In time, Yarico came to him again. Certainly she was as terrified as himself, but she had experienced such a storm before, and besides, she loved. This night he truly realized that. She was a savage, a bloodthirsty cannibal, and he would never be able to forget her as she had been on that terrible day, but she loved, with a protective desire which made nonsense of differences in language, and religion, and outlook, in past and no doubt in future, in present. Where there was a love of this caliber, there could never be sin.

And again, in time, there was dawn. The wind dropped, although it remained a gale, but the terrifying whine and the equally terrifying clouds had passed away, and the sky was a more brilliant blue than he had ever seen, a drenched blue, washed clean by the pounding rain.

He sat up, and then stood up cautiously, because his muscles were cramped and he could not help but wonder if anything was broken. Amazingly, he was unharmed, and so was the girl. In their mossy hollow they had lain in safety. Not so the forest. A giant hand had swept across St. Christopher, plucking and flicking, enjoying itself with all the gusto of the Caribs destroying the man from Dominica. The analogy came strongly to mind as he looked at the uprooted trees, the overturned boulders, the swathes of bushes and scattered shrubs, almost as if a gigantic scythe had been at work. And the wind had come from the east, so there had been the mountain between them and the worst. What the windward side of the island must be like did not bear consideration.

And the beach. "By Christ," he shouted, and ran from Brimstone Hill. Yarico came behind, more slowly. She knew what he would find.

He stood on the lip of the hill. The beach was obliterated beneath the huge foaming breakers which still hurled themselves at the shore, ripping up the sand with horrific force, smashing it and swirling it, and sucking it back out to sea. The village remained above the high-water mark. Tegramond had made them build wisely. Above the high-water mark. But not above the high-wind mark. There had been a village. This much was evident in the discolored sand, the timber which lay scattered across the grass and into the field. But then, there had been a field, and the field had contained an almost ripe tobacco crop. Now it was nothing more than a scar. Even the seed beds had disappeared, the carefully prepared earth demolished as a child might have demolished an unwanted sand castle. He was obsessed with this relationship to childishness, to the childish fiendishness of the Caribs, and now of the weather. He wondered how any responsible adult mind could conceive of destruction on such a vast scale, and then implement such a concept.

But there had been people here. He ran down the path, panting, amazed at his selfishness, for his soul cried out, no, I cannot be the only white person left alive in this terrible community. No love there, no feeling for Tony and Hal Ashton and Berwicke. No love such as had brought Yarico feeling her way through the darkness and the danger to find him last night. Such as brought her behind him now, scurrying down the path, anxious for his friends because he was anxious for them, although her mind must be consumed with worry for her own people; the Carib village was much more exposed.

He reached the foot of the hill, found the sand piled up in huge drifts much like the Suffolk snow, thrown against the grassy banks as if to protect the land beyond. But it had not protected the land beyond.

He kicked his way through the shattered timbers. They had been so proud of their huts, of the way they had been constructed, of the wooden utensils they had carved. They were here too, and so were the remains of the wine bottles, and even one of the muskets, sticking up out of the sand.

"Edward? By God, 'tis the boy." Ashton came staggering out of the trees, bleary-eyed and shaking.

"Ned." Hilton was behind them, face ashen.

Last of all came Berwicke. How he had aged in a night. Perhaps there had always been a considerable amount of white in his hair, but it had been kept sufficiently concealed behind the remaining black. Now it was all in evidence, and his round cheeks had shrunk, and his shoulders were bowed. "Edward," he said. "Thank God for that, at the least."

"The girl saved my life," Edward said.

Yarico stood, some distance away, watching them, as they watched her, for in the tumult of the night she had lost her cloth, and now he, too, realized for the first time that he was naked.

"It was a fierce wind," he said stupidly.

"Aye," Berwicke said. "Well, it matters naught now. There can be no law, no discipline, where there is no colony." He turned away from the boy. "We were not meant to hold this pleasant land. It belongs to the wind, and the sea. And the people of blood."

How calm the sea. Edward paused to wipe his brow, to toss his head and scatter the sweat as did his Carib friends. And to gaze at the water. It stretched forever, a measureless blue carpet, undulating, but no more than gently. That it could have acted the angry fiend of a few weeks ago seemed incredible, looking at it now. Yet it had not been a dream. He had to do no more than walk along the beach and look at the colony, at the empty weal which had been the tobacco plantation, at the scattered huts, at the sand still piled in huge drifts, only slowly being whittled away by the breeze, at the men, as scattered as their erstwhile belongings, lying on the sand, existing, in a tropical paradise which held within it the core of destruction.

He could never have supposed that once these men had been his friends. More, his mentors. He had begged them to work, to make some effort to restore the buildings and replant the crop, and they had thrown stones at him. Berwicke, a man whose entire body, always overweight, had sagged into a coma, who stared at the field and muttered to himself. Ashton, a sailing master come to grief upon an endless reef, gazing at the waters and remembering rather than dreaming. Tony Hilton, strangest of all. Hilton climbed the hill every day, at the least, and looked out to sea. He would do no more. "Plantations," he said in disgust. "Months of backbreaking work. To be scattered into dust whenever He feels the mood? Speak not to me of plantations."

No longer men, but creatures. Edward had taken himself to where men still were men. Now he discovered why the Indian village had given such an impression of flimsy impermanence. There had been storms before, hurricanes, as the Caribs called them, and it made no sense to stand before such a wind. One took shelter, and allowed one's house to scatter, and when the wind was gone, one rebuilt one's house. It was only a matter of a few hours' work.

He had endeavored to ask Yarico and her father if such storms were common. They had said yes, and no, which he interpreted to mean that they were common enough in this part of the world, but that they did not invariably destroy a particular island. But as to time, he could learn nothing. The Caribs thought in moons, and it was apparently a great number of moons since the last hurricane had struck St. Christopher. But as the Caribs regarded any number greater than five as enormous, he was very little further ahead.

It did not matter. He was happy here. He was one of the young men, an important phrase. Theirs was a meaninglessly busy life. They fished, and they swam, and they wrestled, and they practiced the use of their weapons, the long spear which they hurled with deadly accuracy, and the bow, with a range hardly longer, for it was a small and poorly stringed instrument, but with which again they attained great accuracy. They slept together in a larger than usual hut, as they were the unmated ones, and they acknowledged as their leader the chief designate, Wapisiane.

This single fact had disturbed Edward at first. But Wapisiane apparently bore no grudge, or concealed it well. There was no morality in this culture, beyond the necessity to be brave. They reminded Edward of dogs. When a boy felt the necessity, he sat on the sand and masturbated or coupled with another boy. It seldom occurred to them to seek one of the girls for pleasure. Rather was this a duty which would follow manhood, for the perpetuation of the tribe. That their new friend found it enjoyable to trail into the woods behind Yarico they found at once amusing and contemptible. But they also soon learned to respect him. At fourteen he was a full-grown man, stronger than any of the Indian boys, and he had been taught the use of his fists by Tony during the voyage from England, an art which was totally incomprehensible to them. The first time he answered a challenge, and his assailant lowered his head and shoulders to throw both arms around his waist, he had struck down with all his force and stretched the boy unconscious on the sand. He had, indeed, been terrified that he might have killed him, but the other Indians had been delighted, and soon enough his victim had scrambled to his feet, dazed and quite disinclined to continue the fight.

This total personal liberty encompassed even the adults. It was impossible to decide who belonged to whom, mother, father, child, or wife. The small children were herded together and were cared for by the older women. The younger women worked the fields, for they grew corn, and cleaned the fish, and attended to all household chores, which included rebuilding the houses. Even Yarico, the chief's daughter, slept with the girls and worked with them, and possessed only as much leisure as they did. But she saved her leisure for him.

It occurred to him that to all intents and purposes he was married. But far more than that. He wore a breechclout and nothing more, ate raw fish with his fingers, and indeed, caught them with his bare hands, for Wapisiane was a great fisherman, and every morning before dawn he and Edward would scour the shallows off the village, and seldom return with empty baskets. He feared the return of his father, to interrupt this idyll which made so much nonsense of kings and their courts, of titles and towers, of the right to worship or the right not to worship, of the inevitability of growing old, of the certainty of death. There was no death among the Caribs—at least, not to the visible eye. Now he learned the secret of the far north of the island, and the reason for the absence of old people; it was the custom among the Caribs that the moment any man or woman felt old age or infirmity approaching, they walked away from the village and took themselves to the thick forest at the north, there to die of starvation in solitude. At fourteen this seemed an admirable philosophy. Their entire religion was in this simple mold. All things, the leaves on the trees and the grains of sand on the beaches, possessed life. The more powerful the object or creature, the greater the life. Thus the sea, the wind, the clouds, and above all the sun, were dominant creatures, as near as possible to the Christian concept of God, equaled only by the solid mass of the central mountain, similarly immense, similarly immortal. Prayer consisted of a simple appeal. That there could be a life after death had not occurred to the Caribs.

As for their other philosophy, that by eating the living flesh of an enemy a man could imbibe some of his strength and courage, the occasion had not yet recurred. What *would* he do should Yarico come to him with a dripping human steak in her hands or in her teeth? But this was a problem of the future, to be set alongside the return of Father, and other incalculable prospects. Life in the Carib encampment was lived from day to day; only the good or famous events from the past were remembered, and any possible sorrows or problems in the future were not considered at all.

Yet the future must come, and in March, five months after the storm, it arrived in the shape of a small vessel, flying the cross of St. George, announced by a running Hilton, showing more activity than for months past.

They gathered on the water's edge, white men and Caribs, women, girls, and boys, to watch the pinnance making for the shore. Tom Warner stood in the stern, clad in velvet and leather, new doublet and polished thigh boots, tall hat with feather, gleaming hilted rapier suspended from shining baldric, trimmed beard, and a jeweled pin at his throat.

"What?" he cried, as he approached. "There has been some disaster here, I'll warrant."

"A storm, Tom," Berwicke said. "A storm such as you can

never have imagined." He peered into the boat. "Mistress Warner, well, thanks be to God, ma'am. But who is this strapping fellow?"

"Philip, you old fool," Tom said. "Ten years old, by God. And what think you of this, eh? Her name is Sarah."

The little girl clung to the gunwale and stared at the island and the Indians with wide eyes. Like her brother, she closely resembled her father, short and sturdily built, blue-eyed and dark-haired.

Tom lifted his wife ashore. "But when happened this storm? Tegramond, you old villain." He clasped the smiling cacique to his breast. " 'Tis good to see you again. And I bring news. The storm, Ralph, you were to tell me of the storm."

"Some months gone," Ashton said.

"Months, and the village is still scattered. And no tobacco planted? Or have you changed your site?"

"We are still at Sandy Point, Tom," Hilton said. "In faith, it has not seemed worth our while to replant where it can be so easily destroyed."

"By God," Tom said. "Rebecca, I'll have you shake hands with the chief. Now, remember, girl, I have told you all of him. He is not half so fierce as he seems, and he is my friend. Perhaps my best friend in all the world. Ralph, I'm that disappointed in you, old friend. How can a colony prosper without setbacks? Setbacks, storms, illnesses—it is the surviving of these things that makes a man better than these savages. Have we not suffered much together, and still survived, and prospered?"

"Colony," Hilton said in disgust.

Tom rounded on him. "Aye, colony, Tony. For that is what we are." From his doublet he pulled a rolled parchment. "Here is my warrant. Thomas Warner, gentleman, the king's lieutenant of the Caribee Isles. I have much to tell you, lads. Much. Welcomed at court, I was. Mr. North is a true man, and spread nothing but honest tales of our courage, and my lord of Warwick is again in favor. The grant, indeed, is in his name, but transmitted through him to me and my heirs. But where is Edward?"

"Edward?" Rebecca freed herself from the cacique's grasp, for he was staring at her with a bemused expression, taking in her padded skirt and her low-cut bodice, her combed hair and her pale skin. "Where is Edward?"

He stepped through the crowd. Saving his hair, he looked no different from the boys around him.

"Edward?" Tom shouted. "By Christ, boy, what has become of you?"

"He is all of a savage," Berwicke said. "We call him Caribee."

"Edward?" Rebecca whispered. "Oh, Edward."

Her arms were wide. Yet he was strangely reluctant to step into them. There was too much difference here between what he was and what he had been. It had been too long since last he had been close to her, and in that time too much had happened. And she was still a young woman, and an attractive one.

He went closer, felt her fingers on his skin, inhaled her scent. "Mother. 'Tis good to see you."

She kissed him, held him at arm's length. "And is that all you can say? But truly, you are not the child who went away. Now I have two men."

"Two men that you'll be proud of," Tom said, taking his son's hand. "But I'll have no white Indians in my colony. I've brought you some fine clothes, boy. We're rich. Did you not know that? Ralph Merrifield—you remember Ralph? He has bought our tobacco and advanced me a sum against our next crop. Why, my return is all the talk in London. You'll get yourself dressed, boy. I have need of you, I can see that. There's work to be done."

"And have you also come with a shipload of colonists, Father?"

Tom frowned. "No," he said. "I doubt that England is yet the place it was in my youth. Now all they can speak of is the don's habit of torturing to death intruders found in the Americas, and of the cannibalism of the Caribs. I raised six men in England. But they are fine fellows."

"Six men?" Berwicke asked.

"Disappointing, Ralph, to be sure. So I sailed across the ocean to Virginia to search for more."

"And had you success?" Ashton asked.

"Not really. Six more. That is our force for the present."

"Twelve men, to found a colony?" Edward asked.

"There will be more, lad, you may rest assured on that score."

"Twelve men," Tony Hilton said contemptuously. "Warner's Empire, by God. I'll do better on my own." He turned and walked into the forest.

5

The Lovers

"Oh, let him go," Tom Warner said. "He'll be back when he's tired of living like an animal. He had always the spirit of a troublemaker. And 'tis true enough I failed him in his present. But not you, Ralph. . . ." He waved his hand, and two of the young men brought up a large box. "The finest beaver hat in England. Hal, there's enough beer coming ashore for you to bathe in. And, Edward, your sword."

His eyes gleamed as he watched his son take the blade and slowly turn it over. Caribee. But the boy was, after all, a Warner.

Rebecca could read his mind. "And a man," she said softly.

Edward raised his head. "It is good to see you again. So good. How are Uncle Edward and Aunt Jane?"

"Well." But her face was solemn. She anticipated his next question.

"And Mother Elizabeth?"

"Dead these two years. She was old, Edward. Old."

"As we shall all grow old one day," Tom declared. "Meanwhile, there is work to do."

He had been rejuvenated. The doubts and the fears had been swept away by his reception in England. He considered it, and rightly, no more than a just reward for his efforts, for his courage and his determination, and regretted only that he had waited until the second half of his life to reveal such qualities to those in power. Now he bubbled with confidence.

"You may be disappointed," he told Ashton and Berwicke and Edward, "in these lads, but they've the backs for work, and the ambition to be wealthy."

"This wealth you speak of," Ashton remarked. "You did not bring it back with you?"

"Have you not all got new clothes? And weapons? Is there not a sufficient stock of European food, good wine, and cheese to allow us to enjoy this heathen diet?" Tom bellowed. "As for the rest, why, it is invested in the future of the colony. John Jefferson—you remember John Jefferson, Ralph? He will be arriving soon enough with another shipload of men. And he'll be bringing the women to make our lads wives. Then we'll see young Hilton come crawling back out of that bush. And for the meanwhile, fear not, old friends, I have made them all take the same oath as ourselves. There'll be no friction with Tegramond."

He paused and again gazed at Edward. But he was not disposed to make an issue of what remained only a rumor. The boy had been lonely, and going on the evidence of his own eyes, alone. He could not be blamed for seeking some positive company. Meanwhile, it was necessary to dangle the dream always before their eyes. He, at least, never doubted that it would come true.

"Aye," he said. "This island will be the fortune of us all. And many more besides. St. Christopher? What rubbish. We're no papists. We have renamed it, by God. Merrifield and Warner, Mer and War, so Merwar's Hope. That's how it shall be marked on the maps forevermore. Merwar's Hope. Now, here's something to make your eyes gleam."

For another boat was approaching the shore, a noisy boat, with its barkings and yelpings, and soon two mastiffs, a dog and a bitch, came bounding through the shallows.

"We had that trouble, to keep them apart at sea," Tom said. "But now, why, they'll mate and provide all the guards we shall ever need. What say you, Tegramond, old friend?"

For the Caribs had gathered in a huddle, staring fearfully at the bounding dogs, who could sense the fear, and now bared their teeth and set their forelegs firmly in the sand; the chief had his hand on the hilt of his sword.

"They'll not harm you, Tegramond," Tom said. "Unless you make them or I tell them."

The cacique pointed. "Spanish," he said.

"Aye, the Spaniards use them, to be sure. But we'll not, I promise you that, without good cause. Yet a few sharp-toothed brutes will render our numbers more equal," he remarked to his friends. "I've a mind that Tegramond will not live forever, whereas this colony of ours is now planted for eternity."

His energy could not help but be contagious. Within a month the seed beds were again arranged and filled, and they were at work rebuilding the village. He made them clear more land, and in their enthusiasm they encroached across the line drawn by Tegramond two years before. But the Carib chieftain merely smiled and continued his weekly visits to the Warners for his cup of wine.

It was a season of endless labor, reminiscent of their first arrival on the island. Edward seldom found the time to escape into the forest during the day, and he was far too tired at night. And besides, he no longer possessed the inclination. There seemed so much to do at home. So much to talk about with Mama. So much to show Philip, who regarded his elder brother with awe. So many hours to be spent attempting to entertain Sarah.

But the best part of each day was that spent with Mama. The Warner house was the largest in the village, with three rooms and a porch running the whole length of the front, looking out over Sandy Point and the bay. Here Tom had his men construct a chair for Mama, on rounded timbers, so that she could sit in the evening and rock herself slowly to and fro and watch the sun declining into the endless Caribbean Sea. Here her children would gather at her feet, and often enough Berwicke and Ashton would come over as well, to talk, to remember, and to dream. And here Edward could consider her, and think. A great gulf seemed to have been torn out of his life. When he had last seen her, he had known the comfort of her arms as a child, and nothing more. Now she had returned, and he knew the comfort of a woman's arms as a man. Hideous thoughts, but thoughts not to be turned away as he sat on the floor and watched her, her long light brown hair floating over the back of the chair, her gown, so tantalizing in its exposure of sunburned neck and suddenly pale breast, closing in to grip her waist, to trace the outline of her leg under her skirt, for she very rapidly discarded the fashionable hip pads as being quite impossible to manage in a largely physical life such as she had now undertaken. To all of these were matched her face and her smile. Father's possession. The sight and the thought made him sweat, and when he did seek Yarico it was with a desperate intensity which seemed to reassure the Indian girl for their less frequent meetings.

He took to returning to the house at odd moments of the day, to observe her and to gain precious moments of private conversation. She was eager to have him close, having missed him from her life for three years, and compounded his problems by inviting him into her bedchamber, often when she was in a state of undress, and on one unforgettable occasion when she had been frightened by a lizard which had got in through the window and gone scuttling across the floor. Her scream had summoned him, because Father was out at the time, and he had burst through the door to discover her pressed against the wall, naked.

For a few terrible minutes he had acted the role she had chosen for him, that of her still-young son. He had caught the lizard without difficulty, and laughed, and presented it to her as a harmless creature. She had gazed at him for a moment, and then at it, beginning to smile, while he had been allowed to look at the endless white of her legs, the tremendous growth of hair between, the sucked-in belly, even when she lacked the corsets dictated by habit, and above, the huge breasts. She possessed everything Yarico did, and everything Yarico lacked. Only her nipples remained flaccid. He was her son.

And yet, when she had raised her head, the quivering lizard still held between her hands, and looked into his face, she had realized the danger in which she had placed them. Color had flared into her cheeks, and she had licked her lips before saying very softly, "I had forgot how large you are grown, Edward. Here, take your pet, and I will dress myself."

Yet dismay had not lasted. This was the most terrifying thing of all. She was, he remembered, a dozen years younger than Father, and Father was in a mood of constant preoccupation. Could not a woman flirt with her own son, while revealing always nothing more than the admiration of a mother? She was eager to touch him, to hold his shoulders and feel the rippling muscles, to trace the brown flesh, to wonder, perhaps, at his reluctance to be embraced, to kiss her and touch her back. He dared not. To let her go, having once truly held her in his arms, would be next to impossible. The strangest of terrible thoughts kept entering his head, culminating in the dream of Father dead, and Mother a widow, turning to her eldest son for support, and more than support. For now that he was all but a man there could be no question as to who would succeed Father. Berwicke and Ashton had been tried and found wanting. Hilton had deserted the colony. The newcomers were no more than newcomers; it was remarkable how the Caribs treated them with disdain, when they appeared to notice them at all, while their friendship toward the four original colonists remained unchanging. But that they also worshiped the white woman, or at the least found her compellingly attractive, was plain to see; she had to do no more than take a walk along the beach to have them gathered around in admiration.

Only sanity, and the cloying embraces of Yarico, demanded that he wait for John Jefferson and the arrival of the promised females, like the other men.

Her name was the *Hopewell*, and she dropped anchor in the Old Road formed by the isthmus leading to the south peninsula, off the Carib village. As usual, everyone on the island gathered to watch her and to greet the boat which came ashore. For once again they had a splendid crop to be shipped, and the golden leaves were gathered and sheaved.

They stared, and broke into cheers as they saw the flutter of skirts being lowered into the boats. "By God," Ashton said. "My throat feels as dry as a boy's. What a pity Tony did not live for this day."

For they had seen nothing of him since the moment he had taken to the forest, and the conclusion seemed obvious.

Tegramond stood next to the Warners. Even he had managed to learn a word or two of English. He waved his arms, encompassing the sea and the sky, and said, "Many people come." But he smiled, and Tom Warner smiled also, and clapped him on the shoulder.

"Women," he said. "Men, women." He crossed the forefingers of each hand, and Tegramond laughed.

"Tom," John Jefferson cried, as the first boat grounded in the shallows. "Well met. By God, but you told no lies when you described this place. I have not seen such beauty. I wish I could stay. Perhaps I shall, at least, return after I have sold your tobacco. Mistress Warner." He kissed Rebecca's hand. "And this is Edward? By God, sir, you're a giant."

He was himself a large man, dominated by the huge hook of his nose, which threw cheeks and wide mouth into the shade. He wore a broad hat, and sweated right through his doublet, and looked ill at ease, despite his enthusiasm.

"What news of England, Mr. Jefferson?" Ralph asked.

"It changes little, Mr. Berwicke. The king is ailing, and

fear that we may soon be ruled by Prince Charles. Ah, well, they say any change is usually for the better." He laid his finger alongside his nose. "But I am no politician, you'll understand. Now, Tom, tell me what you think of these."

Edward had already been staring at the two remaining boats coming ashore, frowning in a mixture of alarm and dismay. For one thing, each boat contained four sailors, sitting in the bows, armed with cutlasses and with pistols in their belts, and Father had always insisted that there be no display of weapons in front of the Indians. For another, the people gathered amidships in the boats were unlike any he had ever seen before. White-skinned, certainly; in fact, most of them were either yellow- or red-haired, with very pale flesh. But there was no suggestion of breeding or even civilization among them; their hair was wild and curling, the men's beards were unclipped, and their clothes were a collection of rags.

Tom Warner had also noticed the boats as they came into the surf, and had begun to frown. "What's this, John? What's this?"

" 'Tis a difficult question you posed us, Tom," Jefferson explained. "Which we undertook to solve as best we could. This colony of yours still sounds a savage place to English ears, and your crops, if prime quality, are still small. Success begets success, they say. As your colony becomes larger and more prosperous, so will men and women of quality become anxious to join you. Until then, why, it is necessary to prime the pump, so to speak. These people are from Ireland."

"Ireland?" Ashton said, peering at the boats, which were now grounding. "You mean Catholic rebels?"

"Were they not, Mr. Ashton, they would hardly be here. 'Tis becoming quite a custom, in these days, to ship the disaffected off to the Virginias and the Carolinas, there to work for a spell. So I arranged a shipload for you, Tom. You'll find them good, sturdy people, capable of fine work, if properly supervised. Line them up there," he told his officer.

The Irish men and women were made to wade ashore, and arranged in two lines, the females in front and the males behind; there were twelve men and eleven women. None was very old, and they certainly looked strong enough, and cheerful enough, as well, despite the undoubted rigors of the voyage they had just undergone. They muttered among themselves and winked and smiled at the amazed colonists, and the women were not above tugging at the tattered bodices of their gowns to reveal swelling flesh, or combing their hair from their foreheads as they observed Rebecca. But to Edward's dismay there was hardly one he would have called pretty, or even attractive; certainly not when set next to Mama. Although perhaps their filth and the odor which arose collectively from the group had something to do with this.

"By God," Tom was muttering. "What are they, then, slaves?"

"Indentured servants, Tom," Jefferson said. "I have purchased them for you, with some of your profits from the last crop. The last of your profits, I may say. They are now bound to serve you for ten years. For that period of time you may certainly look upon them as your servants, bound to do your every bidding. Your only duty is to feed them and clothe them."

Tom walked slowly down the line of women, frowning as they giggled at him, and glancing at the group of young men behind him, who were whispering among themselves. " 'Tis not what I had expected."

"But all that could be secured, Tom. You should know the difficulties yourself."

"And at least they seem cheerful and well behaved," Rebecca said.

"Ah, well . . ." Jefferson pulled at his long nose. "They are that glad to see dry land again, and to keep them happy we gave each man and woman a glass of wine before bringing them ashore. They're Irish, you'll understand, Mrs. Warner, and given to riot and general ill behavior. They need a strong hand over them."

"And I have such powers?" Tom demanded.

"They are yours, Tom, for a space of ten years. Here, I have drawn up a paper for their understanding. This has been read to them, and they appreciate its worth. I think it would be best were you to continue its dictates."

Tom took the rolled parchment and perused it with a grim face. "By God," he said at last. "For insolence, a dozen lashes on the bare back. For raising a hand against an employer, two dozen lashes on the bare back. For attempting to escape, four dozen lashes on the bare back. John, you've an omission here. There is no actual death sentence."

Jefferson did not appear to notice the sarcasm. "Ah, well, you see, as they are only bound for a term of years, it is your responsibility to keep them alive. To the best of your ability, that is. Should they attempt to mutiny, now, you'd be entitled to use whatever force you considered necessary, and no doubt make an example of the ringleader. It'd be best to leave them in no doubt as to that."

Tom scratched his head. "You pose me a pretty problem here. John. What say you, friends?"

"They outnumber us, to be sure," Ashton said. "But not to any great extent. And provided we keep our wits about us, we should not find ourselves in any quandary. There's no doubt that with those sturdy fellows we could clear a much larger area to put into cultivation."

"And in any event," Berwicke put in, "we can always call on the chief here for assistance, should we need it."

"And the women?" Tom asked.

"Well, they'll be a great help," said one of the young men. He glanced at his companions and flushed. "It seems to me that Mistress Warner is faced with a sight too many domestic duties."

Rebecca smiled. "I won't say no to that, William Jarring. But I've a notion you see more arising from these girls than a mere laundry."

"Well . . ." Jarring stood on one leg and again gazed in confusion at his compatriots.

"As I said, John, a pretty problem," Tom said. "My boys have been bachelors for too long."

"Well, then, why not let them pick and choose," Jefferson suggested. "Ten years is a long time. With fortune. none of these girls. at the least, will want to return to their bogs at the end of it."

"Saving that you quite forgot to bring us a priest, John."

"There's a fault I shall remedy on my next voyage, I swear. But for the time being, you can fill that duty. Tom. You are king's lieutenant, and governor of these islands. You have the right to perform a marriage, at least in common law. provided the banns are read in proper fashion."

"Aye," Tom muttered, pulling at his lip. "I had little conception that there was so much to growing a few sheaves of tobacco."

"Yet was it always your ambition to grow people as well, Mr. Warner," Rebecca pointed out. "Did you not dream of a place where all men could be free, of law as well as imposition, each to attempt to live his life in his own way?"

"And here is my dream coming to an immediate end."

"Only as it is forced upon you, sir," she insisted. "Can you not look upon these people, no, upon us all, as your own children? We have bound ourselves to obey you, and do so faithfully. These Irish folk may need to be shown your fist on occasion, but have not your own sons always needed that, and do they not still love you and obey you? I think Mr. Jefferson is right. We need to grow, and we cannot afford to be too particular about the means we employ. And if I may in any way influence your decision, I shall be happy to play the mother to these girls."

Tom continued to frown and stare from his people to the newcomers, until one of the Irishmen called out, "Sure, and are we to stand here the day, being broiled in this sun? 'Tis better we'd be clapped back in the hold of that tub."

"Hold your miserable tongue," bellowed the officer from the ship, stepping forward and whipping his stick to and fro. The sounds of the blows echoed across the beach, the Irishmen cursed, and one or two raised their fists, only to be checked by the pistols of the sailors. The Caribs muttered among themselves on the far side of the strand, and Tegramond grinned.

"Avast there," Tom growled. "We'll not air our differences in front of the savages. All right, my decision is made. Each man is allowed a male servant, and a female. I'll force no man, by God, and no woman, for that matter. You'll make your choices and abide by them with full responsibility. But whosoever shows me a full belly shall be married within the month. And to his wife he shall show the respect of a gentleman. I'll have that understood."

"Spoken like a Solomon, Tom," Jefferson said. "Come, will you make a choice now?"

"It'd be better done over a bottle," someone muttered.

Tom rounded on them, his face an angry flush. "I'll have no lewdness here," he shouted. "Choose now, or be done with it. And remember, I'll have respect and good manners. We'll make these people serve us best by treating them as we would our own families."

"But there are only eleven females, Mr. Warner," Jarring protested. "And fourteen unmarried men." He ignored Edward.

"Now, there's a fact," someone else remarked.

"Thirteen," Berwicke said. "I'll not be lumbering myself with a wife after sixty years of bachelorhood."

"Still two short," Jarring said.

" 'Tis a pity you'd not a couple more of these girls tucked away, John," Tom said. "There's nothing likely to disrupt the colony more than jealousy. Ah, well, you'll have to draw lots, lads. Mr. Ashton is reserved, as he is one of my original colonists. But two of you'll go short."

Jefferson was tugging away at his nose. "There is another wench," he said in a low voice.

"Eh?" Tom turned. "And you'd not bring her ashore?"

"She's under duress, if you must know. Seems someone responsible for rounding up these beggars made a mistake. This young woman claims some quality. Oh, 'tis vague enough, and nothing that any of us should note, but it's had that bad an effect on her character. She's pushed a knife clear through one of the crew."

"Killed him?" Rebecca whispered.

"No. Although he'll wear a scar to his grave. Still, it was her intent, no less."

"No doubt she had a reason," Tom suggested.

"Well, it was attempted rape, to be sure. But still, she was nothing better than a serving girl, by his lights. In any event, Tom, I'd not burden you with a born troublemaker. She can go back to England, if she survives the voyage, and cool her heels in the Fleet."

"No," Rebecca said. "Bring the creature ashore. I'll wager she needs nothing more than fresh air and kind treatment."

Jefferson glanced from Tom to his wife, and Tom nodded. "If she was protecting her virtue, then I've every sympathy with her."

"Virtue?" Jefferson asked in amazement. "You'll find none in this crowd. They're fornicating before they know the meaning of the word. But I'll have her ashore."

He signaled the ship, and a moment later they saw the young woman being forced over the side; she seemed to feel each touch of a male hand, each command from a male voice, as a drop of boiling water, to be resisted and avoided. Edward felt a sudden compassion for her, and with it, a sudden excitement. The eleven girls on the beach in front of him interested him no more than the Carib women, perhaps even than Yarico, now. She was the most intelligent of them all, but she was still very little more than an animal, and she was capable of filling him with disgust. He could not imagine her, or any of them, deeming it necessary to rebuff an amorous sailor. But here was a girl who had acted very much as Mama might have done, only she was to be punished for it.

And here was some beauty, too. No doubt it was already present, in his mind, but then, he could tell by the expressions of the men around him, and even of the Caribs, that this was not the whole of it. She gloried in a head of the most marvelous auburn hair, which possessed a peculiar sheen to it, even in the afternoon sunlight. Below, the skin was very lightly dusted with freckles, entirely lacking the muddy quality of the other girls. Nor were her features vacantly rounded, as theirs, but rather aquiline, with a straight nose set between two wide gray eyes, and a matching mouth which sat well the way she gazed at the beach, allowed herself to take in the Caribs, with interest but not fear, and then to dwell with the utmost contempt on the group of eager white men. Only when she saw Rebecca did her expression change, but for a moment, before resuming her normal reserve.

She was tall; when she stood up, she matched any of the sailors, and slender, but yet obviously a full-grown woman; she wore no more than a shift, which the breeze flattened against breast and belly, gathered around thigh and buttock. And she had all the instincts of a lady, for when she stepped down onto the beach, and a playful gust threatened to lift her skirt, she held it firm with her hands where her predecessors had cared nothing for their exposed legs.

"Over here," Jefferson said.

The mate gestured the girl in the direction of the others. He seemed to prefer not to touch her at this moment. Still holding the skirt of her shift, she crossed the sand toward them.

"By God," Jarring said. "Now, there is a woman. When do we draw lots, Captain Warner?"

The girl stopped, and her gaze, hitherto studying the sand, came up. "Ye lay a finger on me and I'll take out both your eyes," she said quietly and yet very distinctly. The brogue was there, and yet, hidden beneath, a veneer of education.

"You see?" Jefferson pointed out. "She's incorrigible."

"I do not think so," Rebecca said softly, and stepped forward. "These girls were sent out here less as wives than as servants, were they not? And am I not, as wife of the governor, entitled to a servant for my house?"

"But . . ." Jarring began, to be silenced by a look from Ashton.

"You are, Rebecca," said the sailing master. "I think that is an entirely suitable suggestion. And indeed, given the time to settle herself, and to understand that we are gentlemen and not louts, Mr. Jarring, she may well prove a good wife to one of us yet."

"Provided we can wait that long," Jarring said in disgust, and turned his attention to the other girls.

"What is your name?" Rebecca asked. The two women were of almost the same height.

The girl stared at her and flushed. "My name is Susan Deardon," she said. "And I'd know what ye want of me. I'll not be sold off like a cow."

"That shall not happen, Susan, I promise you," Rebecca said. "Now, firstly, I want your trust. That way we may become friends, and life may take on a more pleasant aspect."

With the coming of July, Ashton, Berwicke, and Edward fell to watching the sky. But it remained clear. There was increased rain, and occasionally they could see the heavy dark clouds forming on the horizon, but always they dispersed before the wind, without assailing the island. Yarico was confident. "Hurricane, no," she pronounced, and would fall to playing with his body, as she invariably did whenever they were alone.

He lay on his back, in the forest adjoining Brimstone Hill, their usual meeting place, as it had been the first. His clasped hands were beneath his head, and he looked down on her glossy black hair as she fingered and stroked, kissed and caressed. She never tired of him, after more than a year, delighted it seemed equally in arousing him and then in reducing him to flaccid impotence. He was her toy, her plaything, and she loved him. This was the disturbing factor. He marveled that she had not yet become pregnant. Three of the Irish girls already had swelling bellies, and there seemed little doubt that there would be others before very long; Father anticipated the arrival of the priest with more anxiety than he worried about the shipment of his crop, for he could not convince himself that the civil ceremonies he had performed had any significance before God.

What would happen should Yarico also give birth did not bear consideration. Because try as he might, Edward could discover no similar feeling within himself. He admitted to an endlessly muddled series of emotions. He loved her physical loving—and yet could not help but imagine how much more marvelous would it be should it be done to and by a white girl. This was Susan's effect on him. She had even managed to replace Mama in his midnight dreams. Not that she ever paid any attention to him. She paid little attention to anyone. Father and Mama allowed her to take her meals with themselves and the children, and in many ways treated her as a daughter, yet they were seldom rewarded with a smile, and when two of the Irishmen had got drunk and fought, and Father, reluctantly, had ordered them to be flogged for causing a riot, her eyes had smoldered as she had watched the punishment.

Edward blamed her not a whit. To be torn from home and family, merely on account of birth and religion, seemed unjust. And the sight of her, the smell of her, for she was most remarkably clean about her person, and the very presence of her, kept him in a state of constant excitement, from which again Yarico benefited, still without seeking to discover whence it arose, without, perhaps, ever suspecting that it had a source other than herself.

He sat up, suddenly decided. Yarico moved her head, to gaze at him, eyes watchful.

"I must go," he said. "I have remembered . . ." He reached for his breeches, dragged them on. "I must go."

Yarico stared at him. He bent over her, kissed her gently on the forehead.

"Tomorrow?" she asked.

He hesitated. "Perhaps. I must go." He ran away from her, over the brow of the hill and down the winding path. Great beads of sweat rolled down his neck, flew from his face. Relief, certainly. She was choking him, slowly, incessantly, with her love. Love? Savage Indians could not love. That girl had torn a man to pieces with her teeth. He must never forget that. He could never forget that. He was her conquest. Her prisoner, she had thought. He would indeed have been her prisoner, had she had the wit to become pregnant. Father would have seen to that, rather than antagonize Tegramond. But now he had escaped.

And there was the sweat of anticipation, too. Because it was Sunday, many of the colonists were asleep. Others were gathered by the water's edge, smoking and talking. The Irish laborers, with the frenetic energy peculiar to themselves, were farther up the beach, playing a remarkable game in which they armed themselves with palm fronds, carefully trimmed of excess leaves so that only the hard, curved spine remained to provide a four-foot-long club, with which they chased a dried husk to and fro, as often whacking each other on the shins as gaining their objective. A truly strange people.

It needed no more than caution to approach the village from the rear, through the tobacco field, past the seed beds and the sheds erected for the drying and curing of the crop, for Father had come to the conclusion that he would save by doing this here, and more, produce a distinctive brand of tobacco. Too much was lost by rot on the way home.

He stood in the little yard behind the governor's house and watched his sister building castles in the sand. She was six years old, and remained a total stranger to him, a small, dark, earnest child with unutterably deep eyes and a perpetually dribbling nose, who spoke little and cried less, seemed wrapped up within herself in the possession of some vast secret.

Sitting on the little step which led to the back door of the hut was Susan Deardon. Her feet were bare, as usual, and her legs drawn up beneath her. Her magnificent hair was loose and fluttered in the afternoon breeze. She looked half-asleep, but her eyes followed the child. Christ, *how* he sweated. But this was all to the good. Father and Mama must have taken a walk along the beach, perhaps to visit Tegramond.

He stepped around the building, and her head moved. "Ye're a strange one, Master Edward," she said. "What brings ye creeping through the grass like a thief?"

He cursed the flush he could feel burning his cheeks. "What makes you sit here by yourself, when everyone else is enjoying themselves?"

"Enjoying thmselves? Is that what they're at?" Her shoulder rose and fell. "I'm to watch Miss Sarah."

"And I came to watch you," he said boldly.

Her head half-turned. There was no change in her expression. But she moved her legs, stretching them in front of her, and arranged her skirt across her ankles. She wore one of Mama's old gowns, pulled in to fit her slender waist, but refused to attempt shoes. And what need, in such a climate and with such beautiful feet?

"Because there's nothing I'd rather do," Edward said, and sat beside her. Now his sister also watched him, briefly, before returning to her game in the sand. "Why don't you admit it?" he asked. "This place is not half so bad as you'd anticipated. You've food to eat, and water or wine to drink. You've as pleasant a climate as anyone could dream of. . . ."

"And I'm owned by pleasant people," she said.

"You're not owned by anyone, Susan."

"Of course ye're right, Master Edward. I'm just borrowed. Do ye know how old I am? Eighteen. So when your mother is finished with me, I'll be twenty-eight. Mistress Warner's castoff."

"You could end that tomorrow." The saliva drained from his mouth, to leave his throat parched.

At last she looked at him. "Marry one of them thick-headed louts? Then I *would* be entering slavery."

"I was thinking that there are gentlemen on this island."

It occurred to him that he had never really seen her before. She had been a face, exposed by its very circumstances, but strong enough to protect the brain within; a body, well concealed beneath her clothes; bare feet, which but promised the beauty that would exist in the rest of her. And the hair. It was the hair which filled his dreams. Would the hair on her belly be that glorious? But now the mask was splitting, from sheer surprise. Her reserve had, after all, been no more than loneliness. And suddenly she looked less an untouchable beauty than a frightened young girl.

Then it was closing again, shutting herself away behind the cool gray of her eyes. "Ye've a mind to mock me, Master Edward."

She was again staring at Sarah.

"No," he said. "Believe me, Susan."

His hand started to move across the step toward hers, and then slipped back again. Christ curse him for a coward, but he was afraid of her.

"Then ye're a fool," she said. "Or a dreamer. Ye know nothing of me. Ye've never touched my flesh."

"A dreamer," he said. "Not a fool, Susan. Would the reality be so different from the dream?"

Her head turned, so quickly she took him by surprise. "There's the girl," she muttered.

"She'll not understand." But he was incapable of movement.

Not Susan. She placed her hands on his cheeks and kissed him on the mouth. She all but sucked the tongue from his throat. And here was no Indian smell. Here was fresh beauty. And breasts. His hands came up, to close on them, to feel the nipples right through the cloth, to feel the surging flesh beneath. Mama had breasts like these. Oh, Christ in heaven.

Her hands were on his chest. "God, I have wanted," she whispered. "And you. If it's my tits ye're after, Master Edward, they're yours. Just don't mock me."

"No," he said. "I'm sorry. I have wanted you. Since you stepped ashore. I fell in love with you then, Susan."

She tossed her head, straightened her shift. "Every man on the island did that. Even the savages."

"And have you yielded to any of them?"

"Christ," she muttered. "To *that*?"

"Listen." He seized her hands. He could do that now, and as they lay flaccid, his own rested on her lap. On her thighs, and on everything that lay beneath the gown. So, was he about to lie? He could not tell. He knew now that he did not love Yarico, that he would never love Yarico. He knew now that he would dream of that day in his mother's bedroom until he died. But at least that dream now possessed red hair rather than brown. "I love you, Susan," he said. "I want you. But all of you. I want you to marry me."

She was gazing at him, and he was no longer afraid of her eyes. "I'm a bastard," she said. "My father was a big man. Oh, he was a big man. My mother was a whore. But she was his whore. Life was good until your English came. They burned Daddy's castle. They hanged him. They laid Ma on her back until she died of exhaustion, and they went on laying her after that. I'm no virgin, Edward Warner. They got me too, but I didn't die, so I was right for slavery."

Christ, how he hated. Them. *Them.* Out there in world. But this world was no more than twenty miles long by ten wide, if that.

"I'm no virgin, either," he said.

"Ye're sixteen."

"I'll be seventeen in a month. I'm a man grown. I've had to be, Susan. I'll care for us. I'll build us a house, back there. I'll give you sons. And one day this colony will be mine."

Now he was afraid again. There was a quality in her eyes which seemed to say: Liar, liar, liar, you want these tits and this belly. You want to own these legs, because you have never seen legs to equal them. But she was wrong there. And if a man could not possess his mother, well, then surely he could love this magnificent creature.

"Then ye'd best act the part," she said softly.

Footsteps, coming through the house. Edward hastily stood up, on one side of the step, and Susan followed his example, on the other. Rebecca came through first, Tom at her shoulder. "Sarah." She stooped and scooped the girl into her arms. "You've been good?"

"Oh, yes, Mama. Edward was with me."

"Mooning about the plantation on a Sunday afternoon?" Tom demanded. " 'Tis not like you, boy. Where is Philip?"

"I have no idea, Father."

"Susan?"

"He . . . he wandered off." Her cheeks were flushed, and now she bit her lip. It was difficult to suppose anyone on this island opposing that bluffly domineering manner. But Edward reminded himself that he had seen his father just as nervous and uncertain as this girl.

"Careless," Tom said. "You'll do better in future, Susan."

"The boy is growing, Mr. Warner," she said quietly.

He stopped in surprise and glanced from her to his wife.

"Why, that's true enough," Rebecca agreed. "And the men are on the beach."

"Aye," Tom said. "But you'll remember your place, girl. Now and always."

Edward sucked breath into his nostrils, felt his heart pounding, and for the second time this afternoon cursed the heat in his cheeks. "Not always, Father. I would like to speak with you."

Now Tom was frowning and looking from boy to girl. "You'll take Sarah inside, Rebecca."

Her turn to hesitate. But she knew better than to increase his simmering anger. She gave Edward a warning glance and closed the door behind her.

"Yes?" Tom inquired.

"I would take a wife, sir," Edward said. "Susan."

Tom looked at the girl. "Your doing?"

"There's no other man on the island I'd rather wed, Mr. Warner. If that is what ye mean."

"Slut," he snapped, and swung the back of his hand. It caught her across the mouth and stretched her on the sand, legs kicking and skirt flying.

"Sir," Edward said. "You have no right."

Susan sat up, straightened her skirt, and only then wiped the trickle of blood from her lips.

"No right?" Tom shouted. "She's that fortunate I do not take the skin from her arse. And you, by God, look at you, sixteen years old, and you'd take a wife, would you?"

Edward refused to lower his gaze. "You made me a man, sir, before I was twelve. You've a thriving colony now. Have you no wish for a grandson?"

"By God," Tom said. "What have you been doing, then? Crawling around the Carib village hoping to thrust your weapon into some cannibal?" He continued without giving Edward the time to consider a reply. "No. They'd not have you. They like men, not boys. And she . . ." His arm outflung. "Do you think *she* cares a damn for you? She seeks to be free. Aye, she'd laugh in your face the moment the words were spoken. Get from my sight, boy. Mention this to me again and I'll flog you both around the camp, so help me God. Now, take to the woods, and do not return before suppertime." He seized Susan by the hair as she would have risen. "Not you, girl. You'll spend the rest of this day on your knees here in this yard. And you'll pray that I forget this afternoon's work."

The anger bubbled inside him, curling his fingers into fists, causing him to rip the branches from trees and slowly strip them to the bark. Once, even, he caught a lizard, and hurled it from him with all his strength, listening to its passage through the bushes with tumultuous glee. Anger, against whom? Father? Or self? He was a coward. There was a fact. He had crumpled like a leaf in the hand. What would she think of him now?

But he hated Father, too. For treating him as a child. Why, if he wished, he could take Father as he had taken that lizard, and . . . If he wished. If he had the courage to oppose not only Tom Warner, but the king's lieutenant, governor of the Caribee Isles. There was a dream.

And Susan. Desire clouded up his body, turned his legs to lead, left his brain a limp rag. Susan, all of that tall, straight, white-skinned beauty, all of that proud face, all of the promise which had surged beneath the shift, all of that abundant fire-red hair, had been granted to him. For the space of a few short seconds.

It could be his forever. To take that would be to reject all else. But what else was there worth having, where that was absent? Especially where all that would be *there*, all the time, perhaps, in time, belonging to someone else. In a very little time. Of course, Father would now seek to force her into marriage with one of the colonists. Then would life truly become unbearable.

His decision was made. He was so happy he felt like bursting into song. And then grew serious again. A time for planning. But it all seemed very simple. Once the decision was made, it all fell into place.

He returned to the village at dusk, as instructed, in time for supper. They sat around the table as usual, Father at the head, Mama at the foot, Edward and Sarah on one side,

Philip and Susan on the other. Father's bad temper had disappeared, as it usually did, and he was, again as usual, determined to make it up to all. He talked and joked. His conversation played around their heads like a sea breeze. Unsuccessfully. Mama was quiet, the children inquisitive. "You looked so funny, kneeling in the yard, Sue," Philip said. "Why were you kneeling there all afternoon?"

Susan stared at her plate.

"She'd been kissing Edward," Sarah said. "Hadn't you, Sue? Like this." She pursed her lips and thrust them forward.

"Be quiet, child," Mama snapped, and looked at Tom.

"Aye," Father said. "Be quiet. You'll not bear a grudge, Susan."

Susan's head raised for the first time. There were tearstains on her cheeks.

"Say so, girl," Father commanded.

"I'll not bear a grudge, Mr. Warner."

Edward tried to attract her attention by staring at her. But she would not look at him.

"Well, then," Father said. "It's done." He stood up. "You'll join me in a leaf, Edward."

There was condescension. They were all adults together now, provided they stopped being adults whenever he so commanded. Edward's anger rose, kept his resolve at fever pitch. He retired early to the hammock in the room he shared with Philip and Sarah. They were already abed, and soon asleep. But he had to wait for the others, to listen to every last creak. At last he fell asleep himself, to awaken with a start only a few minutes later. The house was still, the village quiet, the only sounds the ever-present soughing of the breeze through the trees and the never-ending rumble of the surf.

He lowered his feet from his hammock slowly, cautiously, touched the floor, and stood up. He had deliberately undressed in his most careless fashion, left his breeches under the hammock. These he dragged on, but did not bother with shoes. He seldom wore them anyway, and he would not need them where he was going.

He picked up his sword and crossed the floor, listening to the snoring from Sarah's hammock. She seemed to breathe less than to wheeze, and she was six years old. Pity the man who married her and spent the rest of his life listening to her gasp. Carefully he pulled the door open, watching the hammocks behind him, motionless in the gloom. He would never see them again. Did he care? They were strangers to him, milksops from a milksop society, their inadequacy revealed in the paleness of their skins. No, he would not miss *them.*

He stood in the little hall, listening, and hearing nothing. Well, then, Mama? He would never see her again, either. But he was deliberately escaping Mama. And with Susan at his side he would have no time to think of other women, other limbs, other breasts, other lips.

Susan slept in the front room, which meant that she was compelled to stow and rehang her hammock with each day and night. But at least here she was alone. Cautiously he crossed the room, anxious about a board which had creaked during dinner. But this time there was no sound. He stood by the hammock, his eyes accustomed to the darkness now, and looked down at her. Her hair drifted over the side, seemed almost to touch the floor. She was on her back, her face upturned.

He bent lower, and her whisper reached him. "If ye touch me, Master Edward, I shall scream."

He knelt beside her. He was so close he could smell her; even her scent held endless promise. "Listen. Will you come with me?"

Now at last she moved, to turn her body so that she could face him. "Come with ye?"

"We shall leave this place. This island. I have thought it out. The Caribs keep no night watch, and their canoes are on the beach. We will take one and paddle across to Nevis. It is only a few miles, and the Indians say it is uninhabited. They will never find us."

"Ye're mad," she asserted. "What would we live on?"

"There are fish, and coconuts. Same as here. I would take weapons. Father's pistols are right by the door."

"Such a step takes courage," she said. "I doubt ye possess so much, Edward. Ye'd not defy your father."

"Will you not trust me?"

"With my life? It amounts to that, whether we succeed or not."

"I'd give my life for you, Susan. I swear it. But allow me the chance."

She smiled; he felt her breath on his face, and he could see the flash of her teeth. "Ye're a passionate devil, Edward Warner. And all ye really want is to pull these tits. Here, boy, help yourself." She leaned out of the hammock, and her breasts touched his face; he realized with a thrill of amazement that she was naked beneath the blanket. He seized her shoulders, crushed his face into the soft flesh, felt the erect nipples seep into his mouth, heard the beat of her heart only an inch away. "God," she whispered. "Ye have a way with ye, boy."

But he was pushing her away. He did not know why. Except that he hated Father and every human being on the colony. On the island. Save this one. "I want you as my wife," he said. "I want all of you. Will you come?"

She waited, for the longest moment he had ever known. Then she threw back the blanket, dropped her feet to the floor. He was alone with a naked, beautiful white woman for the second time in his life. He felt a tremendous surge of energy and manhood within him. But it was not merely sexual. Here was an enormous responsibility placed on his shoulders. An enormous honor placed in his keeping. To protect that, he could assail the world.

It was a time to do. As she reached for her shift, he tiptoed across the room to stick a brace of pistols in his belt and hang the pouch with the bullets and powder over his shoulder. Aye, he thought. The world.

He led her through the jungle paths he knew so well, navigating himself by the moon. Often he held her hand to help her over an outcrop; the touch of her sent his heart pounding and his mind soaring. They spoke little. In the strangest way, where down to yesterday he had been master and she servant, now in a matter of hours they had become old friends. Intimate friends, although he had hardly touched her.

But their progress was slow, and soon enough he felt the shift in the breeze which heralded dawn. He stopped. "We'll not make Nevis before daybreak," he said.

She waited for him to decide to go back. What would she do then, he wondered? They could not regain their hammocks before daybreak, either.

"If we go farther into the forest," he said, "we can lie there the day. It will be better, indeed. For they will not suppose us to be so close." He bit his lip as she did not reply. "It'll mean going hungry, but just for one day. And then, tomorrow night, when they have abandoned the search, we may resume our way without difficulty."

"We'll not go hungry." She also carried a bag over her shoulder, and from it took a cheese. "I thought our journey might well be delayed. But the concealment must lie in your care. I know naught of this forest."

Yet she was not afraid of it, or if she was, she did not reveal it. He left the shore and struck inland, using the mass of Mount Misery, for such was the name the white men had given to the central hill, as a guide. They plunged into ever thicker trees, ever more close-packed bushes; had he not by now been certain there were no snakes on the island, he would have been afraid himself. They forded tumbling streams and waded cooling pools, climbing all the while, as the sky lightened and the sun, huge and round and red, came peeping above the eastern horizon, bouncing from all the mountain peaks of the Leewards before reaching Merwar's Hope, the last of them all.

"Here," he said, coming across a fern-filled hollow. "Here we will be safe. They will not come this far to look for us."

Susan flopped onto her face and lay there on the damp grass, breathing slowly, muscles still twitching with exhaustion. "I have not been so weary for years," she said. "But so . . . so clean, as well. Because I have not been so free, for years."

He knelt beside her. He was as exhausted, surely. But he remained excited by her nearness. And now there could be no going back. The village would have been awakened by now, and their departure would have been noticed. There would be a great deal of excitement on the beach. Now it was the pair of them against the world. As he had wanted.

He touched her gently, taking her thick hair and drawing it through his fingers, arranging it so that it lay evenly on her back.

"I must sleep," she whispered. "I must sleep. When I awaken, Edward, dear Edward . . ."

"When you awaken," he said. There must be no forcing of this girl. No antagonizing. No differences between them. They must be as one, now and always.

He moved away, sat against a tree, watched her as he ate some of the cheese. He was tired, certainly, but still too excited to sleep. And just to look at her was to watch a dream come true. For soon she turned on her side toward him, pillowed on the soft ferns, one knee drawn up, her arms extended in front of her and then clasped, drawing her breasts together, glowing white globes which thrust upward from the tattered shift. All his, now. All his.

He slept, and awoke, to watch her again. For she too had

awakened, and taken herself into the forest with a modesty he had not expected; Yarico had never done more than spread her legs as she felt the need. But now he could watch the flaming hair moving through the ferns, without hearing the rest of her.

She parted the bushes, looked down at him. "What time is it?"

"Not yet noon."

A bead of sweat trickled out from her hair and rolled down her temple. Even her sweat was different from Yarico's. "Do ye wish me, then?" she asked.

His throat was dry. He had to lick his lips. "Are you not hungry?"

"Afterward," she said. "I should like to know, now, that we can love, Edward."

"Yes," he said, and felt the blood rushing into his face.

She lifted the shift over her head, half-turned away from him, spread it on the ground, stooping, her back to him. All he had ever dreamed of. All any man had ever dreamed of, except for the thinness. She had none of Mother's voluptuousness. The legs were endlessly long, endlessly straight, smoothly muscled. The buttocks were small and tight; they controlled the equally tight muscles of the flat belly. Even the thighs were slender as a boy's, and the hair was scanty, however thick. The breasts were smaller than he had supposed, but yet they surged, standing away from her chest as if scarce belonging to her, only just beginning to sag from their own weight, with nipples long and pointed like a poking finger. And the whole was shrouded in the white skin, all lightly dusted with the pale brown freckles, firm-textured and amazingly dry, where Mama had been moist to the touch.

He moved behind her, caught her around the waist as Yarico had taught him, hands sliding up her breasts while he brought his body against hers. She uttered a little shriek, and kicked him, twisting her body to and fro, striking behind her with her elbows. He let her go and fell backward, sitting on the ferns to stare up at her in dismay. "Susan?"

She panted, on her knees, turning slowly to face him. "Are ye a monster?"

"A . . . Did you not want me?"

"I wanted ye, Edward. But not up the arse. I'm Christian, no matter what may have happened to me."

"Up the . . . No," he protested, "I did not mean that. Sue, dearest Sue, I but sought to make an entry." He leaned forward to take her hands, so obviously upset that her gaze softened.

"Ye claimed experience," she muttered. "I believed ye."

"Tell me," he begged. "I have no knowledge of white girls."

Her frown was back. "Ye've been with an Indian? Mounted her like a dog?"

"It is their way."

"Christ," she said. "Oh, Christ, what have I done?" She looked down at her body, as if seeing it for the first time.

"I am the same man," he said. "If you would educate me, Susan, I shall submit with pleasure."

"A savage," she said. "Ye've entered a heathen savage. Aye, they call ye Caribee." She pulled her hands free. "Ye must allow me time, Edward. Not long. I swear it. But ye must let me accept ye as ye are, not as I had imagined."

"You thought me an innocent boy," he said, and gasped in horror at the face.

She had picked up her shift. "Aye. With a backyard tumble to your credit." She glanced at him, saw his expression, and followed his gaze. They were surrounded by faces, brown and amused, interested and delighted. Successful faces. As how else could they be? This was their forest. The white people were no more than intruders.

"Oh, Christ have mercy on me," Susan whispered.

"Be merciful to her, Tom, I beg of you," Rebecca whispered. They stood in front of the entire colony, in front of the village, looking down the sweep of the beach as the Caribs drove their two captives toward Sandy Point. Edward's and Susan's wrists were bound behind them, and they stumbled over the sand, heads bowed as the Indians kicked them and prodded them; Susan's hair clouded across her face and hid her tears.

"Merciful," Tom muttered. "I dare not be, sweetheart. I would, believe me. But these people—understand how they watch me. How they wait, to see the temper of Warner justice, whether weak or strong." His throat was dry. Be merciful, she said. Perhaps that would not, after all, be difficult. Did he fear a single one of the colonists? He could truthfully say not. He had measured them all, their abilities and their ineptness, their strengths and their weaknesses, and he knew that against them he could call out the resources of Tegramond and his savages, whenever he wished.

But that was not quite true. He did fear one white person on this island. And that boy was now approaching him, bound and humiliated. There would be a reckoning there, one day, and that reckoning would not be abated by love. Only by strength and determination. And in the end, by fear.

And then, the girl. Oh, Christ, the girl. She was close now, staggering toward him. Sweat drenched her body, rolled from her hair in a steady stream. Her shift was caught against her flesh at breast and thigh and groin. He had never seen a woman quite so perfectly made. But she was an Irish whore. This thought had crossed his mind too often. It had crossed his mind when Rebecca had first elected to have her in their house. He had thought then: What a blameless life you have led, Tom Warner. What woman have you ever sought, what woman have you ever considered, save your wife; if not Sarah, then Rebecca. But of late the zest had gone from Rebecca's lovemaking. The eager woman who had worked her body against his that morning in the Tower no longer existed. Was it fear of another pregnancy? According to Jane Warner, she had all but died. Or was it, despite all her assurances, a deep-seated resentment against his having left her? He often wondered how Rebecca, not yet forty, strongly built and passionate by nature, had spent those three years. With Sarah at her breast she would have been more beautiful, more passionate than ever; he remembered the nursing mother of Edward and Philip.

The prisoners stood before him, feet sinking into the soft sand, breath rasping, sweat staining their faces. The Caribs piled the sword and pistols in front of them.

Tom gazed at his son. "You'll answer a charge of deserting the colony, and larceny."

"Larceny, Father," Edward said. "There is no law against deserting the colony."

"The boy speaks the truth, Tom," Berwicke pointed out. "But this is an omission on our part that were best remedied."

"Aye," Tom said. "I'm assuming the girl led you, boy."

"No, sir," Edward declared. "It was my doing. We meant no harm, sir. We wished only to marry. And as that was impossible here, we sought another, less restricted land."

Tom turned to the girl. After several attempts she had succeeded in tossing the cloud of red hair from her face; only a few strands remained, past which the gray eyes looked with their usual clarity. Those eyes, those lips, that body, possessed by Edward. How he hated her. Hated with all the intensity of a savage jealousy. Hated with the anger of a man who must at all costs remain the disinterested judge.

"Have you no words?" he demanded. "You were on the beach when the articles were read. For absconding the colony, four dozen lashes."

"No," Rebecca cried.

"Be quiet, woman."

He watched Susan's nostrils dilate as she breathed. "Ye'd find it easier to cut my throat," she said quietly. "But not so enjoyable, maybe."

She defied him. She had identified the desire in him. Perhaps she had always known it, in the way he had looked at her.

"Four dozen lashes were too much for a woman, Tom," Ashton whispered. "She'd not survive. And if she did, she'd be good for nothing."

"You'd start sentencing on physical appearances, Hal?"

"You've no right to punish her at all, sir," Edward said. "She is no longer an indentured servant, as I have taken her as my wife."

Tom stepped forward, whipped the back of his hand across the boy's face. Edward took the blow with a jerk of his head, but kept his feet. "I'm governor here, by God," Tom said. "I'm the king's lieutenant. You'd do well to remember that." He raised his voice. "All of you. I act for the king, in his name. My son has reminded me that we suffer from serious omissions here, as regards law. I had hoped that such laws would not be necessary, but as they are, why, by God, we shall set to work this afternoon to draw up a code to manage our conduct. But the girl is a confessed absconder and for the servants there are laws enough. She'll receive four dozen lashes."

"Tom," Rebecca screamed. "You cannot."

"Get away, woman," Tom shouted, freeing his arm with a jerk. He moved so violently that she staggered. Then she regained her balance, gazed at her husband for a moment, and went into their house. Sarah ran behind her, coughing and sneezing. Philip remained standing on the porch, staring at his father and brother with wide eyes.

Susan's mouth slowly opened, as if she would have spoken. Now she slowly closed it again. There were pink spots in her cheeks.

"It shall be done now," Tom said, feeling the resolution seeping away from his mind. "Mr. Jarring, you'll see to it."

"Yes, sir, Captain Warner," Jarring cried in delight, and signaled two of his friends to follow him. "We'll fetch stakes from the bush."

"Four dozen lashes, Tom?" Berwicke whispered.

"She's a sturdy wench," Tom said. "You're bemused by her pretty face, Ralph. She's nothing but a whore from the bogs of Killarney. I doubt Jarring will mark her back."

"By God, sir," Edward said. "You harm this girl, and I'll . . . I'll kill you."

"Beware, boy," Tom said. "That is nothing less than treason, to threaten the king's lieutenant. I'll have order here, by God. She'll be punished, and you'll watch it, sir. We'll see if your belly has grown stronger with age."

Color flooded Edward's face. He had not suspected his father could enter so deep a mood. But now Jarring and his companions were back from the forest, equipped with two cut-down saplings, each about six feet long. These they proceeded to embed in the sand, in front of the governor's house, setting them four feet apart and testing them with their own weight to make sure they would not move. A nod to the Caribs, and the Indians stood aside from their captives, yet remained in a cluster on the beach, watching the white people with great interest, no doubt wondering if they meant to eat the girl. Jarring slit the rope binding Susan's wrists, and she was marched forward, a man holding each of her arms, placed between the stakes, facing the house, and her arms extended on each side of her body, one wrist being secured to each of the uprights. Still she made no sound, but remained gazing at Tom Warner, her face composed, only her breathing a trifle labored.

"By God, sir," Jarring said. "We have no whip."

Tom found his mouth choked with saliva, as it had used to be when superintending an execution. He had to spit and swallow before he could speak. "You've a belt, Mr. Jarring. We all have belts."

"A happy thought," Jarring cried.

"No studs," Berwicke said. "No studs and no buckles, Mr. Jarring."

Jarring nodded. He secured five of the belts, and these he bound together at the buckles, to leave himself with five leather thongs. "Shall I cut her hair?"

"No," Susan cried. "I beg of ye, Mr. Warner."

"Let one of the women bind it," Tom said.

"I'll do it," cried an Irish girl, running forward to grin at Susan as she gathered the long red hair into two plaits, securing each one with a string, and then hanging them in front of the tensed shoulders. "There ye are, sweetheart," she said. "They'll not harm a hair of your head."

Which brought a gale of laughter from her companions.

"Then there's the shift," Jarring said, speaking very deliberately.

"Remove it, man," Tom shouted. "And get on with it."

Jarring hesitated, then seized the material and jerked; the straps parted and it came away without resistance, to fall in a cloud of linen about her ankles. Tom could hear the sucking of breaths around him. Never had he seen such a magnificent sight; the strength in thigh and arm, for she stood with legs spread and muscles tight, waiting for the first blow; the mark of the ribs, one after the other, as her breath was similarly drawn; the spread of pale-forested belly, the composure of the firm-lipped face—Edward had known all this. By Christ, he thought. All this.

Jarring swung his arm, and the fivefold crack spread across the beach and up into the trees. Susan's whole body shook, but she never moved her feet. The second and the third blows followed in quick succession, and her eyes turned up, away from the watchers, to gaze at the sky. But now there were tears rolling down her cheeks.

The fifth blow brought her mouth open, with surprising suddenness. The sixth blow had a moan escaping those parted lips, and now her feet moved, constantly, as she shuddered and stamped. At the seventh blow the rope holding her left wrist began to slip, and at the eighth blow the dam broke; as blood flew from her lacerated back, she screamed, and again, and again, an endless, terrible, and terrifying sound, which brought the morning alive and even had Jarring hesitating. But he was swinging again, the leather straps blood-wet now in the sunlight, each blow causing a fresh cascade of red drops to fly into the air, each crack bringing a fresh scream from the tortured lips. But the screams were losing their pitch, just as those so sturdy legs were losing their strength. Now she hung, her ankles and her knees flaccid, suspended by her wrists, and now the ropes holding the wrists were themselves commencing to slide down the stakes, so that with every blow she sagged lower. She was actually being flogged into the ground. You should stop it, Tom's brain cried. Stop it now, or you will create an enemy for all the rest of your life. *An* enemy? He watched Edward out of the corner of his eye, watched the sweat standing out on the boy's face, the hard line into which his mouth had formed.

"You'll stop this madness, Tom Warner."

The voice cut across the morning, a voice strange to them for upward of a year, so unexpected they turned in horror, thinking to see a ghost, to stare at the tall, thin man, long beard a mass of curls to match the hair which tumbled about his shoulders, yet all the hair unable to conceal the tremendous gash of a mouth. He leaned on a staff as tall as himself, and had a bow slung from his shoulders, and beside it, a quiver of arrows. Nothing else, yet the colonists gazed at him as if he were behind the touchhole of a cannon with a glowing match.

"Hilton?" Ashton asked. "Tony Hilton?"

Hilton came forward slowly into the assembly. The Caribs were shouting and gesticulating. They were unused to having anyone creeping up on them in this fashion, but they had been too interested in the white man's sport.

"By God," Tom said. "We had thought you dead."

"I am not so easily destroyed, Tom." Hilton walked up to Jarring, still moving with great deliberation, took the bloodstained belts from his hand, and threw them on the sand. He knelt beside the girl, still now and perhaps fainted. From his belt he took his knife, gleaming sharp in the sunlight, and cut the ropes holding her wrists. She tumbled forward onto her face, without a sound, and he hastily rolled her onto her back. "I deserted this colony, Tom," Hilton said. "Would you take the flesh from my bones as well?"

"We . . ." Tom licked his lips. He was conscious that Rebecca was in the doorway behind him. "We had just realized that there was an omission in our laws."

"Laws?" Hilton demanded. "I remember your dream, Tom, of a land where laws were unnecessary, where men were free." He looked down at the girl. "I'll take this creature away from here."

"You'll do what?" Jarring demanded, laying his hand on Hilton's shoulder.

A moment later he scattered sand as he stretched his length on the beach. "No man touches me or this girl. By Christ, Tom, you'll have to commit a murder. And be sure I'll not go alone."

Tom chewed his lip. But his rage was past, and with it the

vicious hatred of the girl. The vicious lust to see so much unattainable beauty destroyed as well. Now he felt only the sickness, the self-hatred, the certainty that this day would leave a scar across the face of the colony which time would not heal.

"She's an indentured servant, Tony," Ashton observed mildly.

"The women are available as wives, as I understand it," Hilton said. "You've waved this carrot in front of us for too long. I worked and fought with you, Tom Warner, when this colony was but a dream, and you promised me something like this for my reward. Now I'm claiming my right."

"To skulk in the forest?" Tom asked.

Hilton gazed at the girl; her eyelids were starting to flutter, and even through her unconsciousness her face was beginning to twist with pain. "I've made a home on the north side, Tom. Tobacco growing was never my style. But I'll submit to the laws of the colony, play my part. You need someone on watch over there, and you could use my nets. You'll get a deal more fish on windward than ever over here. But I'll bow to your laws, and to you yourself, Tom, if you give me this girl."

"Let him take her, Tom," Berwicke whispered. " 'Tis certain you'll have a rebel on your hands in her, forevermore. And when there is one troublemaker, be sure you'll find others soon enough."

"And do I not have a say in this?" Edward demanded.

Hilton straightened, Susan in his arms; her eyes were open now, and she stared at him, frowning, while the pain tears still seeped away from her eyes. "No, lad, you do not," he said. "She gave you her trust. You lost your right to her when you let them take you." He walked up the sand. "I'll be back, with my bride. When she's in a fit state to be married."

Tom watched them disappear into the trees, gazed at the grinning Irish, the staring colonists, the bemused Caribs. "So what do you gawk at?" he shouted. "The girl committed a crime, and has been punished. Now a place has been found for her. The incident is closed."

Slowly, hesitating, muttering among themselves, the crowd broke up. Ashton glanced at Berwicke, and the two men left together, strolling down the beach deep in conversation. Only Edward remained staring at his father.

Tom picked up the sword, turned it over before raising his

head. "I'd best keep this. Hilton was right. You have played very little of the man this day, boy."

"Had I done so, I'd have killed someone, and perhaps been killed myself. I had no conception that you would play the savage."

"I did what I had to do, as governor of this colony," Tom said. "You'll not make these people work, and face disaster, perhaps, and rise again, by feeding them milk. As for you, boy, as you say, you would have been killed. Better that, however much the grief to your mother and me. You'll not hold your head high among these people, or the Indians, ever again." He went inside. Rebecca lay in her hammock. Sarah had gone out the back. Tom threw the sword in the corner, took off his hat. "There's not a scene I'd repeat every day of the week."

"You surprise me," Rebecca said. Never had he heard such coldness in her tone.

He stood above her. "What mean you, woman?"

Her eyes came up, gazed into his. "You were all of dripping saliva when you saw that girl lashed. Aye, you, and every man there. I conceived myself in the midst of a pack of wolves. I'd have felt safer with the Indians."

He hesitated. But now was not the time for more anger, especially where she was so nearly right. "Aye," he said. "It was a time for quick and savage justice, and it made us less than men. We must discover a better means of conducting our affairs, where it is less of a spectacle. It is the spectacle that does the harm." He sighed. "There is so much to be done. Every day turns up another problem. Edward will remain one now for too long. Hilton has reappeared to become one. And count upon it, there will be endless others. I had no conception of what I undertook when I landed here so confidently. Yet will we survive and prosper, Rebecca. This land is Warner land. In time we shall seek the other islands, and they too will prosper. The Spaniards have no interest where there is no gold, and in time we shall muster sufficient numbers even to set the Caribs at naught. Do not fear the future, Rebecca. My faith in it grows with every disaster we overcome. But I thank God I shall ever have you at my side in the struggle."

Her head turned away from him. "Perhaps you will have me at your side in the future, Mr. Warner."

"Perhaps?"

"Perhaps," she said. "I know not now to whom I am married, a captain of the king, a kindly man, given only to just anger and legal lust, or some adventurer returned from pirating, filled with the dreams and the wild talk of Walter Raleigh, and yet entirely lacking his greatness of spirit."

"Woman," Tom snapped, "I am not in the mood to be tried by your humor."

She sat up, a suddenly blazing virago. And once he had mourned her lack of fire. "So, then, sir," she shouted, "would you strap me, naked, between those stakes, and tear the flesh from my bones? Ah, you'd not have the courage for that, Tom Warner. You'd give the leather to that boy Jarring."

He stared at her, taken aback, his mouth opening and shutting again.

"So leave me be," she said. "Give me time to get to know this new man. I'd not anticipated more than one in my life."

He hesitated, and then went outside. Edward still stood on the porch, staring at the sea. Philip scraped the sand by the door. "Why is everyone quarreling today, Father? Why did Susan have to bleed?"

"Oh, hold your mouth shut, boy," Tom said. But he had no wish to speak with anyone this day; he could see Ashton and Berwicke returning up the beach. Angrily he stamped through the house again, and out the back, left the village, and surveyed the growing tobacco in the field. His wealth. What he had always sought, and now possessed, in abundance. So let them have their tempers and think he had changed. He had brought them all this, and he would bring them more, and yet more.

A sound had him turning sharply. It was no more than the faintest of rustles in the bushes by the edge of the field.

"Who's there?" he asked.

A moment's hesitation, and then Yarico stood up.

6

The River of Blood

"There she is, by God," Jarring shouted. "A sail. At last. A sail." He seized the conch shell with which the watch was provided, ran to the lip of Brimstone Hill to look down on the village and the tobacco fields, and blew a long, wailing blast, which screamed on the wind across the southern half of the island. Ships were the only punctuation in the endless life of the colonists, and when the ship was delayed, morale immediately seeped away into irritation and quarrels. Thus the conch must be blown only when there could be no doubt that the sail on the horizon was standing in.

Its wail caught every attention on the island, for the sound penetrated as far as the Carib town. The Indians gathered on the beach to gaze seaward. At the foot of the hill, work in the tobacco field ceased, and the colonists and their servants and their women gathered at the water's edge, differences forgotten at this suggestion of news from home, of fresh European food and wine, of reinforcements for the colony, of a vehicle for the removal of their tobacco.

All of these things were necessary, Tom thought, as he stood on the porch of his house and gazed at his people. And yet the sinking of their differences was by far the most important. Would that he could have discovered a means of accomplishing this without the uncertain assistance of Jefferson's vessel. He had assumed that governing an island would be little different from commanding a regiment of foot, or the Tower of London, for that matter. He had assumed so many things. He had found the Irish laborers the simplest to deal with, as, indeed, so many of his foot soldiers in the past had been Irish vagabonds. These men understood command

and the lash, and little else. Yet here again there was a difference. He could not inspire them by standing before them and pointing his sword at the enemy. There was no enemy. There was not an Irishman living—it was impossible to imagine an Irishman living—who would not respond to such a call on his valor and aggression. To hoe another furrow, to prune another leaf, left them sullenly discontented; hence the stocks which had made their unwelcome appearance in the center of the village, close by the whipping post. O'Reilly sat there now, as he had sat there for the previous two days. A big, cheerful young man with a shock of fair hair and a straggling beard, he considered himself their natural leader, apparently felt it necessary to assert himself, and suffer for it, every couple of months.

Then, the women. In many ways they were the most content of all. But even that was a transient phase. Their pleasure at being freed from the ship and the prison they had infested before that, at finding themselves in a tropical paradise with eager young men to love their bodies, was already dwindling. Three were mothers; three others would not be long delayed. It was more than ever necessary for Jefferson to have brought a priest with him; already two of the girls had been whipped for promiscuity. For adultery he could order a more severe punishment.

Punish, punish, punish, Was that, then, to be his role? Had he exchanged the position of jailer to the nobility merely to become jailer to this pack of layabouts? He had punished none of the men. He was too conscious of his weakness, here. They were his colonists. They had to have arms at hand and the freedom to live their lives. So when they sought outside love, he had whipped the women. He was in the presence of a force he could not command and could not otherwise control, because he lacked the strength. It should not have been so. Berwicke might by now be past physical endeavor, but Ashton remained always a powerful aid, and there should also have been Edward and Hilton; he did not doubt that they were each worth six of the colonists. But Hilton was seldom seen on the leeward coast, and since he had removed her, Susan had never appeared in the village. He brought fish and coconuts, as he had promised. He acknowledged the Warners as the leaders of the colony, and no doubt, if called upon, he would lend that strong and angry right arm, that bow and that sword and that pistol, to his governor. But how to summon a man ten miles away, when he might be needed in seconds?

No, if it came to a business of force, it would have to be Edward. If he could trust the boy. If he could trust the boy for anything, whether for him or against him. Near a year now, and he had not forgiven. He mooned the beach, did no more than his share of work in the fields, grew in height and breadth and strength with every day, until already, at seventeen, there was scarce a man would dare lift a hand against him in the entire colony—and remembered.

As did Rebecca. Only in Rebecca's presence did Edward's face soften; only when Edward was near did Rebecca smile. But Rebecca provided a more serious cause for concern. She would have few relations with him, only those she regarded as her duty. But this was not entirely disgust, he was sure. She complained of headaches and was often hot to the touch, while she sweated in a quite unusual profusion. Her dwindling strength could be seen in the gauntness of her face and body, the great shadows which had accumulated under her eyes, the sudden streaks of white which marked her hair. She was ailing, and he knew not what caused it. As with Sarah. Her constantly running nose and her endless sneezes were more a matter of irritation than alarm, but she was nonetheless hardly suited to this climate.

Of all his family, only Philip was unchangingly his, in appearance and health and support. But Philip wanted several years to manhood. He had not been forced to it like his brother.

And did they, did the colonists, did the laborers, did his personal problems, really matter? Was not the colony, despite all, thriving, and had not the ship, after all, arrived? Were not his fears the product of his own imagination, his own guilt? Because he was guilty. He was guilty of so many crimes he dared not stop to count them. Of adultery, merely to begin with. Of breaking his own rule regarding Indian women. Of loving, where he had never loved Rebecca. Of wanting and desiring like the most profligate courtier, when he had refused all during his days at court, had even, on one unforgettable occasion, spurned the advances of Frances Howard. Then he had been a man. Now he was a . . . a dog, summoned to his duties by his bitch, daily.

But no one knew. Of this he was sure. He took himself into the forest from time to time. But he had been given the character of a solitary man, disappointed in his family, in his colonists, in his very island. No one knew how his heart sang with joy whenever he saw her, waiting for him, shrouded in her midnight hair, a bundle of lascivious evil, for she was undoubtedly that, intent on possessing his body with the ferocity of some demon, reawakening in him all the long-forgotten manhood he had delighted in sharing with Sarah. And no one knew, either, the black despair with which he returned from these trysts, his energy and his desire spent, the fascinating laughter of Yarico following him through the trees, flooding his ears to remind him that he, the governor and the lawgiver, was the biggest criminal on the island.

Edward stood by the porch. " 'Tis the ship, Father," he said. "Will you not come?"

Tom raised his head. Excitement, at last, in the boy's tone. He must forget that word. In the man's tone. A fine figure of a man. No, a splendid figure of a man. A dominating figure of a man. He had created this colony for Edward and Philip, to give them property and empire they could never possess in England. "You'd best see if your mother wishes to rise."

He walked down the beach, joined his colonists and their women and children, to stare at the vessel which came around the north of the island, drifting rather than sailing, for there was little wind.

But this ship would hardly have sailed very fast in any event. Her foremast was gone, and her mainsail was a tattered rag. Only her mizzen seemed intact, as she ghosted toward the beach.

"She's been in a storm," someone muttered.

"A hurricane," said someone else.

"In the spring?" asked a third voice, with contempt.

Oh, they were knowledgeable, his colonists. But not knowledgeable enough. "She's been in battle," he said quietly, and their heads turned. The fact that life was a conflict between nations, fought with guns and swords, had passed them by here on Merwar's Hope. They fought among themselves, and were whipped for it, but they had seen no death here. Perhaps they doubted such a thing was possible. Sometimes he doubted it himself, could he but forget the memory of the Dominican savage being torn to pieces at the stake.

"By God," Ashton said. "You're right, Tom. Look there."

For now they could see the shattered bulwarks, the gaping hole in her hull, just on the waterline.

"But she flies no flag," Berwicke said.

"Aye. We'd best approach this with caution. She carries a

deal of metal," Tom said. "Ralph, you'll assemble the women and prepare them to take to the forest. Where do you think she'll come ashore, Hal?"

Ashton studied her through the glass. "I cannot make out the name," he muttered. "But there are men aboard, and able to move. She is under control, and I see them making ready to anchor. She should come in by the Neck."

"Then we'd best down there to see what can be done. Edward, you'll issue arms to every man. Not the Irish. Ralph, you'll remain here with four men to see that no mischief is done to the plantation. Creevey, you've my permission to leave the village. Make your way across the island to Mr. Hilton, and request his presence, fully armed, if you please. Be off with you now. The rest of you men will accompany me."

They gazed at him in some surprise. They had not known such decision, such certainty, since the day the girl had been flogged. Suddenly they remembered that he was, before all else a soldier. And that their natural instincts were in that direction, too. They fell in behind him, hefting their firepieces, with cartridges and powder horns slung from their shoulders, and cutlasses hung from their belts. They might not amount to much in a fight, Tom considered, but they looked the part, every man save himself and Ashton stripped to the waist and browned by the sun, every man eager to relieve his boredom.

They marched along the beach, a full dozen of them, staying close to the trees, in case the stranger should take it into his head to open fire, but easily keeping pace with her. And at the Neck they found Tegramond, wearing his sword, with a score of his braves, also armed.

"Ship, fight," Tegramond said.

"Not with us, I hope, old friend," Tom said. "But she has certainly been in a battle. I have a notion they will want our help, not our enmity."

Tegramond touched the sword Tom wore. "Tom, fight," he said.

"Only if I have to. Let us see what he has in mind, first."

The stranger approached slowly. The men on the shore watched, and sweated, and talked among themselves. They had long broken their ranks, and sat on the sand drinking coconut milk and gossiping.

Edward remained standing, by himself, leaning against a tree, watching the vessel. He had no friends here. His contempt for them, and theirs for him, was too openly expressed. His mind was over on the north side of the island, but Hilton had made it plain he was not welcome, and he would not go against Hilton. Because he was afraid? He doubted that. Not of the man, at any rate.

Or did he seek to convince himself? The colonists regarded him as a nothing. They had watched him humiliated by his own father, reduced to the stature of his younger brother, into helpless obedience. Nor did he deny them that right. He waited. Life was a matter of waiting for something. For Mother to get well again, perhaps. For Yarico to come back to him. He had gone into the forest, to their usual meeting place, and she had not been there. He had climbed Brimstone Hill, and she had not been there. She had not forgiven him, either. Yet she had not come to the village to taunt him. Perhaps he had, after all, had a civilizing effect on her.

So he had waited. On none of those things. He had waited for John Jefferson, determined to leave this island and seek his fortune elsewhere, if he had to stow away. Only by doing that could he hide his shame, at the least from himself, and seek a new start to life. Merwar's Hope was no El Dorado. Like that man of gold, it was a dream, and dreams could not survive the light of day. To reach out for a dream, and attempt to close the hand upon it, was to awaken. And having done that, all life became a nightmare.

A sound beside him. Wapisiane stood amid the trees, pointing at the approaching ship. "Ed-ward, fight?" he asked.

"I hope not," Edward said. "My father hopes not."

Wapisiane gazed at Tom Warner for several seconds, and smiled. "War-nah." He placed his finger on Edward's chest. "Yarico."

"Not anymore," Edward said. "She's all yours, Wapisiane. And I envy you her possession."

"Wapisiane, no," the Indian said. "War-nah."

Edward's head turned. The Carib continued to smile. "You speak . . ." He hesitated. Wapisiane would hardly know the word for lie. He made a quick movement of his hand, from right to left.

Still Wapisiane smiled. "Ed-ward, War-nah." He touched the sword thrust through Edward's belt.

"You're demented," Edward snapped. "Look, the ship is anchoring."

The rattle of the chain spread across the bay, rumbled

through the trees and up the slope of the hill. And now one of the crew unfurled a flag from the remains of the jackstaff.

"A fleur-de-lis," Jarring called. "She's a Frenchie."

"What to do, Tom?" Ashton asked.

Tom chewed his lip. "When last I heard, our countries were at peace. Is not Prince Charles betrothed to a French princess?" When last he heard. Over a year gone.

Tegramond took his bow from his shoulder and drew it, without attaching an arrow. "Psssst," he said.

"No," Tom said. "Not without reason. And not until they are ashore, in any event. See those cannon, Tegramond?" He pointed at the row of a dozen pieces staring at them from the open parts. "Blam," he said. "Big noise, fire, death."

Tegramond grinned.

"They are lowering a boat," Jarring said.

"Aye. We'll remain here until they beach," Tom decided.

Edward studied him. Father? It seemed incredible. Not incredible, impossible. Why, Father was near fifty. And Yarico? Father, on his knees like a dog? Father, on his back like a prisoner, condemned to the most beautiful of fates? That had to be impossible. It was impossible to visualize, at any rate.

The pinnace approached the shore, manned by a dozen seamen, stripped to the waist but armed, and with kerchiefs in a variety of brilliant colors tied around their heads. But the man in the stern was a different sort. He was slightly built, and wore no doublet; his shirt was purest white, and laced at throat and wrist. There were no patches on his breeches, and now that the boat came into the shallows they could see, to their amazement, that he wore no boots, but rather stockings in white as pure as his shirt, and for all they could tell also made of finest linen, tied beneath each knee with a crimson silk garter, and highly polished shoes, with golden buckles and high heels. To add to his strangeness, the chin beneath the broad-brimmed hat was clean-shaven, although he wore a thin moustache. It was a handsome face, lean and yet purposeful, with small tight lips, and a matching nose, and now that he took off his hat, a high forehead made to look more so because, like his men, he had shaved his scalp and wore no wig. The eyes, deep-set and dark, seemed to take in every man on the beach, and the trees and the mountain and almost every grain of sand, without appearing to move.

And, most amazing of all, he was unarmed save for a cane, which he carried in his right hand.

Now he replaced his hat. "Captain Warner?" he asked in perfect English. "Have I your permission to land, sir?"

The English stared at him. Fine manners had been quite forgotten over the past few months. But Tom recollected himself and stepped forward. "It is my pleasure, sir."

The Frenchman nodded and jumped lightly ashore. His men remained in the boat, holding it steady in the gentle surf. The visitor now removed his hat again, and made an elaborate leg. "I am Pierre Belain, Sieur d'Esnambuc, at your service, Captain Warner. I had heard of your colony, and, sir, I am happy indeed that it thrives, and is prepared to welcome a distressed mariner."

Tom frowned. "You've been at war," he said bluntly.

"But no," Belain protested. "The dons, you'll understand, Captain Warner. We sighted this Spainard, cruising alone, and knowing this to be contrary to their invariable custom, we bore down upon him, seeking perhaps to offer assistance." He shrugged. "You will not believe this, sir, but he was a man-of-war disguised as a merchantman. He lay silent as we approached, for all our signals and halloos, and, when we were within pistol shot, opened up with all his iron. By God, sir, it is only surprising that we were not sent to the bottom."

"You returned fire?"

"But of course. We are men. We made it as hot for him as he for us. But there was no advantage to be gained, and so we pulled off. You see a damaged ship there, Captain, in no condition to undertake a voyage of any duration. But then I reminded myself of this English colony on St. Christopher—"

"This is widely known?" Tom interrupted.

"But of course. It is all the talk of Europe, how you live in friendship with the dreaded Caribs." He allowed himself a glance at Tegramond, but there was no fear in his eyes. "And as our nations are now united, so to speak, in the person of your dear queen—"

"Queen, you say?"

Belain raised a finger. "I had forgot, you are not acquainted with affairs at home. Alas, Captain Warner, your noble King James has died, and now your king is called Charles, the first of that name, and long may he rule in splendor, and in amity with our court of France, as his wife is our very own princess Henrietta Maria."

"By God," Tom said. "How the world changes. You are

welcome, monsieur, to beach your ship and make your repairs, and while that is doing, to share in our humble life here, if you will but be honest with me. You are a privateer, sir, who sought an isolated Spaniard, and found her to carry more metal than you had supposed."

Belain frowned, and then smiled. "But of course. How else may a gentleman earn himself a fortune?"

The contempt for the colonists was there, well disguised, but nonetheless evident. Yet now was not the time for quarreling. Tom held out his hand. "Then welcome, monsieur, to Merwar's Hope. May your sojourn here be a profitable one."

Her name was *Madeleine,* and she was the finest ship any of them had ever seen. Every white man on the island was needed to beach her, to pin her on her starboard side, warps secured to trees and anchors bedded deep in the sand, to expose the gaping hole by her port bow. To accomplish this, her guns must be run to the starboard side as well, and hawsers carried out from the stumps of masts. It took them several days of unceasing labor, while the Caribs stood around in amazement at men so willing to work themselves into the ground. But when it was done, Pierre Belain invited the colonists to a celebration.

There was wine on board the *Madeleine,* and fine cheeses, and sweetmeats such as they had not tasted in over a year. They sat around a gigantic fire lit on the beach, and drank, and laughed, and sang, and forgot that Frenchman and Englishman had ever raised a sword against each other, or that either had ever feared a Carib. The scene reminded Edward of that never-to-be-forgotten feast on the banks of the Oyapoc River, saving many essential differences. Here was Mama, raised from her hammock at last and consenting to put on her best gown, her one remaining good gown, to take her place between Father and Monsieur Belain. Here, too, for this special occasion, was Susan. She would have to be called Susan Hilton now, but she was nonetheless Susan, in a homemade gown, to be sure, lacking either the revealing neckline or the frills and furbelows of Mama's, and yet dominating the scene with her beauty and her flaming red hair. And without any effort on her part, for she spoke little and smiled not at all, even at the gallantry of the French officer seated beside her, nor did she eat or drink in any quantity.

But the rest were enjoying themselves, French sailors, English colonists, Irish laborers, and Carib savages; even the mastiffs fought over the morsels tossed their way with apparent good humor. The white women were also having a splendid time, shared out as they were one to some five men, while the Carib women gathered in a group farther down the beach.

And even Father was happy this night. Because Mama was smiling, after so long, and because he had spent the afternoon showing Belain his plantation and watching the Frenchman's initial contempt disappear as his shrewd brain had totted up the wealth of the endless brown leaves.

He was returned to the subject now. "Captain Warner," he said, sipping his wine, "you are to be envied. A beautiful wife, a beautiful family, a beautiful island, a priceless crop . . . and I supposed you hardly better than shipwrecked mariners. Sir, I most humbly beg your pardon."

"And your apology is accepted, monsieur," Tom said magnanimously. Perhaps he had drunk more wine than a governor should, but it was nonetheless pleasant to see the flush in his cheeks and hear him conversing with an equal, no, a nobleman, to be sure, and holding his own. Father? And Yarico? That was impossible. That was nothing more than an attempt by Wapisiane to drive a wedge into the white man's world. Wapisiane was a sly one. He had none of his uncle's affection for the Warners.

"Yet I cannot but wonder, sir," Belain was saying, "if your comfort, your apparent security here, has not lulled you into a false sense. You know, sir, that these islands are shown on the map as belonging to Spain?"

Tom chuckled. "There is no gold to be dug out of this soil, monsieur, unless, as in our case, it is first of all planted there by human hand. The Spaniards have forgot these islands exist, save as refuges for Caribs and the buccaneers. As for the rest, I hold a grant from King James himself."

Belain nodded thoughtfully. "And yet, who knows, who can understand the mind of a don? It but requires a man of action to occupy the seat of power in Santo Domingo, and . . . sir, I tell you straight, were I governor here I would mount a brace of cannon on yonder hill."

"Spoken like a man, sir," Tom cried. "I can see you have campaigned."

"Indeed, sir, although it grieves me now to speak of it, I was before La Rochelle."

"We share no cause of antagonism on that score, monsieur," Tom assured him. "There was an ill-fated venture, best forgotten by all true men. But I will admit it, sir, when first I saw this island, my thoughts centered on that mound. Hence its name! Brimstone Hill. I have never seen anything like it, as a natural fortress."

"I have," Belain said. "Off the southern extremity of Spain, a huge rock sticking up out of the sea and connected to the mainland by a neck of land, rather like the situation on your south coast. But where your Christ Child protrudes into the empty ocean, this rock controls the very entrance to the Mediterranean. Brimstone Hill is hardly less advantageously positioned. Brimstone Hill. I like the sound of that. The general who commands that hill, sir, commands this island and its approaches."

"It is a thought which has been in my mind, monsieur," Tom agreed. "Should the occasion ever arise."

"Please believe me when I say that I speak as your greatest admirer, Captain Warner," Belain insisted. "But *when* the occasion arises, should you ever be that unfortunate, there will be no time to fortify that hill. It should be done now. Is not an ounce of protection worth several pounds of cure?"

"You are right, monsieur," Tom declared. "Cannon. I must spend some of our profit on cannon. When Jefferson arrives, if he ever does. . . ."

"If, indeed," Belain said, and filled their glasses, spending the time to do the same for Edward, on his left, with a smile. "There are cannon on board the *Madeleine*. I have a saker, sir, which will throw a ball upward of two miles, and with some accuracy."

"By God," Tom said.

"And cannon, like love, like life itself, are negotiable."

"You are too generous, sir. I have naught save tobacco to offer you."

"You, sir, are worth a million if you are worth a sou," Belain declared. "And I do not only speak now of tobacco. But here again, I doubt you have realized your potential. Why cling you to this narrow tract? I would estimate this whole south coast is ideal for your tobacco."

"Oh, indeed it would be, monsieur. But we have cultivated all that we may of the land Tegramond gave us."

"Ah," Belain said. "The chieftain claims a suzerainty over this entire land."

"Well, monsieur, it is most certainly his."

"I would dispute that, Captain Warner, if you will allow

me. I have it on authority that this land once belonged to another race, a gentle, mild people, now quite disappeared from the face of the earth. And why, Captain? Because of these very Caribs, who have spread across these islands like the plague."

"No doubt, monsieur. We have encountered some of these Arawaks of whom you speak, in the forests of Guyana, eh, Edward?"

Edward nodded. But his interest centered on the Frenchman. Here was a man talking with a purpose, and he observed that not a drop of wine actually passed his lips.

"Well, then, sir," Belain was saying. "You will observe that their title rests on the strength of their right arms. The best of all titles, I may say, but one open to dispute by a stronger arm."

"There was a treaty and a pact of friendship between the chieftain and me," Tom explained. "Verbal, to be sure, but nonetheless before witnesses."

"Ah, Captain Warner, you are an amusing fellow. These people are heathen savages. Worse, they are cannibals. You know they are cannibals?"

"Indeed, monsieur, we have seen them at their work."

"Mon Dieu," Belain remarked at large. "And you sit here feasting with them? Sir, you are a man of parts. Yet can there be no treaties with heathen savages. You know, sir, that Tegramond would break his word to you without compunction, should the notion enter his head?"

"That I do not *know*, monsieur," Tom said. "In any event, it must be my responsibility to see that such a notion never does enter his head. Else would we find ourselves in a position of some peril."

"Indeed, you are right, sir. What do you muster? Scarce two score men, and there must be a hundred of these savages, if you include the women. I have three score men with me, as you can see at a glance. Good men, Captain Warner, devoted to me."

Tom put down his cup. "Monsieur, you will have to be plain with me. My head swings."

"Well, then, sir. I will be perfectly honest. You English, you are fortunate. Hear me out, sir, without offense or anger, I beg of you. Your late king, bah. I can understand your reasons for leaving your homeland to settle these barbaric shores. But he at the least is now dead, and all the world looks to this Charles for greatness, especially supported as he is in his domestic life. But we in France enjoy no such benefits. We are ruled by a priest, sir, who makes far too free with the queen mother, while our king suffers all the vicious habits of your James, without even the wit to hold his own scepter. Our country is torn by dissension, sir, why, 'tis said the Huguenots store arms in La Rochelle and once again prepare to take the field. Ah, Captain Warner, France presents an unhappy sight to those who love her."

"You would emigrate?"

"I have spoken with some of your colonists, Captain. They feel sadly the absence of numbers. Of European numbers, sir. Our nations are now as one, through the good offices of your king and our princess."

Tom was shaking his head, but very slowly.

"Nor need we encroach upon your land, your profit," Belain said, speaking urgently. "You are settled here, in the very center of the island. We shall not disturb you, Captain Warner, this I swear. But grant to us the two extremes. It can easily be measured to reassure my people that we are not being cheated. And that, Captain Warner, will leave the Caribs mainly my problem."

"The chieftain would not agree," Tom said.

"I would argue that point, sir. A few presents, some old arquebuses I have on board, some trinkets, and a few dozen bottles of this excellent wine of mine, and that fellow will sell his soul. Eh, monsieur?"

He reached around Edward to slap Tegramond on the shoulder, and the cacique's eyes flopped open. He smiled delightedly, and then dozed off again.

Belain burst out laughing. "I promise you, Captain Warner, the problem shall be mine."

It took another week of hard work to raise two cannon to the summit of Brimstone Hill. Ropes had to be bent together, cradles had to be constructed, blocks and tackles had to be installed, not only on the top of the hill, but in various places on the slopes, to enable the huge pieces of metal to traverse the sheer cliff. The work was attended to mainly by the Frenchmen, while the colonists and the Caribs watched and wondered.

"People," Tegramond said to Tom. "Much people."

"People," Wapisiane said in disgust. "Food, no."

"Not so," Tom protested. "We shall plant corn as well as tobacco now. There will be food enough for all."

"I doubt the governor has considered the matter in its entirety," Tony Hilton said to Edward down on the beach. "So he was afraid of mustering only two dozen men to fifty savages. Now he musters no more to fifty savages *and* a like number of armed Frenchmen."

"You are allowing your sense of history to affect your judgment, Tony," Edward said. "My father and Monsieur Belain have signed a treaty of perpetual friendship. Whatever happens in the outside world, on Merwar's Hope there will be amity between us, forever. Why, it could be a new world."

"It could be," Hilton said. "But for the time, it is a worthless scrap of paper. And it does not seem to have occurred to your father that he has obtained nothing from that cunning rascal. So he now has two cannon pointing at the empty ocean. They cannot command the approaches to the hill, should the French decide to encroach upon English land. As for this farce of us maintaining the center of the island while they are handicapped by existing at each end, has it occurred to you to explore the interior, Edward? I have. That mountain and its offshoots effectively divide the windward and leeward coasts as if it were a strait. Susan and I, on windward, are farther from Sandy Point than a Frenchman standing at either end, in point of time."

"If Father elects to trust Monsieur Belain, then I am prepared to trust in him," Edward said.

"You have composed your differences, then?"

"After a fashion. But there can be no future here, for me."

"No future, for a Warner, in Merwar's Hope?"

"You are making sport of me. Tell me of Susan."

The girl was inside, with Rebecca, who had retired to her hammock with one of her fevers. "I would not excite you, or anger you, Ned. I would merely say that she was worth fighting for, and if need be, dying for."

"Her back . . ."

"Is scarred. Her mind also, I think. But scars heal, in time."

"And she loves you?"

Hilton glanced at him. "Now, that I cannot say. She is my wife, at least in common law. I will make her so before God when the priest finally arrives. I would have you remember that, Ned. You are my friend. I willingly apologize for the harsh words I used to you. I used them because you disappointed me on that occasion. But I recognize that as a fault of youth. Yet remember that she is my wife, and if perhaps she still feels some tenderness toward you, I possess her, and will keep her. That apart, I would have you stay. What, man, would you throw away all of this?"

"Think you my father will ever bequeath it to me?"

"I would lay a rich wager on that, Ned. I look forward to it. Because then you shall remember that Susan and I, and our children, are your oldest and best friends. So there's my hand on it. Stay, and rule. And count on me and mine."

A strange promise at a strange time, Edward thought. He sauntered through the house, and as a dutiful son, must stop and wait awhile by his mother's bed. Rebecca sweated, and Susan was drying her forehead with a towel. She glanced at Edward and then returned to her work. Without even a flush. Her mind seemed to be closed.

"Is the cannon in place, Edward?" Rebecca whispered.

"Aye." He knelt beside the hammock. His arm brushed the girl's, and she never moved. Her hair stroked his bare shoulder. "They make a pretty sight."

"This will be a pretty place," Rebecca said. "In years to come, I see houses, and a church. We have sadly neglected that. One day there will be bells ringing across the bay, beneath the protection of those cannon."

"And more, Mama. We will build a fortress, up there."

"You will build that, Edward," she said. "Promise me."

She had ever been able to read his mind too well. He took her hand, so thin, where once it had been as strong as his own. "I will build that, Mama," he said. "I promise you."

Again he glanced at the girl, and this time she smiled at him. The smile of a conscientious nurse pleased to discover filial loyalty. Once she had lain on her back before him, naked. And moments later he had taken her mind and torn it into pieces. He got up and left the house by the back door, away from the toiling men and the hustle and bustle of the beach. He crossed the tobacco field and entered the bushes. Here it was cool and silent. There would always be a cool and silent forest in Merwar's Hope. And he would always walk it. By himself. An endlessly lonely figure in an endlessly lonely world, doomed to a single-handed passage through time of some forty, fifty years or more.

"Many men," Yarico said. "Much bang. Many dead."

She no longer startled him. As she no longer drove him wild with desire. Yet she had hardly changed. No, that was not right. She *had* changed. There was a slyness in her gaze he had never noticed before. Yarico and Father? While

Mama lay dying? What an incredible thought, fit to reawaken all the old hatred. But Mama had made him promise.

"Your world," he said. "And you haunt it like a spirit, Yarico."

She smiled. "Ed-ward," she said. "Yarico." She placed the forefinger of her right hand across the forefinger of her left.

He shook his head. "I have not the stomach for it. Have you no other lover?"

The smile remained bright. "Ed-ward," she said. "Many men, Carib no. Tegramond no. Wapisiane no." She came closer, squeezed his breast as she had done that first day, and then did the same to his buttock. "Ed-ward . . ." Her tongue came out of her mouth and slowly circled her lips, a quite hideous gesture. Almost he could see the blood seeping from the corners of her mouth.

"They'd find me uncommonly tough," he said.

Now the smile did fade. She grasped his arm, pointed at the sky. "Carib no," she said. "Be-lain, no. War-nah, no. Sun, no. Carib . . ." She made the unmistakable gesture of drawing a knife from her waist. "Ed-ward . . ." Her head flopped sideways, eyes staring, tongue lolling.

He frowned at her. "I do not believe you. Tegramond is our friend."

"Many men," she said again. "Many men. Carib no."

"You . . . Why are you telling me this, Yarico? You have not been with me for a long time."

"Ed-ward," she said, and placed her hand on her left breast.

"Aye." He had believed her, once. But she was too savage to understand the true meaning of the word. "I do not believe you, Yarico. You seek to make trouble between your people and mine."

She stamped her foot, her sunny mood disappearing. "Edward, good," she said contemptuously, and rubbed her belly.

"So tell me then, when is this terrible deed to take place?" he demanded. "When, Yarico? When? Tonight?"

She shook her head. "Sun, moon, sun, moon. But moon, no."

He nodded. But to believe her—to believe that this savage bitch, because she was no more than that, would betray her own people, for the sake of a white man who had spurned her—it made no sense. It made no sense of the Tegramond who had quietly fallen asleep at the dinner, who even now stood on the beach gazing at the cannon being set into place.

"I do not believe you," he said. "You wish to cause trouble between our people. Now, go."

She hesitated for a moment, gazed from his face to his outstretched hand, and then turned and glided into the trees as silently as she had come.

He awoke to the sound of footsteps in the room. On the far side Sarah wheezed in her sleep, as ever. Closer at hand, Philip slept heavily. All of Sandy Point slept heavily, after the toil of the past few days. And the carousing. Since the French had arrived there had been a continual celebration, which had caused Father some concern, as the women were clearly inclined to spread their favors. But this night, with the cannon in place, all had slept, saving this intruder.

Slowly Edward dropped his hand over the side of his hammock, seeking his sword. But this was no Indian; he was sure of that.

"Edward?"

He sat up. "Father?"

"Dress yourself and come with me, lad," Tom whispered. "Hurry, now. And bring your weapon."

Edward got out of the hammock, dragged on his breeches, and went outside. The air was chill with the promise of dawn, but the night was at its darkest, although the skies were as clear as ever and the stars winked in an unceasing sweep of glowing red.

"Here, boy." Tom Warner stood outside his house. "I have sent Jarring to summon Monsieur Belain. Hal, are you there? Ralph?"

Figures loomed out of the darkness. "What has happened, Tom?" Ashton asked.

"Grave news," Tom said. Now that his eyes had become accustomed to the gloom, Edward could see that his father had not been to bed at all; he was fully dressed.

"Captain Warner?" Belain, half-dressed, hurried up the beach, Jarring behind him. With them was Belain's brother-in-law, who acted as sailing master of the *Madeleine*. His name was Joachim Galante, a tall, thin man with a remarkably grim face, who made himself appear the more sinister by his habit of always dressing in black. "Are we assailed?"

"We shall be, monsieur, depend upon it. News has been brought to me that the Caribs mean an attack upon us."

"Mon Dieu," Belain said. "But why?"

"Because our numbers are grown too great," Tom explained. "They fear our eventual dominance, and also that there will be insufficient food to feed us all, should we continue in this vein."

"Who told you this, Father?" Edward demanded. "Yarico?"

Tom turned slowly. "She is an honest child."

"She knows not the meaning of the word," Edward said. "This is a plot to cause friction."

"Friction, you say," Jarring remarked. "And us like to be murdered in our beds, and eaten afterward."

"You'll keep your voice down, if you please, Mr. Jarring," Tom said. "I should not like to alarm anyone unnecessarily. Nor should I like the Caribs to know we are aware of their plans. But I deemed the occasion of sufficient importance to call this conference."

"For which we must thank you from the bottom of our hearts, Captain Warner," Belain said. "We must first establish that the event will take place. You believe this girl?"

"I do," Tom said.

"Well, I do not," Edward said.

"Ah," Belain said. "No doubt you are equally well acquainted with this young woman?"

"Now, what do you mean by that, monsieur?" Tom inquired.

"I meant no offense, sir," Belain assured him. "And I would be grateful should you not take any, or I should have to kill you."

"By God," Tom said. "You impudent—"

"Tom," Berwicke said. "Surely this is no time for quarreling amongst ourselves. It matters naught whether we choose to believe the girl or to discover some ulterior motive behind her action. 'Tis certain that we cannot ignore the circumstances. We should arm ourselves, and go openly to Tegramond, and put this rumor to him, and hear the answer."

"A happy thought," Tom said. "We'll deal with him as men, and Christian men, too, by God. Straight up."

"Mon Dieu," Belain said. "Have I landed in a colony of children?"

"I do not expect the chief to admit to any plan of murder, monsieur," Tom said. "I merely wish him to understand that we are aware of what he intends, and prepared for it."

"And you think this will alter his intention, Captain Warner? Then indeed you are an optimist."

"Nonetheless, it is the honest, Christian thing to do," Tom

said. "And after that, why, we shall mount guards on our encampment."

"Forever?" Belain inquired. "And what of our plans, our treaty? We mean to divide ourselves. In time we shall spread over the island, in small groups. Why, sir, are you not immediately condemning your Mr. Hilton and his beautiful bride to being eaten alive? They are alone on the north coast."

"By God," Ashton said. " 'Tis true. We cannot permit that, Tom. And the monsieur is right; if the savages mean to attack us, and discover that they cannot finish the job in one night, then be sure that they will resort to stealth and murder."

"Or summon assistance from one of the neighboring islands," Galante put in.

Susan being torn apart by Wapisiane? There was an impossible thought.

"Well, then, monsieur, do you have a better suggestion?" Tom inquired.

Belain sighed and glanced at Galante, who shrugged.

"Captain Warner, we are here faced with a terrible situation," Belain said. "I am responsible for the lives of my people, as are you for yours. More, we have both elected to make our futures here, to populate these fair islands with our families and their descendants. Now, sir, it seems to me that in the pursuance of such an ideal, which is, after all, nothing less than the propagation of the Christian faith throughout these heathen lands, and in the face of such a tremendous responsibility, we can afford to shirk no task, however distasteful, however horrible it may appear to us, as men and as Christians."

"I do not understand you, monsieur," Tom said. "Speak plain, man. Speak plain."

Belain sighed again. "These people, these savages, these cannibals, seek our destruction. And having once conceived of that, they will never lose sight of it. Our only course is to defend ourselves by first destroying them."

"By God," Tom said.

"You mean array ourselves in order of battle, and await their onslaught?" Berwicke demanded.

"One way, certainly, Mr. Berwicke," Galante said. "But surely a foolish waste of those very lives we are sworn to protect. Are we less men than the Caribs? Why should we not assault them, while they are unaware that we know their intentions?"

"By God," Tom said.

"Indeed, sir," Belain said. "Why should it not be done this instant? We can call our people to arms and undertake the necessary deed within two hours. At daybreak, where they are not planning their venture before tomorrow night."

"The man is right, Tom," Ashton muttered. "Why shed Christian blood where there is no necessity for it? Would any captain, would you, during your days in Holland, have undertaken battle where it was possible to gain the victory by subterfuge and surprise?"

" 'Tis true they sleep without watch, in the most utter confidence," Tom said. "So, we could surround their camp, call upon them to surrender, and ship them off to Nevis or some such place."

"Mon Dieu," Belain said for a third time. "Captain Warner, I beseech you, understand what you are at. These men are not French soldiers or English sailors. They are not Dutch Protestants or even Spanish Catholics, who will solemnly give you their word and march away. They are savages who know only the terrible urgings of their own heathen desires. Send them away, sir? Would that not be to invite them back, on some dark and silent night, to perpetuate a deed far more horrible than anything we could contemplate?"

Tom gazed at him. "You propose wholesale murder."

"I see it, sir, as a necessary surgical operation. This island, these people, governed by ourselves, are all part of a single whole, a body, if you like. But now we discover that in the very center of this body there is a cankerous growth, a spreading gangrene which threatens to overwhelm us all. Now, sir, too often such a growth is impossible to remove without destroying the life of the patient itself. But here, sir, it is isolated. And we are fortunate. With a single cut of the knife, however painful that may be to you or to me, sir, we can eradicate this poison, and leave the body, our body, healthier than before. But it must be done *now*."

Tom glanced at his companions.

"There is a deal of truth in what Monsieur Belain suggests, Captain Warner," Jarring said.

"Hal?"

Ashton shrugged. "I have no wish to be murdered in my bed, Tom. Nor to spend the rest of my life in fear of being so treated."

"And will you ever sleep again?" Edward cried, as he suddenly realized that the Frenchman was carrying his point, that in a matter of seconds his own father would be agreeing to this deed. He traced it back to that dreadful day when the Dominican had perished at the stake. From that moment not one of the Englishmen had regarded the Indians as quite human, however much they pretended to like them. And once the point was conceded, as even Father was tacitly doing, to destroy them was but a logical projection. "Would you not, in fact, *be* destroying this colony, and all within it, by destroying every Christian principle any one of us possesses? By making us no better than the savages you fear?"

"The boy is young," Galante murmured.

"Aye," Tom agreed. "I doubt you know much of what you speak, Edward. A conference like this were best left to men with experience of life. And death."

"With . . . Mr. Berwicke," Edward cried, "I appeal to you, sir."

Ralph pulled his lip. "I can see little alternative, boy."

"My God . . ."

"Be quiet," Belain said, suddenly very brisk. "But the boy's interruption serves a point. We can be under no misunderstanding of what we are about, gentlemen. Otherwise we are worse placed than before. This is no military adventure we consider. I repeat, it is a necessary operation. There must be no survivors."

"You mean we kill the women as well?" Jarring asked.

"And the children. Every last babe at the breast must be destroyed this day."

"You cannot mean that," Edward begged. "You must at least obtain proof that Yarico is telling the truth."

"Be quiet, boy, or take yourself off," Tom snapped. "I take your point, monsieur, and I understand that considering the horror of what we have to do, one or two more lives seem irrelevant. Yet I will not destroy everyone. There are men on this island, yours as well as mine, who sorely lack the comforts of home. I am sure there are sufficient maids of between, say, puberty and womanhood, who can yet be assimilated into Christian thought and European habits."

Belain hesitated, and then smiled. "Including, of course, the Princess Yarico. Yet I imagine you are right. Eh, Galante? Our own people have too long been without the comforts of a woman's arms, as Captain Warner so aptly puts it, and our wives are a long way away. Very well, sir. Any woman who does not actually take arms against us will be spared. But there must be no male survivors. 'Tis understood?"

"I understand," Tom said. "And so will my people."

"Then summon them. We must be at the other end of the island by sunrise."

"By Christ," Edward said. "That I should stand here and listen to anything so dreadful decided in so matter-of-fact a manner. You would compound murder with rape and abduction? Sirs, you sink lower than the creatures you would destroy."

"Be careful, boy," Belain warned. "Your fondness for these people is well known. Caribee. Aye, you are aptly named. And so I have put up with your insults for this while. Be sure that I shall not do so indefinitely. And be sure, sir, that if I turn my blade toward you, not even your father will save your life."

Edward gazed at the man, big fists opening and shutting in helpless desperation. He knew nothing of swordsmanship. Nor was his accuracy with a pistol anything to match a soldier like Belain's. "You outmatch me now, Belain," he said. "But be sure that I shall grow larger, as you grow smaller. As for what you intend, I'll have naught to do with it."

"To be sure," Belain commented. "I had been told that your stomach in no way matches up to your words."

Edward gazed at him for a moment in impotent rage, and then ran into the house.

And beyond, into the forest, his brain a raging tumult. Hilton? But Hilton and Susan had left that afternoon, and would be on the other side of the island by now. And what could one man do, even a man like Tony Hilton? Besides, he could not be certain that Hilton would not agree with the Frenchman. Tony was utterly pragmatic.

Yarico? But she had inspired the whole dreadful deed. No, she would not have known what she expected. She had but sought . . . to accomplish what? Something dreadful. And why? It made no sense. Just as it made no sense to seek her now and acquaint her with what her gossip had inaugurated.

And to do anything would be to arm and prepare the Caribs. Then even more blood would be shed, and among that blood might be Tom Warner's. Christ, how could a son send his own father to his death? But how could any man deserving of life contemplate a deed so terrible?

He checked for breath, and to scratch his shoulder where a

thorn had torn his flesh. He traveled this forest like any Indian, as a rule, yet this day he was stumbling like a white man from the streets of London. Yet was he also moving insensibly toward the Carib village. For what?

The beach, and the canoes drawn up in orderly rows. And the sky beyond, suddenly showing faint pink streaks against the blackness. Streaks which would soon enough turn the color of blood. And a figure, moving stealthily through the shallow water off the beach. Wapisiane, tending to his nets. Belain and Father had forgotten the boy. But then, they knew nothing of his habits.

Edward knelt in the last of the bushes, slowly getting his breathing under control. "Whist," he sounded through his pursed lips.

Wapisiane's head came up.

"Whist," Edward said again, and stood up.

Wapisiane gazed into the blackness of the trees, and then came ashore. He moved with deliberation, stooped and picked up his spear without hesitation, and walked toward the forest.

"Here," Edward said.

Wapisiane came through the trees. "Ed-ward," he said. And looked at the trees, the sky, the darkness before the dawn.

"I have no time," Edward said. "Awake your people, quietly, and take to your canoes. Make for Nevis. Do this now, Wapisiane, and do not ever come back."

Wapisiane gazed at him.

Edward seized his arm and pointed at Nevis. "Go quickly. War-nah, Be-lain, Ber-wicke, Ash-ton, Gal-ante, they come. Many men come. Swords, pistols. They come. Take your poeple."

Wapisiane turned slowly to look at the village. His face was silhouetted against the growing light. No twilight on Merwar's Hope. In one instant it was too dark to see a man's face. In the other it was light enough to see a quarter of a mile. Too far. Wapisiane stared at the village, and beyond, at the dark line which had suddenly spread across the beach, men, their morions glinting dully in the first rays of the rising sun, placing their staffs and resting their firepieces for the initial volley.

Wapisiane looked at Edward, and his face changed. Edward gazed at the other side of the village. Another line of men, waiting, beyond musket shot, armed with swords and pistols, holding the dogs in check.

Wapisiane threw back his head and uttered a tremendous howl, like a wounded wolf. The sound burst out of the trees and screamed across the morning, picked up the breeze, and disappeared over the bay, perhaps over all the neighboring islands.

But he had done no more than signal the destruction of his people. While his yell still hung in the air, it was overtaken by the rumble of the arquebuses and the glow of the exploding powder, running across the beach like a touch cord. Almost they seemed able to feel the hot wind which seared the beach and the huts. Perhaps the bullets did little actual damage, but the noise and the crackling of the ball bemused the slowly awakening Caribs, and into the village there now rushed the white men, swords drawn, preceded by half a dozen mastiffs, snapping and snarling. Wapisiane gave a groan and stepped forward. Edward seized his arm and pulled him back into the bushes. For a moment they faced each other, and then the Indian attempted to free himself. There was no time for a wrestling match, which would cause noise and which he might not win, Edward realized. He closed his fist and drove it with all his strength into Wapisiane's chin; the boy gave a grunt, and his knees sagged. Edward caught him before he could crash through the bushes and laid him gently on the grass. Then he turned his gaze back toward the village.

The first Indians, all men, these, had come running out of their huts, one or two retaining sufficient wits to carry spears, but the majority unarmed. Into them the swords of the colonists and the French buccaneers, and the teeth of the dogs, scythed. Blood scattered, and with it the limbs and the howls and shrieks of the vanquished mixed with the yells of the victors. It was not in the Carib nature to run. Bare-handed they threw themselves at their assailants, clawing and clutching; Edward watched one brave seize William Jarring at the neck, but Jarring held his sword in both hands and thrust it up with such force that it passed right through the brown body, and showed its tip on the other side.

Now the women attempted to join in the fight, and the morning grew more bestial. By Carib law there could be no old women in the village, and the attackers were rendered maniacal both by the blood and the excitement, and their creeping knowledge of what they had done. Suddenly there was no humanity left on this island. Edward watched one of the women thrown on her back by two of the buccaneers. One held her shoulders and cut her throat while the other knelt between her legs. A little boy was dragged across the beach by two of the shrieking colonists, his penis pulled high as they sliced away testicle and flesh beneath, and then rolled him into the shallow water to drown as he bled to death. And yet perhaps he was more fortunate than his sisters, hardly older than Sarah, one impaled on a sword which entered between her buttocks and seemed to emerge at her throat, another the bleeding bone of contention between two of the dogs.

And yet he did not vomit. His belly had hardened, as had his mind. He left the bushes and walked down the beach, watching the sand scattering from his toes. Sand which coagulated into blood, little cakes of red and yellow, mingled, looking almost good enough to eat. Save for the smell. Merwar's Hope had always smelled unbelievably sweet. But it would never do so again. The stench of blood and fear and hate and death rose from the still beach, and even the morning breeze could not waft it away. The water of the stream, rushing down to the sea, was tinged with red. The very surf had turned crimson.

How long had it taken? Not more than a few seconds, certainly. Now a dozen of the girls were huddled in one corner of the village, surrounded by their captors and their tormentors, sure at least of their lives and yet in the process of being picked clean of feeling or even womanhood by a hundred hungry fingers. And around them, in front of them, behind them, and to either side of them, their mothers and fathers, their brothers and husbands, their sons and their daughters were dead. Some still died, swords protruding from their bellies, hands and arms cut off, mouths gushing blood. Others lay in silent humps, still attacked by the beasts who had descended upon them, still being reduced to steaks, as no doubt they would have done to their vanquished had they won.

And over the whole, already, there descended the insects of the forest, the mosquitoes and the sandflies, the butterflies and the bees. They sought their prey with an enormous buzz, to render an already hideous morning unspeakable.

Edward walked up the beach to Tegramond's hut, for there he saw his father. Tom had dropped his sword, or lost it in the melee. He stood by the hammock which contained the remains of his friend. A sad end for a warrior chieftain. Tegramond had been killed before he could even leave his bed. At the least he had fallen to a bullet wound, and he had not been mutilated. His tooth necklace still clung to his throat.

Belain stood on the other side. "It is done, Captain Warner. We have not lost a man."

Tom gazed at Tegramond. Perhaps, Edward thought, he recalled the day of their landing, the firm fingers on his shoulders, the uplifted hands pointing at the sun.

Now he felt the presence of his son. His head half-turned, and then checked, and instead he gazed at Belain. "This day will not be forgotten."

"Nor should it," Belain declared. "This day we have made this island, your island, Captain Warner, a fit place for Europeans to inhabit. Now, come, let us rid ourselves of even the memory of these people, saving their women. We shall accumulate all the dead, here in the village, pull down these useless shelters, and pile them on top, and create a funeral pyre which will be seen for miles."

"And attract other Caribs to vengeance," Tom muttered.

"And frighten away other Caribs for all eternity," Belain insisted. "*Mon Dieu*, we must look upon this day as a victory. It should be a holiday in our annals, forevermore."

"In yours," Tom said. "In ours it will be a day of mourning." He looked down at the dead chieftain. Even in his death Tegramond appeared to smile. "He was a happy fellow."

"Tom." Ashton hurried up the beach. "Ralph has fallen. I would have you come, quickly."

Tom glanced at Belain. "You told me we had suffered no casualties."

"Nor did we. He has been taken ill."

"Aye," Ashton said. "No doubt the heat, and the excitement."

They ran down the beach, kicking their way through the bleeding bodies and blood-caked sand, disturbing mosquitoes rising in clouds above them, and Edward followed. He wondered if he was dreaming, experiencing the most horrible of nightmares.

Berwicke lay on the sand by the water. He had been rolled on his back, and Jarring pillowed his head on his knees. There was blood on Jarring's hands, where he had thrust his weapon clear through the savage who had resisted him. But with these same hands he smoothed the graying hair from Berwicke's brow and attempted to fan some air over the dying nostrils. Berwicke's face was no less the color of blood, and he breathed, but slowly.

"Just the heat, old friend," Tom said, kneeling beside him. "We shall get you to shelter, and a cooling drink, and you will be well again."

Berwicke stared at him, his face suffusing even more, until Edward thought it would burst with effort. But he could manage no words, not even a tremor of his lips.

"It is a seizure," Belain said. "We must bleed him. I will do it."

But Berwicke's face turned ever more purple, even as they watched, and the staring eyes grew ever more fixed, and suddenly he was all veins, swollen and still, in his cheeks and forehead.

"By Christ," Jarring said. "He is gone."

"He was an old man," Belain said. "I am sorry, Captain Warner. I had looked for no such death, today."

"He was an old friend." Tom slowly straightened. "Tegramond was an old friend. They say these things travel in threes." He glanced at Ashton.

The sailing master chuckled. "I am not yet done, Tom, you may be sure of that." He pointed. "Someone had best stop the women."

The men watched the fluttering skirts coming along the beach. A terrifying awakening, for the women of Sandy Point, to discover their men gone. But how much more terrifying for them to come here.

"Edward, you'll send them back," Tom said. "I'll not have your mother see what has happened."

Edward gazed at the skirts, the drifting hair, and felt his stomach rising into his chest. "You stop them," he muttered, and ran up the beach, away from the blood and the stench and the pitiful, helpless bodies. He reached the coolness and the shelter of the trees, and checked. Wapisiane knelt there, staring at the village, his face expressionless.

Edward crouched beside him. "You cannot stay here," he whispered. "You must get away, into the interior of the island. Tonight you must come back to the beach. I will have a canoe for you, and you will get away to Nevis. There are no Indians on Nevis, to our knowledge."

Wapisiane stared at the white man.

"Can you not understand me?" Edward asked. "I am sorry

for what happened. Sorry. By Christ, there is a profound statement. I would not have had it so. They were afraid. But it is done now. Nothing can make your uncle and his people come back to life. I would have warned them, but I was too late. Now you must think of your own life. You are the only survivor. They have kept some of the girls, but you are the only male."

Wapisiane's head remained still, but his eyes seemed to have spread, until his face seemed nothing but eyes.

"Say you will take care," Edward begged. "Say you will make your escape tonight."

"Wapisiane take care."

"Thank God for that," Edward said. "We have had our differences, Wapisiane. But I would remain your friend. Perhaps we shall meet again one day. Until then, here is my hand."

Wapisiane looked down at the outstretched fingers. "Wapisiane take care," he said. "Wapisiane live. Wapisiane return. War-nah . . ." He drew finger across his throat. "Belain . . ." Again the gesture. "Ber-wicke, Ash-ton, Hil-ton . . ." The finger moved to and fro. "Gal-ante, and women. Rebecca. Susan." Now his hands came together, and then moved apart with hurried, brutal strength.

Edward started to protest, and then thought better of it. "Aye," he said. "You are entitled to be bitter, Wapisiane. Time is our best course."

Wapisiane stood up, looked down on the white man. "Edward," he said. And once again the finger traveled across his throat, but this time very slowly. Then he was gone into the forest.

The fire blazed over the Indian village. Additional dry wood had been brought from the forest, and the smoke from the funeral pyre billowed high into the air, up and ever up, for with the rising of the sun the breeze had dropped, and there was nothing to disperse the smoke. And so it rose, in a long column, hundreds of feet into the air, certainly visible from Nevis and Antigua and Montserrat, and perhaps even farther away than that, a signal of the catastrophe which had happened on Merwar's Hope.

Farther down the beach, the white people prepared to bury the first of them to die on the island. They moved in silence, still burdened by the guilt of what they had done. For how long, how many years, would they carry that weight around their necks?

The grave had been dug by the Irish laborers, who now gathered in a whispering group by the houses, their habitual jollity quite forgotten. The Irish women were also grouped, gazing at their husbands with new eyes; they had not suspected that the fathers of their children would be men of blood. Rebecca stood by herself, dressed, at her husband's command, in her best gown, the one she had worn to the feast, not a week ago, beneath the broad-brimmed hat which she used to keep the sun from her complexion. It was a man's hat, and served several purposes. Today it kept the tears and the horror which vied for supremacy in her face from being revealed to the crowd. Sarah stood beside her, fingers clutching her mother's skirt. Both women shook, but this day it might easily have been emotion rather than the fever which was their habitual companion.

Philip and Edward stood together, close by the grave, and in front of the assembled Frenchmen. Like their mother, the boys had put on what they could find in the way of decent clothing. Edward's shoulders had not been covered in months, and the material felt uncomfortable against his skin. He listened to his father reading the service, in slow and sonorous tones. But Father had spoken no service over Tegramond. He had hurried away from that funeral. He glanced at his brother. Philip had not been present at the massacre, and he watched his father with admiration. Father was a man of steel. And Philip admired steel.

As no doubt did Monsieur Belain, wearing all the lace he could muster, and with his garters dripping jewels of silken splendor from each knee. Monsieur Galante affected a more fitting black. But then, Monsieur Galante never wore anything else. And Hall Ashton? He stood by himself at the foot of the grave. Of them all, saving perhaps Tom, he had been closest to Ralph Berwicke. They had lived next door to each other for several years, and had laughed together, when there had been anything to laugh at, and drunk together, when there had been anything to drink, and, to their discredit, despaired together whenever there had been the slightest reason to do so. Now, despite his promise to Tom, he suddenly looked the oldest man present.

Tom closed his Bible and nodded. The burial party withdrew their ropes and picked up their spades. Tom remained standing at the head of the grave while the first shovelfuls of earth were thrown onto the silent body wrapped in its hammock. Then he moved forward, to stand in the midst of his people.

"Ralph left a will," he said. "Which he entrusted into my keeping." Slowly he unrolled the parchment. "It is very brief. He says, 'To my oldest friend and faithful employer, Thomas Warner, gentleman, king's lieutenant in the Caribee Isles, I leave my new hat, that it may shelter him from the tropical sun. All other of my effects that may be worth having I leave to my other old friend, Henry Ashton, esquire.' " He looked up. "It is a good hat. And we have lost a faithful supporter." He hesitated, staring into their faces, one to the other, slowly, hurrying only when he came to his wife and eldest son. "This day will long be remembered in the annals of our island," he said. "Truly, it is not an event which any of us present may ever forget, nor would I have it so. It was a necessary event. The Sieur d'Esnambuc and myself received information that the Caribs, grown afraid of our too rapidly increasing numbers, had resolved to strike when we slept this coming night, and massacre us, saving perhaps only those they kept for the stake. We chose to anticipate that horror. We are white men and women, and we are Christians. We have a duty, to ourselves, our wives and families, to our descendants, to hold this land, and to preserve our portion in it. It will be said that we acted without honor. I will say to you that we acted wisely. There can be no honor in fighting savages. There is seldom much honor of any sort to be gained in war. I speak now as a soldier, and I have seen my share of bloodshed and suffering. The Sieur d'Esnambuc and myself could not risk the lives of a single one of you, for we are responsible for all of those lives. Thus we acted as we did. But I say this to you. A deed like ours today were indeed criminal, and wasted, and horrible, should we ever discard the fruits we seek. There must be no more enmity on this island, no more bloodshed. Let it be our claim that heat and old age are the only causes of death among us, as they were the causes of the death of my friend here. Let this colony grow, and let Frenchman and Englishman live in harmony here. And let this island be the most fertile, as its inhabitants must be the most envied, of any in the world. Thus may we justify our actions for all eternity. For as the Bible truly tells us, out of evil may yet come great good."

He paused, but he had already lost their attention. They gazed not at him, but past him to the left, in twos and threes, and then in increasing numbers, until every head faced the forest, above which the smoke rose in a long column of memory.

Yarico stood there, her hands hanging at her sides, her hair a black shawl on her neck.

"Mon Dieu," Belain muttered. "I had forgot the princess."

They watched her move slowly down the beach. Then one of the Frenchmen gave a yell, and they surged forward, reaching for her with hands still hungry in their lust.

"Avast, there," Ashton bellowed.

"Wait," Tom shouted.

"Arrêtez-vous," Belain bawled.

Edward drew the undischarged pistol from his belt and fired it into the air. The report brought them up, and they looked over their shoulders, their leader's fingers already at the girl's breast.

"There will be no more of that," Tom said. "Of these women, you may take your pick. You will have to draw lots, to be sure, but it is the only way. I'll have no promiscuity. One woman, one man."

Belain translated for him, and then glanced at him. "You include the princess in that, Captain Warner?"

The girl had ignored the men who would have attacked her, and had continued to walk forward. Now she was only a few feet away.

"She must make her own choice," Tom said. "She has that right, for the service she has rendered us, for the great loss she has suffered." He gazed at her. "Yarico," he said, "you must take a man. And live by our laws now. And be sure of our respect and honor."

She smiled. Or did she merely show her teeth? Edward watched her in fascination as she approached. Approached? But she ignored him, went up to Tom Warner, and held his hand.

"War-nah," she said. "Yarico."

Tom flushed, although he was obviously flattered. "You mistake the situation, my dear," he said. "I already have a woman. Rebecca."

Yarico glanced at the white woman with total scorn. "War-nah," she said again. "Yarico." She interlocked her fingers and held them to her belly, and then slowly carried them away from her to her arm's length. "War-nah. Yarico. Son."

7

The Revolution

"There will be a headstone," Tom Warner said. "I would have you bring marble from England, John. I will give you an inscription."

John Jefferson fanned himself with the hat he had originally removed out of respect. "It will be my pleasure, Tom. But she scarce needs one. This entire hill shall be her monument. You see it almost before you see the island itself, at least when approaching from the west. The first lady of Merwar's Hope could scarce wish a better memorial."

"The first lady," Tom said. "When she died, John, she was the *only* lady on Merwar's Hope."

"No doubt. You'd not say that now. She'd have been proud to see this sight." Jefferson walked from the grave, across the smoothed earth of the courtyard, past the two great cannon which stared westward over the Caribbean Sea, and rested his hand on the earthen breastworks as he looked down from the fortress at Sandy Point. This was his third visit. He recalled the eager, almost desperate faces which had greeted his first arrival, and the equal hunger for news and food and reassurance which had met his second, two years ago. The colony had been struggling then, and no doubt the trouble with the Caribs had taken its toll of spirit as well as ambition. This was something he meant to investigate. So many rumors had filtered back to England, not all of them believable. But now . . . Sandy Point was no longer merely a settlement. It was not even merely a village. He looked down on a street, stretching back from the beach, unpaved and dusty, to be sure, but nonetheless a street, lined with houses on either side. These too were in the main modest, but curtains fluttered at the windows, and lines of washing in the back yards, and there were other, larger buildings: Jarring's General Store, halfway up the right-hand block, with its overhanging porch which was a refuge for thirsty planters on a hot day, and close by, the church, with its bell tower rising above all others; it faced the courthouse—this and the solid, windowless jailhouse beside it were evidences that there was more lawlessness than religion as yet, but also evidences that Tom Warner and his officers were capable of dealing with it. The jailhouse was seldom empty, although its inmates were mainly the Irish laborers, who worked hard, driven to it by the lashes of their employers, and drank and fought among each other with equal spirit.

Set at the inland end of the town, where the land rose slightly, was the governor's house. This was the only two-storied dwelling on the island, or at any rate, in Sandy Point. Its floors were fronted by a huge porch, really a continuation of the sloping roof, extending outward and held in place by six great pillars, small tree trunks in themselves, to give the seaward-facing windows shelter at once from sun and rain. The others, like all the houses in the town, were protected by shutters, but these were only needed when the hurricane winds blew, and this was seldom enough. The governor's house was a suitably imposing building; it required suitably imposing inmates. Something else to be investigated.

But the town was only an aspect of Merwar's Hope. The corn fields and tobacco fields spreading away on either side, the ships riding to their anchors in Old Road, these, too, were no more than aspects of the current prosperity which shrouded the island. Its future lay in the manner in which it had pushed its tentacles farther inland. Hal Ashton had been one of those who had taken advantage of Tom's law that any man who had proved his worth by three years of labor for the community could go and claim himself a plantation removed from the town. Hal now lived and farmed tobacco five miles up the coast, with his own two-storied house and his own fields of corn; he had never married, but he maintained a thriving establishment, with half a dozen Irish laborers and three serving girls, and two overseers to look after the whole; a small colony in itself. Even more independent was Tony Hilton's plantation on the windward coast, where he held sway with his beautiful, silent, red-haired wife. Hilton did not welcome visitors, and indeed it was a full day's journey through the forest and the mountain passes from

Sandy Point to the other side. But even Hilton acknowledged the authority of the king's lieutenant.

Jefferson glanced at his friend. "Aye," he said again. "She would have been proud."

"I doubt that," Tom said. "Once . . ." He sighed. "You'll dine with me, of course, John."

"I was but waiting for your invitation, Tom." He followed the governor down the steep slope. "You do not mount a permanent guard in your fortress?"

Tom shook his head. "We should see an enemy fleet approaching long before they could come within range, and have all the time we need to man our defenses. But there are no such things as fleets in the Leewards."

"Aye. There is too much bloodshed in Europe for even the most vicious stomach; they say that Germany is reduced to nothing better than a desert. And the French? You'll have heard our countries are again at war, even if our queen does come from Paris?"

"Harriman told me things were shaping that way. But in Europe. Here we have a treaty with them," Tom said over his shoulder. "But truly, John, I wonder what Belain was at. They lay around the place for a year, and then, their ship repaired, they sailed for home."

"All of them?"

Tom shrugged. "There are some half a dozen, eking out a precarious existence among the crabs and the fishes. I have seen no tobacco planted."

"Yet they were useful, once," Jefferson observed.

They were halfway down the hill, a good place to pause for a rest. Tom took two rolled leaves from the pocket of his coat, and bent low to escape the breeze as he scraped his flint against his tinderbox. "Our prosperity. The greatest comfort a man may know."

"I'd not argue with that." Jefferson drew the scented smoke into his lungs, expelled it again with a long sigh. "You'll not find a gentleman in England without his pipe or his leaf. If he would be a gentleman."

"England," Tom said, and glanced at his friend. "You'll have been hearing rumors, John. Thus these guarded investigations."

"When Harriman returned, he spoke much rubbish."

Tom nodded. "Or much truth. I would know what they say of me in Whitehall."

"You are very well regarded there, Tom. When you are regarded at all. No doubt you have also heard rumors."

"Only what you tell me now. But Harriman at least informed me that his Majesty is not in the least like his father, and this can mean nothing but good."

"You think so?" Jefferson got up, walked to the edge of the path, and looked down on the town once again. "I wish I knew. His Majesty is the most blameless of men, the most affable, too, in his private life. And yet . . . You know that Buckingham is dead?"

"Steenie? Great God." Tom flicked ash from his leaf. "I'd not whisper this to any man but you, John, but I cannot regard that either as bad for the nation."

"You think so? He was at least a nobleman born, an instrument the king could use for the channeling of popular hatred and discontent. As indeed he was used, and thus murdered."

"Murdered?"

"Struck down as he would have sailed for La Rochelle. But now . . . now the king turns to men like Strafford."

"I do not know the name."

"You knew him better as Tom Wentworth."

"Wentworth? But he was one of King James's most virulent opponents."

Jefferson nodded. "Now he has changed his tune and his coat, and incurred much odium in so doing. The rumor abroad when I left England was that soon the king will again dissolve Parliament, and there are no plans for calling a new one. Yet he is as much in debt as ever, and contemplates war, with Scotland as well as with France, and with God knows who else, in the cause of his religious principles. England is a sorry place, Tom, and if taxes are to be collected at sword point, it will become sorrier."

"Which but makes me realize the more how fortunate I am that three thousand miles lie between me and that Stuart court."

"Three thousand miles," Jefferson repeated slowly. "A great distance. But not quite far enough."

Tom frowned at him. "You've something to say which sticks in your gullet?"

Jefferson sighed. "Your grant . . ."

"You'll not say it is revoked?"

"Revoked, no. Taken over. Debts, you'll understand, on

the part of Warwick. The entire Caribee Isles have been leased to the Earl of Carlisle."

"Hay? I remember Hay. Aye. We have had our differences. And yet, you say, the entire Caribee Isles? Where will he find a colony to equal Merwar's Hope, save for a few beachcombers in Barbados? Where will he find the colonists to equal mine? He'll not play fast and loose with me. I have the king's own appointment as lieutenant, and the right to appoint my successor."

"All true. But the king, I say again, is deep in debt. Too deep for comfort, and certainly too deep for scruple. The transfer was a costly business for Master Hay. And so he obtained a slight addition to the lease. That of taxing the colonies for his own benefit."

Tom's head turned slowly. "He'd impose a tax on Merwar's Hope? In what sum?"

"He spoke of a hundred pounds a year."

"A hundred pounds? Is the man mad? Where will the colony support such a sum at this time?"

"I am but a messenger in this matter, Tom. I grieve for the situation. I told him, it but invites discontent among the colonists. I beseeched him to be patient and give you time to grow. But he is adamant. Your next crop, the crop that I take home with me, will be subject to this tax, and so will all others."

"By God," Tom said. "How rapidly a dream can dissolve into air. By God. This Hay must take me for less than a man."

"You'll not resist, Tom. That were madness."

"You'd have me submit, without question? You think we are without our problems here? You think these men down here would see their profits dissipated to keep some lord in his satins and laces, and his whores in their beds? By God We'd best go down. This is a matter for consideration."

"If I might offer advice," Jefferson said, and waited. But Tom was on his feet again, and making his way down the hill.

They reached the beach, from where a dock had been built out into the still waters of the roadstead, to allow boats to disembark without the necessity of their passengers becoming wet from the knees down. Yet here the sea was too shallow to allow oceangoing vessels to approach the shore, and the ships must need lie at anchor in the deeper waters of Old Road, and ply their trade to and fro by pinnace. They were at it now, unloading their cargoes, greeted by a large crowd of colonists, men, women, and children, some just standing and staring, others hard at work under the supervision of William Jarring. Among them were mingled both the mastiffs and the goats, growling and frisking, apparently quite accustomed to each other's company.

"A good man," Tom said, observing his friend's interest in the storekeeper. "A self-interested man, who will carry the colony upward with him."

Jefferson said nothing. He had nothing to say, save the questions which bubbled across his tongue and which he dared not utter. Yet the people were interesting enough. It was possible to tell the length of time they had lived in the colony by merely looking at them, separating the brownness of their skins, the tidiness or otherwise of their dress. But here at least was a legitimate question. "How many people do you muster now, Tom?"

"More than a hundred, to be sure. I have not yet held a census, although it is in my mind to do so."

They walked past the crowd, who ceased their labors to stand straight and touch their hats to the governor, or in the case of the women, to curtsy.

"And they live well together?"

"As I said, we have our problems. Forced upon us by circumstances. You'll remember that the first women you brought were the Irish. They are all married now, to my original settlers. Their children multiply each year. Yet they began life as Irish whores, and we have had few opportunities to change them here. So when Harriman arrived with his shiploads two years ago, you'll understand what happened. The most part of these people are Suffolk farmers and the like. Not gentlemen, certainly, but good yeomen, people of manners and gentility. If they swear, they do so in private, and if they drink, it is seldom to the point of collapse. Yet they are the newcomers, and thus the inferiors, in land and status in the community. There can be no other way to manage the colony."

"Indeed. Yet do they, surely, outnumber your original people?"

"By some four to one."

They walked up the deserted street toward the governor's house, and saw Mr. Malling standing on the steps of the church.

"Good day to you, Reverend," Tom said.

"It is indeed, your Excellency. Well, Mr. Jefferson, what do you think of our colony?" Malling was a very small man, with graying hair and clean-shaven, pointed features. His mildness was remarkable. It was impossible to imagine that, like everyone else on this island, he had found it necessary or at least desirable to leave England. But he was no high-church man, and Laud's assessors had been breathing too heavily down his neck.

"It thrives, Reverend," Jefferson agreed, and the three men walked slowly up the street. "Captain Warner was telling me of his problems, of the jealousies which crop up between the original colonists and the newcomers. And yet I observe very few suggestions of coercion. No soldiers or trained bands. And I would have thought you needed those for your very safety."

"We call such forces a militia in these parts," Tom said. "And every man is bound to serve."

"Saving the indentured labor, of course," Malling said. "There would be a risk we could not envisage, to place arms in the hands of such papist hooligans."

"Well, then," Jefferson said. "To protect yourselves against *them*."

"Hardly necessary," Tom said. "On the one hand, they are divided up among the colonists, and on the other hand, when they do accumulate, it is to drink and fight among themselves. I know the Irish, sir. I fought over their bogs when I was hardly more than a boy. Their lack of discipline, of any care for the morrow, indeed, leaves them totally unfitted for concerted action. Added to which they would require a leader of character and purpose, and in Merwar's Hope they entirely lack such assistance. No, John, when I spoke of our problems, they are matters of fairness between individuals, arising from jealousies and rivalries between individuals. They will be resolved by the reverend and myself. It is our business. And I do promise you this: there has been too much blood shed to secure this marvelous land for any man of us lightly to consider throwing any more away. This is Yarico."

For they had reached the top of the street, and the Indian woman waited for them. At that, Jefferson wondered, was she anything more than a girl? She was very modestly dressed, in a high-necked and wide-collared gown; the color was green, the collar white, all in linen. Indeed, there was a total absence of lace or furbelows about her. She wore a white cap on her head, from beneath which her black hair descended in a straight mass. It was longer hair than Jefferson had ever seen, and in a way the most beautiful hair he had ever seen, because unlike the softness he would have expected in a European woman, this hair had a texture of stiffness, and glimmered in a dull fashion, so as to suggest it would be impenetrable, and in fact, when she moved her head, as she did now to bow before the white men, the entire mass of hair moved in unison.

To complete her incongruity, her feet were bare. But there was more beauty here than in just the hair. The face was handsome, features filled with strength and purpose, and supported by a strong chin and firm, wide lips. Her eyes were black, and remote, except when she looked at Tom Warner; then they came to life, with a possessive purposefulness Jefferson had seldom seen before. For the rest, the gown was sufficiently shapeless to hide the body, but the wide hips and the bulge at the bodice were sufficient, when added to the hair and the feet and the face, and the suggestion of savagery which remained around her like an aura, to suggest untold, and heathen, delights, should she ever wish to share herself.

"My pleasure, Miss Yarico," he said, and to his surprise she extended her hand, and waited, so confidently that he almost kissed it before recollecting himself. But the hand itself was admirable, with straight fingers and a dry palm.

"Chief Tegramond's daughter," Tom explained. "And my housekeeper."

Jefferson glanced at him, but there was no suggestion of a flush, or any indication of embarrassment. Malling, on the other hand, had turned a bright red from forehead to neck.

"Welcome, sir," Yarico said, and stood aside. Two Irish servants, a male and a female, waited behind her, to take the men's hats and relieve them of their swords, and this done, she walked before them, her bare feet noiseless on the uncarpeted floor, across the hall and into the inner room. Here Jefferson halted in the doorway in surprise, for the room was furnished with four well-carved chairs, and an equally stylish table, set against the wall; it lacked only a fireplace to suggest a room in Suffolk. And on the table there were glasses and a variety of bottles.

"You have done well, Tom," he said. "Well indeed."

"You drink, sir?" Yarico asked, taking her place at the table.

"Indeed I shall, madam," Jefferson said. "Whatever you are offering."

"The French wine, Yarico," Tom said, "as it is a special occasion. You'll understand, John, that our delicacies have to be rationed, as we can never be sure of your arrival."

"But now that I propose to leave three of the ships here," Jefferson said, "why, you should never lack for anything, ever again."

"There you have our toast. You'll join us, Yarico."

She handed them their glasses without replying, and raised her own. "Merwar's Hope," she said. She spoke her English carefully, and yet with obvious difficulty.

"Merwar's Hope," the men said.

"Now, come," Tom cried. "Do not lurk there in the shadows. You'll remember Uncle John Jefferson, Sarah?"

The girl was a thin wisp; the mucus gathered in a steady stream beneath her nose, and stained the sleeve of her gown where she had sought to wipe it away. There were dark shadows under her eyes, and she moved without pleasure. But Jefferson was interested less in her than in the child who clutched her hand, hardly more than two years old, a strange combination of Tom Warner's rounded features and Yarico's lank black hair.

"My youngest son," Tom said, and swept the boy from the floor. "I have named him Thomas, after myself. He will perpetuate the name."

The child gazed at Jefferson with the deep, solemn eyes of his mother, and the white man found himself looking from son to mother, and from father to preacher.

"This is not England, John," Tom said. "Things are different here. Tom is but the leading representative of a new peole, who one day will claim this land. Perhaps this world."

Jefferson nodded. "I have read that the Spaniards face the same problem on the mainland."

"Problem? By God, it is no problem, but a just and proper arrangement on the part of Providence. Now, come, where are Philip and Edward?"

"Philip come," Yarico said.

Here at least there was no cause for surprise or distress. Philip must be fourteen by now, Jefferson thought, an absolute image of his father, in height and build and feature. Even in manner. He shook hands briefly. "It is good to see you again, Mr. Jefferson."

"And where is Edward?" Tom demanded. "Does he not wish to greet Mr. Jefferson?"

Philip glanced at Yarico.

"Edward not come," Yarico said.

"Not come? By God . . ."

"You'll not find him, Father," Philip said. "He is drunk. He got drunk the moment the fleet was sighted. Now he has taken himself into the forest. You'll not find him."

Tom rolled his leaf with great care, savoring the scent with every movement, striking the flint, and waiting as the first wisps of smoke rose under his nostrils. Jefferson and Malling were already alight glasses of wine at their elbows. Dusk had come to Merwar's Hope with its invariable suddenness, but it had made little difference to Sandy Point. Rather had it brought the town to life. Lanterns glimmered in Jarring's General Store, and someone was scraping a fiddle down there; people were dancing in the streets. Mosquitoes and sandflies buzzed eagerly through the still air, for they too would feast this night. Merwar's Hope, on holiday celebrating their tenuous links with that life they had left behind in England. Tonight there would be an absence of tensions and jealousies, although fresh causes of dissension would certainly be in the making, as hitherto faithful wife found herself holding hands with handsome, transient sailor, while husband drank himself insensible in the shadows.

But the governor's house was dark, save for a single lantern in the doorway. The three men sat on the porch and looked down the street.

"They are a happy people," Jefferson said. "Despite any differences you may observe among them, I'll wager you are a proud man, Tom."

Dinner had been a strained, silent affair. Now they waited for Tom either to dismiss them or speak his mind. That he so urgently wished to speak his mind was clear to them both.

"A happy people," he said. "I'll not disappoint them. As you say, whatever our differences, they came here to seek some relief from the burdens of living in England, and they have placed their trust in me. I have taken hard decisions before, by God. This one were relatively easy. I'm coming home with you, John."

"With me?"

"Aye, to see the king. To put our position squarely before him. He'll understand. But you'll forgive me, dear friend, this is not a matter that can be illustrated by means of a letter or by the advocacy of the best friend any man could ask. It must be done by me alone."

"Now, there is true statesmanship, Tom," Mr. Malling said.

Jefferson nodded slowly. "You'll understand that Charles is not like his father, Tom. Nor is England still the country you left."

"He can be no more difficult than James, to be sure. And with Villiers in his grave, England must be a better country. And to say truth, I long to see Framlingham again, and Jane and Edward, before they die. And I have another problem on my mind. Sarah. This climate plays the same tricks with her health as it did with her mother's. I'll take her with me, and we'll see if an English spring cannot put the bloom back into her cheeks. There. The decision is done. I'll communicate it to the colony tomorrow."

"And appoint your deputy," Malling said quietly.

Tom glanced at him, frowning. "Aye. To solve one problem, we must create another. It will have to be Hal Ashton. He has the seniority and the experience. And if perhaps he suffers from pessimism and stolidity, well, at the least I'll be sure that there will be no wild flights of fancy in my absence."

"Yet did not he and Berwicke all but cost you the colony, in the old days?" Jefferson asked. "And if there are differences between your people, will Hal . . . well, has he not withdrawn from public life these last few years?"

"That is to the good," Tom asserted. "He'll not have been too intimate with the layabouts, either. Oh, he's a disciplinarian, Hal is."

"Well, of course, the decision is yours." Jefferson watched Malling.

"But you'd have taken another one in my circumstances, eh?" Tom said. "You do not know my circumstances, John. Nor would I wish them on you." He inhaled, found the cigar to his satisfaction, and sighed. " 'Tis ever a mistake to paper over cracks, or to attempt to do so. Edward has not lived beneath this roof since his mother died. He has built himself a house, if you can call it that, for it possesses but a single room, on the other side of Brimstone Hill, and lodges there. By himself."

"He takes no part in the life of the community? I do not see how you can permit that."

"He works. Oh, we'll have no beachcombers here. He takes his turn at the duties of constable, and is a good one.

Perhaps his attendance at church is not so regular as we would wish."

"You'll not find his name in the book more than five times this year, Tom," Malling said. " 'Tis a problem we shall have to face. Should anyone else take it into his head to dissent . . ."

"We'll have him in the stocks. It is something which is continually on my mind. I think the time has come, indeed. To make an example of my own son, by God, And yet . . ." he sighed.

"I can see the difficulty," Jefferson remarked. "In operating one law for the governor and his family and another for the colonists. That can only breed discontent."

Tom got up violently, walked the porch. "You'd not understand, John. You do not live here. You do not know. In any event, that law we made among ourselves has long gone by the board; this was agreed before . . . well, you may as well know the story. By Christ, man, you know me for what I am. There has been no more faithful husband in my experience, I'll swear to that. But since arriving here, Rebecca was always different. She did not enjoy the heat. Like Sarah, she suffered from it. Her health, I mean. And then, she did not enjoy the responsibilities I was, and am, forced to undertake. It began with the Irish girl, Tony Hilton's wife. She formed an attachment to Edward, and they sought to elope. It was necessary to make an example of the girl."

"Of the girl," Jefferson said softly.

"She was an absconding servant. But it caused dissension. Her mind could not stand the pain. By Christ, I was not to know that. She was nothing more than an Irish whore, so far as I could see."

"You mean she became mad? Where is she now?"

"She lives with Mr. Hilton on the north coast," Malling explained. "As for being mad, Mr. Jefferson, perhaps a better word would be dull."

"And this was . . .?"

"Four years ago," Tom said. "But it is not her I'd discuss. I do not regret ordering the punishment, only the outcome. Yet the punishment was necessary, or we'd have no order among our domestics. And now, well, she seems to satisfy Hilton well enough, and between them they fill a necessary role. I must have at least one plantation on the windward coast, to ensure that the French do not spread themselves too far, and Tony is the only man willing to undertake such a lonely and uncomfortable vigil. They suffer more from wind and rain over there, you'll understand. But still we stray from the point. Rebecca would not take my side in the matter, and we quarreled. And while we quarreled, I found myself beside Yarico. Christ, it was a bad time."

"I'd argue with no man for taking a mistress," Jefferson said. "I do not see the reason for your apologia. Although . . ."

"You do not see how she achieved her present position, either," Tom said. "She brought news of an intended massacre by her people, of the French and ourselves, and Belain and I decided to anticipate the event. There was naught else we could do."

"Ah," Jefferson said. "I doubt I would have acted differently. Mr. Malling?"

"I can but thank God I have never been in such a position, Mr. Jefferson," the parson said.

"Aye," Tom said. "But the whole of it is not clear. The Caribs are a vengeful people. It was necessary to do the job completely, you'll understand. Except where wives were needed. And by God I swear that every woman taken was in due course lawfully married."

"In due course?"

"Christ, man," Tom shouted. "It is not a deed of which any man on this island can be proud. Any part of it. It haunts us, every one of us. But the worst was later. I repeat, it was necessary to destroy the entire tribe. There was no time or room for parley, for ascertaining the truth. And when it was done, it was discovered that Yarico was pregnant."

"With the boy?"

"You'll see at a glance he is my son. You, and everyone else. Her own people, had they survived. Now, there is something to haunt a man."

"Good God," Jefferson said. "You mean you think she fabricated the entire plot in order to save herself from the vengeance of the Caribs?"

"I do not know," Tom said. "Christ in heaven, I do not *know*. Perhaps, had I certainty . . . No one knows. Only Yarico, and her mind is her own."

"And yet . . ."

"Yet she now lives as my mistress. She mothered my son. I could not turn her away. Nor could I allow her to be married off to some layabout who'd beat her every dusk."

"And Rebecca?"

"Accepted the situation."

"As you would have it so. And died."

Tom turned. "You accuse me?"

"No," Jefferson said. "It is not my place, and if indeed your marriage was finished, it might have happened anyway. But Edward holds it so. That is why you do not punish his misdemeanors. Why you cannot."

Tom Warner's entire body seemed to sag. "Aye," he said. "I am the guilty one. There is none other."

There was a movement from the far end of the porch. Their heads turned in alarm, and Yarico glided up to where they sat in front of the doorway. Here she hesitated. "Warnah, go?" Her voice was soft.

"Only for a season, sweetheart. I have been before. And come back."

"With Re-becca," Yarico said, and disappeared into the house.

"By Christ." Jefferson wiped his brow. "Do you think she was there all the time?"

"Undoubtedly," Malling said. "Now she . . . I'd not offend the governor."

"Aye," Tom said. "There is a total heathen. She merely laughs when I try to speak to her on such matters."

"I'd not have thought laughter was a part of her character," Jefferson observed.

"It's there," Tom said. "But what laughter. She laughs at death itself."

"By Christ," Jefferson said. "You're all afraid of her, Tom."

Tom glanced at him. "So might you be, if you knew her as I do."

O'Reilly played the flute and Connor danced. The pair were friends, and they were accomplished. The notes filled the night, gentle and haunting. and Connor, although he was a big man, revealed a remarkable lightness of foot as he pirouetted and leaped, crossed his legs and stretched them wide—without ever a stumble, although he had drunk as much as anyone.

The others lay around the sand, clapping their hands, drinking and singing, laughing and telling interminable stories. Theirs was a closed world. No laborer was allowed inside Jarring's General Store unless he carried a note from his master. And celebrations of this sort were seldom allowed. Nor would it go unpunished, should any man be too drunk to work, come sunrise. Yet with their national carelessness of the morrow they were able to enjoy themselves, even lacking female companionship.

And with the enormous good nature which controlled even their hatred, they welcomed into their midst the governor's son. Not that he shared their merriment. The more he drank, the more silent and morose he became, staring into the flames which guttered in the night breeze, holding the bottle by the neck and scorning the cup, careless of slaps on the back or scattering sand across his legs. Like them he wore only breeches. Like them his body was a mass of hardened muscle. Only, unlike them, it was not scarred. No whip had ever fallen across his back, and there was not another man present who had avoided a session in the stocks or at the whipping post.

"Ye'll share the bottle, Ted, lad." O'Reilly sat beside him, wiping the back of his hand across his mouth. " 'Tis thirsty work, a-blowing on that flute. Christ, man, ye's the saddest sight I ever did see."

"Leave the boy be," Yeats said. " 'Tis upset, he is."

"Aye," O'Reilly said. "I've a mind ye once said ye'd not stay here a moment after the ships came, Edward, even if ye had to stow away."

"You'd not understand, Paddy. I've changed my mind."

"Well, 'tis to be hoped for sure ye know what ye're at," O'Reilly said. "Tell us, Jimmy, boy."

Creevey scratched his head. He was reputed to be a trifle daft, and scarcely worth his while in the field. Thus he worked for Mr. Malling, and swept out the church. " 'Twas examining the book, he was, your honor, and grumbling."

"Who?" Edward asked.

"Why, the reverend, may God heap curses on his soul."

"Now, there's an unchristian thought," O'Reilly pointed out. "Ye may be sure that the rascal is going to the fiery place, in any event, as he is as protesting a dog as ever knelt before an altar."

"I wish I could understand," Edward said, "why you hate Mr. Malling so much, for being a Protestant, and yet welcome me into your company."

"Ah, but, ye see, Ted, lad, ye're not a Protestant," Connor said. "Ye're a heathen, so ye've still hopes of salvation."

" 'Tis this we're speaking about," O'Reilly said. "If ye'd let us get a word in. Go on, Jim."

"Grumbling, he was," Creevey said. "About nonattendance. Oh, 'tis a serious crime, nonattendance. I'll have to speak with the governor, he was saying, even if it is his son."

"Aye, nonattendance, 'tis a matter for the stocks," Connor said.

"He'll not put me in the stocks," Edward said. "I care not a fig for his laws. He made them, and he breaks them, as he chooses. Well, one day, the laws will be mine, to make or break as I choose. You'd not realized that, Paddy O'Reilly."

"On the contrary, Ted, lad, I've had it much in me mind these last four years, or I doubt I'd have survived them. I doubt I'd wish to. But I'd thought to see ye in power before now. Creevey has a point. 'Tis your nonattendance made the governor put that dry stick Ashton in your proper place."

" 'Tis drinking with the likes of you, you mean," Edward growled.

"Man, we're all the comfort ye know. Here, let me get ye another bottle."

"No," Edward said. "I'll drink no more this night, or I'll have it all back." He rose to his knees uncertainly, the stars and the entire firmament whirling about his head. But he'd not drop before the Irishmen. With a tremendous effort he reached his feet and staggered out of the circle of light, there to stand with legs spread, sucking great gulps of air into his lungs.

A voice drifted to him faintly on the breeze. "Now, that was right careless, Paddy boy," someone said. "The lad is still a Warner, whatever his present discomforts. He's not to suppose we have a notion, save as he plants them there."

Paddy's protests were lost as the wind died, but Edward did not wish to hear any more. He forced his feet to move, and staggered up the sand toward the houses of the town, darkened now, as even the colonists had retired to their beds. Father would have retired as well. No longer a hammock for Father. A great big tent, wide enough to sleep four, but containing only two. What had Father taught *her* about the art of lovemaking? What was he teaching her at this very moment? The Carib way was not really practical on a feather mattress.

He knelt, staring up at the mass of Brimstone Hill. Mama looked down on the colony and smiled. Or frowned. She had much to frown about, because being dead, her gaze would not be restricted by roof or wall, much less by coverlet.

What rubbish. The dead were dead and could only be remembered. Else was Mama too encumbered by those who would surround her, to gaze down at Sandy Point with bitter hatred in their hearts. More than a hundred of them, an oath of eternal friendship on their lips. But then, Mama had died with an oath of eternal faith and honor on her lips. If there was the price of success, of empire and fame and wealth, it was surely a great deal too dear. He wondered he felt no resentment, no hatred this night. The announcement had been made from the steps of the church to the assembled populace, and more than a hundred heads had turned to stare at the governor's heir, excluded from his rightful post. And yet, this night, he felt only regret and sadness. The hatred would come later, with his hangover.

Another voice, wailing through the night. A dream voice, come from the heights of Brimstone Hill. Edward found himself on his knees, staring at the darkness in horror. It could not be. The dead were dead. And this spirit was not even speaking English all the time.

"Help," it shouted. "Assistance. *Mon Dieu,* but they sleep like the dead. Help."

Edward stood up. "What is it, monsieur? You trespass."

The Frenchman stopped, to pant and stare at him. Gone were the elegant buccaneers who had first stepped ashore from the *Madeleine*; those who had elected to remain and farm the infant colony when Belain had sailed for home had very rapidly become beachcombers, with tattered breeches their only garments. "Trespass? *Mon Dieu.* We all trespass, monsieur. And the owner has returned."

"Eh? What do you mean?" Edward tried to focus his eyes through the haze of alcohol which surrounded his brain.

"Ships, monsieur. Caribs. Score upon score of canoes."

"Where?"

"We sighted them at dusk, monsieur. We could not believe our eyes at first. But they were well out."

"Coming from the south?"

"From the south, monsieur. They appeared from behind Nevis, heading north. So we said, they are passing St. Christopher by, and making for one of the other islands. But then they started to close the shore. It was dark by then, and difficult to be sure, monsieur. But they were hard by the windward beach when last we saw them."

"Oh, Christ." Edward seized the man's shoulders and shook them to and fro. "Now, tell me straight, how many were there? Speak the truth, man."

The Frenchman goggled at him. "Not less than forty canoes, monsieur. This I swear."

"Forty canoes," Edward muttered. "Twenty men to a canoe . . . by Christ but you lie. There cannot be that many Indians in the entire archipelago."

"Well, monsieur, perhaps not so many, but, monsieur . . ."

Edward threw him to one side and ran up the street toward the church. He bounded up the steps and into the always open doorway, seized the bell rope, and dragged on it. A moment later the first peal echoed through the town.

"Edward? What has happened?" Mr. Malling, his nightshirt trailing the ground.

"Caribs," Edward said. "Keep the bell going, Reverend."

He ran down the steps and up the street to the governor's house, every footstep punctuated by a vision of Susan Hilton tied to a stake, or held on her face by some Carib brave; he could not decide which fantasy was worse.

"Edward?" Tom Warner stood in the doorway to his bedchamber, naked but carrying a sword. "What is the reason for this tumult?"

"A Frenchman has seen a Carib fleet making for the windward coast, sir," Edward shouted. " 'Tis only the Hiltons over there."

"By Christ," Tom said. "But we shall not reach them before dawn."

"Then you'd best hurry." Edward snatched up his sword belt, buckled it around his waist, found his pistols and thrust them into the belt, slung his cartridge pouch over his shoulder, and ran for the back.

"You'll come back here," Tom bellowed. "There is naught you can do by yourself, and you'll be needed to guide the foot."

"Yarico can do that," Edward said over his shoulder. "She knows these woods even better than I." He dashed across the fields behind the town, climbing now toward the forest. Susan, Susan, Susan. The thought drove him on, while the alcohol poured from his blood in endless sweat.

Yet it was light before even he found his way down the pass on the far side of Mount Misery, toward the windward shore. Now he faced the eastern ring of islands, fringing the Atlantic itself, and the breeze had already freshened, driving into his face, and driving, too, the constant big rollers which pounded on the beach below him. By now, too, exhaustion haunted his steps. Yet he was still sufficient of the Indian to have paced himself; he had loped through the forest, neither walking nor running, but traveling as fast as he could without dropping. He sweated, but this was clean sweat; the alcohol haze had quite gone from his head, and only a dull ache remained. But with it, the ache of despair, creeping up out of his belly. From this vantage point he looked down on an empty beach, but not an empty sea. The horizon, to which clung the island of Antigua, a glowing cloud in the path of the rising run, was dotted with canoes. Not forty. Not even twenty. Six of them, already several miles from the beach, rising and disappearing again into the swell, hurrying southward. With what on board? And with what accomplished?

The smoke drove him on. Hilton had cleared a deal of land, considering the size of his work force. Now it was a layer of black ash. And beside it, only the main timbers of the house still stood, and these surely not for long, as they still glowed, and sent wisps of smoke upward into the clear air. Edward panted down the last slope and reached the sand, staggered and dropped to his knees, to stare at the destruction in front of him. Now he could even feel the heat, driven toward him by the wind. A successful raid. How successful? Tony's dog lay on the sand, dried blood stretching away from its open mouth like a hideously elongated tongue.

He stood up, tiptoed forward slowly. He stood as close to the ruins as he dared, gazed at the smoke and the ash and the flame, inhaled, and tried to imagine whether burning white flesh would smell different from the holocaust which had marked the end of Tegramond's people. But surely, if the Caribs had taken the place before setting it alight, the bodies would also be scattered about the beach, the remains of a human butcher's shop.

"Edward?"

He refused to turn. It had to be a dream, a delusion, like the voice from Brimstone Hill, not only because she could not be alive, but because if she was alive she would not have spoken his name. Not after four years of silence.

"Edward?" It was so close it could touch him. And then it did, a handful of fingers on his arm. Warm fingers.

He turned, slowly filling his lungs, preparing himself for something horrible. Red hair, drifting back from her face in the wind. The strong, purposeful face, revealing at this moment only pleasure. She wore a cotton nightdress, torn in several places and soiled from a night in the forest. But she was unharmed.

"Susan?" he whispered. "Where is Tony?"

"I don't know," she said. "We could not defend the house, so we went into the forest. All of us. They left me and returned to see what could be done. I think I fell asleep. But when I woke up it was light, and I could see the smoke. I came down here."

In the forest a musket exploded, and another. "They're looking for you now," he said.

She gazed at him.

"Oh, Christ," he said. His hand left his side without any impulse from his brain, touched the line of her jaw, stroked down her cheek and neck. She put both hers up, clasped them around his wrist, and turned toward the trees.

"Tony will be out of his mind with worry," Edward said. "And there are men coming from Sandy Point."

"They can rebuild our house for us." She released his wrist to walk into the forest. "Do you know the windward coast?"

"No." Now they were hidden from the beach. That quickly.

"It is more steep than the west. You can see that. When there is a storm, the waves come right up the beach and pound on the rocks. So there are caves. There is one here." She went through the bushes with the utmost assurance. A white Indian, with flaming hair. But then, was he not also a white Indian? That was the opinion generally held of him.

"Four years," he said.

She parted the bushes in front of them, showed him a cleft in the rocks. "And then we were interrupted."

"You mean you remember that?"

"No one knows of this place." She had disappeared into the darkness. He sat on the lip, allowed himself to slide down the slope behind her, feet scrabbling on the suddenly dry earth. But it was not far, hardly six feet. "I can't see you," he said.

"Wait," she whispered from beside him. "Just wait."

Slowly the light came, seeping out of another hole in front of them, and at a distance, allowing him to understand the vault of the cavern, rising a score of feet above his head, and then dwindling away at the far end, where the glow came from.

"What is it?" he whispered.

"I don't know. I have never been farther in than there."

He glanced at her, crouching beside him.

"I have a lot of time to myself," she explained. "I go for walks. But there is so much to be afraid of in the forest."

"They think you are mad," he said. "They think the lash drove you from your mind."

She crawled away from him over the strangely smooth rock. "No doubt they are right," she said. "Will you come? I have always wanted to explore in there, to see where the light comes from. But I waited for you."

"For me?"

She was at the foot of the next rise, where the floor almost met the roof, where the light seeped through. "I thought you would come back one day. When you stopped being afraid of Tony. When you stopped being afraid."

"You were in Sandy Point when Belain came."

"Three years ago. And you were still afraid. I could see it then."

"And what makes you think I am not afraid now?"

"You are here."

"I thought of you being torn to pieces by savages. I was afraid of that."

"Well, then," she said, "is not all life a layer of fear, which is uncovered by discovering something you fear more than anything you already know?"

She crawled again, upward, and he followed her. His sword scraped on the rocks, and he took off his belt, left his pistols behind as well. He caught her as she reached the lip of the rock, and lay on his belly beside her to look down on a pool of still water, so clear and so bright they could see the white sand at the bottom. All around the pool the rocks glistened, with a tremendous bright light which welled up toward them and spilled into the outer cavern.

"The very rocks are burning," she said.

"Not burning," he said. "Just glowing."

"So, now I am not even afraid of that anymore," she said. "It will be somewhere to come."

He waited, slowly threading his fingers through her hair, while his body swelled. But he could wait now. She would not have brought him here without meaning more than to show him the burning rocks.

"I am not mad," she said. "I wished to go mad, when the

leather was biting into my flesh. I would like you to look at the marks."

Her voice was even, her chin rested on her hands as she gazed at the water. But she had slightly raised her body from the rock, to permit him to ease the skirt of her nightdress high, past thigh and buttock, to leave it resting on her shoulders. There were stains on the flesh, discolorations, but no marks. It was as firm and as strong as he remembered; stronger. And below . . . His hands caught the curve of her buttocks.

"Caribee," she whispered. "But I did not go mad, even then. And afterward, I think I was ill, for months. I caught a fever, and cared not whether I lived or died. I owe my life to Mr. Hilton."

"Do you love him?" He caressed the flesh, parting it and allowing it back together. But he could wait, still. There was no risk of him losing her this time.

"I do not know what love is," she said.

Very gently he rolled her on her back, and she sat up to allow him to draw the nightdress over her head. "Do you sleep with him?"

The air was cool on the cavern, and her nipples were enormous, and splendid to touch. But then, so were his, as she now satisfied herself. "He is my husband."

"And is he passionate?"

"He is very passionate," she said, and kissed him on the mouth, and while holding him with her lips and her tongue, attended to his breeches. She held him close, her hands between them, accomplishing all that should have been accomplished four years before, and finally drawing him into her body, without ever releasing his mouth. He felt conquered, just as much as he had ever been conquered by Yarico, but in a totally different fashion. Yarico's had been bubbling enjoyment, as she might have dived into the cooling waters of the pool, as she had sucked the dying penis. Susan's was all detached. She sought passion, and she found it. She did not have to guide his hands, and she swelled beneath his touch. But the morning was controlled by her brain, hovering above them. She would remember.

"I am not mad." Her hands left his body, and her arms outstretched. She lay beneath him, crucified on the rock, sucking air into her lungs. "I learned to think, under those lashes, under Mr. Hilton's body, and I learned that there is no greater pleasure than thought."

"You did not share, with him."

Her eyes were only inches from his face, very bright. "No. This hurts him. I see it in his face. He loves me. In him, I can see and understand love."

"But you love me."

She gazed at him. "I wished to know that."

He rolled off her and sat up. "I would like, one day, to know a woman who would seek nothing from me. Who would lie in my arms because she has no wish to be anywhere else on the face of this earth. Because she has no wish even to be in heaven, when she can lie in my arms."

"To accomplish that," Susan said, "you would have to be an altogether exceptional man yourself. You have much talent within you. But it is restricted by fear."

"Still? Of what would you say I am afraid now?"

"Many things, Edward. Your father. Mr. Hilton. Hurricanes. Caribs. Death. Perhaps even of life. And of yourself. You fear your instincts. They say you are a coward, a man who will not fight for anything. Because you did not fight for me. Because you did not take part in the raid on the Caribs. Because now you drink. We hear these things, even on windward. Mr. Hilton is troubled by them. He remembers that you are not a coward. He has told me of you in the hold of his ship, when you were just a child. That is why I think you are afraid of yourself. You feel something tremendous stirring in your belly, and you fear that should you ever follow the dictates of your belly rather than your head, you would uncover something that you do not know how to control, that you will never know how to control."

He gazed at her. An Irish whore, Father had said of her. Who had spent three years thinking, and now wished to love again. "And if I did that, you'd leave Tony? For me?"

"We were married in the church." Slowly she got up and picked up her nightdress. "But he is a Protestant."

Tom Warner and the militia from Sandy Point had put out the last of the fire. They stood in a group gazing at the shattered remains of the plantation. With them was Tony Hilton and his three laborers.

"Edward, by God," Tom cried. "Where in the name of heaven have you been?"

"I found no one when I arrived here," Edward said. "And so I went hunting in the woods, and found Susan. Mistress Hilton."

"But . . ." Tom gazed from his son to Tony.

"They could not have heard our gunshots, Tom," Hilton said. "But I am right glad to see you again, sweetheart, safe and sound. I would you had stayed where I placed you."

She allowed herself into his arms for a kiss on the forehead.

"I became afraid," she murmured. And flushed. Tony was frowning as he released her.

"Aye, well," Tom said, suddenly in a bustle. "You'd best return to Sandy Point with us. There is naught you can do here. And those devils may come again. Fortunate we are that we have suffered no human loss. If only . . ." He pulled at his lip. "We have lived here now for four years, with no trouble from the neighboring islands. What can have brought this venture?"

"They may have learned that there are no longer any of their own people living here," Hilton suggested.

"But how?" Tom demanded. "There has been no embassy, no investigation of our affairs."

By Christ, Edward thought: Wapisiane. He had all but forgotten Wapisiane. Three years since the massacre. Three years for Wapisiane to make his way from empty Nevis to Dominica or one of the other populated islands. Three years to survive the stake which would have been waiting for him there. Now, how had he done that? But if he had, it could only have been by rising among his people. So, three years in which he had become a leader, the cacique, as he had been selected by Tegramond. And thus, after three years, he was in a position to begin his campaign of vengeance. By Christ. If these people knew that, they would hang him on the instant.

"However it came about," Hilton said, "it has done so. But I do not agree, firstly, that they will return in a hurry. It can scarce be even a Carib's idea of pleasure to paddle up and down these waters all day and all night. In the second place, if we are to be subjected to visitations like these, I think it all the more important for me to remain on this coast, at least to give you warning of their next appearance. But spare me some of your Irish people to rebuild my house, and be sure that this time it shall be intended to withstand a siege."

"By God, Tony, but I bless the day you elected to follow me," Tom said. "Of course you are right, and of course you shall have all the labor you require. I only wish I had others of your stomach in my colony." He glanced at Edward. "I'll requisition from among my planters. But you're sure you'll be able to keep order among the rascals? Had I not better also send you some able-bodied men to maintain discipline?"

Hilton smiled; the huge mouth became the gash which could be so terrifying. "I'll manage, Tom. But leave me Edward. He's a likely lad. And it's about time he entered upon his manhood's duties, would you not say?"

Edward opened his mouth, glanced at Susan, and closed it again. He felt he was acting in a play, in which everyone on the stage save himself knew plot and lines, and yet in which he was the leading character.

"Aye," Tom said. "It would be better than lying about the beach drunk, to the detriment of discipline and my reputation. You'll stay and overseer Mr. Hilton's works, Edward, for as long as he requires your services. It would be best for all if that period does not end until my return from England." He hesitated, and then held out his hand. "I'll say good-bye, boy; I'm truly sorry it has to be this way, but we'll put our trust in the future."

"We'll not rebuild on this ruin." Hilton stood on the high land overlooking the beach, hands on hips. "We'll let that scar remain there to remind us and keep us watchful. There's our site."

The men turned their heads to look at the thick grove of trees a hundred yards to their right, standing on a shallow bluff, and then trooped across the beach toward it, behind their leader.

"From here we'll command the sweep of the beach in both directions," Hilton said. "And this is going to be a fortress, lads. Solid wooden walls, with loopholes, and when we're ready, the governor will let us have a cannon. The ships will put it ashore here before they return to England. We're to be more than just a plantation, lads. We're to be the windward bastion of Merwar's Hope. Now, fall to. The first thing I want done is that copse reduced to logs."

The twenty Irishmen exchanged glances. "There's a lot of work, Mr. Hilton," Paddy O'Reilly remarked softly. "Are ye and Mr. Warner going to give us a hand?"

"Me and Mr. Warner have things to do," Hilton said. "We've the future plantation to plan, and some talking to do. So they're a lot of logs, Paddy. You're fortunate in having your building materials close at hand. Is there a man among you'd rather go back to Sandy Point? I promise you this, lads: work well for me from sunup to sundown, and you'll have all the liquor you can drink. You'll eat what we eat, too. You've my word on that. My wife will seat you around our own campfire. There'll be no stocks and no whip, but so help me God, any man who wants to question my authority can get down on that sand and put up his fists now."

He stood above them, tall and broad and filled with strength. His beard remained thin, and thus did nothing to hide the power of his face, the strange attraction of the pock marks and the deep-set eyes. It occurred to Edward that in calling him a would-be buccaneer Roger North had shown a shrewd judgment of character. He glanced at the forest, into which his father and the militia had disappeared but an hour earlier. Was he afraid? He looked down at the beach. Susan stood there watching the men. She still wore nothing more than her nightdress. She possessed nothing more, at the moment, although no doubt the women of Sandy Point would come to her aid with a few spare garments. Now the breeze stretched the linen sheer against her flesh. Twenty men, one lover, and one husband. She did not look the least apprehensive. But then, neither did her husband.

O'Reilly spat on his hands. "I'm thinking that's a fair proposition, Mr. Hilton. We'll build your fort, if ye'll promise not to return a man jack of us to Sandy Point. We've no mind to stifle."

"Aye, Mr. Hilton," Conner said. "Ye'll need a lot of labor to plant your tobacco all over again. For a long time."

"You'd have me get into debt, you rascals?"

"Sure, and ye're a gentleman, Mr. Hilton," O'Reilly pointed out. "Gentlemen are ever in debt."

"You've a mind to practice your popery in private, I reckon," Hilton said. "Build me a fortress, O'Reilly, and I'll be prepared to consider the rest. But by Christ I'm offering no haven for layabouts. Work, God damn you, and then we'll talk. You're overseer, O'Reilly. See to it."

"Ye're a fair man, Mr. Hilton. I'll see to it." O'Reilly picked up the ax, looked at it for a moment, and swung it against the bole of the first tree. His followers gave a whoop and seized their tools with the avidity of children seeking their toys.

"You have a way with you, Tony," Edward said. "You'd make a good governor. A better governor than Father."

"I doubt I quite possess his purpose," Hilton said. "But

then, you could say that I also lack his years. You'll follow me?"

"Where?"

"Why, Ned, we must choose a site for the planting. I'm superstitious. I'll not return to that mangled field."

"And you'll leave Susan alone with those Irish vagabonds?"

Hilton smiled. "You've forgotten she's one herself. Oh, they're to be trusted, Ned. They only want to be allowed to live their own lives. The promise of that will keep them at work."

He stamped through the earth and the trees, away from the sound of the axes and the rasp of the saws. "When last were you on the windward side?"

"But once in my life. During the spell I lived with the Caribs."

"Caribee. And so you took no part in the slaughter."

"You criticize me for that?"

"I envy your courage to be a coward on such an occasion." He went down a slope; the trees thinned, and they reemerged onto the beach. The sea pounded the shore in front of them in an unceasing roar, and they had to shout to make themselves heard. "I have no regrets that I was on my way back here when it happened. I only wish the Caribs were themselves aware of that fact."

"You think this raid was a reprisal? How could they know?" And how his heart pounded. Wapisiane. Wapisiane. Wapisiane. What was it Bloody Mary had said of Calais?

"Now, that I do not know," Hilton confessed. "But it would be appropriate."

"And would you have ordered it differently, had you been the governor?"

"Probably not. When you undertake grave responsibility, you must needs undertake all the unpleasant tasks that go with it. You'll have to strengthen that stomach of yours, Ned, if you'd rule."

"Me?"

Hilton glanced at him, and continued on his way, down the beach toward the water, while Edward followed, and wondered; surely he could not mean to plant tobacco here.

"It will be your responsibility, one day, no matter what decision he has made this time. My only quarrel with your father is his admittance of the French, and in such numbers. But then, no doubt he is born under a lucky star, or there was some arrangement of which the rest of us know nothing.

As Monsieur Belain has sailed away with the most of his men, having paid two good cannon and his good name for the privilege of settling here. It makes a man wonder, indeed it does." He stood before the sea, hands on hips. "Over here life is different, Ned. You feel it every morning when you awaken. The breeze has a bite to it, the sea a roar. And when the wind blows, lad, 'tis that hurricane all over again. And we have not yet been hit by a proper storm. I see, in time, this island, small as it is, breeding two separate races of people, the leeward settlers and the windward. Much as your Yorkshireman differs from your man of Kent."

"And then there are those," Edward said, "who are able to span the pair. Like the men of Suffolk."

"To be sure. You wear a sword. Have you any knowledge of its use?"

It came so suddenly that he jumped backward in alarm. And yet, he had never doubted that Hilton had an ulterior motive in bringing him here.

"You're nervous," Hilton remarked. "I thought I'd made myself clear, why, two years ago."

Edward licked his lips. Was dissimulation possible? Was it what he wanted? Was he afraid? Yes. But incredibly, not of facing Tony Hilton with a sword in his hand. They were much of the same size, and there was no difference in muscle. Nor, he was sure, had Hilton ever received any fencing lessons. The difference, if it existed, lay in the mind, in the determination to kill. He had never killed. He had never done a great number of things. As Susan had said, so shrewdly, he had never shaken off the protecting, smothering cloak of boyhood, of being Tom Warner's son, however much he hated his father.

"It was my doing," he said. "She was alone on the beach when I came, and I remembered too much about four years ago."

"By God," Hilton remarked at large. "You have all the instincts of a gentleman." He drew his sword, thumbed the point. "And yet she neither resisted you nor screamed rape. Indeed, as we searched long and hard and found nothing, nor obtained a reply to our signals, and by your own admission you are a stranger over here, it would seem that she certainly played her part, to some extent."

"And you'd revenge yourself on a mind already weakened by adversity?"

Hilton smiled, but there was no amusement in his eyes. "In due course, Ned. Unless you'd stop me."

Edward dragged the blade from his scabbard, thrust his right leg forward, and swung, right to left and then back again, the sword scything through the air with an audible whistle, such was the force of the sweeps. But Hilton was back out of range, although now he thrust forward to meet Edward's third swing, and the blades clanged together with an echo which rang across the beach.

"Spirit, by God," Hilton said. "Now, that I like. I'd thought you were beyond it."

Edward panted for breath, looked along the sword. Did he want to kill his friend? If he did not, he must stop now. There was no point in fighting, except to the death. Age against experience. Only quite different from what he had once feared. And did Tony have any experience?

He moved forward, point drifting from side to side. Hilton watched him, and then brought up his own blade. They touched with the faintest ping, and then slithered against each other; when Edward moved his blade to the right, Hilton went with it, forcing his right arm wide, and then whipping back toward Edward's unprotected chest. Now it was his turn to leap backward, but not before a sliver of flesh was removed from his breast, to bring blood rolling down his belly and into his breeches.

"Stop it. Stop it, ye silly men."

Susan ran across the sand, hair flying, and nightdress too, feet scuffling sand into the breeze.

Hilton lowered his sword, still gazing at Edward. "I did not mean to scar you."

"You . . ." Edward looked down at the blood, and then rushed forward. But Hilton was not there to meet him; he had skipped aside, and there was only Susan, tangling up his legs, to bring them both tumbling to the ground.

"Now, put up your sword," Hilton said, standing above them. "And, Susan, you'll tend to his chest."

They stared at the great smiling gash of a mouth. Then the woman crawled away from Edward and rose to her knees.

Hilton sheathed his sword, extended his hand. "Come, Ned."

Edward got up. "You were but waiting her coming. I do not understand. Christ, my head is in a whirl."

"And you, Susan." Hilton took her hand as well. "You'd

not know the light in your eye, girl. I have seen nothing like it these three years."

She bit her lip and then pulled hair from her eyes. "Last night, this morning, I wished to live again."

He nodded. "I'd never supposed your brain was dead. Only asleep. Can you stop that blood?"

She hesitated, then stooped to tear a strip from her nightdress, which she took down to the water to soak, while Edward cleaned sand from his blade. "Then we have a problem, still, Tony. Or were you playing a game?"

"A game?" Hilton sat down. "Oh, we have a problem, Ned. But 'tis only a symptom of the whole. There is a problem here on Merwar's Hope. A problem of freedom. I would be free."

"My father has granted you that."

"You think so? Provided I practice Christian morality. Suppose I chose not to? Would he not set his militia at my throat?"

"Christian morality?"

"You've never considered the matter." He pointed at his wife coming up the beach. "I love that girl, Ned. I love the feel of her. I love to lie on her, and I love to feel her lying on me. Without her I doubt I'd stay here. I'd go to sea and become a pirate. And hang, within a year, as they all do. And I have known nothing from her save passive obedience. You have known the fire in her eyes, felt the fire in her belly."

Susan came up to them, knelt before Edward, cleaned the already drying blood from the scratch on his chest.

"A good reason for you to hate me," Edward said.

"Oh, indeed. Were I a Christian gentleman. But then, I am not, in my heart. Are you a Christian lady, Susan?"

She glanced at him. Color hovered in her sun-browned cheeks, threatening to overwhelm them and then fading again. She was uncertain and a little frightened. But then, Edward realized, so was he. "You know me, sir," she said. "I do not understand your drift."

"Would you thud your belly against mine, girl, if Edward possessed your lips?"

"By Christ," Edward said. "That is . . ."

"A heathen point of view. Oh, certainly. But I make no claim to so much virtue."

"You'd take me, sir, on those terms?" Susan muttered.

"I think I'd take you with a wooden leg," Hilton said.

The saltwater burned into Edward's chest; but not half so much as the sudden salt which burned his eyes.

"So, what is it to be?" Hilton asked. "I ask for you to live again, Susan. If you need Edward for that, then I am content. I ask you to have the courage to live with me, with us, Edward. One woman, two men. What I suggest is no more than sensible, in a limited community such as ours."

"My father . . ."

"Will suspect nothing, Ned, for it would never occur to him that so monstrous an arrangement could exist. In any event, he will not be here over the next year. As for our laborers, neither will they suspect anything, and if they should, it is not in their nature to criticize others, so long as they are not criticized themselves."

Susan turned to face Edward. "And are you still afraid of your father, Edward?" Her voice was low, and still the color alternated in her cheeks.

"You . . . you'd agree to such an arrangment?"

She smiled, and the sunlit morning seemed to overflow with light, and life, and love. "Am I not entirely the gainer? I have been dead for too long. I have hated for too long. I have wished for love for too long. I honor and respect Mr. Hilton. I would love him, had I the nature. But that I have not. In many ways I despise ye, Edward, and yet ye make me pant within myself, the very thought of ye. So, in possessing both of ye at the same time, I fulfill myself as a woman. I am a very eastern potentate, enjoying a role no woman can ever have done more than dream of in the past." She crossed her arms, lifted her nightdress above her head, and threw it on the sand. "Catch me if ye can." She ran down the beach to the water.

"Alive, by God," Hilton said. "Alive." He threw his sword and breeches on top of the nightdress. "You'll stay on windward, Ned. If you do not, you are at once a fool and my enemy." He ran behind his wife.

Edward looked down at the dried blood on his chest, and scratched his head. Then he laid his sword on top of Hilton's.

A fortnight later Jefferson's ship dropped anchor off the windward beach, to ferry ashore one of its brass cannon. It took most of the crew as well as all of Hilton's Irishmen, and even Tony and Edward, to unload the huge gun and drag it across the sinking sand to the rocks, and then it took another day's labor to hoist it up the twenty-foot face and embed it in the outward-looking wall of the house, where it nestled behind the wooden logs. It was time, because the roof was ready to be erected, so handsomely had O'Reilly worked his men. By then the ship had raised anchor, and was bearing north, with Tom Warner and his daughter on board. But Tom had not come ashore to say a last good-bye to his son. Nor had Sarah. Edward's exile from his family no less than from Sandy Point was complete.

"Now, there's a pretty sight." Hilton stood on the beach below the house and gazed up at the ugly barrel which protruded above his head. "I'm almost wishing those red-skinned devils would come back. A ball from that beauty would blow a bit of sense into their canoes."

Wapisiane. A savage of above-average capability. That first expedition to windward had been intended as nothing more than a reconnaissance. Next time his destination would be Sandy Point.

"Sure, and it'd be better if they'd wait until the roof's on," O'Reilly said. "Just in case it starts to rain, like."

Hilton clapped him on the shoulder. "You've a general's mind, Paddy. I see you yet, leading your wild Irish against the king's men, when you get home."

"Aye," O'Reilly said. "Except that I'll not be going home."

"Not even when your time is up?" Edward asked in surprise.

"What, be off to hang? Not me, Ted, lad. I'm staying in these blessed islands."

"And so say all of us," Connor agreed.

"Think your father would give us land, when we've served our time, Ned?"

"Now, that I really can't say."

" 'Tis a few years off yet, Paddy," Hilton said. "And in a few years a lot can happen. Who knows, we'll be having a new governor by then, maybe, eh, Ned?"

"I'll drink to that," O'Reilly said. "Now and any time."

"That's treason," Edward declared. "The governor acts as representative of the king, and to wish for his death is as serious as wishing for the death of King Charles himself. I'll hear no more of that."

"Why, sir . . ." O'Reilly began, but was halted by a quick shake of the head from Hilton.

"We've no politics on Windward," he declared. "And we're better off without them. And I'm right happy with the work you lads have put in these last few days. This afternoon is a holiday."

They gave him three cheers, and within minutes had fallen to fighting among themselves as the wine bottle was passed. Edward left them to it, and sought the encampment on the beach, a hundred yards upwind. Here he would find Susan. It was incredible that he should be able to think that, with Tony at his heels. Incredible that Tony should be able to think that too, and that they should remain friends. Friends. Now, there was an understatement. They were blood brothers. Hardly appropriate. Semen brothers. Brothers in sin and crime, who worshiped at the same shrine.

But this, surely, was what woman was created for. She sat on the beach in front of her tent, wearing a shift, which remained always her favourite garment, alike for its coolness and the absence of restrictions it placed on her movements, and brushed her hair. She was fond of this, and never tired of the long, exhausting sweeps of her arm. Perhaps she too found her hair exciting. He suddenly wondered what she would look like bald. What she would feel like bald. But his brain was always becoming filled with these devilish, irrelevant, dangerous ideas.

There was a remarkable thought. As if any idea could ever be dangerous again after the one which Tony had implanted in his brain, and which they now implemented to the full.

He threw himself full length on the sand beside her, and leaned forward to kiss her toes.

"They're a good lot," Hilton said, sitting beside his wife. "Do you not think so, sweetheart?"

"I'll not argue against my own people."

"And yet, how wasted they are, laboring in this hot sun. If ever there was a race created by God to fight and love and drink, it is the Irish. Certain it is they are good for nothing else."

"I'd not argue with that, either," Susan said, and brought her legs together for Edward to roll in his back and rest his head across her thighs. "Why so solemn today?"

"Solemn? Not I, sweetheart. Not I." Hilton pointed at the sails which were almost hull-down on the horizon. "There goes Jefferson, and the governor. And now we are more of a colony than ever before. We are recruited, and he has left us three ships, so that we need never again be cut off. This place will thrive from now on. It but remains for us to decide how the thriving will be. Will Merwar's Hope always be no more than an extension of England, as the ancient Greeks would have it, a true colony, or will we seek to make a new nation, here in the Caribbean, with new laws and perhaps a new religion, with a new conception of what our lives, or deaths, or *meaning*, are all about."

Edward's eyes opened. Here, then, was what he had been expecting the past week. Tony had clearly been working up to something from the very beginning.

"Ye are uncommonly serious this afternoon," Susan said. "If your wild Irish are indeed holidaying, I shall have to go up the beach to bathe. Will ye gentlemen accompany me?"

"Stay awhile," Tony said. "I wish to speak with Edward, and he will listen while he can touch you at the same time."

"You are a vulgar, blasphemous, traitorous dog, Tony Hilton," Edward pointed out.

Hilton smiled. Incredible how winning was that smile, breaking through the loom of the pockmarked features.

"Because I wish you to think? You may have forgotten that your father himself dreamed of such an outcome to our travels, before he became obsessed with propriety."

"No doubt because he discovered that propriety is an essential part of life. There seems to be no more than two choices. Either we preserve our identity as Englishmen, as loyal subjects of King Charles, or we descend to the level of savages, or perhaps lower. We have experienced both, Tony, and so we know how true that is."

"I would scarce agree with you. We knew less of the climate, then, and the people. And ourselves, perhaps. We lacked numbers. And I would hold us three up as examples of how people may make a new life, and lose nothing of their essential beings." He turned on his hands and knees to face them. "I must speak my mind, Edward. We three, we share too much for us to have secrets from one another. Is that not so?"

"Aye," Edward said.

"I understand not a word of what ye are saying. I'm going to bathe." Susan dropped her shift on the sand and walked down the beach. No doubt she expected them to follow her.

"So listen to me," Hilton said. "There is deep unrest in Sandy Point, and not only among the Irish. Your father thinks it is a constant difference of outlook between the new arrivals and the old. But he is wrong. He knows nothing of what goes on among his people, because he cuts himself off from them, sees them only in church. No doubt he has a lot on his mind. And no doubt he has a lot to do with his spare time, and that red-skinned temptress of his. And no doubt she but nightly increases the burden weighing on his conscience. You'll hear me out, Ned. The fact is, the very newest arrivals are all he can count on for support. The old hands are that discontented with their lot. 'Tis the church that bothers them most. The main left England to escape the constant quarrels between Laud and the Covenanters, the conception that a man should go to jail or lose all his wealth merely by choosing to worship God in a house not ordained and selected by the government. And that is why they come here, why they flock to the Virginias and the Massachusetts colony, far more than merely to escape paying a little ship money. So what do they find? Malling has grown as high church as any archbishop, and he records absentees in that book of his. Your name figures prominently."

"O'Reilly has been whispering in your ear."

"Not just him. I get word from Sandy Point. 'Tis an explosive situation, boy. And when a situation get this combustible, 'tis best to light the fuse yourself, before someone else gets careless with a match. Now, there is not a man on this island, myself included, would willingly go against Tom Warner. But Hal Ashton . . ."

"You preach mutiny," Edward said quietly. "Against my own father, and against your own friend, whether he is here or not. Nor do I understand why you turn to me. You seek to find some resentment within me at being passed over? I would be lying should I pretend that I do not feel some resentment. And yet, this is justice. I am still not twenty-one, not yet a man in the eyes of the law. And in addition, I am regarded as a drunken layabout entirely lacking in backbone by the colonists, as a joke by the Irish. These opinions were shared by yourself until very recently."

"I regretted them, and I hoped to be prove wrong. As I think I have been, by your willingness to draw on me. I'll tell you why I turn to you, Ned. There are two reasons, closely connected. Firstly, as you say, Tom is my friend. It was his will drove us to this island, drove us to prosperity. I'd not have the name of Warner dissociated from our future. The second reason is ever more important. We must grow. How we do that is our concern, that is what we are speaking about. But for the time being we are yet an infant, like to be choked out of existence by any armed fleet. We must dissemble, and continue our loyal obedience to the English crown, until we are strong enough to care for our own, until every house on the island sports a cannon like that one over there, until there are enough houses to make it beyond the ability of any Stuart king to assail us. For that, we must continue the grant as it is. Tom has read it to us often enough. It is to Thomas Warner and his heirs. Any successor who does not bear the name of Warner will indeed be a felon and a traitor. But you, Ned. In the eyes of the world, you are his natural heir. And let me add this. He has little enough justification for his position now. He has broken his own laws, and not only in the matter of Yarico. Should the truth of the massacre at Blood River ever come out, be sure that he would be impeached. And returned to occupy that very Tower which was once your home. We can save him that, Ned."

Edward got up. "Treason," he said. "No matter how you dress it up, Tony, it remains treason. Treason by you against your lawful lord, and treason by me against my own father."

"It is a sport of kings, treason. Their only sport, one would suppose, looking over the pages of English history. Aye, and Scots, and Irish. Yet the institution survives, more often than not to the good of the country."

Edward faced him. "I do not quarrel with much of your reasoning. Father has lost his way. I sometimes wonder if he ever possessed as much certainty of purpose as he pretends, as others suppose in him. Certainly his being in this part of the world at all is much of an accident. Yet he has always followed a dream, to the best of his ability, as do we all. This colony, this island, is his life, and his reason for life. Take that away from him and he will have nothing. Perhaps he is unduly stern at times, and perhaps he seeks to re-create aspects of England. It will take the weight of history to determine whether or not he is right or wrong. You and I, we have the time to wait and see, in the certainty, as you say, that I must succeed him. I would prefer to do it legally, and not while his back is turned."

"The dutiful son." Hilton sighed. "I'd not want to disturb your spirit, Ned, but you're forgetting that you're not the only Warner left on this island."

"Philip? Why . . ."

"He is but a boy, to be sure. Scarce fourteen years old. I remember you as a man, at fourteen, Ned. Perhaps you should look more closely on your brother. Study him. You will not find a more industrious, sober, God fearing youth on this island or any other. The very apple of his father's eye. I can see no certainty that the eldest son must succeed."

"Why, you . . . It is the law."

"Provided there is no impediment. Where the eldest son is a lawbreaker, who will not attend service, who drinks with drunken Irish laborers, who has already been guilty of at least one act of mutiny . . . for make no mistake, your refusal to take part in the attack on the Carib village was mutiny, Edward. Punishable with death, under any other commander. And when, to top it all, it becomes known that the boy lives in open sin with another man's wife . . ."

"You scoundrel," Edward cried. " 'Twas your doing."

"And I bear no grudge. Indeed, I admit it freely. These past few weeks have been the happiest I have known. And Susan also. And you, I'd reckon. Yet we'd be fools to suppose we can continue our arrangement indefinitely, without word creeping back to Sandy Point. What then? I at the least have no governorship to lose."

"By God," Edward said. But of course Tony was right. One could not steal paradise. One entered it boldly, with a clear conscience and the blessings of church and man.

Or one seized it, sword in hand. Had any man ever succeeded in doing that?

Hilton was on his knees beside him. "As we are now speaking openly, Ned, let me say more. You have been the subject of much discussion between your father, and Jefferson, and Malling, and Ashton. They know you are the obvious rallying point for the discontented. But you are Tom's son, and he would have nothing done against you while he was here. Ashton, now, has been left with instructions to proceed against all wrongdoers in the colony with much severity, being assured of Tom's support when he returns. You'd do well to bear that in mind. Those he has imprisoned are those he would estimate to be your supporters, should it come to a confrontation. It will not be long before you join them. In fact, I would estimate that you are safe only so long as you remain here on windward."

Edward chewed his lip. Certainly there had been no love between himself and his father for too long now. He could not help but blame Tom for Mama's death. And the open flaunting of Yarico was more than his belly could bear. Or had that been nothing more than jealousy? Was he too eager to blame himself and excuse Father? Christ, to know what to do. But he had not needed a glass of wine for several weeks now. Not since coming here to stay. Not since knowing Susan again. Not since being included in the wild wild dreams of Tony Hilton.

Dreams? Then where was the reality? But the step was irrevocable. Once taken. How easy, then, not to take it. But then, as Tony pointed out, this opportunity, once passed, would not be regained. There would be no room for rebellion once Father returned. Rebellion. Because that was what it would be.

He watched Susan returned up the beach toward them. She strode the sand like the naked goddess she was. Drops of water sparkled at neck and breast and groin, and her hair lay in a dark crimson mat on her back and shoulders. To lose all that, why, it was impossible.

What rubbish. Did he possess all that? It was part of a scheme, a gigantic conspiracy which lurked in Hilton's mind. When had the idea been born? When he had marched away into the forest five years ago to brood on his own and develop plans on his own? And now he saw the opportunity to put those plans into practice. Tom away, and his son discontented and unpopular with the established government.

But suppose he was right? There could be no denying his ambition, but might it not have been brought to a point by the looming disaster he foresaw?

Susan came up to them. "Ye've solved the problems of the world, I've no doubt." She dropped to her knees between then, put an arm around each of their shoulders. "Now, ye've had enough serious matters. Ye could devote a little time to a poor shipwrecked waif. Ye know what being rolled up in the surf does to me. And for me."

Her mouth was loose, and her eyes were liquid. And they were looking at Edward.

"We'll settle this matter first," Hilton said. "It affects us all."

A threat, allied to a promise. The girl still gazed at Edward. Oh, they were conspirators, all right.

"I'll have no bloodshed," he muttered.

"I'm all for that. But you'll not avoid it by being halfhearted in the matter. We've twenty wild Irishmen over there, and enough arms for every man. There's a force to be reckoned with."

"And the arms were given you by my father," Edward said. "You've planned this a long time."

"Let's say I've seen it coming a long time," Hilton said.

They left Windward at noon and made their way through the forest, Hilton, Edward, and Susan in the van, the Irishmen bringing up the rear. They reached the high woods overlooking Sandy Point at dusk, and waited there the night. Hilton stood in the midst of his men and glared at them, huge mouth wide, but not smiling tonight. "You'll mark my words," he said. "There'll be no drinking, and no singing. And no playing on the flute, Brian Connor. Paddy O'Reilly, I'm putting you in charge, and you'll answer to me for any breach of discipline."

"I'll do that, Mr. Hilton, sir," O'Reilly agreed. "I'll break the jaw of the first man who pipes up."

"Aye. Now, as to tomorrow. You'd do well to listen. We aim to make this colony a free place and to restore Mr. Warner to his just rights as the governor's son, confident that when he has those powers and responsibilities, he will take care of them who supported him. And all other Irishmen in the colony. But not one of us must in any way prejudice his position. There's to be no firing, not even a raised sword, without the express orders of either Mr. Warner or myself. I want no bloodshed if we can avoid it. As for rape or robbery, by God, the first man who lays a hand on anything which is not his, be it woman or piece of cloth, I'll hang him from the clock tower within the hour, and leave him there to rot. You understand me, O'Reilly?"

"Oh, yes, sir, Mr. Hilton. I'll keep me lads in order."

"See to it. Now, eat your food and get some rest." He returned through the trees to where Edward gazed down at Sandy Point, so quiet in the gathering darkness. The breeze was off the land, as usual at dusk, and no sound came up from the town. Nor was any movement to be discerned. But lights were starting to wink in the windows, and on the ships riding at their moorings in the roadstead.

"Satisfied?" Hilton demanded.

"You're a born leader of men, Tony. I wish I had your confidence. Yes, friend, I am satisfied. But yet disturbed. You say you have word that the main part will support us when we make our play?"

"I have Jarring's assurance, certainly. And he knows his people, as they do their drinking in his tavern."

"He knows we are here now?" Edward asked in alarm.

"I'm not that stupid. He'll know we're here, like everyone

else in the town, when we choose to let them know. And then it will be too late to do otherwise than acquiesce."

"There are points I doubt you've considered. Not everyone will join."

"I expect no more than half. But these will be sufficient."

"And the others? Malling and Hal Ashton?"

"I've no mind to harm them, or anyone, Ned. Provided they are sensible about it. They can take one of the ships."

"And return with an army?"

"I doubt that. We'll make this colony so strong it *would* take an army to reduce us. And if King Charles is that in need he is reduced to taxing colonies at a distance of three thousand miles, where will he afford an army to send against us? 'Tis certain he'll not be able to promise them plunder."

"You've an answer for anything. So tell me what we do with our Irishmen when the victory is won? Twenty fighting men, with arms in their hands."

Hilton laid his finger on his nose. "There's the point. Jarring claims to favor you, Ned, but who knows how deep that favor lies? He'll have no choice tomorrow. He *must* favor you, and he must rally every man he can, and every woman, too, by God. It's that or being ruled by Paddy O'Reilly. They'll not accept that."

"By God, but we gamble, Tony."

"All life is a gamble, Ned. And I for one would not have it otherwise. Look on this gambler, Ned, and say I have not done too badly."

"You have not hitherto aimed so high," Edward pointed out.

"You'd not backslide now, boy? Those men back there would tear you limb from limb."

"I'll not backslide," Edward promised.

"So come and get some sleep. There'll be none for the next day or two."

"I'll sleep," Edward said. "In time. Just leave me here."

Hilton hesitated, and then nodded, and withdrew into the bushes. But, as Edward had supposed he might, he soon sent a replacement. Tony Hilton might be a gambler, but he believed in controlling the odds where it was possible.

She lay on the grass beside him, looking down on the village. "I can never do that without a shiver."

He nodded. "You above all of us have cause to hate, for wishing a change, maybe."

She rolled on her back, lay pillowed on her hair, looking

up at him. "Ye'll be a good governor, Ted. Ye've compassion."

"I'd not been aware that was a requisite. A governor must govern, and sometimes that is hard."

" 'Tis still easier to lead than to drive. I've a mind this colony has been fortunate, because of the state of affairs in Europe. Should England and Spain come to war again, and it could happen any day, then it might be necessary to make these people fight, and then ye would count yourself happy had ye not to look over your shoulder."

"Schemes, intrigues," he said. "Even from you. Tell me straight, Susan; were you no more than the bait of Tony's trap?"

She gazed up at him, and past him, at the darkening sky. "I know nothing of Tony's plans, Ted. I plan nothing. Whatever I do, I do from my heart. I have always done that. But now I am happy. I think I need ye both. And ye will *have* to share me now. My belly is full."

"You . . . Does Tony know this?"

"I have not told him yet."

"And who is the father?"

She smiled. "Now, there is a problem, would ye not say? Will it not bind us closer together?"

Edward looked down at the village; only the lights were visible. "Or drive us irretrievably apart. And how can you be sure?"

"I can no longer bleed."

"It cannot have been more than once. That can be caused by too many things."

"Yet a woman knows, Ted. I have life within me. I would have ye know this."

"Tricks," he said. "Plans. What would you have me do?"

"I would have ye love me tonight. I wish that more than anything else in the world."

"And when I tell you I cannot? I am the possessor of the limpest rag in the Caribbean Sea. Or maybe the world."

"Then I must remain chaste." She put her arms around his neck and pulled his head down to hers. Her lips were as inviting as ever, but not even their touch could awaken him. As she very rapidly realized. She sighed and sat up. "And sorry. Why are ye this way? Because I am pregnant, or because of tomorrow?"

"Tomorrow," he said. "All things wait on tomorrow."

It came at last, the first glow of light rising around Mount Misery in their rear, and stretching long pink fingers over the sky toward the dark western horizon. It brought a crow from the cock, walking his empire in Jarring's backyard, and a responding bark from one of the dogs. The waiting was at an end.

Edward had not slept, although he had scarce moved, had remained watching the winking lanterns slowly die, except where they rode by the anchor watches on the ships. Beside him the girl had slept, breathing slowly and deeply. No girl, if indeed she was pregnant. No girl, anyway. But Hilton had not come looking for his bride. He had let her remain close by Edward. There was always intrigue here, surrounding him like a morning mist, and no less thick and clammy.

But this morning there was no mist. The air was as clear as ever in this climate, the skies were also empty. Once before he had watched the dawn coming up while crouching in the bushes. The memory of that day, of the screams and the smells, and above all the bestiality which had overtaken the white men, haunted him, and would haunt him to his dying day. And these men at his back were not even civilized, by the standards he would set. Wild Irish, clutching sword and pistol and musket like the pirates they would rather be.

"Time," Hilton said. "Now, then, Paddy O'Reilly, Mr. Warner and I, and ten of your people, will make straight for the governor's house, and there we will seize Mr. Ashton and Mr. Philip Warner, and place them under restraint. You will take the chapel, and place Mr. Malling under arrest. And remember what I said about violence. But you will need no more than half a dozen men for that. Send your remainder around the houses, waking up your compatriots and summoning them to meet in the street before the church. No noise, now, and all quiet. When we are ready, I will fire a pistol into the air, and you will then toll the bell. Understand me, Paddy, I'll cut down the first man who disobeys even the thoughts in my head."

"You have 'me word, sir," O'Reilly said with considerable dignity. "Me boys will be quieter than the grave."

"But what happens when the ships learn there is something amiss on the shore, sir?" Connor asked. "Will they not fire into us?"

"They will not," Hilton promised. "For two reasons. Firstly, they are only half a dozen men on board each ship, and secondly, they will not risk firing into the town where are the women and children, as well as their own shipmates. They'll wait upon the outcome of the business ashore, and we all know what that will be." He glanced at Edward. "You give the signal."

"Then we do no good by waiting here." He scrambled to his feet. "But you have forgotten the most important task of all. The men Ashton and Malling have imprisoned. There is our surest support."

"By God," Hilton cried. "But you are right. Paddy, you'll see to them."

O'Reilly grinned and nodded. "That I will, Mr. Hilton."

"And have ye no task for me?" Susan demanded.

"Aye," Hilton said. "A severe one. To remain here in patience until either Edward or myself comes to you. Mark this well, now. It should not take long, and you can oversee whatever happens."

She nodded. "Well, then, Godspeed to you all."

"Godspeed," Edward whispered, and set off down the hill.

Slowly it became lighter, but the village seldom awoke at dawn, although there would be stirrings in the houses, children crying, women getting up to boil water. It was a time for haste. He led them down the hill at a steady jogtrot, although they traveled with commendable silence, twenty ghosts going about a dreadful task. They reached the beach, and Hilton waved his arm. He, Edward, and the main party dashed straight up the street, leaving the others to take up their positions more slowly.

A dog barked, and then another, but Edward was already at the porch to the governor's house. Here he paused to draw his sword, and heard the rasp of ten others being made ready behind him. No door was ever locked on Sandy Point; he pushed it gently back. The parlor was empty. Empty, too, of the scent of stale tobacco, which it always held during Tom Warner's residence.

Behind the parlor an open doorway gave access to the hallway, off which opened the kitchen and scullery; at the end of this hallway the flight of straight steps gave access to the upper floor. At Hilton's signal two of the Irishmen remained on guard, one at the front door and the other at the back. The remainder tiptoed up the stairs behind Edward.

They entered another corridor, off which opened the three bedrooms, their windows overlooking the front of the house, beneath the huge porch. "Yarico sleeps in the first one," Edward whispered. "You'll secure her, Tony. Gently, now. She is not likely to scream, at the least. Connor, my sister used to sleep in the center room, so it is odds on that Mr. Ashton will be occupying that. Place him under arrest. Again, gently. I will see to my brother. Wait for my signal."

He tiptoed along the dark corridor, only dimly illuminated by the morning light as it drifted through the closed shutter at either end, paused outside Philip's door, raised his hand, and threw it open.

"What?" Philip sat up, hair tousled. "Edward? What?"

Two of the Irishmen had followed Edward in.

"I wish no trouble, Philip," Edward said. "In which event you will not be harmed. For the time being you are under arrest. Fetch those weapons."

One of the men darted across the room, picked up Philip's sword and pistols.

"You have lost your wits," Philip said. "Father will have you hanged."

"Father is in the middle of the Atlantic Ocean," Edward pointed out. "You'd best remain here, Jocko."

"Aye, aye, sir," Jocko agreed, taking his place by the door.

"Mr. Warner. Mr. Warner." Connor's voice was anxious. "The center room is empty, sir."

Edward ran into the corridor, heart pounding, a dreadful weight seeming to accumulate slowly in the pit of his belly. The door to Sarah's room stood open, and the bed had not been slept in.

"Bad." Yarico's voice came to him. "You will die. You, Hilton, and all your people."

Edward stood in the doorway. She sat up in bed, naked, only half-concealed beneath the covers, nor did she seek to protect herself in any way as she gazed at the intruders with angry eyes. Little Tom lay beside her, pillowed in the crook of her arm, staring at the white men in terror.

"Ed-ward," she said. "War-nah will flog you."

"Oh, she's a tiger cat," Hilton said. "But she's only talk, at the moment. All secure?"

"Ashton isn't here," Edward said.

"What do you mean?"

"He isn't here," Edward shouted. And at that moment the bell began to toll.

"What in the name of God . . . ?" Hilton ran to the shutter and threw it open. "By Christ."

Edward stood beside him. The street below was filled with

men, all carrying arms, milling about at this moment, but being brought to order by Hal Ashton and William Jarring.

Yarico gave one of her utterly delightful laughs. "You look for Hal?" she asked. "He no sleep here. Not this night. He got friend. You ain't know that, Ed-ward?"

"That old lecher," Hilton said. "That we'd be knocked up by an overactive tool. By Christ . . . I could drop him from here."

"No," Edward said. "What of Jarring?"

"He has made *his* decision. We have time to withdraw, Ned. We can escape across the field and into the forest. They'll not follow us there. And if they do, we'll break a few heads for them."

"What of Paddy O'Reilly?"

The door to the chapel was shut.

"He'll have fallen by now. How else were the people to be alarmed?"

"Not by Paddy," Edward said. "We cannot desert him. We must negotiate."

"Negotiate?"

Edward ran to the head of the stairs. "Close that door," he shouted. "And push furniture against it. Connor, get down there and help him. And then close all the shutters and bar them, and stand by them."

Connor hesitated. "You'll not let them take us. Mr. Hilton? There'll be no negotiations for us. It'll be the rope."

Hilton chewed his lip.

"They'll take you over my dead body, Connor," Edward promised. "But hurry."

For the crowd was moving up the street.

"There's to be a fight," Hilton muttered. "They'll come to us without Ashton. I can drop him, Ned. His chest sticks out like a flag."

"You'll not," Edward shouted. "Hal? Your oldest friend, after me? Before me, by God."

Hilton sighted along the barrel of his pistol and then lowered it. "You're an honorable man, Edward. Or you entirely lack stomach. I hope you've sufficient to stand on the gallows without shaking."

"Bar those windows," Edward said.

"You frightened, white man," Yarico said. "You die."

"Edward," Philip said, "you'd best surrender at discretion. There are sixty men out there. You'll not stop them."

"For Christ's sake, shut up," Edward shouted. "I'll gag the next person who speaks."

He leaned on the window, looked down. From below there came the bangings of the windows and doors being boarded up. This was the strongest house in the town, after the church. Between them they could sustain a long siege; there would be no lack of food and water in either building, for Mr. Malling lived in a room behind the vestry. But it would cost lives. And it would raise a fund of bitterness not to be alleviated in a few days, or perhaps even a few years.

And what would happen to Susan, alone on her hilltop? What had already happened to her, indeed? She would be able to see that something had gone wrong.

He threw the shutters wide again as the men approached. "You'll stop there, Hal," he called. "I've armed men posted."

Ashton looked up, blinking; Jarring pointed to the window. "Edward?" the sailing master called. "This is madness, boy. What do you mean?"

"To claim my rights as Edward Warner," Edward said.

"Why, boy, you have just thrown them all away," Jarring said.

"I speak to you, Hal," Edward said.

"Mr. Jarring is right, Edward," Ashton said. "For God's sake, boy, I count myself your friend, and I would assist you in every possible way. But this is mutiny against the lawfully constituted government of this island." He took off his hat and wiped sweat from his face. "And to ally yourself with the laborers, why, boy, that is not only criminal, 'tis downright madness."

"A man must find his friends where he may, Hal," Edward said. "I demand safe conduct."

"You demand?" Jarring asked. "By God, boy, you're in no position to demand anything. You're outnumbered and besieged."

"And armed," Edward said. "And, if need be, desperate. We'd not have bloodshed, Hal, but by God you'll find our lives expensive."

Ashton spoke sharply to Jarring, who would again have replied, and then faced Edward.

"Safe conduct, you say? Where would you go?"

Hilton appeared at the window. "There's ships in the harbor, Hal," he called. "We'll take one of them."

"I might have known you'd be involved in this, Tony," Ashton said. "You were ever a pirate at heart."

"No more," Hilton said. "Not unless I'm forced to it. We'll take ourselves to Nevis. There's a fair offer, Hal. 'Tis sure that to remain here will but perpetuate unrest. In Nevis we can go our own way."

"You and how many?" Ashton inquired.

"My wife and followers here, for a start. And anyone else who chooses to accompany us. 'Tis fair."

"To allow mutineers to escape, free?" Jarring cried. "What would the captain say? By God, he'd hang the lot of us. And be in his rights."

"Then take your chances, scoundrel," Hilton shouted, and fired.

The ball did no more than kick dust in front of the assembly, but it acted like a cannon shot. Men ran in every direction, taking shelter behind houses and in ditches; several returned fire immediately, and the bullets thudded into the wooden walls of the governor's house.

Edward stepped away from the window. "Now, there was a cursed stupid thing to do, Tony. I'd have persuaded them."

"You," Hilton said contemptuously. "You have no stomach for revolution."

Edward looked through the window again. How empty the street looked, on a sudden. But there were faces at the windows of the houses, women and children, and now from below there came the explosion of a musket as one of the Irishmen fired.

"Big fight," Yarico said from the bed. She had prudently lain down to keep out of the way of the bullets; Philip sat on the floor beside the bed. Young Tom, remarkably, seemed to have gone back to sleep.

"Many dead," Yarico said, and smiled. "You dead, Edward?"

"I did not intend this," he muttered. "Wait," he shouted. "Cease firing."

Still the explosions rang out, and still the bullets crumped into the thick wooden walls. And now there was firing from the church, while at the far end of the street Jarring and Hal Ashton reappeared, with a dozen men and three bound prisoners; clearly the three laborers who had been arrested trying to alert their compatriots and were now bound for the gallows.

Edward ran down the stairs. His heart pounded and sweat rolled down his cheeks. He was afraid, and yet he had become filled with a wild exhilaration. He had tossed, and lost.

This seemed to be the entire story of his life. But he had no right to involve countless others in his defeat. And most of all, he had no right to involve Susan and her unborn child. His unborn child, maybe. She believed it to be so. Else why tell him and not her husband? And indeed, only that made sense; Tony and Susan had lived together for three years, without result. Edward had but to appear on the scene, to impregnate her.

He burst into the parlor. Connor had arranged his men well, one to each window, front and back; they crouched there, muskets at the ready, firing whenever they saw a movement in the village.

"Hold your fire," Edward said. "And unbar the door."

"Ye're crazy, sir," Connor said. "They'll shoot ye down like a dog."

"They'll not shoot a Warner," Edward insisted. "And I must stop this business. I know how it can be done. Now open that door."

Connor looked past him, to where Hilton stood in the doorway.

"You'd best let him through," Hilton said. " 'Tis sure he's all the hope we have of surviving this fiasco."

Connor shrugged and moved the bar to the door. Edward pulled it open, took a deep breath, and stepped outside. There was an immediate explosion from down the street, and the bullet smacked into the wood beside him.

"Hold your fire," he shouted, and reversed his sword. "I'd speak with you, Hal."

He walked out from under the porch, to stand on the street. It was well into the morning now, and the sun was above Mount Misery, already steaming heat from the ground and sending it back through the still air.

"You'll surrender?" Ashton called.

"I'll negotiate, Hal."

"From there?"

"I'm but one man, Hal. There are twenty others, armed and desperate. You'd do well not to push them to extremities."

There was a short silence, and Edward took three more steps into the street; his heart pounded; he was an easy target for anyone so minded. But he kept his head high. He was the Warner heir, and no matter what had happened in the past, or might happen in the future, they could not afford to forget that. And what *would* happen in the future? He was sure of nothing. Only that he had made a dreadful mistake this day.

Hal Ashton emerged from a house farther down the street. His sword was sheathed, and he carried no other weapon. "Well?"

"I'd talk with you, Hal, not the entire colony." He went forward again, was now opposite the church, which was perhaps the most dangerous place of all. O'Reilly and his five men were in there, and should they take it into their heads that he would betray them, they might well shoot him down. But Ashton was also coming forward, to halt not ten feet away. Two men on a lonely street.

"What have you to say, boy?" Ashton demanded. "This is mutiny. Revolution, indeed. There can be no mercy for revolutionaries."

"I had thought the watchword of this colony, and its rulers, was expediency," Edward said. "You followed that course with the Caribs."

"And you've hated ever since, boy. 'Tis unnatural for a man to hate his own kind."

"I'm yet to find out who are my kind, Hal Ashton," Edward said. "But I did not come here to quarrel. These Irishmen, and Tony Hilton, will fight, as you know. They'll fight much harder than anyone at your back. They'll happily die, with weapons in their hands, rather than return to slavery or the noose. And for every one of them that dies, be sure at least two of your people will go too. Would you offer my father a colony populated by women?"

"I'll not offer him a colony seized by revolution, Edward."

"Nor need you. We realize that we cannot win here. We had been informed there was popular support for me in the town, but it seems we were optimistic. So you'll allow Tony and his men, and his wife, a ship, and let them depart. Hear me out, Hal. We have committed treason and revolution, at my command. It was my doing, and my will, and it is my will that we now end it. I will take the responsibility for all that happened here."

"You think it will be an easy matter?" Ashton asked. "On your surrender you'll be an admitted felon."

"Yet you'll not try Tom Warner's son until he returns," Edward said.

Ashton hesitated. "Aye," he said at last. "You can wait for your father. In that jail over there. But if you suppose he'll encourage leniency toward you, you'll be making a mistake.

Tom has had a bellyful of you, Edward. You'll hang. I do not wish you to be under any misapprehension concerning that."

"Nor am I. You're that angry, at this moment, Hal. But I'll also have freedom for the people in jail now. They must be allowed to go or stay as they choose."

Ashton frowned at him. "You're demented for sure, lad. There is no one in that jail."

"But . . ."

"It was the governor's express wish that we proceed to extremes against no one until his return. If you believed differently, you've been misled."

Misled. Oh, yes, he'd been misled. To the very steps of the gallows. By Susan as well? He could no longer doubt that. But she carried his child.

"Do you agree to my people manning one of those ships?"

Ashton pulled his nose. "They'll be going to their deaths. Hilton is no navigator."

"I suspect he'll live. He means to go no farther than Nevis, for the time being. There's diplomacy for you, Hal. At least in a way you can put to Tom. No bloodshed here, and should he return with sufficient men and a ship of war, why, then, you can easily take the sea against them, over there. Why, man, here's your opportunity to rid the colony of all its malcontents. Offer your own people, such of them as wish to take the risk, passage to Nevis with Tony."

Ashton frowned. "You play a deep game here, Edward."

Edward smiled. "Have you no confidence in those at your back? You can disarm them first."

Ashton pulled his nose some more. "It is certainly a way out of our problem. And we'll have the leader." He glanced at Edward, apparently understanding what had been agreed for the first time. "And you'll stay? To face your father and then the noose? By God, lad, you've courage after all. Of a sort."

Of a sort. The cell was pleasantly large, when he was alone, some eight feet square, room for a man to walk to and fro and to breathe. When he was alone. But this was seldom. Only the twenty Irish who had followed Hilton from windward had been allowed to depart; those who had not immediately jumped to arms at the bidding of their compatriots had been allowed to regret at leisure; now they were more harshly treated than before, and not a day passed but one was hauled to the whipping post or locked in the stocks or clapped into the cell with Edward. Then only his size and his ability with his fists allowed him survival; it was the law in Sandy Point, as indeed it was in England, that once the door closed on a prisoner, he was left to the mercy of his friends.

He'd have starved but for Yarico. She came every day with food. The first morning he had stared at her in amazement and mistrust. The boy Tom lurched at her side, hanging on to her skirt. But then, the skirt itself was unnatural, shrouding as it did those muscular brown legs which had first made him a man.

"Food," she had said. "You eat, Ed-ward."

"Why?" he had asked.

"Ed-ward, Yarico."

"Oh, for Christ's sake, don't start that again. Aren't you my father's woman? By God, you're all of a stepmother to me."

"Ed-ward, Yarico," she said firmly. And shrugged. "Edward, Susan, Yarico, War-nah. You eat, Ed-ward. You must not die."

"They are going to hang me, Yarico. Hadn't you thought of that?"

She tossed her head scornfully. "War-nah not hang his son."

"But he has others, of whom he is proud." Yet he had by then picked up the bread and fried fish. It had smelled so good, and he had been starving. And then she had stood so close. Yarico, the savage. Yarico, the lover. Yarico would survive, as she had always survived. And he still did not even know her age. No doubt she was unaware of it herself. But as he was only twenty, he doubted she was any older.

And now her gaze was as soft as ever he remembered it. "You want Yarico?" she had asked softly.

Yarico, who had destroyed her entire nation to ensure her own existence.

" 'Tis neither the time nor the place," he had said. "But you'll come again, Yarico?"

"Every day," she had promised. "Every day, Ed-ward."

Thus she was able to keep him informed of events in the colony, of the departure of Hilton and Susan and their followers. Quite a band, apparently, for a dozen of the colonists, ... wives and three children, had elected to accom- ... rebels. Not one of them, not even Susan, had come ...d-bye. No doubt, had he led them to battle against their friends, and seen half of them killed, they'd have called him a hero. He wondered that he hated none of them, Hilton most of all. Certainly he had been completely hoodwinked into accepting responsibility for a harebrained scheme which he now knew had never the slightest chance of popular support, and very little more of success, even had they discovered Ashton asleep in his bed.

But the scheme had worked for the Hiltons and their followers. They had put to sea and gained Nevis easily enough, and Sandy Point had been left in self-righteous security, glowering across the narrow passage, remembering and preparing to avenge. As no doubt Hilton was well aware. Yarico brought news, after only six weeks, that the ship they could see anchored off the smaller island had left again, under full sail, for the northeast. Another dream gone forever, Edward thought. Only one among hundreds. But on board that ship would be Susan, and with her, growing in her belly, his son. He had to believe this, as he wanted so desperately to believe it. Without that, his life was indeed wasted, and his brain doomed to extinction.

Those that remained behind found themselves in a new world, dominated by William Jarring and the Reverend Malling. Jarring might have given out that he favored the freedom advocated by Hilton, but clearly he had decided it was more worth his while to support the parson; whatever Mr. Malling's professed repugnance for the high-church principles of Archbishop Laud, he now introduced a rigorous system of attendance at chapel, refusal to comply being punished without fail by a term in the stocks for a first offense, and a spell in jail for the second, while similar measures were meted out to the slightest case of drunkenness, or the slightest altercation. Hal Ashton, however good his intentions and however great his desire to obey the precepts of Tom Warner, very rapidly found himself a cipher in his own colony. The limit to drink no doubt slightly interfered with Jarring's profits, but he clearly regarded this as a worthwhile investment in his future, for with the parson's backing there could be no bounds to the heights at which he might aim.

He visited Edward regularly, to talk of the plans he had for the colony, as if Edward were already hanged, and Philip . . . There was no mention of Philip, and he never visited his brother; while there was no window in the prison, merely a skylight which did not admit of looking at the street. Yet the boy was well, and seemed hardly disconcerted by the turn of events, according to Yarico. But she herself was an enemy of Jarring's, permitted her liberty and her place in the community only by the fear of Tom Warner's return. Edward wondered just what would happen should news arrive that his father was dead, or too ill, perhaps, to resume his duties. Then would this ill-assorted group utterly disintegrate, he had no doubt. He wondered, too, if Father had ever really understood how precarious was the peace of this colony, even with the rebels departed. There were far too many factions, too many memories, too many ambitions, for there ever to be peace here. What had they said so contemptuously of Walter Raleigh's Virginia colony? An ill-chosen lot, hence failure. What would they say of Tom Warner's Merwar's Hope? Nothing different. But at least their leader lived in the colony himself, and could hold them together.

His importance was sounded with the explosion of a cannon from the summit of Brimstone Hill, and a moment later the door opened to admit Mr. Malling, another regular and unwelcome visitor. "You'll be pleased to learn, Edward, that a fleet has been sighted, and is approaching Great Road. 'Tis your father, returning with six big ships. You'd best prepare yourself to meet your trial."

"I'd have thought you'd say my maker," Edward remarked. "You are that determined to have my blood."

"Aye," Malling said. "You'll hang, and stay in chains until you rot, boy, as a warning to all other would-be troublemakers. And you'll not be alone. There are people yet on Nevis, we have learned, left behind by Tony Hilton. They'll be brought back to dangle beside you. We'll have no revolution on Merwar's Hope."

He banged the door behind him, and Edward was left to wait, and remember Father's last return from England, when he had been such a bubbling mass of energy and determination. And optimism. Not the sort of man to hang his own son. But then, he had never supposed that was possible. Or he would not have sacrificed himself. There was an admission of cowardice. But perhaps there was no argument with that. Any other man would have defied the worst the colonists could do, and gone down fighting, rather than tamely surrender himself and his dreams. Because Father might not hang him, but there could be no question as to his exclusion from the succession now.

Meanwhile he had naught to do but wait. Yarico had already been, and would not return before tomorrow. If then.

By tomorrow the fleet would have anchored, and Tom Warner come ashore. Tomorrow. He listened to a hubbub outside, to noise and excitement. Tomorrow. Or this evening? Things might happen more rapidly than he had supposed. But then, would not Tom Warner's first action on landing be to seek his errant son?

Footsteps at the door. Many footsteps. The governor and his advisers come to see the leader of the revolution. Edward stood up, his back to the wall.

The door was thrown in. There were a great many people outside. Strangers, most of them, but very well armed, and very well dressed, too. And closer at hand, Henry Ashton, looking pale and worried, and Joachim Galante.

The Frenchman smiled and bowed. "You are surprised, Mr. Warner? Did you not suppose I would return? We made a treaty with your father."

"A treaty you would now destroy," Ashton growled.

Galante continued to smile. "Circumstances have changed, Mr. Ashton Our two countries are at war. It is my duty to call for the surrender of this colony, and I should prefer to receive such a surrender from you, Mr. Warner, rather than from any temporary deputy governor appointed in your father's absence."

8

The Guns of Spain

The French fleet lay at anchor, perhaps half a mile from the shore. But even at this distance the watchers on the beach could see that every gun was run out, and that the sails remained ready to be unfurled.

"Christ, to know what to do." Ashton chewed his lip.

"By God, that seems simple enough." Edward sucked fresh air into his lungs. To be free, away from the fetid atmosphere of the jailhouse and its uncovered cess bucket. To see blue sky and feel the trade wind on his face. He felt that he could challenge the world. "Monsieur Galante, you seek to bluff us, I assume. Were we to man those cannon which your leader so graciously granted to my father, you'd not land here without loss."

Galante shrugged. "Perhaps not, Mr. Warner. Yet I do assure you that there are three hundred fighting men to be spared from those ships, and still leave them capable of maneuver and action. Should you defy us, why, we shall land farther down the beach and assault you from the land."

"We are capable of turning our cannon to command the beach," Edward said.

"Then will our ships approach and bombard you from the flank."

"In the name of God," Mr. Malling shouted. "That would be nothing less than a massacre."

"Aye," Jarring said. "There are the women and children."

"Of course, gentlemen," Galante agreed. "And we are not murderers. Hence you will observe that we have not even fired into your ships. There are two of them. Sufficient to permit you to evacuate the island."

"And go where?" Edward demanded.

Once again the gentle shrug. "That is entirely up to you, Mr. Warner. It is a large world, full of empty islands. This merely happens to be one of the most attractive of them, and more, it is the one chosen by the Sieur d'Esnambuc on which to create a new France."

"And if we decide to surrender but remain?" Jarring asked.

"That also you are welcome to do," Galante replied. "Our colony will certainly need all the labor it may obtain. Indeed, I am instructed to inform you that the offer of evacuation does not extend to your Irishmen."

"By God," Ashton said. "You'd seek to set us alongside those rascals?"

Galante permitted himself a smile. "To us, Mr. Ashton, it is all a matter of degree. You are both from islands off the coast of Europe, and you both possess a certain indiscipline which renders you bad neighbors, except under duress."

"We are wasting time," Edward said. "My name is Warner, Monsieur Galante, and this island was granted to my father, firstly by Chief Tegramond and then by King James, for him and his heirs in perpetuity. We'll fight, by God. You'll get nothing but a desert, when you force your way in here, and be sure your people will also have suffered."

Galante gazed at him for a moment, and then allowed himself to look at the other colonists, and up the street at the women and the children, waiting at the rear. "Spoken like an English gentleman," he remarked somewhat sadly. "It is but as I expected. However, I must be clearly understood on this point. The Sieur d'Esnambuc will allow no renewal of his offer. Should fire be exchanged, Sandy Point will be reduced by storm, and all within it become the property of the victors. No doubt, Mr. Warner, you have been at the storming of a town? It is not an occasion you would forget. What took place at Blood River will become merely amusing in retrospect."

"In the name of God," Mr. Malling said. "You cannot permit this, Ashton."

" 'Tis the women," Jarring said. "And the children."

"And you call yourselves Englishmen?" Edward shouted. "By Christ, what crawling curs have we here?"

Ashton pulled his lip, took off his hat to scratch his head. " 'Tis a grave responsibility your father placed on my shoulders, Edward. I would he had not done so."

"Then resign your post," Edward said. "'Tis certain you are not suited to it. You never were." He walked away from the group. "You'll remember, Hal. Father did this in Guyana. He called for support. Who'll stay with me and fight for Merwar's Hope?"

The men stared at him, and then at the ships of war waiting in the roadstead. Galante smiled.

"You preach bloodshed and warfare," Malling intoned. "Beware, Edward Warner. Those who live by the sword shall perish by the sword."

"God give me patience," Edward cried. "You'd thus yield to anyone who presents a weapon to your breast? You talk of sailing away to safety? Where will you go?"

"Why, we'll return to England," Ashton said. "This colonizing business has turned out to be a failure, unless supported in strength greater than we have ever commanded."

"England," Edward said contemptuously. "And what of Father? He will be at this moment on his way back here with a fleet of war."

"I doubt that," Ashton said. "He has never obtained such support before."

"Nonetheless, he will be coming, to a colony he left in *your* care, Hal Ashton. Only you'll not be here to greet him. You'll have betrayed your trust."

Ashton licked his lips. "I never wanted the responsibility. He forced it upon me because of his disappointment in you. Well, I resign now. This business is too much for me. I am a sailing master. I was trained to that, nothing more. These five years have brought me nothing but troubles. I'll sail those ships home to England. I will leave tomorrow, and I will take anyone who wishes to come. In my absence I appoint Edward Warner as governor of Merwar's Hope. Now, make your choice, and quickly."

"Spoken like a sensible man," Galante said. "Let us have done with this business. Now, Mr. Warner, will you strike your flag?"

"Touch that flag, sir, and I'll break you neck," Edward said. "For God's sake, are there no men on this island? Do you not understand what these people are about? This is an act of war, perhaps justified by war. France seeks the surrender of Merwar's Hope. Now, should we acknowledge the presence of a superior force, and surrender, our case remains to be decided when peace is agreed. But should we evacuate the colony, why, we will have no claim upon it in the future."

They stared at him yet again. Then Philip pushed his way through the crowd. "I will stay with my brother," he said. "As I too am heir to this land."

Galante burst out laughing. "A boy, a child, and a woman. There's an army, Mr. Warner."

How history does repeat itself, Edward thought. And now for the first time he realized how Father must have felt that day on the Oyapoc. Only here there was not even a John Painton standing by with a reasonable alternative.

"Do not be a fool, Edward," Ashton said. "Why expose yourself to ridicule and mistreatment?"

"Aye," Galante said. "For make no mistake, Mr. Warner; do not suppose that you shall be treated differently from any other prisoner, should you elect to remain. Nor the woman. Nor the boy."

"And there is a place for you on board the ships, Edward," Ashton said. "For all of you. Why, I will go further. Come with us, and the charges held against you will be dropped. I'll enforce an oath from every man present to that end."

Edward seemed to see a red mist rising out of the forest behind him, to come shrouding down over the houses and the beach, to encircle every head. Once he had dreamed of leaving this island. Driven to it by his own uncertain desires. But now, to be driven to it by a pack of cowards and traitorous Frenchmen? Then indeed was he a traitor himself to the colony, to the dream, to the very name of Warner. Better to stay and perish, here.

And he no longer possessed even a sword.

"My father left this colony in the certainty that no matter what happened," he said, "there would be a Warner here when he returned. I shall not betray him. I surrender Merwar's Hope to your superior force, Monsieur Galante, but I do so under protest that it is an act of war, and I intend to remain here, in whatever capacity I may, to await the conclusion of peace, and whatever arrangements may then be made, or the return of my father with sufficient force to regain what is rightfully his, whichever may be the sooner."

The prisoners stood in line, to be inspected by the victors. The sun was high, the sky clear, the day hot. The sails of Ashton's two ships had disappeared during the night, and the fleur-de-lis fluttered from the flagpole in front of the courthouse. Edward stood at one end of the line, with Philip beside him, and Yarico and little Tom beside Philip; beyond them the seventeen Irish laborers and the three Carib women deserted by their erstwhile husbands also waited, with the four other children. All that remained of Merwar's Hope.

"A barbarous name," Belain remarked, taking a pinch of snuff. "We shall restore the original, St. Christopher. It has a ring to it, and is more fitting to a Catholic government. Would you not say, Cahusac?"

The Sieur de Cahusac bowed. Although he sported as much satin and lace as Belain, with his silk stockings and the ridiculous high red heels to his shoes, he was less of a dandy and more of a seaman, both in appearance and in speech. "Nor is this the best position for a seaport."

"Indeed, you are right. We shall leave this place, of course, with its quaint little buildings, as the center of our tobacco industry, but I had already intended to build myself a real town, indeed, a city, in the bay over there, where the ships may lie close to the beach and the land is low for some distance back from the shore, giving us more space to grow. Hence the architects. But wait, the ladies have arrived."

The soldiers from the ships had been drawn up in a guard of honor, and now, walking up the beach, there came the flutter of skirts. Not less than twenty women, in all the splendor of silk and satin, with hair pulled back in great mounds on their heads and little black patches on their faces and chins, with masses of jewels on their fingers, with bare shoulders and plunging bodices, although each lady was protected from the sun by a bright colored parasol held above her head by an attentive young Negro wearing coat and vest and breeches and stockings and shoes in materials and colors hardly less splendid than those of their mistresses.

"You'll bring your men to attention, Joachim," Belain said. "We must give the ladies a treat."

Galante nodded, drew his sword, and signaled his officer. A bugler blew a blast, and the pikemen brought their weapons upright with a clatter and a slap of hands on hafts. The women clapped their hands and exclaimed with pleasure, a babble of high-pitched French. Edward avoided looking at them. They represented the enormous confidence which accompanied Pierre Belain like an aura. He had sailed from France to conquer Merwar's Hope, but not merely with a fleet of war. He had brought his officers' wives, and even the women for his common sailors and soldiers, and he had brought architects, and God alone knew what else, to create his conception of a colony. The idea of failure had not crossed his mind.

But if Edward would not look at the women, the women seemed determined to look at him. They wandered down the ranks of the prisoners, talking to each other behind their fans, laughing and exchanging comments, stopping to gaze at Yarico, and then at Edward, no doubt acquainted that one was a member of the terrible Carib race and the other the surrendered governor of the colony. They exuded perfume, but little beauty, to his eyes; he disliked the caked eyes and the puffy cheeks, the flashing insincere eyes, the obvious layers of clothing which must be clammy with sweat, all the effulgence of court ladies. He had not known this style for too long.

"Now, then, Mr. Warner," Belain said. "I would have you and your people put forward your best appearance. Stick out your chest, man, and take on a manly look. You have a reputation to uphold."

"A reputation, monsieur?" Edward inquired.

"Oh, indeed. Terrible people, the Warners and their colonists. Men who would massacre even the fierce Caribs in their beds."

"And you played no part in that, monsieur?"

"It is not really my style, Mr. Warner," Belain said. "Besides, I would seek to tarnish none of *your* glory. For to these ladies it *is* glorious, you know. As they have naught to do with their lives save their flirtations and their amours, it amuses them to consider men, whom they conquer with such ridiculous ease, as very devils incarnate when opposed to other men. For where is the satisfaction in conquering anything puny?"

Contempt. All contempt. But none to match the laughter of the girl.

His head turned, without meaning to. She stood next to Captain Galante, and was obviously his daughter or his very young sister, for she had his height and even his face. But the features which in the man were gloomy and even sinister, in the girl were almost beautiful. Almost. Her nose was strangely short, and looked out of place beneath the wide-set green eyes and above the equally wide mouth. Symmetry was supplied by the chin, which was also too small for the rest, as it came together in a point. Her neck was long, her shoulders bare, and the cut of her bodice revealed swelling breasts. Yet strange to say, the possible delights of her figure did not at this moment hold his attention. Nor even the splendor of her pink satin gown, not quite brushing the sand and allowing her shoes, of similar color and material, to be seen. Her gloves were white, and her hat, broad-brimmed and drooping over her eyes, was of a dark shade of pink, and sported a tremendous white feather. Her hair was a splendid rich brown; she also wore the fashionable bun, but her ringlets undulated gently from beneath the huge hat to rest on her shoulders and wisp behind, with just a strand in front. It all added up to a picture of grace and health and confidence and wealth he had not seen since leaving England, as if an entire rose garden had mysteriously been picked up and transplanted to this empty shore. Certainly she dominated the other women. Yet none of these obvious attractions equaled the laugh. Here was no simpering smile and no coquettish giggle, no suppressed amusement, and not even the delightful wicked shriek which was Yarico's. This girl laughed with genuine humor, mingled with, he feared, a good deal of contempt, and above all, with a joyous pleasure in being alive, in being where she was and what she was. He received an impression of pink tongue and gleaming white teeth, of head moving backward to display neck and chin.

And then the laughter died for just a second, as she said something else to Galante, before another peal of amusement drifted across the sand.

Clearly she was not the most popular of the ladies, among the ladies. They muttered to each other behind their fans and moved on down the line of men.

"Now, there," Belain said, "you have already caused a disappointment, Mr. Warner. My niece cannot believe that you are the pirate you have been depicted. You must impress her. And she speaks English, you know. Aline, would you care to meet the monster?"

She came closer. She carried a fan, dangling by its string from the forefinger of her right hand. And her dress had a sash, in the same color as her hat, sucking in her already restricted waist, so that it was a miracle she could breathe at all, while every breath brought a vision of swelling white up to meet his gaze. The Negro boy with the parasol hurried behind her.

"Aline, I would have you meet Edward Warner, eldest son of the famous captain. A very devil in his own right, I do assure you." Belain watched Edward.

"I am enchanted, monsieur." Her voice was liquid, but it sparkled.

Edward bowed. "And I, mademoiselle. It is seldom that Merwar's Hope—I beg your pardon, St. Christopher—is graced with such beauty."

"A gentleman," she said. "And a pirate, and a murderer." Her voice had dropped to a whisper, but now suddenly it exploded into sound, bringing all her scented breath into his face. "Monsieur, monsieur, quickly."

He swung around, as did Philip and indeed everyone present, to gaze at the empty street.

Aline Galante's laughter rushed around his head like a tumbling wave. "My apologies, monsieur," she said. And once again her voice dropped to hardly more than a whisper. "I thought I saw a Carib warrior sneaking from house to house. And I was sure you would wish to be informed."

Her gaze held Edward's for a moment, her mouth widely smiling.

"And you were mistaken, mademoiselle," he said. "And perhaps disappointed."

"Oh, indeed, monsieur. But then, so much of life is disappointing. Or have you not yet discovered that?"

"Enough," Belain said. "I would address the prisoners." He stood before them. "Now, mark my words well. I have accepted your surrender in good faith, and would place no more restraint upon you than is necessary. You will work the fields, as in this you are more experienced than my people. You may build yourself some huts at a suitable distance from this town of yours, for my people shall require those houses until our own city is built. Now, your governor has elected to remain with you, and so far as you are concerned, his authority is undiminished. I would have you know that. As for you, Master Warner, I hold you responsible for the behavior of your people, and also for their work. Be sure that you understand me."

"I understand you, monsieur." He attempted to meet Belain's stare, but always his gaze kept straying to where Aline Galante stood next to her father, once again laughing at something, it could have been anything, which had caught her fancy. A woman who either had lived too much, and found all life contemptible, or had not yet lived at all, and therefore found all life excitingly amusing. He wondered which it could be.

"By the great God Himself, I'll work no more this day." Yeats threw down the ax, and threw himself with it.

His compatriots exchanged glances and then slowly lowered their own tools. It was the middle of the afternoon, and the day had been one of extreme heat. But it wanted yet three hours to dusk, and there was a great deal still to be done. Over the past week they had cut down the trees that Edward had estimated they would need, and this day they had commenced cutting the wood into planks. Houses were their first necessity; since the coming of the French, they had slept like savages on the beach. Savages? Why, that was all they were. At the least they had all been so exhausted that even Yarico had gone rapidly into a deep sleep, and he had feared her more than any other. Although perhaps even Yarico, as she cuddled little Tom to her breast, had changed.

Yet he had known all along that the Irishmen would become his most pressing problem, and this confrontation bore no comparison with the brawls he had indulged in during his months in jail. Then he had still been the governor's son, with all the weight of government there to preserve his life until the return of his father. Now he lowered his own saw and wiped the sweat from his forehead. At least they were all in front of him. Only Philip, still chiseling away at what would eventually be a door, was behind him. And Philip, at this moment, he could trust. His plight was no different.

Now, as he straightened and pressed a hand to the aching muscles in his back, the whole afternoon seemed to wait upon his reply. It did not, of course. Even at this distance he could hear the rumble from farther down the beach, beyond Brimstone Hill, where the French were commencing their city, their Basseterre, as they called it. And on Brimstone Hill itself the sentries patrolled between the great cannon; unlike the Warners, Pierre Belain was not the man to risk surprise. He had less faith in human nature. In Sandy Point, the ladies were gathering for one of their soirees, for the first thing brought ashore from the ships had been a virginal, and the last few evenings even the Irish had gathered in a group on the beach to listen to the clear sweet sounds drifting through the breeze.

Perhaps there was reason for the absence of hate. The French had behaved with treachery, no doubt. Yet war had been declared, and if the English were uncaring of it, the fault was surely theirs. Nor had Belain, in seizing the colony while the governor was absent, behaved any differently to

Tom and himself in assaulting the Carib village; he was in pursuit of the most profit for himself and his people. And the French knew more of living than the English. In scarce a week they had changed the very air on St. Christopher. The music was but a symbol of the whole, of the perfume and fine clothes and the styled hair and the glittering jewels and the lilting laughter. Mama should have lived for this, for them she would have lived forever. This was, indeed, the dream that had given substance to the colony. But it would take men like Belain and Galante, and women like Galante's daughter and Belain's wife, to give that dream substance. Because they were gentlemen, and their women were ladies.

And for the Warners? A disappearance from history. A disappearance which had already begun, and was now to be hastened on apace. For the Irish were watching him, knowing too well his reputation for sliding away from violence.

"I agree with you, Yeats," he said. "It is damnably hot. Yet are we not our own masters, and must continue working until dusk. Or we shall have the Frenchman standing over us with whips."

"Let them come," Yeats said, stretching. "They can hardly be different from Jarring's bully boys. And this time they'll take to you and your brother as well. Aye, and the brown-skinned bitch. That'll be amusing that will."

Someone laughed. Philip also stopped work.

Edward walked across the sand.

"Ed-ward," Yarico said. She would warn him, perhaps, that these were wild Irish, who did not fight in any way he had been taught. But then, neither had the Caribs.

He stood above Yeats. "You'll get up, Yeats," he said. "And you'll work until I tell you to stop. We'll maintain our discipline, by God, until my father returns."

"Discipline?" Yeats inquired. "Faith, we'll have none of that from ye, Ted, lad. And ye'd do best to forget your father. He'll not return. And if he does, it'll be to naught of value. Even the Frenchies don't understand that. That sail we saw three days ago, that was a Spaniard, Ted, lad. Ye recognized her yourself. Attracted, she was, by Cahusac's fleet. There won't be a house standing on this island in another month. So where's the point in building more for the dons to burn? If I was ye, Ted, lad, I'd go bargain with the monsieur for a bottle."

Edward seized the ax. "Up, or I'll split your skull."

The sucking in of Yeats's breath was accompanied by similar noises from all around. The Irishmen seemd to be gathering themselves.

"Ed-ward," Yarico warned again.

But he could not look over his shoulder. He could not take his eyes from the man he must dominate.

From the hilltop there came shouts. The guards had seen the coming trouble.

Yeats sat up slowly. "Leave him be, lads," he said. "I'll not need ye."

"Up," Edward said, praying that there would be surrender.

And knowing differently the next moment. Yeats hurled himself to one side, at the same time kicking his feet with vicious accuracy; each toe in turn took Edward at the knees and threw him full length on the sand. Before he could turn, a foot descended on his wrist, pinning it and the ax to the ground, and Yeats stood above him.

"Aye, Ted, boy," he said. "We'll have discipline here. I'll see to that."

His foot swung back, and the toes crashed forward. Edward released the ax and brought up his knees, but not in time; the blow smashed into the pit of his belly and sent rivers of pain streaking away from his groin. And the foot was swinging again.

But it no longer mattered. He knew only the redness which rose out of the sand and the trees and the man in front of him. It was a blood mist which blocked his eyes, because it arose from inside his own brain, clouding all his instincts with the desire to hurt, to maim, to destroy, and to kill, as it had that day in the hold of the *Great St. George*. He moved his whole body at once, caring nothing for the seething pain of the second kick, for the numbing weight across his arm. His other arm, his feet, his knees, and his thighs wrapped themselves around the foot as it ground into his belly, and Yeats fell with a grunt of astonishment. The weight left Edward's wrist, and he turned, fists closed and flailing, landing twice on Yeats's face with spurts of blood, leaving a red mask where they had torn the flesh.

Still on his knees, he reached forward to seize the Irishman by the hair and drag him close for another blow. And was surprised in turn. Yeats twisted and brought his face against Edward's arm, and a thrust of real agony coursed across the muscle and up into his shoulder. He jerked backward with a cry of horror, watched the blood welling from the terrible gash torn out of his forearm by the razor-sharp teeth.

"Get him, Terry," howled the Irish. "We have him now."

Yeats reached his feet, in the same moment as Edward did also. Dismayed by the quick recovery, the Irishman hesitated, and Edward closed again. Blood flew right and left, his own blood, from his arm, and blood from Yeats's face as the tremendous blows smashed into the unprotected flesh. Yeats's knees buckled and Edward caught him by the hair while he hit him again and again and again. The Irishmen fell silent. Yeats was on his knees, still held up by the hair, while Edward hit him time and again, his own hand now starting to swell into mushy ruin.

"Enough." Pierre Belain gave a signal, and two French soldiers moved forward. "Enough, Edward. Will you kill the man?"

Fingers closed on his arm and dragged him back. He stood still, and yet trembled, muscles, fingers, even knees. Sweat rolled out of his hair and down his shoulders, mingled with the blood draining down his arm and dripping from his fingers. And with the sweat and the blood went the hate. He gazed at Yeats, lying a crumpled, unconscious, bloody mess on the stained sand in front of him. By God, he thought, I did mean to kill him. With my bare hands.

But now he was also aware of people. Almost the entire population of Sandy Point had turned out to watch the fight, aroused by the sound of alarm given by the sentries. The music had stopped, and the women were there, too. He looked at them through pain-filled eyes, caught her face for an instant. This afternoon she was not laughing; indeed, for a moment he almost caught a look of admiration, certainly of concern. And it was she who looked away.

"I understand that such an event may be necessary, from time to time, for discipline," Belain said. "And I would not interfere with your methods, Edward. But I can afford no deaths in my labor force. We are short-handed as it is. I have made arrangements, but until new recruits arrive, why, you must take care of your men, and yourself. Now, will you have my surgeon see to your arm?"

"I care it," Yarico said.

Belain glanced at her and nodded. "Then do so, Princess. And the other man."

Yarico tossed her head. "His friend care him. You come, Ed-ward. You fight like Carib. Tom proud."

"Aye," Philip said. "I'd never have guessed you had that much spirit, Edward."

"You'll tend Yeats," Edward told the stricken Irishmen. "And then get back to work."

"And you come," Yarico said. "I have leaf for wound."

He nodded, and looked over his shoulder at where the French ladies and gentlemen were slowly strolling back to the town, their entertainment completed. A burst of magnificent laughter drifted to him on the wind.

From the forest behind Blood River it was possible to watch Basseterre taking shape. In only a month the streets had been laid out. These were marked by no more than stakes driven into the earth, but there were sufficient of them. And there could be no doubt that they would eventually be filled with houses. Pierre Belain possessed all the energy of Tom Warner at his best, and twice his vision. Already he had his men digging drains, over which his city would rise like the new Paris of which he dreamed.

Edward sighed and turned away. He had no business to be here, as the prisoners were strictly confined to the tobacco and corn fields and the small area of beach beyond. But when he chose to disappear into the forest, no man could stop him, or could tell where he was going. That was his prerogative. Caribee.

Yet he must return, in good time, to his people. It was already dusk. An important dusk, this, the Sieur de Cahusac's birthday, and for the occasion Belain had even sent down some flagons of wine to the prison camp. There would be a good deal of revelry tonight, and no doubt a fight or two, which would need ending. How confidently he considered the prospect, while the frightful scar on his forearm throbbed with both memory and anticipation. No man quarreled with him now. And even Philip looked at him with admiration. While Yarico snuggled close to him every night, and grew morose when he would not touch her. As if he did not wish to do so. As if his constantly encouraged manhood over the past few years was now not making itself felt too vigorously. But Yarico, Father's woman, the murderess of her own people, the mother of his half-brother . . .

He crept through the tobacco field, stood in the shelter of the porch of the governor's house, watching and listening. It was a hot night, and the shutters were raised on the courthouse; even from here he could see the glitter within, the acres of bare shoulders and breasts, the swaying, carefully curled hair, the swinging skirts on the magnificent gowns, the brilliant doublets of the men, and flashing jewels and the even more flashing smiles. He could not smell them. There was a shame. But he could imagine the scents rising in that room, the strangely satisfying mingle of perfume and perspiration, overladen with wine-filled breaths. And he could imagine, too, the conversations, the flirtations and suggestions, as he could hear the laughter.

And the laughter made him dream. Of all the French people on the island, he hated only her. Of this he was sure. But it was a hate composed of so many things. She was the epitome of everything a woman should be, and thus everything any women ever possessed by Edward Warner could never be. She was the unattainable, as Mama had been the unattainable. And she laughed at him. But she also found him interesting. He remembered the expression he had caught, for just an instant, the afternoon of the fight with Yeats. She would not have liked to see him harmed, perhaps. But there was a dream, truly unattainable. Yet a dream he was unable to resist.

His responsibility to his own people was forgotten. He crouched in the shadows by his father's house, hour after hour after hour. He watched the moon rise and begin once again its decline behind a broad band of silver stretching forever across the Caribbean Sea. He listened to the noise of revelry also dim, as minds became fogged with drink, and then occasionally burst out again in tremendous sound. He listened to the endless scrapings of the fiddles. He enjoyed strange fantasies. With fifty men at his back, armed and determined, he could this night regain the colony for England and Tom Warner.

In time he dozed, on his knees, slumped against the farthest upright of the porch, and awoke stiff and shaking with the chill that crept over the island in the few hours before dawn. At last the fiddles were silent, and the town, too. Silent, and dark, in most places. Yet not asleep. The noise was now stealthy, but nonetheless obvious to his Indian-trained ears. For there was much to be done, between ending the dancing and the drinking and retiring. Much that could only be done when the brain was befuddled with drink and the body brought alive with endless contact.

The prison camp had also sunk into silence. Yet now he must return there. Perhaps he had been lucky this far to have escaped detection. And detection would certainly bring a flogging. Belain had made it perfectly clear that the town was out of bounds for any of the prisoners. Cautiously he stretched, and then shrank back into the shadows as he heard footsteps.

A couple came out of the forest, on the far side by the porch, but they did not pass the governor's house by. Instead they walked under the porch itself. His heart swelled, and he stood against the pillar, straining his eyes in the darkness, and making out nothing more than the sheen of the woman's gown. Yet, coming here, it could only be one of two. And what had she been doing, whichever she was, this past hour? They whispered constantly, as they approached, but in French, and if she laughed, she did so silently, so that he could not hear her.

Now they had reached the door, and stood there, bodies close as they faced each other. And now there could be no doubt. She was too tall for Madame Belain. Edward sucked air into his lungs, a disturbingly loud sound in the pre-dawn stillness. For a moment indeed he all but took to his heels, for he was sure they checked. But the man was kissing the woman's hands, and leaning forward, as if he would do more.

She made him stop. He hesitated, and then he kissed her hands once more and released them. He stepped away, half-bowed, and made his way down the street.

Aline Galante stood in the doorway gazing after him, not moving, until he was clearly out of earshot. Once he turned, to raise his hand, and she fluttered her kerchief in response. Then he was swallowed by the darkness.

Aline stepped out of the doorway, slowly closing the door behind her, so that the porch was utterly dark. "Who is there?" she asked.

How his heart pounded. How his whole body glowed with desire. He had never known anything like this before. Even with Susan, patient possession had been all he wanted.

"Speak," she said. "You are no Frenchman, that is obvious, Master Warner." As she had known all along, else why address the unknown in English? Why address the unknown at all, in the deserted darkness? But she found him ... interesting?

He stepped aside, inhaled her scent.

"Ah," she said. "It is not the act of a gentleman to lurk in the darkness and watch another man courting."

"Was that what he was doing?" Edward asked. "Courting?"

She came closer. "And of course it is unwise for a prisoner

of war, like you, to lurk close to the house of the governor general. There are two reasons to have you whipped."

Now he could see her face, with opened mouth, smiling, and perhaps even preparing to laugh. Certainly she felt no fear of him. Yet she had watched him very nearly destroy a man. But not a gentleman. Only an Irish laborer, a prisoner like himself. And it had been done with his fists, not a rapier. She knew nothing of him, save his name and his present status.

"You are silent," she said. "Perhaps you are dumb with fear. My father says you are a coward. And yet, I saw you fight. Or were you fighting from fear, Master Warner? It is said that this can drive a man to desperation."

She asked the question with genuine interest. She was investigating an emotion she had only heard her father speak of. Because there was nothing on earth that the daughter of a man like Joachim Galante, the niece of a man like Pierre Belain, should fear.

"Your silence does you no credit, monsieur," she said. "I was disposed to forgive your insolence because I found it flattering that you should stand there and watch me, but now I find it annoying. Be sure that I *shall* have you whipped."

Then be afraid, he thought, and hit her on the chin.

He knew now the power of his fist, when supported by arm and shoulder. Her head snapped backward, and her knees buckled all in the same instant. He caught her before she struck the ground, already unconscious, and threw her across his shoulder. He even had the presence of mind to stoop and recover her fan and the kerchief which had fallen from her hand. For a moment he was enveloped in lace and satin, in beckoning softnesses and strange hardness as his fingers sought to hold her; when he was upright again, he shivered. For now at least he had thrown away life itself.

But before they could seize him and hang him, or worse, there remained a few hours. Perhaps longer. No one knew the island so well as he, save Yarico. And she would not lead them after him. Not this time, he was sure.

He hurried through the fields and into the forest, his shoulder aching where he held the girl. The trees clouded around him, and the branches plucked at his arms and face, and at her legs, held fast against his chest. Yet he made his way with purpose toward the looming height of Mount Misery, with the promise of the windward shore beyond. Hilton's house, not yet completed, but still a house, with its single cannon staring at the other islands of the Leewards, awaiting the return of the Caribs. And Susan's cave, where a man and a woman might lie hidden forever, if they chose.

Her body stirred, and he was exhausted. He took her from his shoulder and laid her on the ground. Already the darkness was tinged with gray, and now he was above the tree line he could look at her with more to see. Her skirt billowed against him, and she breathed slowly and evenly. There was no more reason for clothes now. He intended rape, at the very least. Yet he would not touch her. The wild anger was already past, and he was distressed to discover that her shoes had fallen off.

She sat up, touched her chin, stared at him with a frown. "*Mon Dieu,*" she muttered, and winced. She pulled off the star-shaped black patch on her cheek.

"We've a distance to go," he said. "You'd best get up."

She looked down at herself. "They will hang you."

"This is a big island, mademoiselle. My island."

"But . . . why did you do it?" Her head came up as she gazed at him. "You have the Indian woman."

"And you are not half so intelligent as I had supposed. But you still smell sweet, and look clean, and wear pretty clothes. On your feet."

She started to move, instinctively, and checked herself. "And if I refuse?"

"I . . . I'll hit you."

"Ah. Of course, Monsieur Warner, you are a famous fighting man. With women as well. But not, I think, a famous lover." She threw back her head, and a peal of laughter disappeared into the trees. And then died. "Ouch," she said. "That was very painful. Oh, do not hit me again, monsieur. I am coming with you."

She climbed to her feet, while he gazed at her, big hands opening and shutting in angry impotence. Yarico had been his teacher in every sense. Susan had dominated his every thought. And when she had beckoned, he had gone without thinking, and walked into the deepest of bogs. And now this girl laughed at him. At her own kidnapper. At the man who would soon . . .

"Well, monsieur?" she asked. "Which way?" Again the glittering laughter. "Or have you forgotten? I can show you the way back to Sandy Point, if you wish."

He lunged forward, and she realized that she had after all

made a mistake. Her laughter ceased, and she attempted to sidestep, but he caught the skirt of her gown with his left hand as he lost his balance. She seized the skirt with both hands and attempted to pull it free, found she could not, and tried to stamp on his arm with her feet. But he was on his knees again, both arms thrown around her legs as she kicked, to bring her full length to the ground. The fall seemed to knock the breath from her body, and for a few seconds she lay and gasped. He thrust his fingers into the bodice of her gown, pulling with all his strength. White flesh seemed to leap at him as it was released from its prison, exploding into huge, distended nipples surrounded by the largest aureoles he had ever seen, glowing pink in the first light.

She reached for breath, staring at him and trying to speak, but he would not look at her face. His tearing fingers encountered stiff material and boned corsets, too strongly made for him to rip. His hands slid over them and resumed tearing below. He panted and grunted like a wild animal. And now she had recovered her breath, and sat up to hit him, closing her hands together and swinging them left and right against his head, and having no effect at all except to increase his madness. His last tug was so violent he fell away with it, and lay on his back with the dress billowed on top of him.

Aline Galante turned on her knees as she attempted to get to her feet, a magnificent white-skinned surge of womanhood, all that he had ever dreamed of since that day in the bedchamber with Mama, with long rich brown hair, loosed by the struggle and scattering over her shoulders, with belly still tightly constricted by the corset, and legs still clung to by cotton stockings, and between a wonder world of thick, dark-forested riches, the whole clouded by the perfume she wore, an excitement not even Mama had ever offered, and still dominated by the laughter he seemed to hear ringing from tree to tree.

He caught her ankle, and she tripped, and fell again, and rolled on her back to kick at him, once again realizing her mistake as he retained his grip. "Monsieur," she shouted. "Edward, I beg of you . . ." She knew now that she could not stop him with words, and sat up as he released her to take off his breeches, but he was still quicker than she was, and before she could turn again he had seized her around the waist and laid her flat. Her hands came up, swinging and scratching at his face, and her knees drummed against his thighs as his body slid up hers. They were almost the same height, and his face pressed against hers as he forced her legs down. Still she fought, sobbing and gasping, for breath and with anxiey in the beginning, and then with pain, as his grip on her arms tightened, and as her kicking pelvis became absorbed in his weight, while the ribs of the corset ate into his flesh with a force equal to the thrust of her breasts.

Passion left him with male suddenness, and he was aware only of the softness under him, of the urgency behind her knees as they flopped against him, of her gasps for breath, which mingled with her sobs. In time he moved, or was moved, and rolled into the bushes to gaze at the sky. Never had he wanted woman more. Never had he so hated himself as now.

Aline was on her knees, retching and panting. "Monsieur," she begged. "I cannot breathe. I cannot . . ."

He knelt beside her, fingers tugging at the corset. Now he could see, and now it was easy. And now he could see, too, the blood on her thigh. And now, too, he wanted to weep.

"I'm sorry," he mumbled. "I did not know . . ."

"You took me for a street woman?" The tight bones slipped from her waist, and she inhaled with tremendous satisfaction.

"I saw you with that man . . ."

"*Mon Dieu,*" she said. "But of course, you English are savages. In France, monsieur, a lady's virginity is at least safe until her marriage. That man did no more than kiss my shoulder. Nor would it have occurred to him to do otherwise."

Edward got up, turned away from her. Gone was the exultation and the ecstasy, the anger and the hatred. Now he felt only disgust.

He heard her moving behind him. Doing what? Preparing what tragedy?

"*Mon Dieu,*" she said again. "You have destroyed my dress. You will at least do me the courtesy of returning to the town for another."

He looked down at her. She was quite the most splendid object he had ever seen, with the body of a voluptuous athlete, the slender legs, so white and so absurdly stained with earth, reaching up to the wide woman's thighs, the wonderland beyond, the magnificent breasts, the hauntingly unforgettable face, so beautiful in its very lack of symmetry. the masses of waving mahogany hair, above all else the total distraction with which she examined her tattered garments.

"As you said just now, they will hang me."

She did not bother to look at him. "It is more than likely," she agreed. "But not immediately." Now at last she raised her head, and to his utter amazement burst into a peal of magnificent laughter. "Oh, you look so miserable, Monsieur Warner."

"You . . . you can laugh?"

"Would you have me weep? I did, when you were hurting me and when I supposed that I might stop you. To continue would be to introduce wrinkles into my face, and I should not like that. And why should I not laugh? My maidenhead had to be wrenched from my body at some time quite soon, and there are worse ways to lose it. Why, I would wager you have done me a service."

"A service?"

She stood up. "But of course. For now we must be married."

"Be married?" he repeated stupidly.

"Of course, monsieur. I cannot go to any other man lacking a maidenhead. And you are a gentleman born, are you not? Oh, yes, Papa will insist upon it. And I promise you, Edward, if you are good, I will allow you a wedding night."

"But . . . my crime . . ."

"Oh, for that you will be hanged," she said, and burst into another peal of amusement. "You do not really expect *not* to be punished?"

Edward scratched his head.

"And I," she explained, "will then be a widow. Now, no one expects a widow to possess a maidenhead. Indeed, to a widow all things are possible." She extended her arm. "You may kiss my hand, Edward, and I will accept your troth."

He seized her hand and pulled her forward.

"Oh, no, monsieur," she cried. "Nothing more. Let us endeavor to conduct ourselves, at least in the future, with propriety."

"Propriety." He released her slowly, allowing himself to enjoy her beauty, hoping to be rewarded, and was, with the slightest flush, but only the slightest, and she returned his inspection with interest.

"Well, monsieur," she said, "we can both at least be sure of what we are getting. Are you not satisfied?"

"Are you?"

She wrinkled her nose, a fresh extravagance of sheer delight he had not before observed. "I doubt I shall ever find a body quite to equal yours, monsieur."

"But you will still have me hanged."

"Well," she pointed out, "you have committed a most serious crime. To most fathers, rape is no less than murder, especially of an unmarried daughter." She wrinkled her nose again. "You would not wish to beg for your life?"

"No."

She shrugged. "Then you are at once a gentleman and a fool. Truly, I have often wondered where the one left off and the other began. If you do not hurry to obtain some clothes for me to wear, there will be search parties out looking for me, and I should not like to be discovered naked in the forest."

He clenched his fists in indecision. So easy to take her again, to drive her in front of him, over to windward. Over? They were already there. He gazed through the trees at the beach, at the great rollers pounding on the sand, at the islands beyond, at the ships. Endless ships, one, three, five, seven, ten, fifteen, twenty, more than a score of sails, filtering through the windward passage.

"By God," he whispered.

She stood beside him. Her moist shoulder touched his own. "*Mon Dieu*," she echoed. "But that is an armada."

"You're right. From Santo Domingo. By God, but Yeats is nothing less than a prophet; your uncle has raised a hornet's nest." He turned and ran back through the forest.

9

The Phoenix

"But, monsieur," Aline cried. "You cannot leave me so far from town."

Edward checked. "Then come on."

"Like this? That is impossible."

He faced her. "Aline, that is a Spanish fleet. Have you any idea what they will do to your father, to your aunt and uncle, to you yourself, if they manage to make a landing here?"

"And the Sieur de Cahusac will stop them?"

Edward smiled. "We shall see if your Frenchman are any more courageous than our English."

Aline was pointing. "You smiled. Do you know, that is the first time I have ever seen you smile? Will these Spaniards not also kill you?"

"Undoubtedly," he agreed. "But I have been told that one death is much like another, when it comes to the point." Almost he laughed, less at his own bad joke than at the sheer situation. He was reminded of the middle-sized fish swallowing the little fish, and then in turn swimming too close to the big fish. In the Americas there was no bigger fish than the Spaniards. Besides, it was such a treat to discover Aline looking concerned.

"Well," she grumbled, "at least help me, monsieur."

He knelt beside her, discovering the torn shift and sorting it out from a variety of other undergarments. " 'Tis certain you'll not need this." He threw the corset into the bushes.

"But . . ." she rested her hands on her knees as she knelt, and gazed after it. And then laughed, as only she could laugh. "But of course. Why put it on when a Spanish sailor will soon be dragging it off."

He helped her dress, and they began their return journey, as slowly as they had come out, although it was well into the morning by now, because Aline's feet were soft, and often they had to stop while she massaged her insteps, or Edward had to carry her over outcrops of rock. Yet she never complained, although very soon she panted for breath, and perspiration began to mark that splendid face. Indeed, by the time they regained the forest behind the town, she was a sorry sight, her hair scattered in every direction, the last of her paint gone, her gown torn and stained with dirt and leaves and sweat, her feet coated with dust beyond the ankles, for her stockings had disintegrated.

"Well, now," he said. "You'll be all right here, Aline. You can watch what is going on, and I'll try to get some clothes out to you. And if you begin to worry, you can always come in as you are."

"I am starving," she pointed out. "Do you realize that it is past noon? And what are you going to do, anyway?"

"First of all, inform Monsieur Belain of what is sitting on his doorstep."

Again the tremendous laugh. "And do you not think he knows?"

He followed the direction of her pointing finger. Brimstone Hill was a mass of soldiers, their officers gathered at the seaward parapet, gazing through their telescopes; and indeed, on the faint breeze he could now hear the rumble of cannon.

"Nevis, by God," he muttered. "I had no idea there was anything there worth bombarding."

The French fleet was also active, with boats constantly plying to and from the shore, and sails being made ready.

"You'd best forget about your appearance and come now," Edward suggested. "I doubt that Monsieur Belain intends to pit six against thirty, after all."

"*You* had best hurry, Edward," she said. "Fetch me a cloak. That will do. And some bread and cheese and a bottle of wine."

"One day, mademoiselle, you are going to have to look at life a little more seriously."

"One day, monsieur, I shall be old and gray and have grandchildren, and I hope that they too will be able to make me laugh. Now, do not say that you will not kiss your betrothed farewell, even if only for a few minutes."

He hesitated, and then lowered his head and brushed her on the lips.

"Oh, Edward," she said. "That was the kiss of an old married man. Not an ardent lover."

He pulled himself away and ran through the trees, followed by her laughter. He gained the beach north of the town, to find his Irishmen, with Philip and Yarico and Little Tom, and the Carib women, gathered on the sand to watch the ships. From here Nevis was out of sight, but there was no mistaking the anxiety of the Frenchmen, nor the fact that they were packing up; boxes and bales had appeared on the street, and the women were hurrying back and forth.

"Thank God you've come back," Philip said. "Where in the name of heaven have you been?"

"I went over to windward, and saw the dons. Seems there must have been more of them than I thought, and farther south. 'Tis fortunate we are that they chose to stop at Nevis first. Why have you not been to Belain to inquire his arrangements?"

"Sure, and those beggars will not let us past, Master Edward," Yeats declared.

For there was a platoon of French marines, fully armed and looking suitably determined.

"Spaniards bad people," Yarico said. "Many dead."

"And this lot ain't staying," muttered another of the Irishmen; the first pinnace was loading with women, to take them out to the ships.

"Come on," Edward said, and went along the sand.

"Halt there, monsieur," said the young officer in charge. "My admiral will have no panic."

"Panic?" Edward demanded. " 'Tis not us that are panicking. What, does your commander mean to cut and run?"

"The governor has the safety of his people in mind, monsieur. That is a fleet of war out there."

"And what about *my* people?"

"I do not know, monsieur. No doubt his Excellency will acquaint you with his plans in due course."

"I'd speak with him now, if you will permit it, lieutenant."

"I do not permit it, Monsieur Warner."

"Then tell Monsieur Belain, and Captain Galante, that I have news of Mademoiselle Galante."

The officer frowned. "News, monsieur?"

"You are aware that she is missing, are you not?"

"I had heard . . . You'll come with me, monsieur."

"We'll all come," Edward said. "Will you lads stand by me?"

"Well, sir," Yeats said, "we might, if we knew what ye was after."

"I'm after bargaining for our lives, Yeats, and I think we'll do best by staying close."

"Then we're with ye, sir."

The officer chewed his lip. And then came to a decision. "You'll march in close order, monsieur. And you'll obey my commands."

"Willingly," Edward agreed, and fell in at the head of his men, with Philip at his side and Yarico immediately behind him. The marines took their places on either side of the group and marched them toward the town.

"What do you seek?" Philip muttered. "Belain will not find us a place on those ships."

"Then he must let us make for the interior of the island now. To stay here is to be murdered," Edward pointed out.

They approached Sandy Point. From the street to the landing stage an avenue of soldiers had been formed, and down this the women, assisted by the sailors, were carrying their belongings, chattering at each other in French, alarmed, certainly, and yet apparently still confident that they could escape the coming holocaust. By now, too, Brimstone Hill had been abandoned, and the officers were returning to the beach.

The prisoners and their escort were halted by a captain, who exchanged remonstrances with the lieutenant, waving his hands in the air, shouting, and gesticulating, and being at last interrupted by Belain himself, accompanied by Galante. They also spoke with the lieutenant before turning to Edward.

"What means this demonstration, Warner?" Belain demanded. "Where is Mademoiselle Galante? We have had a patrol out searching for her this last hour."

"They'll not find her," Edward declared with a sinking heart. Because however modest she was, she would certainly have heard and no doubt responded to their halloos.

"But you know where she is?" Galante demanded. "Why, you insolent young puppy . . ."

Belain made a remark in French, and his brother-in-law fell silent.

"You abducted her?" Belain asked very softly.

"I asked her to become my wife, Monsieur Belain."

"You . . ." He burst into laughter. But there was a little humor in his eyes. "I see. And when she refused . . ."

"She did not refuse, monsieur. She accepted, and we took a walk in the forest to plight our troth."

"To . . . By God," Galante shouted, reaching for his sword.

Once again he was checked by Belain. "I have no doubt my niece will confirm your story, Edward. So, then, why keep her hidden?"

"I but wish to know your intention regarding my people, and myself," Edward said.

"Ah. Well, as you will have observed, the dons appear to resent our settling in their islands, so we shall have to take ourselves off. There is a pity, now, but I have no doubt at all that we shall come back when the power of Spain has been whittled down a little further. I tell you the truth when I say that I had no idea they yet mustered thirty men-of-war in Santo Domingo. Why, they must have scoured the entire Caribbean to find them. But they are here, and the odds are unsuitable."

"You mean you will abandon the colony?"

"Indeed we must. Our investors will not be pleased. But who knows, we may be able to use our time well, before we finally leave the Antilles. If every ship the Spaniards can muster is here, there must be one or two unprotected ports which *we* can visit with profit."

"And us, monsieur?"

"Why, Master Warner, as you so gallantly insisted on remaining to watch your property when Monsieur Ashton left, I naturally assumed that you would not be prepared to allow the Spaniards to make free with your town. Do not tell me I was wrong?"

"I admire your humor, sir," Edward said. "You'll know as well as I that the Spaniards admit no rights of warfare to intruders in the Indies. They will treat anyone they can catch as a criminal. And a heretic."

"Indeed, I have heard that," Belain agreed. "But then, of course, in landing here with your father and three other men, you were prepared to risk Spanish wrath. I find your attitude at once unexpected and disappointing."

"And the fact that I am betrothed to Mademoiselle Galante has no effect upon your reasoning?"

"By God," Galante growled. "Give me half an hour with him . . ."

"There will be no need, Joachim," Belain said. "I assume you are jesting, Monsieur Warner. I do not know what witchcraft you practiced upon the poor child, but you must know that I could never permit such an alliance between a niece of mine and a half-savage such as you. Now, come, tell us where the girl is, and we shall let you go with your lives, at the least. Otherwise, by God, I shall hang every man of you within the hour. And the women."

Edward hesitated, pulling at his chin.

" 'Tis the best we can hope for, Edward," Philip muttered. "You said we could take to the wood. The dons will not stay long."

"Aye," Yeats said. "Better comb the beaches here in St. Christopher than live as French slaves for the rest of our lives."

"Come, come, Edward," Belain said. "Time is passing."

"You'll let me and my people go," Edward said. "As soon as I have told you where Mademoiselle Galante is?"

"You take us for children?" Galante growled. "Suppose she is dead."

"She is not dead. And by our lights, she is not even harmed. Refuse me this, sir, and I will cheerfully hang. And I observe that the firing from Nevis has stopped."

"We have got to be away, Joachim," Belain said, "and we waste our time here. Edward, will you give me your word as an English gentleman that you will direct us truly, and that Mademoiselle Galante is unharmed?"

"I do, monsieur. And you will let my people go, on your word as a French nobleman?"

"Here is my hand upon it."

"Bah," Galante said. "Dealing with these dogs. I'd as soon hang them anyway."

"Mademoiselle Galante is in the forest immediately behind the town, monsieur," Edward said. "At least, I left her there. Her gown was torn, and so she asked me to procure a fresh one before she would return here. I am sure she is waiting with much impatience. And now, gentlemen, we shall bid you farewell."

Belain gave a stiff bow. "Perhaps we shall meet again. Edward. If the Spaniards leave you a head on your shoulders. Adieu."

He led them along the beach at the double. Yeats would have stopped to pick up what gear they could carry. but Edward would not give them time for this. He did not trust the Frenchmen, and he wanted to be away from the beach when the dons arrived.

"But where will we go?" Philip asked.

"Mount Misery for a start," Edward said. "And then windward. From Mount Misery we will be able to see what is happening, and on windward we may well lie safe until the dons have departed."

"And then what, Mr. Warner?" Creevey, the half-wit, asking the one question he dreaded most.

"Why, then we shall build ourselves a new town," Edward said with all the confidence he could muster. "And plant ourselves a new crop. This is all my father and I, and Ashton, and Berwicke, and Hilton did when first we landed. And then we had the Caribs to worry about."

"And when the dons come back again?" Yeats panted.

"I doubt they will. They were but offended by the sight of the Sieur de Cahusac's fleet. We order things with more modesty, and so have remained untroubled these five years."

And soon after this exchange they ran out of breath, which was all to the good. Edward could not help but wonder what would happen when the Irishmen remembered that there was no longer any outside force to fear, save the Spanish, which would equally affect them and their masters. Against seventeen men he could pit himself, Philip, and Yarico and the three other Carib women. Persumably they would follow the lead of their princess.

They climbed through the forest, listening to the dying sounds of pandemonium from the beach. The jungle grew thicker, but Yarico knew more ways through it than even Edward, and they made good time, stopping only to slake their thirst from the various mountain streams which cascaded down from the summit of old Misery. And by the middle of the afternoon they had reached the very place, just above the tree line, where Edward had been the previous night with Aline. A place of blessed memory, but of strange memory, too. He could hardly believe that it had happened, that he had committed rape and that the girl had laughed. He had lied to Belain and her father about her physical well-being. To them she was no doubt as badly hurt as if he had cut her face with a razor. But she had laughed. Aline Galante, a face, and a body, and a mind, and above all, a laugh, to remember. And what, he wondered, would she remember about Edward Warner, the white Indian? He thought she would forgive the lie, even if her father was unlikely to. She might even honor that memory of him, for risking so much to save his people.

The Irish had collapsed in exhaustion, and Philip was also sitting down, the boy Tom beside him. Yarico stood at the edge of the forest, gazing at them, her face expressionless. Edward wondered what *she* thought of it all. In the five years since the English had first landed, her life had gone through too many changes. And now she was watching him.

He climbed a few feet higher up the mountain, and found himself somewhere to sit. From here he looked down on the leeward beach no less than the windward; back there was utter confusion, still; men running back and forth, the ships already breaking out their sails, although yet at anchor and clearly not possessing their full complements, and muskets being fired, into the air, he presumed; he could see the puffs of black smoke. It almost suggested a mutiny. Belain would have his hands full. But more likely they were endeavoring to recall the search parties which had been seeking Aline, now that she would have rejoined them.

It was time to forget the French; Nevis held more promise of catastrophe. From his vantage point the island was more than ten miles away, and yet he could see the column of smoke rising from the shore. He wondered if the smoke rising from the destroyed Carib village had looked like that, say, from Antigua. But from this distance, too, he could also make out the Spanish fleet, apparently still at anchor, but endless ships dotted all over the bay. There was a deep game being played here. The Spanish admiral was clearly under orders to destroy all foreign settlements in the Leewards, but he had no intention of engaging the French fleet if he could avoid it, even with a superiority of five to one. He was giving Cahusac and Belain every possible opportunity to escape, was no doubt watching them through his glass with as much anxiety as Edward was watching him.

Yarico sat beside him. "Ed-ward," she said. "Yarico. Philip. War-nah." She laughed.

"Just as we began. With less, maybe."

"War-nah," she said again. "Ed-ward War-nah. Philip War-nah. Yarico War-nah." She waved her arms. "All War-nah."

"If we live that long, sweetheart, to be sure."

"Ed-ward . . ." She looked down at her gown. "I take off?"

"No."

"Ed-ward . . ."

"You don't seem to realize that you're all of a stepmother to me now."

"War-nah speak to me of this," she said. "I mother, you

son, you obey. I take off dress, and you come with me in forest."

"No."

She frowned. "I beat you, Ed-ward."

He caught her wrist. "You're a funny child, Yarico. You must try to understand. You and me, that is over now. When my father returns, I doubt not that he shall make you his wife. Before the priest. Then indeed you will be my stepmother. And then, if you like, you may beat me."

She pouted. "No," she said. "They say . . ." She tossed her head at the Irish. "War-nah not marry Yarico. Yarico got brown skin."

"The color of your skin doesn't matter to Tom Warner," Edward said. "You're the mother of his son, just as Rebecca was the mother of Philip and me. And Sarah. By our law, our religion, a man may have only one wife. But now that Rebecca is dead, why, he may marry whomever he chooses. And he has chosen you, Yarico. That will be a great day. You will be Mistress Warner. You will be part ruler of this island."

She did not look mollified. "Yarico already ruler of this island. Yarico last of Tegramond's people."

He hesitated, but decided against telling her that Wapisiane had survived. That secret he would have to take with him to his grave, as it came back to haunt him in the small hours of the night. "Aye," he said. "But then you'll be the first of Warners' people as well. Come. They've rested long enough."

Hilton's house remained as they had left it on that unforgettable night five weeks in the past. The roof timbers lay waiting to be set in place, and the thick wooden walls rose out of the rocks of the bluff he had selected, like the bones of some gigantic skeleton. A skeleton with but a single tooth, for the cannon still pointed aimlessly seaward.

"You do not think they will look for us over here?" Yeats asked.

"Not this night, at any rate," Edward said. "And here at least there is food and wine." For no one had been to windward since Tony's departure, and the carefully constructed cellar containing the salted beef and the barrels remained unopened. "Tomorrow, Yarico, you must show us how to gather food from the forest itself, which berries are edible and which poisonous. And we must get Tony's fish nets working again as well. We shall do all right over here; the forest is thickest, and there are also caves in which we can take refuge, so the dons will not find it easy to pin us down. But nonetheless, we shall take care. This night we shall all sleep sound; as from tomorrow we shall post guards."

They gazed at him, reminiscent of a flock of sheep. For the moment they were too frightened and too tired to do more than think of their immediate needs. And too thirsty. Their eyes kept straying to the house.

"Aye, help yourselves," Edward said, and with a whoop they ran for the trapdoor.

"Is that wise?" Philip muttered.

"The sooner it is consumed, the better. And it will give us time to think. It may not have occured to you, brother, but we do not possess a weapon between us save our knives, and we are outnumbered ten to one by our servants."

"Yarico will show us how to make weapons of wood, as the Caribs do," Philip said. "Yarico?"

Yarico continued cuddling little Tom, who was already asleep.

"She's preparing to sulk," Edward said.

"A strange woman," Philip said. "How Father can ever . . . But what has she to sulk over now?"

Hardly stranger than you, Edward thought. At fourteen I'd have found her attractive enough; I did. "Who can understand the mind of a woman?" he said with suitable pompousness. "And you'd do best not to criticize Father. He is all the hope of survival we have at this moment."

Yarico pointed. "Canoe come."

"Eh?" Edward scrambled to his feet, peered into the darkening sky. "By God."

For now that it occurred to him to look, the tiny bark could be seen cautiously negotiating the surf.

"Indians, you think?" Philip whispered. "Shall I call the men?"

Already sounds of song came from the house.

"Not a war party, that's certain," Edward said. "It is too small a vessel. And there cannot be more than four people in it." He knelt beside Yarico. "What do you make of it?"

Again the disinterested shrug of her shoulders.

"Yarico," he said. "In a moment you are going to make me angry. And it would not be good for a son to spank his own stepmother."

Her eyes gloomed around him. "Spank?"

He seized her shoulder, pulled her body toward him, and

struck her smartly on the left buttock. "Like that. Many more like that."

"Ed-ward," she exclaimed in delight. "We go in forest, for spank?"

"Oh, for Christ's sake," he shouted. "All right. We go into the forest for spank. Just tell me what you can about that canoe."

She released Tom and stood up. It was quite dark by now, the boat no more than a silhouette on the suddenly still evening. "White people."

"White people? But . . ."

Yarico tossed her head. "Hil-ton."

"Tony? There's a gift from heaven. Come on, Philip . . . ."

"Not Hil-ton," Yarico said. "Hil-ton woman."

"By God." He ran down the beach, sand flying from his feet, Philip beside him. Yarico and Little Tom followed more slowly. "Susan?" he shouted. "Susan, is that really you?"

The canoe came into the shallows. It was paddled by O'Reilly in the stern and Connor in the bow; amidships sat Susan Hilton and Margaret Plummer, the wife of one of the colonists who had volunteered to accompany Hilton to Nevis, a small, quiet woman of about thirty, presently looking as if she had seen a ghost.

But Edward had eyes only for Susan; he bounded into the water to help her, and to look at her, too, for her belly was beginning to swell.

"Edward?" she whispered. "Oh, Edward. I had not thought to see ye over to windward."

He smiled. "Maybe you thought I'd be hanged by now. It's not so easy to dispose of a Warner."

She put up her hand to stroke his chin. "And ye've a beard, all but. Ye'd naught but a little down six weeks ago."

"So maybe you'll grant that I'm a man, at last. And you are well?"

"Well?" She shivered, and he set her on the sand.

"Ye'll know the dons have taken Nevis, Ted, lad?" O'Reilly demanded.

"We saw them," Edward said. "But I'll confess I had no idea any of you remained there. You told me naught of your plans before you left, remember?"

"Aye. Well . . ." He nodded to Connor and between them they pulled the canoe clear of the water. "The business was done in haste."

"He's dead," Margaret Plummer muttered. "Dead. Do you think he's dead, Paddy?"

O'Reilly scratched his head. "Well, he'd be dead by now, Mrs. Plummer, that he would."

"Oh, aye, Mrs. Plummer," Connor agreed. "He'd be dead by now. Is that our boys we hear over there, Ted?"

"You can join them in a minute, Brian. Tell me what happened on Nevis. How many of you were left there?"

Susan led the way up the beach, still moving with all the vigor he remembered, despite her handicap. "Just a dozen, Edward. It was Tony's decision. He knew we could not make a go for the colony without more people, and he feared to be dispossessed when your Father comes back. We held a conference, and decided it was best for him to return home and obtain the grant of Nevis, before Ashton could spread lying tales about him."

"But he left you behind."

"I am pregnant, as he then knew. And I was in good hands. We anticipated nothing from the dons. Especially after the French left us alone. 'Tis what your father did, Edward. Successfully."

"He screamed," Margaret Plummer whispered. "I heard him scream. Christ, I can still hear him scream."

"What happened?" Edward asked again.

"Took by surprise, we were, Ted, lad." O'Reilly stopped beneath the house and gazed up at it, hands on hips. "Sure, and 'tis good to see the old place again."

Susan sank to the sand beneath the outcrop. "Maybe we'll get a roof on it at last, Paddy."

Edward looked from one to the other. No mistress and servant, there. But then, had they not been members of that first shipload, so long ago? "You were telling me of the Spaniards."

"Well, we saw the ships, Ted, lad," Connor said. "But it never occurred to us they'd pay attention to Nevis. When suddenly they pulled aside and opened up. We'd only a few huts on the shore, and these they scattered with their first balls. But then they landed. Must have been near a thousand of the devils, all crimson and silver. A pretty sight."

"A pretty sight," O'Reilly agreed. "A column of maneaters, coming ashore like if they was on parade."

"He would go back," Margaret Plummer whispered. She had dropped to her knees beside Susan. "He would go back."

"Aye, and he took his friends with him," Connor said.

"Against our advice, Ted. But there was gear on the beach, and the Spaniards had camped upwind of where we'd been. Two of us had been killed in the bombardment, it had been that sudden. Harry Plummer took Billy Smith and his brother and the other two girls back to see what they could pilfer. They'd not have us along, ye understand. Wild Irishmen who'd make a noise, they said. Christ Almighty. And we've forgotten more about that kind of thing than they'll ever learn. Not that they'll learn anything now."

"The dons caught them?"

"We watched from the hilltop. There was firing, and Billy Smith fell. Maybe he was killed. He was that lucky. They got the girls, and Harry and Joe Smith as well."

"They cut off his feet," Margaret Plummer said tonelessly. "Just cut them off at the ankles, and left him there. And his wrists. They cut off his hands at the wrists, and smeared the stumps with honey, and left him on the beach, to the sand-flies."

Edward stared at O'Reilly in horror.

"Fact, Ted. 'Tis what they have threatened to do to every interloper they find in these waters."

"He screamed," Margaret said. "And screamed, and screamed. I asked Paddy to go down and put a bullet in him, but he wouldn't."

"They'd have got me too," O'Reilly objected. "Long before I could have got close enough to hit him right. But I'll admit it was a terrible sound."

"And the women? What happened to the girls?"

Connor grinned. "Well, Ted, they was taken too, like we said. They screamed too."

"But afterward?" Edward demanded. "What about afterward?"

"Now, that we don't know, Ted, lad," O'Reilly said.

"You left them?"

"There was nothing we could do," Susan suddenly shouted. "What, two men and two women, one of them pregnant? There was nothing we could *do*."

"So you came here."

"Man, it takes a lot of guts to paddle a canoe across that strait," O'Reilly said. "More than once I figured we was for it."

"Aye," Edward said. "It takes a lot of guts. Your friends are over there, Paddy. And they've found a couple of bottles. Mrs. Plummer, Yarico is with us. She'll look after you."

They hesitated, and walked up the sand. Susan started to follow them, and then checked. He could not see her face properly in the darkness.

"Ye'd have done the same, Edward."

"Maybe." Edward knelt beside the canoe. Three muskets, but less than twenty balls and scarce sufficient powder for two discharges. Two swords, and a pistol without any charge at all. Oh, they had left in a hurry, all right.

"Maybe? Ye'd not fight at Sandy Point."

"My own people, Susan? No, I'd not fight on those terms."

"And that sticks in your craw?"

"That you'd not say good-bye. Neither you nor Tony. Nor Paddy O'Reilly, nor any of the others."

"Maybe we thought ye'd let us down. Oh, for Christ's sake." Her shoulders rose and fell. "I'm sorry it turned out that way, Ted. I still dream about ye. But it'll not do me much good now, will it?"

"And the boy?"

"His name will be Hilton."

He took her elbow, and they walked up the beach behind the others. "That's fair enough. You expect Tony back?"

"He's my husband."

"Well, you'd best pray he comes soon. You'd not figured the dons will be here next?"

"They're on their way now, Edward," Aline Galante said from the bushes close by the beach.

"For Christ's sake," Susan said.

"Aline?" Edward peered into the gloom. "What in the name of God . . ."

"I followed you through the forest," Aline explained. "But when it got dark, I lost you. And then I heard your people singing."

"She is French," Susan said in wonderment.

"I wonder *what* she is," Edward said. "Aline, did you not hear the shots and the shouts of the men searching for you?"

"Oh, yes," she said. "But I could not go out. My gown is torn, and my shift as well. And then I saw you take your people along the beach, and knew that you intended to remain, so I thought I had best do the same. Edward, I am so terribly hungry."

"But your father . . ."

"Was like a madman on the beach. He had to be forcibly carried on board the ships. I think Uncle Pierre must have convinced him I was dead. Edward, I am also terribly thirsty."

"But . . ." He scratched his head. "You saw the dons, you say?"

"Yes. They weighed anchor at sunset. The breeze is light. They will not be here before morning."

"But do you not understand? They will land and burn the town. They will come looking for us. They will hunt us like dogs. We shall have to exist in the forest, if we can exist at all. You have all but condemned yourself to death."

"But I will have you to look after me," she pointed out. "And you know this forest better than any Spaniard. *You* must understand, Edward, that I could not possibly return alone to Papa and tell him of my situation. With you gone, he would surely had whipped *me*. But when he returns, after the Spaniards, why, then we will be able to explain the circumstances to him. They may even seem more natural then."

"Your situation?" Susan inquired with interest. "Ah, I see that Master Warner has been up to his old tricks."

"We are betrothed, madame." Aline gave a contemptuous glance at Susan's belly. "I am assuming it is madame? But unfortunately, we cannot make our love known at this moment, because our two countries are at war, and Edward is indeed nothing better than an escaped prisoner. Yet I cannot desert him."

"By Christ, she's a lady," Susan said. "Ye'll be the second lady on St. Christopher, mademoiselle. 'Tis not an attitude we're accustomed to."

"Indeed?" Aline demanded. "Then I had best see about redressing the situation."

"God give me patience," Edward cried. "Will the pair of you stop chattering? Aline, your father is not *coming* back. Belain has abandoned the colony and means to return to France. If he does ever return here, it will not be for years."

She stared at him, frowning.

"And in addition, we are not betrothed. I raped you. Can you not understand that? I felt lust for you and anger against your people, and the pair of those emotions got the better of me. How can you talk about love?"

"I must grow to love you, monsieur," Aline pointed out, her voice suddenly cold. "As it appears that now most certainly we are to be man and wife. This is a duty I have long known would be required of me, and I do promise you that I shall endeavor to perform it to the best of my ability."

"God's truth," Susan said.

"Of course," Aline continued, "if *you* find it impossible to love *me*, then I shall be forced into a solitary existence, yet it is your duty, as a gentleman and as my husband, to honor me and respect me, at least in our outward relations. I do not know what this woman is to you, but I did understand from my uncle and even my father that you were a gentleman born, and I expected to be so treated. Which is to say that our private affairs should not be discussed in front of anyone."

"God's truth," Susan said again.

Edward scratched his head.

"So I would be obliged, monsieur," Aline concluded, "if you would either provide me with food or kill me now. That would be preferable to a slow death from starvation."

Edward sighed. "There is food at the house, mademoiselle. And I apologize for any rudeness I may have shown or any inconvenience I may have caused you. You are of course welcome to share in whatever I and my people have *to* share, until some better arrangment can be made."

"God's truth," Susan said a third time.

"I'd be obliged if you'd take Mademoiselle Galante to the encampment, Susan, and see that she is fed and given something to drink. And, Susan, she is in your charge. Be sure that if any insult is given her I'll break the head of the man responsible."

"*You'll* do that?" she asked.

"Aye, me. Tell Paddy O'Reilly to have a talk with Terry Yeats. Now, be off with you."

"While you do what?"

"I've a spell of thinking to do."

He walked away from them and into the forest. A spell of thinking. It seemed as if all the problems in the world had suddenly closed in on him, in a matter of hours. That the Spaniards would land and destroy Sandy Point, and everything else they could find, seemed certain. That they would launch themselves into a full-scale hunt for any white men on the island was at least likely, and that they would torture and maim whoever they found was as certain as anything else on this earth; they did not regard heretic intruders in their world as human. That twenty-odd people condemned to exist in the forest would very likely starve to death was no less likely, even with the aid of Yarico. The Indians were used to a diet of fish, and fish required the spreading of nets off the shore, in the open and with a great deal of time at the disposal of the fishermen.

That Susan and Paddy O'Reilly and Brian Connor would prove disruptive elements was no less certain. They felt contempt for him, and Paddy O'Reilly would regard himself as a different proposition from Yeats. That Yarico would do nothing to make life easier for him was also not open to doubt. And that Aline Galante would prove a continuing problem was most certain of all. Aline Galante. Truly it could be said that one's sins came home to roost. He dared not allow himself to consider his own feelings toward the girl, beyond a compulsive admiration for the remarkable way in which she had accepted the consequences of her ghastly mistake. It occurred to him that she was probably the most remarkable woman he had ever met.

He climbed, for hours, up and then down. He found the place he was looking for, and eventually slept, on his belly, face pillowed on his hands, worn out by exhaustion and tension. And awoke soon after dawn, to peer down at Sandy Point and Great Road and the armada which had appeared there. Endless ships, all he had seen at sea yesterday morning and perhaps more, most at anchor but some still arriving and taking their positions. Boats ferried men ashore, and the beach seemed to have become a solid mass of glittering pinpoints as the first rays of the sun picked out the shining morions and breastplates, the halberd points and the sword handles. It was a splendid picture, the steel being set off by the crimson doublets and the flutter of their flags, dominant among which was the red and gold of Spain. There were too many to be counted, but he could estimate several hundred men on shore already. And now he could see the dogs. Would he had his own to set against them. But they had gone with Belain, and the French fleet was lost beyond the horizon.

He waited for the puffs of smoke to arise from the town, and saw nothing. Save the men, patrolling the street, no doubt exploring the houses. The dons had not come to destroy yet. For others were investigating the corn fields and the tobacco plantations, talking among themselves, good fellows and honest husbands, who had yesterday raped two girls to death and cut off the hands and feet of their male victims because they were not considered part of the human race.

He watched a group of officers on the beach. A table had been erected, with stools, and they were spreading maps, rough sketches, apparently, for each peak had to be identified with pointing fingers. But they were planning a campaign. They meant to scour the island. Hardly more than thirty square miles in which to hide, and the dogs would soon reduce that to nothing. Already a file of men was ascending Brimstone Hill; the two cannon would be the first to go.

He got up, turned his back on the invaders, and climbed once more into the woods. Caribee. He was still more than half-Indian in his strength, the ease and the purpose with which he traversed this forest. Yet would even that strength avail him, running, before the dogs? And how could he teach the Irishmen to move as he did? Or Philip, for that matter? Or the pregnant Susan? Or Aline, used to ballrooms and topiaried garden paths?

He checked, as he approached the windward shore. The sun was high now, and sweat streamed down his body. He was afraid of them, because it had always been his nature to be afraid. He was, despite his victory, afraid of Yeats and his companions, afraid of Paddy O'Reilly, his strength and his determination, should he ever seek to use it. He was afraid of Susan's tongue, as he was afraid of Yarico's anger, as he was equally afraid of Aline's trust. And Philip? He was afraid even of Philip's eventual usurpation of his rights.

But was he not, of them all, the only one without cause to fear? Did they not fear him in even greater proportion? Could he not turn his back on them, and survive? Even on Yarico, encumbered as she was with little Tom. He needed none of them. Without him, without his leadership no less than his knowledge of this forest, they would be helpless, easy victims for the dons and the dogs.

He walked across the sand. An amazing thought, because it was just as likely that the dons, unaware of the massacre at Blood River, knowing only that the French had sailed away, would also be afraid. It would be no more than the nervous tension of men about to go into battle, uncertain of what was opposed to them, unknowing which of them would survive the coming days. But it was nonetheless fear. A fear which could be made to grow.

Of them all, only he had no cause. Provided he kept his wits about him, and remembered that while he was in his element, they were like fishes cast on the shore, and left to drown in fresh air.

He stood before the house. No guard, naturally. Such a thought would not occur to Paddy O'Reilly. They had drunk all of Hilton's wine, and lay scattered about the sand, snoring. The women were absent. What had happened here last night?

"On your feet," he shouted, and kicked O'Reilly in the thigh.

The big Irishman sat up and scratched his head. "What? What? By Christ . . ."

"Aye, and if I had been a Spaniard you'd have been looking Him in the face, if He'd have you."

O'Reilly scrambled to his feet. "Are they coming, then?"

"They are," Edward promised. "Get your friends awake, and be sure they're sober. Where are the women?"

"They took to the house," O'Reilly pointed.

Skirts fluttered, as Susan and Yarico climbed down, followed more slowly by Aline and Philip, and then by Meg Plummer and the other Carib girls and the children.

"We thought they'd taken you," Susan remarked.

"I'm not that easy to take. But they'll be here in a couple of hours."

"*Mon Dieu*," Aline said. "But why should they come here?"

"Because they mean to make sure there are no human beings left alive when they leave. They know we've spread over the island." He frowned at her; her face was pale, and it was evident that she had scarcely slept. "Are you all right?"

"Yes, monsieur." She glanced at the Irishmen, who were gazing at her. "I suffered no more than threats."

"For that night," Susan said. "I'll not stand in front of her again."

"They remember too well she's French, Edward," Philip said.

Aline's pointed chin was thrust forward. "I am one of you now."

Edward nodded. "You are that. Well, Yarico?"

Yarico shrugged. "Ed-ward, woman," she said. "Ed-ward must care."

"I intend to. And what will the rest of you do when the dons get here?"

O'Reilly looked at the canoe. "There's Antigua."

"Ten miles of open sea in that piece of bark? And there are Caribs on Antigua, Paddy. They'd have you strung up before you got landed."

"We'd best take to the woods," Yeats said.

"For what?" Susan demanded. "The dogs will hunt us down."

"True," Edward said. "If they're set to it. And they will be."

"By Christ," O'Reilly said. "Are we done, then?"

"Very likely," Edward said. "And we'll be done quicker by either sitting here and quarreling or skulking around the bushes waiting to be dragged down to the beach."

"So what do we do?" Connor demanded. "Flap our wings and fly away?"

Edward faced them. "They've come here to destroy a rival settlement, made up of tobacco farmers, not soldiers. They're not considering a fight."

"Oh, sure," O'Reilly said. "Right cowards they are."

"I never said that, Paddy. I'm just stating what's in their minds. They want to destroy all foreign settlements in these islands. Otherwise they'd not have gone on to Nevis and given Monsieur Belain time to leave. That's clear as day. And now they're expecting no resistance. And why should they risk their lives? There's nothing here to interest them. Some tobacco, a little corn. They'll have that aboard by tonight. And they don't know what's in that forest."

"And you aim to tell them?"

"Just that, Paddy. We'll make up a story and tell them that."

"Ye'll fight them?" Susan cried.

"You think they'll just look at you because your belly's got a bulge?" he shouted. "It'll make for variety. Aye. I mean to fight them. Every Spaniard we kill gives every one of us a better chance of survival. I'm telling you, they didn't come here to die."

"And we've our hands," Connor said sarcastically.

"Yarico and I will show you how to make bows and arrows. We have our knives. And we need but one success to gain all the arms we need. By Christ, what are you staring at? You just agreed we were done. This way at the worst we can take a couple of dons with us. What are you, men or cattle? You're men, by God. Irish men."

"It'll be like old times," Yeats muttered. "But who'll lead?"

"I'll lead," Edward told him.

"You?" O'Reilly demanded. "I doubt ye've the belly for a game like this one, Ted, lad."

"Maybe you'll find I've changed, Paddy," Edward said. "You'd best ask Yeats."

"Fisticuffs," O'Reilly said. " 'Tis not the same as cutting a man's throat, now, is it?"

"I'll lead, by God," Edward said. "Because my name is Edward Warner. Because this island is mine. And if you care to dispute that argument, Paddy O'Reilly, you'd best do so right away."

O'Reilly hesitated, glanced at his fellows, at Susan, at Yarico, standing there with solemn faces. He shrugged. "Ye'll lead, Ted, lad. At the beginning, to be sure."

And at the end? The end meant just one unsuccessful engagement. Thus he sweated, as he lay on the ground on an outcrop of rock above the windward beach, and looked down at the smoke rising where Tony Hilton's house had stood yesterday. And counted the Spaniards; twenty men and an officer. Exactly even, in numbers of men. But those down there carried swords and pistols and halberds. And they had two dogs, now casting about the beach, sniffing, and finding, as they were intended to. Oh, God, he thought, if Father were here. Then there would be no question as to the success of the coming engagement. If only Father were here. But to gaze at the horizon in the anxious hope of seeing a sail was to lose resolution in a dream.

A rustle had him turning, knife thrust foward. Just three days ago this girl had smelled of perfume, had laughed with the confidence of a lady making her way through a world filled with eager admirers, had preferred to remain in the jungle rather than walk the street in front of her friends in a torn gown, and had made up her own rules for the living of life itself.

Three days ago it might have been possible to doubt just how much of a human being she was, and how much of a fancy doll. Not any longer. She had discarded her gown and wore her shift, as did Susan. Indeed, he had watched her staring at Yarico, who had preferred to revert entirely to the Indian, with thoughtful eyes, where it would never have occurred to Susan to go that far in the search for forest freedom. Aline's feet were bare, as were her shoulders and the curves of her magnificent breasts, and now they were tinged pink by the continuous sun, as were her cheeks and forehead. In places the flesh was rough and threatening to peel, as his had done on the voyage from England, how many eternities ago? Her fingers, long and delicate, were still topped in places by the slender nails, but these also were no longer white. Just as her mind could no longer be the web of cultured artificiality he had taken and crumpled beneath his hands, as he had done to so many minds. She cleaned fish with Susan and Yarico, she disappeared into the forest with them for her necessaries, and she endured the glowing gazes of the Irishmen without embarrassment any longer. Only in one respect had she preserved her individuality; rather than leave her mahogany-brown hair to float in the wind and catch on tree and twig, as did the other women, she tied it back with a length of cloth torn from the hem of her gown, by her action leaving her face curiously exposed, almost like a boy's, and thus increasing at once its strength and its beauty.

There should have been another aspect of her unique personality to be admired, but for three days she had not laughed. Perhaps that first night had revealed to her with too startling a certainty just what situation she had placed herself in. Or perhaps she doubted him. Because for three days he had done nothing more than treat her as any of the other women, and in this she lacked the intimacy, as she had lacked the knowledge and the experience, of Susan and Yarico. But there was no other way. The Irishmen were as hungry as he, and for him to give way to his desires, even for a moment, would be to expose her to everything they dreamed of, and their dreams filled their eyes and their faces every time they looked at her.

So now she was risking too much. "You should not have come," he said.

"No one saw me leave. They are too excited and too frightened."

"And you are not?"

She knelt beside him. It was remarkable how the traces of perfume came to him, even above the sweat. But it was the sweat more than anything, the moisture which accompanied her, which made him want her more than any woman since he had wanted his own mother. "Yes," she said. "But I am happy to be so. These past few days I have wondered how I ever managed to exist, before. Was not all mankind intended by God to live like this? And womankind, too?"

"You'll find it uncomfortable if it continues too long," he said.

"Never. I but lack your affection."

He sighed and turned back to watch the men on the beach. "You understand our situation."

"Yes. But that is no reason for you never to smile on me. And now we are alone."

"You think so? They will have missed you by now, and now they will know whence you have gone."

"Well, then," she said, "the damage is done."

He could not stop his head turning. She was not three feet away from him, the skirt of her shift pulled up to reveal her knees as she knelt. "Can you not wait until we are married, mademoiselle?"

"I could, monsieur. Supposing I was certain of that event. I do not speak now only of the Spaniards. I speak of surviving them."

"Then you have lost your faith in me."

"I would know whether it was no more than lust."

No more than lust. No more than lust, at this moment, certainly. Compounded not only by her nearness and her loveliness, but by fear, of the coming few minutes, of his own reaction to it, and of what might happen afterward. "You have lived with my people for three days. You have talked with Susan and Yarico. Do you think I am worth much as a husband?"

"They tell me very little."

"Yet their contempt for me must be evident. You'd do best to wait until our situation is resolved. I am no less confused than you. To claim you now, of your own free will, were to damn you forever to living at my side. And you may prefer to seek your comfort elsewhere, given time."

"Thus you say I made a grave mistake in deserting my father."

"Aye," he said. "You did that, Aline. Now, hurry back and tell them that the dogs have picked up our scent."

As they had been intended to do. The two mastiffs on the beach were casting into the trees, and baying their eagerness into the morning air. And the officer was giving orders to his men.

Aline stood up. "You are a savage, Monsieur Warner. I suppose I understood that from the moment of our first meeting, and yet I could not believe it of a white man with a background of gentility. My father was right. I apologize for forcing my company upon you, monsieur. Be sure that I shall not do so again."

She went through the trees, and he sighed. Christ, how complicated life had become. But if he were a savage, would he not merely have thrown her on her back, at this moment, and taken his pleasure from her, and then gone to battle without anxiety, in the sex-induced euphoria which would carry him successfully through whatever lay ahead?

If he were, indeed, a savage. But now, at the least, he must fight like one. He was on his knees, watching the last of the Spaniards enter the forest below him. He turned and made his way back through the forest to where he had left his people. He could have arrived only seconds after Aline, and found them staring at him. Whatever she had said, they would have no doubts as to what had happened in the woods. And, thinking in terms of savages and savagery, what had he here? He gazed at the sweating faces, the loose mouths, the tongues which came out and circled the thick lips, the sharp teeth beyond, the straggling beards, the tattered breeches which were all any of them wore, the naked Carib girls and the three white women, standing with Philip—Philip, so like Father, who still wore a shirt. They knew nothing of his plans, for he had told them nothing; not even Susan suspected what was in his mind. They knew only that in two days they had been unable to master the small, light Indian bows Yarico and her companions had made for them. For missle power he must rely on himself and the four Caribs. But the Irish were nonetheless fighting men, who would do what he commanded, a wolf pack who would follow him at least once. He wondered if Aline realized that as she stood beside them. But no doubt Aline, with the still-undamaged self-confidence of hers, supposed that in experiencing Edward Warner at his worst she had actually experienced mankind at his worst, and having survived, she had nothing more to fear.

And then, had they not been savages, would success have been the least possible?

"They are coming," he said. "Down there will lie our salvation." He pointed, and heard Susan's breath as she caught it.

"Down there?" O'Reilly peered at the crevasse. "We'll be naught but bits of meat hung out for the dogs."

"You'll be surprised," Edward said.

"Bad place," Yarico said. "Spirits of dead down there."

"I've no doubt they will be," Edward agreed. "In an hour or two. Down you go, Susan. You'll have to show these bold lads there's nothing to be afraid of. You too, Margaret, and take these children with you. Over the inner lip, Susan, and into the burning cave. You'll keep the children quiet, and no matter what happens, you'll not come out until all sounds of battle have ceased. You understand me?"

She hesitated, and then nodded. "And the Frenchie?"

"Stays here," Edward said. "I've a task for her."

Aline's hair flew as she turned her head sharply.

"All right," Susan said. " 'Tis a fact I'll be small value in a set-to. Come on, Meg. And ye lot. Godspeed, Edward. And to your boys, Paddy O'Reilly."

O'Reilly cocked his head. "Them's the dogs."

"So we'd best hurry," Edward said. "You'll take your lads down, Paddy. You'll find more space than you suppose, so you'll split up, ten to each side. It'll be dark as the pit, but after a few moments you'll get used to it, because of the light coming over the back."

"And what will ye be doing, Ted, lad?"

"My job is to get the dons into the cave. As many of them as possible. But you'll not move, Paddy, and not one of your people will move, until Philip here gives the signal. The dons are as superstitious as anyone. They'll be worrying about the dark and the glow from the inner cave long enough. When the signal is given, you'll fall on them. But you'll mind out for mademoiselle here. She's going to be more use than any one of us, and you remember that. But there's another thing. This is just the first shot in our war. There mustn't be any survivors."

Now, where had he heard someone say that before?

The baying of the dogs was close. Paddy O'Reilly looked at Brian Connor. "Ah, well," he said. " 'Tis certain we'll die more quickly if we stay up here, Brian boy." He sat down and disappeared. The rest of his companions followed.

"Now, Philip," Edward said, "you'll take command. When you hear my call, you'll give the word down there. Arrange your men along the outer walls, and tell them not even to breathe until they get the signal. And be sure that Susan and Margaret Plummer and the children stay in the inner cavern."

"Man, 'tis sure a wondrous place." O'Reilly's voice ghosted up to them.

"But what is that light, to be sure?" Connor's voice shook.

"A natural phenomenon," Edward reassured him. "Now, be quiet." He held Aline's arm. "Would you assist us, mademoiselle?"

"But of course. It is all of our lives, is it not?" She freed her arm.

"Then listen well. I wish you to remain here, to allow the Spaniards to catch a sight of you. They will certainly like what they see. Then you must run away from them, and jump down into the crevasse. Once in there, you must run through the cave and join Susan and Meg."

"And the Spaniards?"

"Most of them will wish to follow you inside, or my estimate of human nature is sadly at fault. You'll understand there is a risk there. Should you slip, or fall . . ."

She tossed her head. "I am not so easily overcome, monsieur, when I am prepared. You took me by surprise."

"Aye. Well, it is less the men that worry me than the dogs. Now, prepare yourself."

He showed Yarico and the other three Carib girls that he wanted them to climb the trees close to the entrance, with their bows and a supply of arrows. "And you'll shoot straight, Yarico," he said.

"Yarico always shoot straight," she remarked.

"I've no doubt about that. Who do the Caribs pray to, just before battle?"

She pointed to the sky. "The Caribs pray to Sun, Edward. Sun is cacique of all things, unless sleeping."

"Well, he's wideawake now. Ask him to keep an eye on things, will you?"

He climbed the tree he had selected for his own, carrying one of the heavy muskets and all the powder and balls; he was himself not sufficiently accurate with a bow. It was nearly noon, and the heat came boiling down through the thin tree curtain. And now he could hear the dogs quite loudly, and even the cries of the men; they could tell their animals were onto a human scent. He flicked sweat from his forehead, dried his hands again, and watched Aline. She knelt by the crevasse, as he had instructed her, apparently busying herself with gathering some bark. But she too was listening; he could see the color in her cheeks, and he could watch the rise and fall of her breasts. She was a young woman of rare courage. And rare beauty. And even rarer spirit; it was possible to suppose, watching her expression, that she was enjoying herself.

A dog yelped, close at hand, and Aline stood up. There was a shout in Spanish, followed by a chorus of excitement. Aline glanced through the trees, and then ran for the cleft, sitting down and sliding out of sight.

Through the bushes came the dogs, held on leashes by two of the soldiers. The rest followed in a close group, discipline forgotten as they hurried for the picture and the promise which had been presented to them. But discipline, as Edward had hoped, was slender—at this moment, in any event. The crimson jackets were made darker by sweat; more than one morion had been removed and was carried under the arm, leaving the man at once vulnerable to a blow on the head and incapable of quickly drawing his sword.

The dogs came up to the crevasse, and shied away from the utter darkness within. The men gathered in a cluster before the aperture. But now the dogs were casting on either side of the entrance, beginning to show an interest in the trees, clearly scenting the Carib girls and perhaps Edward. Once again he flicked sweat from his forehead, and leveled his already primed weapon.

The officer in command of the search party came to a decision and signaled half his men. The girl had gone into the cave, and he was not going to let her escape. The officer sat down and slid into the darkness; he had not even bothered to draw his sword. His men followed, one by one, a dozen of them, leaving eight standing around the entrance. The odds were not as good as Edward had hoped, but they obviously were the best he was going to get. He threw back his head and shouted, "Now."

Pandemonium broke loose. From inside the cavern there came shouts and howls, as the Irishmen, their eyes by now accustomed to the gloom, laid about them on the temporarily blinded Spaniards. The men at the lip insensibly gathered closer together. They could hardly be missed, although as they all wore cuirasses it was still necessary to be accurate. Edward fired. His ball caught one of the men in the thigh, and he gave a scream and fell to his knees. Yarico and her companions were far more deadly; one of the dons took a barb through the neck, and hit the ground with scarce a sound. Two others were wounded about the face, and the remainder gazed in horror at the forest as four more arrows struck home. There was one survivor, and he dived for the entrance to the cave, again as Edward had hoped. Three of his comrades were dead, and the other four lay on the ground vainly tugging at the barbs lodged in their flesh.

"The dogs," Edward yelled, for the mastiffs were at the foot of the trees. A moment later they were stretched on the earth, and Yarico came sliding down with the utter ease common to the Indians' prehensile fingers and toes. Edward followed more slowly, then ran to the entrance of the cave. The wounded Spaniards stared at him with wide eyes, and one said something, clearly a plea for mercy. But he had no means of coping with prisoners of war, even had he been able to forget the people on Nevis. "You'll see to these men," he told Yarico, and slid into the entrance.

The battle in the darkness was also over. Now the Irishmen moved around their victims, completing their dreadful work where it was necessary, loosing morion and breastplate, sword belt and pistol holster.

"*Mon Dieu,*" Aline said from the inner lip. "But I was afraid, Edward, I confess it now."

"And they're dead." Susan sat beside her. "Every last one of them? Ye have a way with ye after all, Edward. I never doubted that."

"By God," O'Reilly shouted. "He's the kind of general we've needed. With this armor and these weapons, why, we'll show them dons a thing or two. Aye, Ted, lad? Nay, I'll not call ye that again, I swear it. General Warner. Aye, General Warner, ye'll tell us this is but the beginning."

Edward gazed up through the aperture at the forest outside, and the brown-stained grass, where Yarico and her girls were stripping one of the living Spaniards, to slice the raw flesh from his buttocks.

"Aye, Paddy," he said. "This is but the beginning."

10

The Crisis

Edward knelt on the sand to draw with the end of the stick he held in his hands. "We can start to take the offensive now," he said. "I'd judge they're more scared of us than we of them."

He gazed at the men standing around him. They wore armor, cuirasses, and morions over crimson Spanish doublets and new Spanish breeches; they carried pistols and arquebuses, and every man wore a sword. Yet they were the same Irish devils who had once mocked him. Lacking two of their numbers, alas. But Yeats and his friend had died well, fighting a rearguard action on the day they had been caught too far from the cave.

And the women. Susan, who seemed to grow larger every day; she still wore no more than her shift, which drew tight against her belly. Aline and Meg had actually found themselves breeches to fit their thighs and shirts to cover their breasts and shoulders; if the result was the display of more white leg than any man present had ever seen before at one time, they were actually far more decently clad than when reduced to their tattered undergarments. Yet they had not really changed, either. Meg Plummer still fought like an avenging angel, and Aline . . . Aline played her part as required, but she had withdrawn her mind. The brutality, the bestiality, the utter absence of civilization with which she was surrounded had at last proved too much for her. She spent much of her time with the children, talking to them and entertaining them. But this was to the good, because the children were always a problem. Little Tom more than most, as his mother reached back into the savage recesses of her mind for survival. But little Tom was Aline's favorite. He was a Warner.

Yarico. She stood immediately behind him, her shadow falling across the plan he would draw. Her three compatriots were beside her. They had lived long enough among the white men to know that they no longer belonged there. White men did not live as they did because they had fine clothes and big houses and huge ships and noisy guns. They apparently believed that it was best *to* live as they did. But survival depended upon these four women, in more ways than one, and they had utterly reverted to their native state, wearing no more than the aprons of their childhood, carrying their bows at all times, and waiting eagerly for the next occasion to pounce upon an unwary Spaniard.

That first day, that first victory, Paddy O'Reilly had vomited, and Aline had all but fainted. And Edward had found the officer's pistol and shot the Spaniard through the head before he could suffer further. And only then stopped to think. What a terrible word for the commander of a desperate band of human beings fighting for their lives. Thought implied so many things, involved so many aspects of the business of living he had always rejected as utterly horrible. Thought composed the entire reason for the hatred between his father and himself. Thought had convinced him that the Spaniards must also be convinced that there were many, many people, savages no less than white men, lurking in the forests of St. Kitts. This was the name the Irish had give to the island, and it was far more fitting than the papist St. Christopher or the pompous Merwar's Hope.

So, of them all, only he had truly changed. He was shocked every time he saw himself reflected in a pool of water. But this was a pleasant shock. His size, for he dominated them all alike by his height and his breadth; his full fair beard, which fitted naturally into his uncut hair; the firmness of his mouth—here was a far cry from the vacillating creature of only a few months before. But here, too, was a man who understood only death and destruction, survival by whatever means came to hand, however horrible.

Thus he had taken his decision. The dead had been neither buried nor burned. They were stripped of their clothing, mutilated and carved, and heaped on the beach by Hilton's house. There the ghastly, stinking remains had been discovered by the next patrol. Then the forest had come alive. But he had taken his people back into the recesses of Susan's cave, and there they had remained in utter security, to venture forth again and annihilate another patrol two days later. And give one of the living captives to the women, so that nothing could be left as doubt in the dons' minds.

This second catastrophe had stung Don Francisco de Toledo into action. The Spaniards had moved forward as an army, so quickly and in such numbers that the guerrillas had been taken by surprise. Hence the loss of Yeats and his friend. But thanks to that sacrifice they had got back to the cavern, and while over a thousand Spanish soldiers and sailors had tramped the beaches and the forest trails, they had remained in safety hidden away beneath the earth. Yet the character of the cave had certainly changed. It had changed that first day, when a dozen men had died inside its eerie half-light. And it had continued to change ever since, as more than twenty people had used it as a home. Its beauty had dissolved in oaths and blasphemy, in crude jokes and cruder songs; its air had become filled with the stench of human sweat and human excreta; and its dark corners had been filled with eyes watching and wanting. Theirs was a sexless society, because Edward Warner so ordained it, and because they knew that they lived by virtue of his leadership and his determination, and his ability. By his talents and his courage he had gained an ascendency over these people in a way his father had never done. This was a remarkable thought, but it was nonetheless true.

And yet he never doubted by how slender a margin his superiority ranked. His biggest headache lay in the fact that the women were as eager as the men. Not Susan, perhaps. But then, Susan merely hated the destruction of this private world in which she had spent so many hours. The Caribs, certainly. Aline, at least as regards himself. Even Meg Plummer, perhaps. They were young, strong women, living close to death and in circumstances of utter intimacy with a score of young, strong men, whom they daily watched killing and hunting in their defense. Only by working them all to the point of utter exhaustion could he keep them from each other's crotches, and, by an almost inevitable sequence of emotions, from each other's throats. Certainly there was work to be done. The fish had to be caught and gutted in the black hours before dawn, when the Spaniards did not venture over to windward. And they could not live on fish alone. They suffered from a food shortage as it was, even if Yarico and her girls managed to keep them supplied with fresh fruit. But yet the spur was action against the dons, for which they relied upon Edward's imagination and leadership. And for two days now no Spaniards had appeared on windward. Thus it was necessary to take the fight to them; last night four of the Irishmen and two of the Carib girls had been late returning to the cave, and no one doubted the cause of their delay. Tonight it would be an increasing problem.

So he drew his map upon the sand. "Like us," he explained, "the dons need fish to eat. They spread their nets in the shallows off Blood River, where the Indians used to spread theirs. The nets are guarded, to be sure, but by not more than a dozen men; I have seen them. And they are well removed from the main force, which is encamped in and around the town, as you'll know. Now, there is the obvious way to discourage those bastards. Destroy their nets."

" 'Twill be risky," Paddy O'Reilly objected.

"For Christ's sake, Paddy, just kneeling here is risky," Edward pointed out. "Why do you think there has been no patrol over here these last few days? Because they are afraid. We have made them afraid. They think of us as ghosts, because we disappear whenever they come close. We must be sure that they remain afraid. That they grow more afraid. And that they become more uncomfortable. Deprive them of a couple of days' food and there will be rumblings of discontent within the Spanish camp itself."

O'Reilly shaded his eyes. "Maybe we won't have to go so far."

Edward stood up, watched Brian Connor staggering up the beach, kicking clouds of soft sand into the air behind him.

"He looks as if *he's* seen a ghost," Philip remarked.

"Well, there's sufficient of them on this island, to be sure," Susan said.

"What is it, Brian?" Edward shouted. "Are the dons mounting another expedition?"

"They're away," Connor shouted. "They've embarked," he shrieked. He came up to them, threw himself full length on the sand, and rolled on to his back, arms and legs outflung. "They're licked, Ted."

Edward glanced at the Irishmen, watched the emotions—relief, delight, surprise, joy, and frustration—flitting across their faces. Then without a word to each other they ran for the path which led up Mount Misery. They climbed and kicked each other, hurried and tripped, tumbled and rose again, barked shins and knees and shoulders, exchanged excited opinions and ambitions, and gained the open space above the tree line, from whence they could look down on Leeward. But long before they reached their vantage point they saw the smoke, rising above the remains of Sandy Point. From the ledge itself the erstwhile town made a sad picture, somehow more horrible than Edward remembered the same site after the hurricane. For this day the sea was calm, the breeze light, and Sandy Point had been more than an accumulation of huts. But now they all burned, individually, to reveal the dons' attention to detail, and generally, as the smoke from each blazing roof merged into the smoke from the next blazing roof, as the pillars supporting the huge porch of Government House crashed outward, and the roof itself fell in, through the bedrooms and into the chamber where Tom Warner had entertained his guests.

But the desolation was not confined to the town; behind it the tobacco plantations and the corn fields were flattened areas of dusty earth. And still the horizon was dotted with sails and pennants and flags, with mahogany brown hills and curling white wakes, as the fleet gathered way before the gentle southerly breeze.

Philip knelt beside his brother. "By all the rules of warfare, we can claim a victory, Edward. *You* can claim a victory. We are left in possession of the field."

"Aye." Edward glanced at the awestruck Irishmen. "Our misfortune is, Philip, that there are no rules on St. Kitts. We make them up as we go along."

Even from a hunderd yards away, the heat clung to the air; the smoke had mostly died by now, and only the glowing ashes remained. Occasionally there was a rumble as a pillar or a roof, made from greener timbers than the rest, came crashing down to send a shower of sparks upward.

"It'll have cooled by morning," Edward said. "We'll get to work then."

"To work?" Connor demanded. "And what work were ye considering, Ted?"

"You'd spend the rest of your lives lying on the sand?"

"There'll be a ship along," O'Reilly said. "An Englishman or a Dutchman. We'll beg passage on that."

"You'll desert the colony?"

"Colony? For Christ's sake." O'Reilly removed his helmet and unbuckled his cuirass. Here was the problem; beside his armor he was carefully laying his brace of pistols and his sword. And most of his companions still wore theirs.

"And for the meantime," Connor said. "We'd best come to an accommodation. We're entitled to relax and enjoy ourselves."

Another of those occasions he had long known would come. He had Philip by his side, but there were seventeen men opposed to them. Aline and Meg and Susan stood with the children, a little to one side. They watched, and waited, and endeavored to preserve their composure. The Carib girls had gone to see what had become of the fish nets.

"What sort of an accommodation were you thinking of, Brian?" Edward said quietly.

"Well, our creature comforts, mostly, Ted," O'Reilly said. "Now we no longer have the need of a leader, we're thinking of a democratic society, like. Share and share alike. Now, there's nineteen of us, all told, and there's seven women."

"Saving that Susan ain't good for nothing," Connor pointed out.

"Aye, so it really works out to one woman to every three and a half men. But I've a better idea, Ted, lad. Your brother ain't hardly even a half, yet, and ye've no taste for the flesh, now, have ye? In any event, the brat in Sue's belly is likely yours, by all accounts. So we'll let ye take care of her, and the rest of us will take care of the others, which'll give us better than three to one. We'll work it out."

"No," Meg Plummer said. "Edward, you cannot permit this."

Aline said nothing; she breathed deeply and there were pink spots on her cheeks.

"And if I'd not agree?" Edward demanded.

"Why, then, lad, 'tis sorry we'll be, to be sure, but we'll be inclined to take what we require. Ye'll not draw a sword against me, Ted. We'll have your throat cut before ye can get it clear of your scabbard."

"For God's sake," Susan shouted. "Can ye never stop fighting? Where would ye be without Ted? I'll tell ye. Ye'd be lying on that beach, bits of ye."

"Sure, and we know that, Sue," O'Reilly agreed. "So we're content to leave him be, and leave ye be as well. All we're claiming is our just rights as men. 'Tis what we fought for. Just as, make no mistake, he fought the dons not for us, but for this island. Well, he can have it, after we're gone. Now, then, Ted, lad, take Sue and your brother and make tracks into that forest."

Edward hesitated, glancing at Philip.

"You cannot leave Aline and me to these men, Mr. Warner," Meg begged.

"Be off wi' ye," O'Reilly growled. "Be off wi' ye, before I changes my—"

The *phssst* cut the afternoon air like a physical impact. The shaft slammed into O'Reilly's chest with such force it knocked him off his feet, reducing his words to a bloody froth.

"By Christ," Connor yelled, reaching for his sword, to be halted by another singing arrow, which sliced into his thigh.

"You stop," Yarico called from the bushes. "I kill you all."

The Irishmen gazed at the trees, and waited; they knew too much of her accuracy. O'Reilly tried to sit up, and fell back, coughing once again. Susan hurried forward to kneel beside him.

"God's truth," she whispered. "He'll not survive."

"You come," Yarico called. "You come, if you want. We go. You come, Ed-ward?"

"I come," Edward said. " 'Tis sorry I am about this, Brian Connor, but you brought it on yourself. Get that arrow out and patch up the blood, and you'll be all right. Aline. Meg. You'll bring the children."

He drew his pistols, and Philip followed his example, and they slowly withdrew up the beach, while the Irishmen gazed after them and muttered to each other and O'Reilly coughed his last on the sand, the arrow sticking skyward from his chest like an avenging finger. After a moment's hesitation, Susan laid his head on the sand and followed the other women. Yarico stood at the edge of the trees with her three companions.

"I owe you my life," Edward said. "And not for the first time. I wish I could understand you, Yarico."

She tossed her head. "Yarico War-nah," she reminded him. "Ed-ward War-nah. Philip War-nah." She smiled at her son. "Tom War-nah." She extended her arms to embrace the entire island. "War-nah land."

The Irish knew too much about the cave and the defenses of the windward coast. Edward preferred to make camp on the upper slopes of Mount Misery, from whence they could command both coasts and even the sea beyond, and where there was a spring they could use for fresh water. Food remained a problem, which necessitated a trek down to the beach every day to clear the nets and to search for fruit. But for this he was grateful. It was necessary to keep occupied, or he had no doubt that the women would in time become quite as unruly as the men had been. And soon enough they relaxed most of their precautions. The Irish never came to Windward. They never seemed to go anywhere, but camped on the beach beside the burned-out ruin of Sandy Point, fishing where they could, living on the coconuts which grew in profusion along the shore. O'Reilly had died, and Connor was not quite in the same mold. Lacking leadership, they were content to lie on the beach for the rest of their lives, if need be.

For the rest of their lives. From the upper slopes of Mount Misery, the other islands—Nevis, Antigua, Montserrat, even the more distant peaks—were clearly visible. And the sea between. An empty sea. The Spanish fleet had sailed north, and left desolation behind them. Not even a Carib canoe. For the word would have spread across the islands that the dreaded dons were out in force, and even the Caribs preferred to remain hidden until quite sure the danger was past.

And Pierre Belain? Back in France, no doubt. Grieving for the death of his niece, for the loss of his investment. Although perhaps he had managed to recoup himself as he had hoped. But, assuming Aline to be dead, he would be vowing vengeance on Edward Warner. So would Joachim Galante. Another pair to set beside Wapisiane. And how many others?

And Tom Warner? And Tony Hilton? It was now near a year since they had sailed away. To be lost at sea? To decide that it was not worth their while to come back? The news of the French assault on St. Kitts must surely have filtered back to England by now. Not come back? Tom, not return to his dream? To his island, to his family? Tony, not return to Susan? There was an impossibility. Certainly it was not something his brain would accept.

Movement, in the bushes behind him. He only half-turned his head. It was of interest to know who would be the first to seek him out on his own. But he did not really doubt. They each had reason to hate him, saving the three Carib girls and Margaret Plummer. But then, Meg Plummer had no reason to seek him, either.

"You risk much, mademoiselle."

She knelt beside him. "They are all asleep."

"Yarico does not sleep. At least, not in the manner you or I would understand."

"And you fear her?"

He turned to look at her. "Why, yes, Aline. I think I fear her."

She wore her shift, and had untied her hair. So then, in what way was she different from Susan Hilton, or even Yarico herself, in the dark? Except that the moon had risen, and it was not that dark. She differed in the whiteness of her skin, even after two months in the tropical heat. She differed in the length and shape of her legs, so thin when compared with the rest of her, and yet, now that constant walking in the forest and on this mountain had given her the muscle she needed, so flawlessly shaped. She differed too in what he could see heaving against the thin material, the nipples swollen and anxious, because of the slight chill in the night air, certainly, but anxious because of what?

But more than any of them, she differed from the others, from Mama herself, because of what he knew of her. Because of the humor he knew to lurk beneath that occasionally petulant exterior. Because of the breeding he knew to control that mind. Because of the mind itself.

"You are strange," she said, having allowed him several seconds in which to inspect her. "I understand that she is all of a stepmother to you. Does that not make you precious to her?"

"You'd not understand," he said.

"And you'll not tell me."

"No," he said. "Why have you come?" He turned away from her and lay on his stomach. "I had assumed that you had decided our betrothal was a mistake."

"Perhaps I would dream."

"Of what?"

"Oh . . ." the leaves rustled as she sat. Her knee brushed his thigh. "There is much of which I must clearly dream, for the remainder of my life. Of hot baths. Of perfumes. Of clothing of which a woman might be proud. Of the jewels I used to wear. Of the men who would kiss my hand. Even of the men themselves, perhaps."

"When my father returns," Edward said, "I will have you shipped back to Europe. You can tell your father and your uncle that I lied to them, that in reality you were bound and gagged at some distance from the town, and therefore escape was impossible for you. And that afterward, why, you were my slave. They will certainly forgive you. They will be too overjoyed to have you back. As for your virginity . . . well, its loss will have been none of your doing."

"Your understanding of society is indeed limited, Edward," she said. "Certainly they would be overjoyed to have me back. But equally certainly they would see me to a nunnery the same day."

"They'd shut you up, for being raped?"

"Would they not bury me, for being murdered?"

"By Christ," he said.

"So I would ask you this," she said. "Last week on the beach, supposing that Yarico had not come to your rescue, or perhaps even sided with the Irishmen, what would you have done? Would you have left me with them, or would you have died in my defense?"

"And on that answer depends your decision, a nunnery or marriage to me?"

"Oh, no, Edward. I will still marry you. No matter what happens, I will marry you. I could never contemplate shutting myself away from life and laughter. I would rather be dead, and I am not prepared to contemplate that either, at this moment. I merely wish to know whether it will be possible for me to love you."

"I would have left you."

She caught her breath. "You . . ."

"As you have just said, death, for either of us, is not worth contemplating unless it is inevitable. I would have left you, and hoped to rescue you in due course."

"And would I have been worth rescuing?"

"Your body would have been bruised. You would have been entered by several men, perhaps by all of them, instead of just one. Yet I think both of those things would have been set right by one of those hot baths of which you dream. As for your mind, Aline, had it also been bruised, then I doubt whether you would have been worth having back. But then, could your mind be bruised by such an event, you would have not been worth dying for, either."

"*Mon Dieu*," she whispered. "And you call yourself a man? Have you no notion at all of honor?"

"I would rather say that your society has no notion of honor, Aline. Honor must surely be related to Christianity, as we claim to be Christian. So then, is it honorable to kill a man? It is certainly unchristian. It can surely only be justified by dire need, the preservation of another life, perhaps. Those men would not have killed you, Aline. You are too beautiful."

"*Mon Dieu,*" she said again. "That I can have been so unfortunate . . ."

"As to find yourself encumbered with a man such as I? Well, then, how does your nunnery seem now? I do assure you, that were the honorable thing to do."

Her breath came sharply. "And you," she said. "If indeed you lack all conception of honor, do you not at least feel the stirring of manhood? I kneel beside you, wearing but a single garment. Perhaps I would scream were you to assault me, but I doubt that anyone lying over there would care to rescue me."

Of course she wanted him to rape her again. She wanted sex, and she wanted reassurance, and she had found his sex at once exciting and reassuring. And also, from her point of view, victorious; he had been her subject for a while afterward.

"Are you are so determined to marry me, Aline," he said, "I can wait. For the return of my father. He will surely have a priest with him."

Her nostrils dilated. "Ah, yes, Master Warner," she said. "He will have a priest with him. And the first thing he shall do is marry us. And then you will make me pregnant, Edward. Again and again and again. I want a great many children, Edward, so I can raise them all to hate you."

She got up and walked back toward the others. Edward sighed and watched her go. How hard his weapon, how anxious his mind. She did more to arouse him than any woman he had ever known, save . . . horrible thoughts. But thoughts to be thought, as he was being honest with himself. And he would possess her one day. But on his own terms.

"You strange," Yarico said.

He dared not turn. "Do you watch me constantly?"

Her laughter tinkled, but softly. "Yarico not watch, Edward die. All die."

"You think so?" He rolled over, found himself against her, and she was naked. "Oh, Christ almighty, go back to your couch."

She cupped her hands on his breast, squeezing the hard-muscled flesh as she was so fond of doing. "Why you not take that girl?"

"I intend to marry her. Before the priest and before God. I wish it to be done properly."

"Proper," Yarico said. She put her arms around his head and pulled it against her breasts. Her breasts had grown with motherhood, and sagged where once they had pointed. He could hear her heart beating, and before he could stop himself, his arms went around her waist and his fingers sought the roundness of her buttocks.

"You are my stepmother."

"I am your woman, Ed-ward. You not forget that."

"My father . . ."

"War-nah not come back."

"Aye," he said. "You could well be right." Besides, this night he wanted her to be right. A combination of pride and guilt kept him from taking Aline, however much he desired her, however much she deliberately inflamed his desire. But there could be no pride, and there could be no guilt, where Yarico was concerned. They had earned each other.

Yet the ships came, as Edward was fast coming to believe they always would, eventually. Two ships, flying the cross of St. George, and large, well-found vessels, too, with a dozen guns in each broadside. And crowded with colonists.

He led his brother and his women down to the beach, wearing Spanish armor and carrying their weapons, for the Irish were also fully accoutered, and stood in an uncertain group in front of the ruins of Sandy Point.

"What, Brian Connor, would you fight Englishmen?" Edward called out. "Be sure you'll not have me to lead you."

"The devil take ye, Edward Warner," Connor said. "Aye, and your harem." They fell to muttering among themselves, and Edward wondered if they'd try to settle matters by an assault at this moment. But by now the ships were furling their sails as their anchors plunged into the clear waters of Great Road, and the beach was clearly overseen from the decks.

And soon the first boats were approaching the shore.

"Tony," Susan yelled, and waded knee-deep into the surf, for all her swollen belly.

Hilton jumped overboard himself to sweep her into his arms. "Sweetheart. By Christ, but I had feared."

" 'Twas Edward," she said. "He saved our lives. He led us against the dons, and drove them away."

"Edward." Hilton came forward with outstretched hand. "I never doubted you, lad. I but knew it would need something tremendous to draw you out. Well, Sir Thomas, you're a proud man this day, I'll wager."

Edward gazed past his friend to his father. No change, except a renewal of that confidence which had accompanied him on his first return from England. And a renewal of the velvet and lace he had sported on that occasion, too, with a new sword, and a jeweled hilt, and a feather in his hat, and a carefully trimmed beard, perhaps a trifle spotted with gray, but nonetheless suggesting active strength.

"*Sir* Thomas?" he asked.

Tom Warner smiled. " 'Tis easy enough to say, Edward. Boy." He took his eldest son in his arms, kissed him on the cheek. "We had heard so many rumors. And when we saw the remains of the town . . . Philip. By Christ, but it is good to see you."

"And you, sir," Philip said. "What news of Sarah?"

Tom frowned. "She ails. Yarico . . ."

"War-nah. Is good." But she made no move toward him.

"And this is little Tom?" Tom swept his youngest son from the sand. "By God, but you'll soon be a man. Meg Plummer? By Christ, what has happened here? And this lady?"

"Mademoiselle Galante, Father," Edward said.

"Mademoiselle? You have some explaining to do."

"As have you, Father, and all good, I swear. Sir Thomas Warner, by God. You've settled your differences with the king, then?"

Once again the quick frown. "Aye, well, in a manner of speaking. We'll talk about it. God's blood, you've armed the Irish?"

"It was necessary, Father," Philip said. "They were all the army we possessed."

"And with that band of rascals you licked the dons? By God. They'll grow fat on that in Europe. I'll hear that tale, lads. Day by day. Blow by blow. Brian Connor, quit your skulking and come here."

Connor advanced reluctantly, limping from the wound caused by Yarico's arrow, and taking off his helmet. " 'Tis welcome ye are, Captain Warner."

"Sir Thomas Warner, you blackguard. But uniform suits you. We'll have to talk, we will. We'll have to talk."

"That we will." Connor glanced at Edward.

"But first"—Tom waved at another boat, which had been rowing to and fro some distance from the shore—"I had but to make sure all was well here, you understand."

The boat approached, and the people on the shore stared, while a sudden band seemed to constrict around Edward's chest, and he glanced at Yarico. Was not this what he wanted? Or was it what he feared most of all?

The woman sitting in the stern wore a dark blue silk gown, her skirt pinned up at both sides to show her taffeta petticoats; her bodice was deep-cut, but her breasts were concealed by a double lace falling band, and the cuffs on her wide sleeves were also of lace; her sash was of pale blue silk, and she wore a pearl necklace with a huge ruby brooch. These things were obvious even from a distance, and long before any judgment could be formed regarding her figure or her face, which was in the shadow of her wide-brimmed hat. But there was a quality here none save perhaps Aline had ever previously known, and that Aline was aware of it was revealed by the way she slipped to the back of the crowd and attempted to straighten her shift.

The boat grounded in the shallows, and Tom himself stepped into the water to swing his wife ashore. "Lady Warner, gentlemen," he said. "And ladies, of course."

She smiled at them. Which is to say, she arranged her features to widen her mouth and show her teeth. It was a small mouth, somewhat tightly lipped when in repose, and looked the smaller because her face itself was broad, and shaped like the most perfect heart, dwindling from a high, clear forehead to a pointed, thrusting chin. It was not a beautiful face, and not even a handsome face, but it possessed a great deal of strength, which in turn gave it a beauty of its own—Edward was reminded of what Sir Walter Raleigh had said of Queen Elizabeth. And if she was nervous, she did not show it.

While that *she* would be worth possessing was no longer to be doubted. Even the huge falling band could not entirely conceal the swelling flesh beneath, no doubt thrust upward by her corsets, for her waist was sucked flat, and her complexion was as clear as Aline's had ever been. Her hair was dressed in the fashionable ringlets from the bun on the back of her head.

"My eldest son, Edward," Tom was saying.

Again the quick smile. She extended her hand. "I have heard so much about you, Edward."

He held the pale blue kid glove, gazed into her eyes with stupefaction.

"You'll have a kiss for your new mother," she suggested, and presented a cheek.

His lips touched the soft flesh, and he was enveloped in a perfume he had not experienced since Aline.

"You have few words," Lady Warner remarked. "I like a man of few words. My name is Anne, Edward. I'd not have you call me mother. I doubt there is more than five years between us. And this will be Philip."

"Ma'am," Philip said.

"I'd have recognized you anywhere."

"Susan Hilton, ma'am. I am Mr. Hilton's wife."

Anne Warner inspected the Irish girl. "You should be confined, my dear."

"Yarico," Tom said. "You'll remember, Yarico."

Anne Warner smiled at the Indian girl's naked body. "I must thank you, Princess, for looking after my husband in his hour of need. And this is your son?" Her gaze drooped to little Tom for the briefest of seconds. "You are to be congratulated." She glanced at Aline, who had flushed the color of a beetroot.

"Mademoiselle Aline Galante," Edward said. "She is the only survivor of the French colony."

"Indeed," Anne Warner said. "I wonder she has managed to make ends meet."

"I would hear about these French and their treachery," Tom said.

Anne Warner was regarding the Irishmen. "And these?"

"Our Irish lads. Presently playing soldiers."

"And intending nothing less, Captain Warner," Connor said.

"By God," Tom said. "Mutiny? You have twenty-four cannon directed at you, Brian. You'd do well to brood on that. But we'll have a discussion, soon enough."

Anne Warner had walked up the beach to look at the blackened timbers of the town. "I had not suspected such total destruction, Sir Thomas."

"It seems every time I leave this place it falls apart," Tom grumbled. "I shall not do so again. This time I am home to die, eh, sweet?"

"Not for a few years, Sir Thomas, I do trust," she said, continuing to inspect the wreckage. "But I wonder you have the desire to start again."

"I have that, sweet. This is our land. Warner land. We'll build again, by God. For our children and grandchildren. Oh, aye, there's much to be done." He stamped back down the beach to where the first of the horses were being disembarked, whinnying and squealing.

"Horses?" Edward asked in amazement.

"And why not? They're a sight better than humans, when it comes to labor. Because we're going to have a road, boy. I've planned it. A road from Sandy Point across to windward. No more surprises from that quarter." He glanced at his son. "We'll sit down to a conference when the heat leaves the sun. We've much to discuss."

It took place on the beach, as all of their conferences had always taken place on the beach. Tom sat with his wife on his right hand, and Major Harry Judge on his left. "Harry has been a soldier all his life, by God," he announced at large. "He'll know how to help us here, to hold and to build. He knows discipline, by God."

Beyond Judge sat Tony Hilton and his wife, and then Edward and Philip, while completing the circle, between Philip and Anne Warner, was the Reverend Sweeting.

"Not you, Brian Connor, not you," Tom had cried as the Irishman would have taken his place.

"I've a right to speak my mind," Connor growled.

"Aye," Edward said. "They have a part to play, and not as servants."

"Indeed?" Tom demanded. "I have heard too much about the part they have played. I'll call on you, Connor. When the time comes."

Connor retired, muttering, to join his fellows; they still wore their armor and clutched their weapons. But they were aware just how futile was their gesture. Although the sun was setting low into the western horizon, cutting across the calm sea like a gigantic beacon, the work went on in Great Road. Men and women and children, horses and dogs, goats and pigs, barrels and boxes; St. Kitts had returned to life.

"St. Kitts?" Tom Warner asked. "Now, there is a ridiculous title."

"Merwar's Hope was unlucky," Hilton said bluntly.

"Maybe it was. Maybe . . . St. Kitts. By God, it comes easily off the tongue, would you not say, sweet?"

" 'Tis your colony, Sir Thomas."

"Why, by God, so it is. Now, then, we'll deal with first things first. You'll understand that Hal Ashton and Will Jarring and the Reverend Malling regained England without loss, or at least without such loss as can always be expected in a journey of that sort. They made no good report of you, Edward."

"Am I then on trial?"

"Only in a manner of speaking. I was then fitting out, and asked them to return with me, and they refused. They had had enough of beachcombing, they said. Beachcombing, by God. It was not long after that Tony himself dropped anchor in Plymouth. And he had a different tale to tell, of how Hal's tyranny and Malling's downright popery had driven you to despair. Word against word. But Tony was willing to fit and return with us. And indeed, he was easily secured in the governorship of Nevis, so winningly did he present himself to his Majesty. So I must needs reserve judgment. Now, I would have you tell me straight what happened in my absence."

Edward glanced at Hilton, who was gazing into his wine cup, and then at Philip, who had flushed scarlet. "Why, to say the absolute truth, Father, my resentment at having been excluded from the governorship grew until I sought to seize what I thought had been denied me."

"By God," Tom said. "You admit to mutiny? By God, sir . . ."

"Hear the boy out, I beg of you, Sir Thomas," Anne Warner said softly.

"I thank you, madam," Edward said. "My conception was of taking the leadership by force, Father, as I knew of the discontent in Sandy Point, and I had no wish to watch Hal Ashton attempting to cope with a revolution. I desired no bloodshed, nor would I have any. When it was obvious that the majority of the population would not support me, I surrendered myself, after negotiating for the release of Tony and his people."

"This does not tally with your tale, Tony," Tom remarked.

"Before we left, I was granted a full pardon by the acting governor." But Hilton's face was angry.

"Ashton admitted that. It would appear that every word he spoke was nothing more than the truth. And we parted on bad terms because I supposed he was but presenting his side of the matter. Truly, I am sometimes distressed at the deceit with which I am surrounded. Well, boy, you surrendered at discretion. Have you any reason to offer why I should not hang you on the instant?"

"Sir Thomas," Anne Warner exclaimed.

" 'Tis the authorized punishment for mutiny."

"But you cannot, Father," Philip protested. "You do not know the whole of the matter."

"I'll conduct my own defense, Philip," Edward said. "If you will be good enough to act as my witness. Aye, Father, I surrendered at discretion. But when the French fleet arrived, Hal was quick enough to resign the governorship, which he placed on my shoulders. He then elected to evacuate the colony, leaving it entirely to Monsieur Belain. I chose to remain, with Philip and my stout Irishmen over there, to make sure that Warner's land remained in the possession of the Warners. And when the dons came, and Belain left in a hurry, it was those very Irishmen and ourselves who fought them and made this island too uncomfortable for them to stay."

"By God," Tom said. "By God."

"And this is why I say, whatever our differences, and there have been many, those Irish have deserved the right to be treated as better than slaves."

"By God," Tom said again. "Brian Connor, you'll have been listening, I have no doubt."

The Irishman approached. "I have, your honor, and Master Edward has spoke nothing but the truth. We fought for ye, sir. At the least, we fought for your son. And now ye have your colony back. And more than one of me friends have died for that. Terry Yeats and"—he glanced at Yarico—"Paddy O'Reilly."

"Yet it is still a problem. Not of labor. I have made other arrangements for that. But we cannot have papists and the like running free to disrupt the life of the colony."

"Then give us a ship, Sir Thomas," Connor said.

"What? To go pirating?"

"No, sir," Connor said. "We want nothing more than that overgrown pinnace ye have there. It will take us to Montserrat."

"Montserrat? By God, man, you'll be wanting to make a Carib feast?"

"We have talked with the Indian women, sir," Connor said. "Montserrat is not inhabited. And we have looked at those green peaks too often from here. But allow us to go, and take the three girls with us, sir, and we'll trouble you no more."

"Will the girls go with you, Brian?" Edward asked. "I'd not force them."

"Nor would we, Ted. But they followed Yarico and yourself because it is their nature to accept authority. Now there's naught for them here. We'd offer them a good life. Why, sir, grant us the permission and we'll acknowledge ourselves to be a colony of St. Kitts, subject to your ultimate jurisdiction, so long as we can practice our religion in peace."

"By God," Tom said. "It would not be approved in Whitehall."

"And yet, Father, it is the dream you first possessed," Edward said.

"And of spreading across these islands, by God. Brian, you've fought for my land; I'll give you yours. And I'll lend the weight of my authority to your right arm, because by God you'll need it, if I understand those rapscallions at your back."

"Aye, sir," Connor said. "I'll lick them into shape, Sir Thomas."

"Be sure that you do." Tom stood up. "Mr. Connor is your leader," he said to the Irish, who had assembled in a group just beyond the fire. "Appointed by me, by God, and answerable only to me. My magistrate . . . no, by God, my deputy, in Montserrat. Brian Connor, you'll be first deputy governor of Montserrat. Take your people and the girls, and depart as you are ready. But mark me well. You'll work for yourselves, but you'll work, by God. I'll have an inspector over there every six months, and I'll want to see tobacco growing and houses building. You understand me, Brian?"

"I understand ye, sir." Connor turned to his people. "We're free, boys. Freer than ever before in our lives. Who'll give three cheers for the governor, now?"

They responded with a will, and the beach echoed with their shouts.

"So I am grateful to you," Tom said. "Now, be about your preparations and leave us to our affairs." He sat down.

"You'd have them grow tobacco, Tom?" Judge asked.

"It would be best. They have neither the labor nor the knowledge for sugar."

"Sugar?" Edward asked.

"Sugarcane. Oh, tobacco is all very well. But it requires too much area to return but a small profit. And each crop has to be replanted. Now, cane, boy, why, 'tis in the first place planted closer together, and in the second, each plant throws off little shoots, called ratoons, which can be used time and again, maybe up to a dozen or more years. Why, 'tis said that the dons have taken sixteen ratoons from a single plant."

"The dons?"

"They have introduced it in Cuba and in places on the mainland. And it thrives in this climate."

"And there is a market for this sugar?"

" 'Tis this new drink which is spreading across the world. Coffee. You'll not have sampled it. It is dark, and strong-smelling, and strong-tasting, too, and of a similarly strong substance. It needs sweetening. A drop of honey but merely loses itself in so powerful a concentration. But the juice of this plant, when suitably crystallized . . . mind you, 'tis a deal of work. The juice must be extracted by crushing, and then it must be boiled into granules. We shall need special equipment, rollers and vats. But I have an expert. Major Judge has seen it done when a prisoner of the dons in Cuba."

"And it also needs a vast amount of heavy labor," Judge said. "Too heavy for white men, it is considered, at least in this climate. Thus you'll see that we are happy to have seen the last of your wild Irish."

"I'll have to confess I do not understand you at all," Edward said. "We need more labor than ever before for this cane, you say, yet you are happy to let our only labor go?"

"We shall replace them," Tom said. "I have made arrangements for a shipload of Negro slaves to be brought here. John Painton, you remember John Painton, Edward? He's now turned to slaving. Oh, 'tis a thriving business for those who can stand the stench. He'll be bringing them here within the six-month. By then we must have the land cleared and the factory built."

"Negro *slaves*?" Philip asked.

"Well, they'd not come any other way. But you see the point, lad. We buy these people, and they are not cheap, I'll tell you that, and then they are ours. No ten-year term."

"Ours to work to death," Edward said.

"No one said anything about death," Tom insisted. "Indeed, it would be unprofitable. The point I am making is that these people will be here for the term of their natural lives, and they will understand this. Thus there will be no cause for revolts or thoughts of revolts, or even for insubordination. And there will be women as well as men, so they will be a self-perpetuating labor force. Oh, we are thinking here not of ourselves alone, but of the future. Of generations of cane planters and their people."

"From being a governor you'll have become a god," Tony Hilton remarked softly.

Tom Warner's head came up, but Judge hastily broke in. "And an even greater advantage, Edward, is that they are born and bred in a climate very similar to this. So the heat will affect them not a whit."

"You'll explain that remark, Tony," Tom said. "By God, sir, I have not forgotten that you were an able assistant to my son in the revolt here."

"Nor will you have forgotten that I bear the king's commission as deputy governor of the island of Nevis," Hilton pointed out. "Secured by your own good offices."

"And under my ultimate jurisdiction, by God," Tom shouted.

" 'Tis best we not quarrel on our first night in this charming place," Anne Warner said.

" 'Tis best we not quarrel at all," Tony said. "I'll speak my mind, Tom. It is something I have considered for a good while, and now, since I have had a chance to discuss the matter with Sue here, and discovered her to be of a like opinion, why . . . that ship over there is mine, secured by my own backers, and paid for by the gold I took out of that Frenchman in mid-channel. You'll not deny that."

"I'll not deny the truth at any time."

"Then I'll take her and bid you farewell. Do not worry, I shall abscond with none of your colonists. I've my crew, recruited by myself. I've my wife. And I'll soon have a son. And I've too many memories both of this place and Nevis."

"You'll sail away? By God, you've a mind to become a pirate."

"There is a war on, Tom. I've no need to look for ships to take other than Spanish or French."

"You cannot do this," Edward said. "Susan?"

But the expression on Susan's face confirmed Tony's words, that it had been at least partly her decision, and perhaps even her suggestion.

"But you have . . ." He gazed at her belly, and thought better of bringing their relationship into the open. "At least offer me a berth with you."

Hilton smiled. "Your father has just mapped out your future, Ned. Maybe for the next century. He'll need you, boy. And this is your land. But it is not mine."

"But . . ." He chewed his lip. He did not love the girl anymore. He could never love her again, after knowing what she and Tony had done to him. But for the child he would wave good-bye to them with a lifting heart. But the child was lost to him in any event.

"And when there is peace?" Tom asked.

"Why, then, maybe I'll settle down. But while there is a war on, I'll be serving king and country." Again that magnificent grin. "And my own pockets, Tom Warner. Come, Susan, we'll see to our goods. You can bid us farewell in the morning."

He helped his wife to her feet. She hesitated for a moment, staring at Edward, and then hurried behind her husband.

"By God," Tom said.

"I do not doubt that it is all to the good," Anne Warner said. "He *is* nothing more than a pirate. He will do well, until they catch him and hang him. And the red-headed whore. And I for one have no doubt at all we shall do better without him. But we must not leave Nevis deserted. His Majesty was adamant about that. Edward, what say you to a deputy governorship, of Nevis?"

He gaped at her. "Madam? I am still under trial."

"Oh, fie upon you." She smiled. "I am sure the governor has it far more in his mind to honor you for preserving our colony than for attempting to oust an obvious incompetent like Hal Ashton." She spoke without the slightest suggestion, certainly in her mind, that Tom Warner would disagree with her. And without, indeed, any of the respect Edward had been used to hearing in Mama's tone.

He glanced at his father.

"Oh, indeed," Tom said. "I have been considering that very point while we sat here. You showed great courage, Edward. And more than that. You showed ability and responsibility. I only wish you had done so sooner. What say you to Nevis?"

Nevis? Where every tree, every stone on the beach, would remind him of Susan? "I thank you for your trust, sir. But Nevis is not for me. If you would forgive me."

"Why, of course we shall." Anne Warner smiled. "I am sure we shall find a willing governor from among our people here. And now I think we have sat talking long enough, and to be sure these mosquitoes have found me out." She looked up the beach. "I observe that our people have pitched tents and made an encampment. We shall retire, and resume our deliberations in the morning."

She rose, and the men followed her example.

"There is but one more matter of great importance, Father," Edward said.

"Can it not wait?"

"No, sir. It affects a lady's honor. Mademoiselle Galante."

"The French girl?" Tom Warner peered into the gloom, where Aline had remained standing throughout the conference. "By God. I assume she is a prisoner of war. And will be treated as such."

"On the contrary, sir." Edward sucked air into his lungs and wondered what devil made him take up these indefensible positions. "She is my betrothed wife."

"What?" Tom demanded.

"Marry a Frenchwoman?" Anne Warner asked. "And a papist? Surely you are letting your notions of honor run away with you. So no doubt you have had your pleasure with her. . . ."

"Madam?"

"Mother, Edward. Mother. Or, as I would prefer it, Anne, as we are so much of an age. Your father told me that we indulge in no false words, no false sentiments, upon Warner's land, and that is a point of view I greatly welcome. Now, if this girl has found it necessary to share her bed to survive, that is oft the lot of prisoners of war, or indeed of women in war generally. Yet should you always remember that she belongs to a nation which foully betrayed a sacred treaty between your father and themselves."

"As her name is Galante . . ." Tom growled.

"Indeed, you are quite correct, sir," Edward said. "Her father is Joachim Galante. Yet does this alter my resolution not a whit. We are betrothed, and seek to make our marriage legal as soon as possible."

"By God," Tom said.

"You love this girl?" Anne Warner demanded. "A papist?"

Edward hesitated. "I wish to make her my wife," he said.

Anne Warner stared at him for a moment and then turned away. "We shall discuss it further in the morning."

"And Yarico?" Yarico asked in a low voice.

Anne Warner checked, and looked over her shoulder. "Why, Princess Yarico, you may be sure that you will be treated, now and always, with the deference your rank deserves. As will the French girl. I will arrange a tent for you to share."

Aline remained standing by the fire. "I am surprised and delighted by your generosity, Edward."

"Did you ever doubt that it was my intention?"

Her turn to hesitate. "No," she said at last. "I did not doubt that, in my heart, at the least. Yet I observe you found it difficult to express your love for me. If you are driven entirely by your notions of honor, I would not have it so."

"Now, there is a change of attitude," he remarked.

"Perhaps I am coming to understand the differences which exist, which must exist, between your life here and the life I knew in France."

"Nonetheless, you will marry me, now," Edward said. "Because I wish a wife, and there is none better than you. None more suited, either, as you know the worst of life in these islands, as well as the best, and there can be little promise of the one in the future without very probably the other as well."

She tossed her head. "And you still will not say the word that matters."

"No, mademoiselle, I will not say the word that matters. You yourself told me it was unimportant, once the event was arranged. Thus you may regard this event as being arranged, in either heaven or hell, as you choose. It is now inevitable."

She gazed at him for several seconds before walking up the beach. Why? he wondered. Why treat her so? Do you not love her? Do you know the meaning of the word? Have you been bewitched? Is she to suffer because of what you have suffered from Susan? But did not Susan suffer because of you in the first place? And Yarico . . . did she not give you her love, entirely and without reservation, and did you not accept that love, until something more compelling came along?

She stood at his elbow. "Ed-ward, stu-pid," she remarked. "A-line happy for love Ed-ward."

"I know that."

Yarico smiled. "Anne happy for love Ed-ward, too."

He glanced at her sharply. "You'd do well to keep your evil thoughts to yourself."

Yarico shrugged. "What happen with Yarico now? Yarico ain't got no man. Yarico ain't got no people. Yarico best go to forest, Ed-ward." She pointed to the north end of the island.

"No," he said. "You'll not do that. You'll . . . I will arrange it for you, Yarico."

"What?"

"I'll . . . I'll speak to my father. Something will be arranged, I promise you."

She smiled. "Yarico, Ed-ward. Ed-ward, A-line." She gave a shriek of delightful laughter, and went to find her son.

Edward watched his father standing in front of the tent, talking with the Judge. New people, once again. And father was the newest of all. Sir Thomas Warner, by God. When would the lordship follow? He had found favor at court, as he had always found favor at court; but once he had been too forthright, too honest, ever to capitalize on that hypocritical advancement. Now that too had changed. And Merwar's Hope? Why, that no longer existed. Merwar's Hope was to become nothing but a copy of all the Spanish colonies in the Americas, breeding grounds for hate and fear and cruelty. He had fought the dons with a savagery he had not supposed he had possessed, to preserve a dream which had already been ended. His only achievement was to free the Irishmen. But in that cause even Paddy O'Reilly had died. There was a sorry history.

He walked up the beach. And now, to preserve himself and his friends, he must play the courtier. Thank God his friends were so few.

"Edward," Tom said. "I had hoped you'd stop by. You'll excuse us, Harry."

"Of course, Sir Thomas. A good evening to you, Master Warner." Judge bowed and withdrew into the darkness.

"Sit down, boy. Sit down. You'll take a pipe?"

"I'd not keep you, sir."

Tom Warner smiled. " 'Tis best I wait awhile. She is a ravishing creature, is she not?"

"Oh, indeed, sir."

"But young. And passionate. This day I am all but exhausted. But then, so is she, I imagine. Give her an hour and she will be fast asleep. And we have much to discuss, you and I." He lowered himself to the sand with a sigh, began filling his pipe. "I am not a man who finds words easy. You'll know the number of times we have quarreled, and indeed come close to blows. But I have always borne in mind the lad who came with me from Plymouth those long years ago. A boy of singular courage and ability. I never doubted that in time that boy would return, and by God he has done so. I am proud of you, Edward. I would have you know that. By God,

I have ever been quick enough to speak my mind when displeased."

"I have no doubt that I deserved every word of condemnation, sir. Perhaps your original judgment was no more than right, and I was too young to embark upon such an adventure. I thought myself a man while still some years away from that state."

"Ah, but without such precocity would you yet have achieved such a state of manhood where you would defend an island like this against a fleet of Spain? I doubt that." Tom held out his hand. "There'll be no more differences between us. You have my word, and here is my hand."

Edward grasped the hand, and sucked on his pipe. "I did not have the chance to congratulate *you*, properly, on the honor done you."

"My knighthood? If you'd know the truth, it is nothing but a farce. Our noble king has made it a law that every man in the kingdom possessing forty pounds a year must present himself for this honor, as you call it. A means of raising income, you'll understand, as it cost me a pretty penny, I can assure you."

"You no longer favor the king?"

"I'll hear no talk *against* him, if that is what you mean. There is enough of that already in England. But he arrogates for himself rights and authorities not even claimed by her late Majesty, God bless her. We'll not talk of Charles Stuart, Edward. We will but thank God we are so far removed from Whitehall."

"And my lord of Carlisle's tax collectors?"

"Will be back, and will be paid. I but secured us a stay on the grounds of changing from tobacco to cane. Capital expansion, you'll understand, which will hardly involve a profit for a year or two."

"But it *will* involve a profit?"

"Oh, indeed, if all the figures of which I am possessed are in the least accurate. A profit many times that of tobacco. There is too much waste, and too much replanting, required in tobacco. But in cane now, the only problem is labor. Why, the very fires which evaporate the liquid into crystals are fed by the discarded crushed stalks. It is a self-supporting industry."

"And you have solved the labor problem."

"You have an Englishman's dislike of the word 'slavery.' "

"I'll not deny that, Father."

"But these people are not like us."

"They are human beings, surely."

"Indeed they are. But they have no knowledge of civilization, or Christianity; they live their lives in superstition and bloodshed. We will be doing them a service, I do assure you. And provided they work with a will, they will come to no harm. Would that same precept not apply to an English servant? And if you suppose that Painton intends to invade Africa with gun and chain, you are mistaken. The slaves come from the interior of that dark continent, and are secured by the coastal tribes of their own people. This trade has been going on since time began. In days gone by the buyers were usually Arab merchants, and the fate of the slaves was to die in the desert. Or be gelded as playthings for the women of the harems. We offer them an altogether more noble future. But if we did not, be sure that they would still be sold, to other, less Christian masters."

"You have an answer for everything, Father, and I have no doubt at all I shall become accustomed to the idea, as indeed I must. I'll not quarrel with it, believe me. Now, sir, if I can mention the matter on which I came here to talk with you."

"I'd not supposed it was an entirely social call. You have ever been a forthright young man. Why change your style now?"

"I am concerned for Yarico."

Tom knocked out his pipe and commenced filling it. "She will be treated with all the respect due to her rank. As will her son. He will take his place behind you and Philip."

"Yet . . ."

"Yet is she distressed at this moment. That is a perfectly normal female reaction to her situation. She will outgrow it."

"She conceives herself quite alone in the world, her people disappeared, her lover, whom I have no doubt she thought of as a husband, now allied to another woman. . . ."

"Hardly the way to talk of your new mother, Edward. I perceive a certain dislike here. Indeed, I thought I saw as much over dinner, and concluded that I must be mistaken. Come now, speak frankly."

Edward sighed. "Perhaps I remember Mama too well."

"As do I. I also remember my first wife, whom you never knew. But to some men, marriage is an important part of life. I am one of those men. I need the constant comfort of a woman's arms, the unending encouragement of her spirit at my back."

"She is less than half your age, Father."

"Which means what, exactly?"

"I . . . I merely meant that she cannot have seen enough of life to give you the comfort and encouragement you require."

"She will learn what I require, and that is more than half of the delights to be obtained from her. But there is more. She is well connected, Edward. So was Sarah, and hence my feet were planted on an upward road."

"And Mama?"

Tom's turn to sigh. "Less so. Her father was a merchant. Oh, a very respectable man, and with some solid wealth behind him. But no influence at court. Indeed, I doubt he had ever been there. Anne now, she grew up in Whitehall, to all intents and purposes. Her mother was a lady-in-waiting to Queen Anne, God bless her memory, hence my charmer's name. She will not only be good for me, Edward, she will be good for all of us. You will but wait and see. I make this request of you."

Edward nodded. "And Yarico?"

"For the third time, boy, she has naught to fear. She will have a house of her own, and will be treated as a princess of the Caribs. And believe me, Anne will also attend to that."

"I hope so, Father. Well, I will leave you to your charmer."

"And seek yours?"

"No, sir. I will wait until, like you, I am wed."

"To a Frenchwoman? By God, boy, I had hoped for better. That scoundrel Belain . . ."

"She is his niece."

"By God, but you amaze me, Edward, truly you do. Your spirit is the most wayward I have ever encountered. By God, sir . . ." He checked himself and laughed. "But I'll not quarrel with you. You're a man now, by God. Even in the eyes of the law. Take whoever you wish to wife, by God. I'll have Sweeting see to the banns in the morning."

The morning. The dawn of a new day on St. Kitts, of a new era, of prosperity and progress. Somehow, this time he did not doubt that, Edward realized. His instincts told him that this new brood of colonists, bearing none of the guilt of Blood River, and lacking even the disturbing turbulence of Tony Hilton, as well as the constant problem of the Irish, would be set upon far firmer foundations than the previous ones.

Because here was nothing but purpose. Merwar's Hope had been too much of an accident. There was nothing accidental about any of these people being here. Even Father had changed, was no longer the same man who had landed here with dreams and hopes. Now he knew what had to be done, what had to be avoided. Over the past fortnight a new town had already commenced to spring from the ruins of the old, and Brimstone Hill was once again armed. And now Tom even had a new wife.

So, out of all the past, only three remained. Yarico, reminder of the horrors which had gone before; Aline, an accidental intruder upon the scene; and Edward. Philip had already found himself quite at home with the newcomers. Only three, to stick out like sore thumbs for the rest of their days. No doubt these new settlers would respect him. They all knew how he had defended the island, their island, against several thousand Spaniards. They might respect him, and they might even fear him, the white savage, Caribee. But they would not know, and no doubt they would not wish to know, how to become his friend. He would be alone in the future, as he had been alone in the past, as he was alone this night. He had no need for a tent, as he seldom slept in one in the past. He preferred to stay away from the encampment, away from Yarico, and Aline, who waited for her approaching wedding, with what emotions, he wondered? The banns had been twice read, and in that time they had hardly exchanged a word. He was unsure of his feelings himself, beyond a certainty that this must be done. But he was also away from Father, and Mother.

He lay on the sand and watched the moon drifting across the sky before beginning its plunge into the ocean beyond. Watched, too, the first pale fingers of dawn creeping across the Caribbean Sea before him. Those fingers he had watched too often, and not many of the memories were pleasant.

He got up, stood on the water's edge, gazed at the endless dark sweep of the Caribbean, and listened to the soft crunching on the sand behind him.

"An early riser?" Anne Warner asked.

"As are you, madam."

"Anne," she said. "I sleep badly. I am too excited. I have dreamed of this island for too long."

He turned. She wore an undressing robe, and her hair was loose. "And now it is all yours."

She smiled. "Surely it is yours as well? Will you walk with me?"

"Madam . . ."

"Anne. If you will not call me Anne, then you must call me Mother. The choice is yours, but be sure I shall respond to your choice. Your father is disturbed by your aloofness, and I am disturbed when your father worries. I would walk, and I know nothing of this island or its creatures. I wish you to accompany me."

He fell into step at her side. "There is nothing on this island for you to fear. No animal, at any rate."

"You have destroyed them all? But then, have you not also destroyed anything human I might fear?"

"Yes," he said. "I have destroyed them all."

She walked up the beach, and gazed into the forest. They were beyond the limits of the burned-out tobacco fields now, and where the path hacked through the trees commenced. "What lies beyond there?"

"Another house, once. Hal Ashton's plantation."

"Can we go there?"

"If you feel you can walk five miles."

"Ah." But she walked down the path anyway. In a moment they were lost to sight from the beach. "Why do you dislike me, Edward?"

"I do not dislike you, Anne. Perhaps I am still too surprised at discovering you here. My father had not suggested that he was proposing to marry again."

"And of course, he had the Indian woman to warm his bed," she remarked. "But a savage can only be a poor substitute for comfort."

"And you seek to give him comfort?"

"It is my duty, as a wife."

"And duty is everything."

She stopped. "I would have you explain that remark."

"I meant that you made a strange choice of husband, to come halfway across the world to a life which must necessarily lack the refinement of that you have known, and which does possess a certain aspect of danger as well, all for a man old enough to be your father, and indeed, I would estimate, somewhat past the age at which he can *be* a father."

"There is quite a speech. Would you have me repeat it to Sir Thomas?"

"You may if you choose, madam. I am known for my forthrightness."

Her forehead was clear, although her cheeks were pink. "I see," she said, and continued her walk. "I am well aware that it is unlikely I shall be blessed with motherhood. But then, it is a mixed blessing, is it not, leaving as it does the woman incapacitated for long periods, and no doubt shortening her life into the bargain, and leaving her, too, at the mercy of that most debilitating of instincts, the desire to protect her child." Her head half-turned. "I assume you have no objection to *my* being forthright?"

"I respect you for it."

"Good. And then, of course, I may also claim to have a ready-made family, might I not?"

"Indeed, madam, if you choose."

Once more she stopped. "I do so choose, but I would order it, also, as I choose. I see myself as the link between your father and yourself, between his ideas of how such a colony as this, such a community as this, should be governed, and yours. For make no mistake. I am aware that your points of view are as different as it is possible to suppose. He has told me all he can remember of you, and every opinion he has ever held of you. He respects you from the bottom of his heart for the part you played in recent events here, but he knows too that you are less of his son than, say, Philip, when it comes to opinions and ambitions."

"My brother and I are different, madam, most certainly. Yet we have proved that we can work well in harness."

"As brothers should. But there cannot be a joint governor in St. Kitts."

"Madam, you project too far and too fast. My father may not provide you with all the satisfaction you desire in your bed, but he is very far from approaching death."

Her head came up, and her eyes seemed to gloom around him. "You are very blunt, sir."

"It was a quality you desired, but a moment gone."

"And you, of course, know much about satisfying a woman in her bed, Edward, with your French lass."

"I am a man, madam. As perhaps you have observed."

"Indeed I have." She moved suddenly, grasped his hands. "I would not quarrel with you, Edward. I shall *not* quarrel with you, no matter what may occur. I brought you here this morning because this last fortnight I have sensed your mistrust. You have asked yourself questions about me, and found no answers. I would have you ask them of *me*. Indeed, there is no need. I married a man old enough to be my father. As you have just said, he is still a *man*, and at the court of King Charles there are not so many of those to be found. Besides, England is an oppressed country; the very air is heavy with the taint of treason and mistrust. Your father promised me a new life in a place where the air is sweet. I believed him. I still believe him. Do I love him? I will say truly, perhaps I do not, as a girl should love her lover. But I honor and respect him, as a woman should her husband." The fingers were eating into his flesh as she reached for breath. Her voice lowered. "And yet I would be an empty-headed little fool did I not consider my situation in its every aspect. I have left all behind, for the sake of Tom Warner and his St. Kitts. And *his* family. He is not an old man, yet he is approaching age. And who may say when death will strike? Then indeed I would be at your mercy."

"My mercy, madam?"

She smiled. Her breath rushed against his face. "Perhaps not in law. Your father has written a new will, in which he has appointed me executrix. I have a certain knowledge in these matters."

How casually she let it slip. But her eyes continued to shroud him, seeking his reactions.

"You are fortunate, madam."

She pretended to pout. "How many times have I asked you to call me Anne? Now I beg you, Edward. I look to that future, while determined to play my full part in the present. Thus I could not bear to have you opposed to me. Give me your friendship, Edward. More. Give me your love. Do not look on me as a mother. And especially as a stepmother. Look on me as a sister, and be sure that I shall be the truest sister man could ever possess, could ever desire, an eternal source of aid and comfort, and of love, Edward."

He gazed at her, from a distance of not more than six inches, shrouded in breath and eyes, in perfume and anxious womanhood; her lips were parted, and her teeth gleamed at him. By Christ, he thought; Yarico was right. Sister? She means to make more sure of me than that.

With a violent tug he freed his hands. "Are you mad, madam? As well as criminal?"

She frowned and stepped back. "You had best explain."

"No, no, madam. You take me for a fool, I think. Is my father that old and decrepit? Are you that voracious? I have a sister, who lies dying in England. I shall have no other. And I do not lack for lovers, I assure you."

She smiled yet again; her mouth widened while her eyes remained cold. "You should be careful, how wildly you speak, Edward. Sir Thomas is presently well disposed toward you, but he still has much to remember, and he would take it badly should you insult his bride."

"His . . ."

"I am that still. Certainly to him. He trusts me, for that very patience with which I submit to his inarticulate desires. For the very frustrations which I so willingly suppress in order not to embarrass him. He values me above all other creatures, Edward. You would do well to remember that. Only those who have *my* trust and support can prosper here."

He stood in impotent rage, and then turned and stamped down the path.

"And be sure you regain control of your temper and your expression before you reach the beach," she called after him. "Or shall I have to explain to your father how you sought me privily in order to assault me, at least with words?"

He checked. But to go back would be fatal. And yet, now that their enmity had come into the open . . . He burst through the trees and ran down the beach. Tom Warner looked up from the plans over which he brooded with Harry Judge, while early as it was the sound of axes rang through the still air, and the morning chattered with vibrant activity.

"Edward? What has happened? You look as if you have met a ghost."

"And did not Lady Warner accompany you?" Judge demanded. "No harm has befallen her?"

"No harm, sir," Edward said. "Father, I have come to a decision."

"A decision?" Tom queried.

"To leave this place."

"To leave St. Kitts? By God." He looked past his son to where Anne Warner was just emerging from the path. "You have quarreled with your stepmother. I saw it coming. Now, come, I will have a reconciliation."

"No, Father," Edward said. "She but confirmed a resolution which has been running through my mind for some days." He became aware of people, downing their tools and waiting, and listening, to hear the outcome of this crisis.

"And you'd leave? To go where? These islands are your home. Your past and your future. Above all, your future. I'll not have it."

"Nor would I leave these islands, sir. You offered me Nevis."

"And you refused. I have appointed Tom Hawley."

"I know that, sir. But does not your dream encompass more than just *these* islands?" He dropped to his knees, marked the sand. "Here is St. Kitts, with Nevis just south of it, and Montserrat farther south yet. Bastions, you could say. Here on the west is the open sea. Naught to fear from there, once this island is held. But to the east, where the remainder of the Leewards cluster fast . . . you'd do well to have an outpost in Antigua."

"Antigua, by God," Tom said.

"The boy is right," Judge said. "It is something I meant to discuss with you."

"But it will take more force than I can spare. There are Caribs on Antigua."

"Not many, to be sure. And I am used to dealing with the Indians, Father."

"And I will go," Yarico said.

Tom gazed at her, frowning.

"Philip?" Edward asked.

Philip flushed, and glanced up the beach to where Anne Warner waited. "I'd as soon have done with fighting and pioneering."

So he had already been made the object of her advances.

"Well, then," Edward said. "I must recruit from among your people, Father. Not more than a dozen will be needed. With Yarico and my wife."

"There is another problem," Tom said. "The banns are not yet completed."

"Then forget the banns," Edward shouted. "We can be married this afternoon. You are ruler here. You make the laws, and you dispense with them, when the occasion arises."

"And this is such an occasion?" Tom demanded. "You come bursting out of that wood with all of the impetuous haste I remember and dislike from your youth, and claim that everything must be done to your satisfaction on the instant? I had looked for your support, here in St. Kitts."

"You shall have my support, in Antigua. I swear it."

"And will you not need mine, in even greater proportion, while I have not the means to provide it?"

"I shall call upon you for nothing, Father."

"By Christ, if I could understand what is happening," Tom

said. "Anne, sweetheart, can you explain this situation? You have heard what this madman wishes?"

Anne Warner came down the beach, her hair fluttering in the slight breeze. "I have heard, Sir Thomas. And I understand. I think your son feels constricted by his surroundings, since our arrival. He is too used to having the entire island at his disposal, at his command. You have told me how he was ever a wayward youth. And how he was ever a disappointing youth, while bound by your laws and your penalties. And we have all seen how he has blossomed forth into a veritable leader of men, when forced to his own devices." She was close now, and smiling at Edward. "I say let him fulfill his ambition, and yours, and spread the Warner wings a few miles farther afield." The smile was cold.

11

The Carib

" 'Tis not so mountainous as St. Kitts, to be sure," remarked Peter Willett. He stood on the poop deck of his ship and conned the approaching shore through his glass.

"And green," Edward said. "If anything, greener than St. Kitts."

"Unless it is merely because it has not been burned out so many times," the sailing master observed. "And like all these pesky islands, it has naught but an open beach. It is my opinion, Master Warner, that the true reason the Spaniards have ever passed the Leewards by, and the Windwards, is that they like their ships to lie secure during the storm months. And so do I, or any sailor. Lacking proper harbors, these colonies you and your father plan will never be aught but huts scattered along a shore."

"I have no doubt that you are right," Edward agreed, peering through his own glass at Antigua. "But as these islands are all our present situation permits us to inhabit, why, we must do the best we can, and hope that one day fortune will be our friend." He frowned, his eye pressed hard against the copper rim of the telescope. "As, by God, she may well have elected to do. Is that not a break in the shoreline, Mr. Willett?"

The sailing master frowned in turn, and checked his compass. They had sailed around the southern end of St. Kitts, taking the narrows between the Christ Child and Nevis, and with the wind, unusually, in the northwest, they were now beating up toward the southern part of Antigua, where the island was to some extent flat in the front it presented to the sea. " 'Tis a fact the beach ends, and then resumes some distance farther along. But I would say it is naught but an outcrop of rock, and best avoided."

"Mr. Willett," Edward said. "I do believe you are a pessimist. Look at the beach, man. Even on the sand there is a thin line of white. If that darker area were rock, there would be endless surf. But there the water is unbroken. We'll stand toward it, if you please."

" 'Tis your father's ship we risk."

"And my father's instructions were for you to set me ashore where I chose. And I choose that bay, if indeed it is a bay. If not, with the wind where it is, we shall have ample time to run back out to deeper water. I would have you stand in. Now." He left the poop and went down the ladder to the waist, pausing for a moment at the top of the next ladder to consider the group huddled there, staring at the land which was to be their home. If they could make it so. There were eight of them, five of them hardly older than himself, already opting for the increased danger but, they would be hoping, increased freedom of the subcolony, removed from Tom Warner's iron discipline. The other three men were married, and had their wives clustering close, homely females, pink-cheeked and buxom, peering with anxiety at the forested slopes ahead of them. They too were young enough to work hard, and not yet burdened with the problems of motherhood. He had had to refuse two couples because they already had children. He had no means of knowing whether survival, even for adults, was possible on Antigua.

Much would depend on Yarico, the only mother. She stood by herself, as she nearly always stood by herself. Except for little Tom, of course. He never left her side, and whenever he seemed tired, he was in her arms. Father had insisted that she wear a gown on St. Kitts, but today she had once again reverted to her loincloth, and remained, as ever, an entrancing and bewildering sight, the more so to the white women than to anyone else, he supposed. She gazed at the approaching land without expression. There were her people there, and only she would be able to talk with them freely. Not even he would know what she would be telling them, just as not even he fully understood what went on inside her mind. She looked at ease and at peace. But then she had looked at ease and at peace when she had stood close to him at his wedding ceremony yesterday afternoon. Throughout the festivity she had stared at him, and none other.

Aline stood by herself, close to the rail. Anne Warner had

found new clothes for her to wear, but no doubt with some malice, had dressed her as one of the ordinary women, in a plain gray gown with a high white collar, which shrouded her figure in a shapeless sack. But Aline had refused the equally anonymous white cap which the other women wore, and had left her hair free and undressed, save for a bow at the nape of her neck. And no garments could hide the splendor of that face. Yet today it was not laughing. This morning, when she had dressed herself, and regarded herself in Anne's glass, she had burst into a shout of that tremendous sound he had almost forgotten. For now she was married. And yet, not married. They had spent not a moment alone since the deed had been pronounced. Of course, there had been far too much to be done, with the accumulating and listing of all the equipment they would need, with the farewells, with the celebrating which had gone on long into the night. But for that morning on Mount Misery she would yet be a virgin, although a bride of more than twelve hours. Yet she had herself shown no great anxiety to be with him. No doubt she was as apprehensive as himself. And now? She glanced at him, as he approached, and then looked away again, pink spots in her cheeks. Aline Warner. Assuming that Anne Warner would see to it that little Tom never took his rightful place, Aline was the cornerstone of the Warner dream, the woman on whom the continuation of the family in the West Indies would depend.

And at this moment she did not wish to speak with him. He stood next to Yarico instead. "What do you know of Antigua?"

"An-tigua people, pouf," she remarked.

"Your people have fought them?"

"My people rule. . . ." she waved her arm. "Until Warnah."

"We think we see a break in the shoreline. Have you heard of this?"

She shook her head. The breeze caught the heavy black hair and floated it. Edward patted little Tom on the head and returned to the poop. The sailors were already aloft, trimming the sails, and the orders were being passed down to the helmsman. Now the little ship came as close to the wind as she could manage, heeling as she approached the shore.

Willett closed the telescope with a snap. " 'Tis a gap, all right, Mr. Warner, but once we enter there we shall lose the wind, and if there should be a current, we shall be at its mercy."

"Then break out your boat and have it ready," Edward said. "You can always anchor until the oars are ready to take the strain. By God, man, are you a ship's captain or an inexperienced apprentice?"

Willett flushed, and went to the rail to give his orders. Edward remained staring at the approaching shore. Now the gap could clearly be seen; the sand and the outcrops of rocks on either side, with a ripple of surf against them, allowed in the center a deep green gash, and the land in there was farther off. Willett, in addition to swinging out the longboat, also ordered sail to be shortened, and with the wind coming ever more onto the bow the ship slowly lost speed. But there were no breakers, no heads, peering through the waters of the gap. It scarce seemed to move, indeed, a slow sway of deep water, to and fro, and beyond, a wonderland, once again of sandy beaches and outcrops of rock, but curving around to form a vast lagoon, to which access could only be gained by this one narrow entrance.

The ship was now almost without way, and the longboat entered the water with a splash. The crew were already at their oars, and a moment later the towing warp took up the strain, while a leadsman climbed into the bows to call the depths. But there was no need, surely.

"By God," Willett said. "I have seen nothing like it. You could hide the Spanish Armada in here, in comfort and security."

"Aye," Edward said. Antigua. His island. In all the group, to their knowledge, the one island with a natural harbor. And it was his.

And once he had called himself unfortunate.

Willett chose his spot, dropped the bower anchor in four fathoms of clear green water, into a bed of the most perfect white sand. It reminded Edward of the interior of Susan's cave. Now they were in, there was no breeze to be felt at all. Nothing moved; the trees in their profusion on the shore, the unscarred sandy beach, the endless tree-covered hills beyond, the quiet, sheltered sea. No mountains on Antigua. No hills to be called misery, no hills to be defended with brimstone. Was the island, then, defensible? It looked larger than St. Kitts.

So, then, would it be defended?

Willett was all of a bustle, now his ship was safe. "You'll require a large armed force, to begin with," he said. "I'll give the orders. The women and the child had best remain behind until we have taught these Indians a thing or two."

"Your instructions from my father were to bring us here, nothing more, Mr. Willett. Although I thank you for your wish to see us safe ashore, the Indians, if they are hostile, are not likely to come out and be shot at, and unless you are to stay here forever, with your guns trained on those trees, why, then, we must make some other arrangements. I shall come to an agreement with these people."

"As your father did with the people of St. Kitts?" Willett asked. And had the grace to flush.

"Aye," Edward said. "And perhaps mine shall be the more lasting. Ladies, your bundles, if you please. I will carry yours, Aline."

"I am quite capable of carrying my own belongings, Mr. Warner," she said. "I am sure you have a deal to do."

Difficult times ahead, but not to be thought of now. "You'll keep Tom by your side, always, Yarico," he said.

"Tom good." She continued to stare at the shore.

"And what of Caribs?"

She shrugged. "If they there, they there, Ed-ward. They come."

"Well, we'd best give them something to come for."

They embarked, a nervous huddle in the center of the longboat, while the seamen pulled to the beach. Willett himself took the tiller, but there was no surf to be navigated, and only seconds after they left the ship they grounded on the sand.

They waited, the sailors with their oars backed, the colonists with their cloth bundles and their weapons clutched to their breasts. Edward stood up, made his way to the bow, and jumped ashore. He was fully armed and armored, but he left his sword in his sheath. In his right hand he carried the staff with the cross of St. George fluttering from its top. He walked up the sand, slowly and deliberately, raised the flag high, and then thrust the stock hard into the ground. He turned to face them.

"I, Edward Warner, take possession of this land, in the name of his Majesty King Charles I of England, Scotland, France, and Ireland, defender of the faith, and in the name of his lieutenant of the Caribee Isles, Sir Thomas Warner of Framlingham. And I name this place . . ." He hesitated. All manner of grandiose titles had flitted through his mind as the ship had entered the landlocked bay. But simplicity were best. "English Harbor. You'll disembark, if you please, ladies and gentlemen."

The colonists climbed out of the longboat and lifted their wives ashore, and then returned for their weapons and their goods. The pile of stuff, enough food and wine for several weeks, muskets and shot, pikes and swords, saws and hatchets, grew on the sand, but remained pitifully small.

"I'll not return this night," Willett declared. "We shall lie at anchor until dawn, and our guns will remain loaded and directed at this forest. Bear that in mind, Mr. Warner."

"And I thank you, Mr. Willett. But I say again, we must surely make our own way here. You'll tell my father that we are safely ashore, and you will tell him more, of the wondrous harbor we have discovered. I prophesy here and now that Antigua is the future of the Caribee colony. You may tell him I said so."

Willett nodded, and gave orders to return to the ship.

"I doubt that was wise, Mr. Warner," Aline remarked. "As it will but encourage your father to supersede you in the governorship."

"My father is a man of his word."

"Indeed?" she asked. "But is it his word which now rules St. Kitts?"

He glanced at her, and she returned his gaze without altering her expression. His wife, by God. His bride of not yet twenty-four hours, and already setting up to be a shrew.

He turned away from her. "Joseph Brown, you'll see about setting up these tents. For this night we'll place them midway between the beach and the trees. The Indians, should they prove hostile, lack distance with their missiles. Hal Leaming, you'll take one of these young men and secure us wood for a fire. It will drive away the sandflies. Mistress Ganner, you'll see to our supper this night. And one bottle only. We are here to work, not to get drunk."

They stared at him. "And you, Mr. Warner?" Robert Ganner asked.

"I will investigate the forest behind us, and locate fresh water. You will accompany me, madam."

"Me?" Aline asked.

"You are experienced in forests, are you not? Put your goods with the others." He walked up the beach, not deigning to glance at them. They had volunteered to follow him, or at any rate, to escape St. Kitts. The first few days here would prove what they would make of this colony. Their respect for him was based on hearsay. No doubt he would have to knock one or two heads together, beginning, he suspected, with Ganner, a short, thickset man with a thin wife—ever a bad combination. But his first priority must be to make sure of those who stood behind him. He could not depend on Yarico alone.

"And the Indian girl?" Harriet Ganner was flanked by the other two women.

"Will also investigate the forest," Edward said. "She knows it better than any of us."

Yarico glanced from him to the women, and then to Aline, who, skirts held in her hands, was walking up the sand behind him.

"I go so," she said, and set off in the opposite direction, little Tom as usual toddling by her side.

Edward parted the first of the bushes, forced his way through them, extricating his feet from the clawing branches which covered the earth. Behind him Aline came crackling.

"I doubt you need me, sir," she panted. "When last I knew a forest I was not encumbered by a gown."

He stopped. The beach was already lost to sight. "Then take it off."

"Sir?"

"Take it off," he said. "I command you as your husband and your governor."

"You seek to humiliate me, sir. Those people . . ."

"Will not leave the beach, I assure you of that. We are as secure from their prying eyes as if we were on the moon. And I am your husband."

She stared at him, a flush rising out of her neck; then she slowly released the ties on the back of her gown, shrugged it free of her bodice, and lowered it past her hips.

"And the shift," he said.

The flush deepened. "Do you, then, mean once again to make me lie upon the ground, Mr. Warner?"

"It may well come to that. I would see if you, once again, will excite me to that pitch." As if there could be any doubt. As if he was not already as excited as a young boy. As if he had not been so for the past months.

"And you are my husband, so I must obey, or risk a whipping." She raised the shift over her head, threw it on the ground behind her gown. And then faced him, deliberately inflating those swelling breasts while sucking her belly flat. And watching his eyes. "Although, sir," she said, "if such a course of action would relieve your mind, then would I be content. It is a sad thing, to be taken with hatred. To be married with hatred."

And how well she understood him. He hated her at the very moment that he loved her. And why? Were the two emotions indistinguishable? Hardly likely. He had known no hate with Susan. But he had always feared Yarico's love. Because he feared to be possessed, and he knew that this girl but waited to possess him, and more, knew her power? Or because she had tormented him from the first, and tormenting, had set his feet upon a path from which there was no turning?

Or because, above everything else in life, he wanted possession of *her*, and not her body, which was there for the taking, but her mind, which could laugh, and in that magnificent sound raise life itself from the level of the ditch and the pasture, which was all he knew, onto the mountain peaks and the high valleys, above the clouds, and where the sun and the moon held eternal, equally magnificent sway? Possession. But possession of Aline Galante's mind was not to be had by wishing it. There was a door there, with a key in it, and he did not have the knowledge to turn it.

And yet, no doubt to her sorrow, she was no longer Aline Galante, but Aline Warner, as she knew too well. The flush had faded into a paleness which spread down to the still-glowing white contours of her breasts. "Do I then, disgust you, sir?"

"No," he said. "No, I should have to be a sorry man were that possible. But as you say, here is neither the time nor the place. The wife of the governor should lie on soft sheets, and as those are not available as yet, she should at least lie in her own tent. But as you are here with me, I would speak with you."

"You do not have to take me away secretly, and force me to inflame your passion, to speak with your wife, Mr. Warner."

"You think so?" He came closer, put his hand on the nape of her neck to grasp her hair and hold her, only inches from him. "You have just proved how necessary it is, Aline. You can use words, and expressions, and even glances, in a manner that is beyond me."

Her eyes were wide from the pressure on her scalp, but she never flinched, nor asked him to release her.

"So now that I am to be governor," he said, "and in addition I am married, it may be possible for a sharp tongue and a more ready, and educated, wit than my own to make sport of me. I will not have it so. Those men on the beach I can handle. If need be I can destroy them. And in doing that I can frighten their women into submission. My own wife is a different matter. If it pleases you to chide me, to make fun of me, or to ignore me when we are alone together, that is your privilege. I will not encroach upon it, I promise you. But in public, at all times, you will be my faithful wife and my most devoted supporter. And my most loving helpmate. Understand that, madam, or I shall indeed bring you into this forest and tie you to a tree and whip the flesh from your back."

His fingers relaxed. Slowly she put her hands behind her head to straighten her hair and rub her scalp.

"I understand you, Mr. Warner, and as, on occasion, you frighten me more than anyone, you may be sure that I shall obey you."

He nodded. "Then there should be no more cause of difference between us. Now, get yourself dressed."

Still she stood there. "And yet, sir, as we are alone, and you promised me the privilege of an independent mind in such circumstances, I would observe that you cannot treat life, and more especially marriage, as if it were a military campaign. Indeed. I have heard it said that even the most successful military commanders rely upon the love rather than the fear of their men. How much more important must it be for the people of a country to love their leader. And where a wife finds it impossible to love her husband, then indeed are they both doomed to a lifetime of loneliness."

Almost could she be said to be threatening him. He chewed his lip in indecision, and was relieved by the rustling of the bushes which announced the presence of Yarico. She glanced at Aline with interest, but her mind was clearly occupied. "Indian come," she said.

"By God." He started to follow her, checked, and looked over his shoulder. "You'll dress yourself, and approach the beach, but cautiously, Aline."

He hurried away from her before she could protest, reached the sand only a few seconds later, to see his colonists accumulated into a circle around their belongings and the first of the tents, weapons in their hands, gazing at the twenty-odd Caribs, men and women, who stood farther down the beach.

"Are they peaceable?" he asked Yarico.

"An-tigua people, pouf," she said. "You come."

She walked toward them, confidently enough, and he followed, with an equal show of bravado. She halted when some yards short of the group, who watched her approach while muttering among themselves and fingering their weapons. Yarico now stepped in front of Edward, spread her arms wide, and began to speak loudly and with fierce declamations, every few words turning around to point at Edward, and the ship which still lay at anchor, punctuating her sentences with the one angry pronouncement, "War-nah . . . War-nah . . . War-nah. . . ."

The Caribs watched and listened, and then one of them replied, briefly, and the whole group turned and made their way back along the beach.

"They not trouble us," Yarico said. "Not War-nah, who is Caribee."

"But we'll post guards, nonetheless."

She shrugged. And then smiled, and placed a finger on his chest. "War-nah, Caribee, much feared. Much man." How she smiled, and how she knew, how much he wanted. And indeed, why else had she come? "I find water," she said. "You come, Ed-ward? I show?" She put her head on one side.

He looked down the beach, to where his colonists still stared at him, and beyond, to where Aline was just returning from the bushes. "Get back to work," he shouted. "The Indians will not trouble us. The princess has located a spring, and would show it to me. We shall not be long." He glanced down at her. "Aye, sweetheart. You show me."

The moon dipped low over the entrance to English Harbor, cutting its brilliant silver road across the calm sea, beginning to illuminate even St. Kitts in its path as it dropped toward its bed. Another dawn, soon approaching. Dawn was the most fateful time of a man's life. His life, certainly, but Edward believed it applied to all men. The dawn of a new day, of another day, of, eventually, the last day. Except for those who died in their sleep. But he did not suppose that would be his fate.

How would he die? Cut down by some Spaniard? Or by some rebellious colonist? Or indeed, as Father would have it, some escaping slave? Any one of those fates would be deserved. Even the thrust of a woman's knife between the ribs, a wife's knife, perhaps, urged on by jealousy and hatred. Not undeserved.

And the other? To lie in a vast bed surrounded by wife and children, and grandchildren and great-grandchildren, and watch them weep, knowing that they all loved you too well? Now, there was a dream.

But dawn was the time when men stirred, and planned deeds, whether great or small, magnificent or murderous. Dawn excited him even as it frightened him.

But he was anticipating. It wanted yet four hours to dawn, and as the moon was declining fast the utter darkness welled up out of the forest and the sea to envelop the island.

Footsteps crunched on the sand as Robert Ganner approached. "By God, 'tis dark, Mr. Warner."

"So you'll keep a sharp lookout. No sleeping, Mr. Ganner. I'd treat that as a military offense."

"I'll not sleep, sir." Ganner sat down, his back against a tree, his musket across his knees. "I wonder any of us do that. Would you not estimate that those people we saw today constituted the entire Carib nation on this island?"

"Possibly," Edward said. "I had heard they were not numerous."

"Then, sir, would it not be a sound idea . . . well, sir, as at this moment we have the support of Mr. Willett and his sailors, and his cannon, whereas from tomorrow we shall be left to our own devices . . ."

"And seeing that we Warners have already practiced such a maneuver, with success," Edward said.

"Why, since you put it that bluntly, sir, yes. Surely there can be little prospect of two peoples as diverse as are we and them ever living together in peace and harmony. Which means that we must continually look to ourselves."

"I think you are wrong, Mr. Ganner." Edward stood up. "I think there is every prospect of the Caribs and the English living together, in peace and in harmony. I think we proved that in St. Kitts. Our action there was hasty, and undertaken through a combination of fear and ambition. My ambition can be contained by what we already have, and I am not afraid of any Carib. And I'll not have my people fearing them, either. Or hating them. You'll remember that, Mr. Ganner. They but require treating as human beings to be our friends."

He walked down the sand toward his tent. Not afraid of

any Carib. What bold words. Was it not the very fear he felt for Wapisiane which made him want to be friends with these people? But, Wapisiane was surely dead by now. Nothing had been seen or heard of him since that raid on Hilton's plantation, and that was close on a year ago. And he had no certain knowledge that Wapisiane had been a party to that, even. It was merely his conscience dictating his feelings.

He parted the tent flap, entered the even more utter darkness of the interior, inhaled the perfume. Her wedding present, from Anne Warner. At her own request. So now they would smell alike, and in the darkness it would be impossible to tell them apart. He lay down, rolled on his back, and watched the faint white loom of the tent above his head. He was tired, but not sleepy. Was he apprehensive of a Carib raid? Yarico had said no, and Yarico knew her people. Nor, in this case, was there any reason for her to lie. If the Warners fell, then she must fall as well.

"Do you love her, Edward?" The voice was soft, whispering through the darkness.

"I did not mean to awaken you."

"I have not slept. And I would have you answer my question."

"I would know why you ask it."

"I ask it because, if you do not love her, then surely you must hate me. No one doubts why you took her into the forest this afternoon. If there are any doubts about you, it is that Tom is not your brother, but your son. Indeed, I wonder if that might not be your reason for leaving St. Kitts so precipitately."

"And you spend your leisure listening to such rumors?"

"Should I not, sir, as that is all the conversation I am granted, or indeed am likely to be granted, so far as I can see? So I ask you again, do you hate me? Have you married me merely to be revenged upon Monsieur Belain? And my father? If you have, why do you not beat me and torture me into the bargain?"

He sighed. "Sometimes I hate you, Aline. Sometimes I hate every living soul on earth. Sometimes I hate Yarico. I loved her once. She was the first woman I ever loved, and she taught me how to love. And I believe she loves me still. But her love is a terrible thing, and she can be a terrible creature. So there you have it. I also fear her. And yet I know that I can trust her, in every way. She is there, and I am here, and she understands me as no other human being can do. I am a savage. Your father was right about that, and when my people call me Caribee, they speak no more than the truth. I came to these islands while I was still young enough to be formed, and these islands took me and formed me. I lived with the Indians for a while, as you know, and I became attached to their way of life, brutal and heathen as it is. There is no hypocrisy among the Indians, no false values, no obscure treasons, and no absurd notions of honor. A man has but to live his life, as a man, and a woman has but to be, a woman. Nor, indeed, are the women the chattels that they are in our society. They fight shoulder to shoulder with their men, when the occasion arises, and they live their own lives, mating with whom they choose when they choose and are able. No doubt you will say that is a society of animals."

"And that leads you to hate me?"

"That leads me to confusion within myself, Aline. When I am in the company of Europeans. And now I am forced to such company forevermore, and must behave as them, and practice their laws and their religion and their morals. And know that they look at me, and wonder, what does he really feel, what does he really wish to do."

"So, on occasion, you seek the company of the one person who has no questions to ask of you," Aline said.

He rose on his elbow. "You can understand that?"

"I would share that, Edward. I, too, will have no more questions to ask of you, if you will but treat me as your wife."

Surrender. What he had wanted and worked for. Without knowing what he would do with his victim when victory was achieved. For now he felt only humility. "Then I am indeed fortunate," he said.

"And I?" she whispered. "Cannot I be granted ... fortune?"

He crawled across the tent to lie beside her, and her arms went around his neck. She was naked beneath the blanket, and warm, and moist, and eager. How eager. He had known nothing like this from Yarico, carelessly enjoying herself, to Susan, all tensed anxiety. But here, suddenly, was love without apprehension or regret, conscience or ambition. And here were the largest breasts, the hardest nipples, the tightest belly, and the most welcoming thighs he had ever known, the whole enveloped in the sweetest smell and the most delicious taste he had ever known. And here, above all, was time, not merely the four hours to dawn, but the certain knowledge that here was an eternity, forty, fifty years of possession. As she also was certain.

And yet it was only four hours to dawn. Four hours in which he felt her shudder beneath him more than a score of times and in which he himself achieved orgasm on five occasions; in which their sweat mingled to soak the blanket and the ground, and their lips and tongues grew sore with the passion of their caresses. Four hours which ended in a tumult, which still left them uncaring or unmoving until the tent flap was torn aside.

"Mr. Warner. Mr. Warner? By God. My apologies, sir. I did not know."

Edward sat up and reached for his breeches, blinking at Ganner in the sudden daylight. "What ails you, man? Are the Indians upon us?"

"No, sir. No, sir. But . . ." He gazed in stupefaction at Aline, only now reaching for the blanket to cover herself.

"Then get outside." Edward followed him. The entire colony was awake, standing before their tents and staring at the entrance to English Harbor. Edward stared with them, at the canoes, more than a dozen of them, oars flashing in the morning sun as they hurried toward the open sea.

"They are leaving," Aline whispered. She stood in the entrance to the tent, shrouded in her blanket, her wet hair plastered to her shoulders and neck, her face bruised and puffy.

"By God," Edward said. "But why?"

Yarico stood by herself, little Tom clutching her hand. "War-nah come, Carib go," she said. "Carib fear War-nah." She turned her gaze on Aline and smiled. "Now, War-nah truly rule this land."

This land. Shakespeare had described it, without knowing of its existence. This blessed isle. Not quite so fertile as St. Kitts, perhaps, but for that reason easier to clear and to cultivate. And with more arable land, as it lacked the backbone of mountain which dominated the sister isle. As yet the harbor was empty, save for the sloop they had built to communicate with the senior colony, but this was his decision. He did not encourage casual visitors from St. Kitts, or indeed visitors at all. St. Kitts was the depot from which they obtained their more essential supplies and through which they shipped their tobacco. And from whence, also, they obtained their colonists. For the Antigua settlement had grown, and would continue to do so. In the three years an additional forty families had joined the original settlers around English Harbor, so that he had planted a subcolony on the northern coast, as a precaution; they had found another possible harbor over there, and named it St. John's.

As a precaution against what? he sometimes wondered. Since the day the Caribs had emigrated, fleeing from the very name he represented, they had seen no intruders. At least, none who would invade Antigua.

Three years, in which he had not left the island. Aline chided him for this. She could, now, for was she not his wife and the mother of his children? Joachim was two, a sturdy fellow; Joan was not two months old—this evening he waited for her to finish with her mother's breasts and be sent to bed. But never were breasts more certainly made for motherhood, for feeding, than Aline's. Unless they had also been specifically shaped for caressing, for filling a man's hand with endless delight.

So then, they were lovers. Of a sort. Her love for him could not be gainsaid. Even he did not doubt that anymore. In some strange and entirely feminine way, she had fallen in love with him during the hours and days after he had raped her, when she had understood the endless complexities of his personality, and understood, too, the good things about him, the virtues which largely dominated the rages and the lusts. Now, if anything, she understood him too well, was too passive regarding his relationship with Yarico, and thus postponed her own dominance in his mind and his life. Or perhaps, being considerably more intelligent than he was, she understood that his mind was still not yet ready for her alone, and was prepared to wait. True happiness had still not found her; she seldom loosed that magnificent laugh. Never might be closer the mark. Now she smiled, and after twenty years of life and two of motherhood, she bubbled less.

Because to love Aline would mean the abandonment of all else. This *he* understood. Hence her gentle chiding. The colony had prospered and would continue to do so. There could be no shame in governing Antigua, and he could meet his father on terms of equality. Yet he kept aloof from St. Kitts. Those who came from Sandy Point, and those who traveled from English Harbor to supervise the shipment of the tobacco, brought tales of prosperity, of a colony numbering more than three thousand souls, of endless fields of gracefully waving sugarcane, of large ships and larger houses, of gangs of Negro slaves slowly making their way to work in the morning, and back to their huts in the evenings. Was it this kept him away? Was he then a paragon who would suffer no man to be his slave? There were floggings enough in Antigua. His colonists had found in him a man who could be every bit as hard as his father, when driven to it. As Aline had warned him, his people felt little love for him, however much they feared him and welcomed the good life his strict management ensured them.

Or was it, despite that progress, jealousy? Father had certainly been right in his prophecy, that sugar was the crop of the future. But to grow sugar on Antigua would mean asking Father for slaves, asking Father for credit. It would mean asking.

Or was it the presence of the French? For they too had returned. Their ships often filled the narrow passage, but always with peaceful intent. His colonists said that Basseterre was taking all the shape that Pierre Belain had intended for it, but not under Belain's direction, and with even more beauty than he had hoped. The new governor general was the Sieur de Poincy, a man of distinction whose greatest love was botany. He and Tom Warner were close friends, it was said, and where Tegramond's nation had died there now stood a garden of flaming blooms, shared by both the conquering nations. But no Belain, and no Galante. The Sieur d'Esnambuc was dead, but Aline's father knew, by now, that his daughter was alive and married to Edward Warner. There had been an exchange of letters which had left her unnaturally solemn for a few days, and into the contents of which he had preferred not to pry. But without their presence, was there any reason why she could not visit her countrymen across the passage? He had forbidden it.

Why? Or did everyone know the real reason, and prefer not to whisper it, at least in his presence? For wherever Tom Warner went, or sat, or gave judgment, or granted rights and privileges, there too went his wife, and by her side, always, her remaining stepson. They were the heirs to that land and that grant. And they meant to make sure of it. Thus he must make sure of his own. Already his thoughts roamed to the possibility of a return to England, in search of a grant for himself and *his* heirs. And no doubt more. Sir Edward Warner. It was not a matter of friendship with the king or his ministers, according to Father. It was a matter of possessing forty pounds a year, and his tobacco was worth that.

And yet, Father was and always had been a friend of the

court, and so he could joke about it and treat it with contempt. Edward Warner would appear in London as a savage, no matter how fine his clothes. He lacked manners and he lacked polish. His very skin, burned the color of the mahogany wood by the unending sun, would set him apart from the courtiers at St. James, even more firmly than it set him apart from his own colonists.

And to travel to England would mean leaving Antigua to what? And to whom? Robert Ganner, a reincarnation of William Jarring, if ever there was one? Father's appointee? That was impossible. He watched little Tom walking up the beach, dangling three fish from the line he carried around his wrist. Tom was seven, and until Joachim could grow to responsibility, he was the natural aide and successor to his half-brother. But even Tom meant a wait of ten years. He almost smiled. He could leave the colony to joint governorship of Aline and Yarico. Petticoat government. Now he *was* being fanciful. And yet, he could not really do better, could he possibly suppose that Father would accept such an arrangement.

So what did it come down to but fear? Fear that with his back turned—no, his eyes shut for a few seconds—his every possession would be whipped away. Perhaps he was deluding himself, and far from Aline being unwilling to dominate his life until he was ready for it, she was unwilling to involve herself that closely with him until he had conquered his fear. Susan's words. But Susan was as perceptive as any of them. She had loved him too. She had given him several chances to prove himself her kind of man, and in the end she had given him up and gone with a man who truly knew no fear. To be hanged? Not Tony Hilton. They had heard how he had settled on a rock called Tortuga, just north of the Spanish mother colony of Hispaniola, and there gathered around him a band of the remarkable *boucaniers,* the shipwrecked seamen and escaped prisoners who for so long had roamed the jungles of the huge island and slaughtered the Spanish cattle, which occupation had given them their name. Now they called themselves the Brethren of the Coast, and in their fast little sloops were said, if it could be believed, to prey upon even large Spanish merchantmen, were the dons so unfortunate as to find themselves becalmed as they left the windswept Atlantic for the uncertain breezes which eddied down from the mountain peaks of the islands. No wonder the viceroy had no longer the time or the men to waste on the peaceful English and French and Dutch tobacco and cane farmers, with this band of vipers sitting on his doorstep. And dominating even the vipers was the tall, thin man with the gash of a mouth, accompanied always by the redhaired beauty who shared his bed, and now, no doubt, by a son as well. Would the son have fair hair or black? Or would he be safely concealed beneath his mother's red?

"What have you there, Tom?" he called.

The boy stopped, half-turning his head to glance at his stepbrother. "I got grouper."

"Now, that I had supposed," Edward said. "That big fellow looks like no flatfish to me. But you'd not catch a grouper in your shallow nets."

"I dive." Tom made the motion with his hand.

"You're more than half-Indian, that's to be sure. But your mother would not be pleased about that. You're still a trifle young to go diving after big fish."

"Mother there," little Tom said, and hurried up the beach.

"Now, what do you suppose is ailing him," Edward remarked, rubbing his son's mat of fresh black hair. "How goes it, sweetheart?"

"She is hungry," Aline pointed out. "She is always hungry. She will be a large woman, like her father."

"Which will not be so good, eh?" He watched Yarico coming up the beach. Unlike her son, she hurried. "You'll have a stick for little Tom?"

She checked outside the porch, panting, glancing at him. "He come?"

"And went straight by. He'd been diving."

"I too."

"Now, there's a relief. I had supposed the little devil had gone in by himself." He frowned. "You've not hurt yourself?"

"Carib come."

"What?" He was on his feet in the same instant.

She held up four fingers. "Not many."

"They were making for here?"

"For windward."

"Aye." Wapisiane, back to his tricks. He had nearly said the name itself. And he had supposed him dead. "How far off?"

"Far," she said. "Long time for land."

"There's a blessing. We'll have a reception committee waiting for them this time. But the boy . . . did he not see them?"

She nodded.

"And he'd not say a word? Why, by God . . ."

Yarico shook her head. "He got for grow, Edward, and choose. You got for let him do that."

Aline came outside, her undressing robe pulled across her shoulders. "What is the matter, Edward?"

"Nothing to be alarmed about, sweet. Yarico has sighted four canoes making for the windward coast. We'll be across to St. John's, and lie in wait for them."

"We?"

"I meant such force as I command. I'll leave Leaming in charge here, with three men. You'll stay as well, Yarico."

Aline grasped his arm. "I had thought to be done with fighting and killing."

"Life is hardly more than that, dearest. Even between lovers."

There was no humor in her eyes. "Yet you will take care, and come back to me, Edward. I have built my life on that rock which is your determination, and should that crumble, for any reason, be sure that I would sink with it."

He kissed her on the nose. "Then you be sure I will come back, Aline. Now I must hurry." He seized the conch shell which waited by the door and gave a long wailing blast which counted as an alarm signal. Wapisiane. But thanks to Yarico's timely warning he could at last settle that account.

"We have to hit them, and hit them hard," he told his men. "These people understand nothing but force, and should we let them suspect for a single instant that we are not capable of destroying them, they'll be back time and again. So shoot straight. And if we go in with steel, be sure that every blow counts."

The men nodded. There were thirty-two of them, stout lads, the more so when defending their own homes and families. Thus the eight from St. John's itself were his vanguard. The settlement had been abandoned, and yet left exactly as it had been to encourage the supposition that it merely slept. The women and children had been sent into the forest, and now the men crouched in the bushes a hundred yards upwind of the little harbor, in which the small lugger, their pride and joy which they had launched only a few weeks before, lay at anchor. But to move the ship might be to alert the Indians that their arrival was expected.

And now Robert Anderson came hurrying through the trees, hot and sweating with his rum from the lookout bluff.

"An hour," he gasped. "Four canoes, Mr. Warner, as you said. Maybe a dozen men to a canoe."

"Long odds," Peter Doughty muttered.

"I've taken longer," Edward reminded him. "And these are not even long, when you come down to it. We wear cuirasses and helmets, to which they will oppose nothing but soft flesh. And be sure our dogs will play their parts."

For the half-dozen mastiffs were already panting at the leash.

"Now," Edward decided, "we'll each have a glass of wine and a biscuit to fortify us for whatever lies ahead. And Peter, you'll grant the dogs water, and some of that raw meat; we'll not have them starving, or they'll be too hard to hold."

"And prayer, Mr. Warner," someone said. "Should we not pray?"

"We should," Edward agreed. "Did I know a prayer which would suit us all." Did I know any prayer at all, he reflected, would be the most honest. "It would be best did we each ask God for guidance and strength in our own hearts."

The sun came higher, and from an immense swath across the water the light spread and the heat grew. Birds sang in the trees and the surf rumbled on the beach below them. Dawn. Always dawn. Men should not die at dawn, he thought. Dusk was more fitting. Just as they should always die on the ebbing tide. But here too, the tide, such as it was in these latitudes, was making, the beach slowly being covered.

A dark shape came around the headland, followed by another, and then another. A whisper of excitement drifted through the watchers, and Edward rose to his knees. "Easy," he said. "You'll make no noise, and fire no shot, until I say so."

The canoes approached the shore, paddling more slowly now. Each man on board would be kneeling, using both hands for his oar, his bow and his arrows and his spear lying in the bottom of the boat beside him. But now they were within hardly more than thirty feet of the shore, rising and falling in the beginning of the surf, in the very last water where they could float, and yet they made no effort to drive their craft up the beach.

Edward frowned. Could there possibly be something about the village to betray the English alarm? But it lay quiet, bathed in the soft golden light of the dawn, utterly peaceful. Too peaceful? Perhaps they were alarmed at the absence of dogs. Perhaps he should have left one or two roaming the beach. The Indians were well aware that wherever the white man went, there too went his faithful companion.

"They don't mean to land," Anderson said in amazement.

"Well, then, we'll discourage them just the same. Come on, lads." Edward rose to his feet, parted the bushes, and ran down the sand. The Indians certainly saw him. One pointed, and they began a loud jabber.

"Set your pieces," Edward shouted, and the men hastily placed their staves and lit their matches. The canoes were backing off now, but several arrows were discharged, to fall harmlessly into the surf.

"All right," Edward commanded, sword raised high. "Give fire."

The cloud of black smoke accompanied the rumble of the exploding powder into the morning air, and the sea around the canoes became peppered with the falling ball; it did not appear as if anyone had been hit. In any event, the battle, if it could be so called, was over. While the dogs ran up and down the shallows barking, and the men hastily refilled their pans, the canoes turned and rowed for the open sea, with twice as much speed and energy as they had shown when approaching the shore.

"Now, there is the most remarkable thing I ever saw," Anderson said. "You'd almost suppose they came to see rather than to carry out a raid."

"What say you, Mr. Warner?" Doughty asked. "You've a sight more experience of these people than any of us."

Edward stared at the canoes, already commencing to vanish around the headland. He was aware of no exhilaration, not even of that overwhelming feeling of relief which comes to a man who has prepared himself to kill, and perhaps even be killed, and discovers that such an end will not now be necessary. On the contrary, his belly had suddenly become filled with lead. Why, and from whence, he did not know. The canoes had been sighted, four of them, and four of them had appeared. They had all been fully manned. But there was the point. They had been manned by the fiercest human beings on earth.

But his name was Warner, and they had run from that name before. Except that, having run once, from a name, why come back? He was being less than reasonable. They had wished to try him out, his speed and decision and determination. And no doubt someone had recognized him when he had gone running down the beach. It was as simple as that. Something to be proud of.

Except that he had only gone running down the beach when it had been apparent that they were not going to land.

"Anderson," he said. "They are leaving, and that is certain. You can get your people back into their homes."

"And we'll cook you the best breakfast you ever tasted, Mr. Warner."

"No," Edward said. "I must take my men back to English Harbor."

Anderson frowned at him. "Back to . . ." He glanced at the last of the canoes. "Because of them? They cannot make the harbor before you, Mr. Warner, not even if you dally here half the day."

" 'Tis not those canoes I am afraid of, Bob. Collect your weapons, lads. We had best hurry."

His urgency, no less than a sudden almost telepathic communication of fear, gave them haste. Within minutes they were on their way back down the rough path which joined the two settlements, and three hours later they were at the south of the island. In all that time they had exchanged not a word, but neither had they slackened a step, two dozen men driven by unspeakable fear. So, having gained the landlocked beach, they did not speak now, either. They stopped, and panted, and stared at the huts with their swinging doors. Untended doors. No fire, because the Caribs had not wished to alert them too soon. No fire. But sufficient evidence of what had happened, even without the shattered wreckage of the sloop sticking up out of the shallow water.

Ganner was first to speak. Or rather to cry, as he stumbled down the shore and knelt beside his wife. Her clothes were gathered in a bundle on her chest, and above them her throat was cut. Her face revealed every single thing that had happened to her in the seconds before she died.

The other women were also scattered on the sand, with their children. The men were dead in a group, on the porch of the governor's house. They had been killed by arrows, and in this were lucky. Lucky in that the Indians had come with a purpose, which they had intended to fulfill in haste. But there were only three dead men; Hal Leaming was missing.

A purpose. Heart swelling, very veins seeming about to burst their contents to flood his system, Edward stepped past the dead men and into the house. But the house was empty.

"Mr. Warner. Mr. Warner, sir."

How hot the sun. How goddamned hot. How many times would he stand upon a destroyed village site and look at the bodies of human beings who had sought to do nothing more than grow tobacco? Was any crop, any possession, any freedom, worth this much brutal filth?

He followed the man, through the other stricken men, his own grief lurking, waiting to be released. On the beach by the water's edge there were strong wooden posts driven into the sand for the mooring of dinghies. On the sand between two of the posts lay Joachim Warner, his head a bloody pulp where it had been smashed against one of the posts.

"The devils," Doughty said. "Oh, they are devils from hell itself."

Doughty could utter thoughts like that. Doughty was not married, and Doughty had not been present at Blood River.

"Ed-ward?"

He turned, the tears, released by the unexpected voice, rolling down his cheeks. Little Tom staggered down the beach toward him, top heavy and lurching, because in his arms he carried Joan Warner.

"Tom." Edward bounded forward, seized his half-brother and his daughter together. "By Christ, boy. Where is your mother? And Aline?"

"Indians come," Tom said. "Three, four hours after you leave, Ed-ward. They come sudden, across the land. Our people fight, but no good. Mama run outside, and Aline pick up Joachim, she try for pick up Joan too, but then Indian come in house. He see only Aline and Joachim, so I lie on floor, on top of Joan, with rug over back, and he go again."

"You saved her life." Edward knelt before the boy. "You'll never want, boy. This I swear, so long as I have my life. But you must tell me what happened with your mother and Aline."

"Indian take them, Ed-ward. Them and Joachim."

Edward got up. "No," he said. "They did not want Joachim. They wanted only Yarico and Aline." They had taken Leaming as well, but out of all this, they had *wanted* only Yarico and Aline.

Wapisiane.

12

The Empire

The grating of the bottom of the canoe on the sand seemed to seep upward through the wooden bark and through Aline's flesh into her belly. It was the first physical feeling of which she had been aware for several hours. How many hours? Even that was not a question she could answer. Memory came to a full stop with the swinging body of Joachim. He had been half-asleep and had uttered not a sound. For that, she supposed, she should be grateful.

She had screamed, and tried to run forward, and been held by fingers she would never forget. She could feel them yet, even if now they clutched their oars instead of her. They had gripped her, and bitten into her flesh, while she had been held close against their leader. And his eyes had eaten further into her body than even the fingers. She had been unable to think, had not wanted to think, had not wanted to listen to the screams and the shrieks from all around her, had not wanted to inhale, because that would mean inhaling Indian, and inhaling blood, and inhaling fear, and inhaling lust. She had wanted only to bridge the few seconds, for surely it could only be a few seconds, between her present misery and her death.

But she had not died, and had instead been thrown into the bottom of a canoe. When? Yesterday? There it was. Yesterday morning, because in the interim there had been darkness, just as there had been unending motion, up and down and occasionally from side to side, and sheets of spray which had come flying over the bows of the canoe to scatter across the oarsmen and their captive, to drench her hair and back, and leave her gown stiff with salt.

She lay on her face, pillowed on her arms. Why her? Or had they taken other captives? The Caribs did not take captives, except . . . Her stomach welled up into her throat. But she had already vomited all she could on the turbulent sea crossing. She could do no more than retch, as her brain seemed to coagulate with horror, and the fingers returned, to seize her arms and pull her to her knees.

The canoe was tilted on its side, and she was rolled out onto the sand. She lay on her back and gasped for air, and stared at the savage, grinning faces above and around her. A day and a night, and it was again dawn. They must have come a considerable distance. But without even getting up, she knew where she was, where she had to be. The colonists of Antigua lived on a single legend, the horror island of Dominica.

The man was back, the cacique. He was not tall, but his face seemed even harsher and grimmer than those of his companions, perhaps because there was more intelligence directing the bitter stare from the black eyes. He wore a necklace of human teeth, and his genitals were protected by a pouch secured around his waist. Apart from that he wore no clothes, and his only weapon was a spear. Now, without warning, he grinned at her and drove the spear downward. She gasped, unable to move because of the terror which gripped her limbs. Her breath only slowly left her body as the sharpened wooden point bit into the sand next to her left shoulder.

"War-nah woman," the cacique said. He withdrew the spear and brought it down again slowly, reversing it as he did so, to direct the blunt butt into her belly. It rested on her navel. "War-nah woman, shout."

The butt pressed, and she gasped again, and attempted to sit up, hands clasping the haft. But still it pressed, and she screamed as he wished, only a thin sound, but satisfactory. He grinned, and the paralyzing pain was withdrawn. Aline rolled on her side, clutching her stomach, watched another canoe coming into the beach and more Indians get out, saw Yarico being dragged toward her. Yarico? She wanted to shout with joy. Yarico. She was not alone.

The men holding Yarico gave her a push, and she landed on her hands and knees next to Aline. But she only glanced at the white girl, so apparently bemused was she to see the cacique. "Wapisiane?" she whispered.

The Indian grinned again, and spoke in his own language.

Yarico listened, all the character seeming to drain from her face as she stared at him. There would be no strength here, to be used as a prop, Aline realized, and realized too, in that moment, just how much she, and everyone else in Antigua, had relied on Yarico's strength.

A third canoe had grounded, and from it was taken a third captive, Hal Leaming, who had been left in command of the settlement while Edward was away. He was bruised and battered, and also plainly terrified, stumbling across the sand toward them, but Aline hardly saw him. Edward. Edward would have returned to English Harbor by now. He would have found the bodies of his children, scattered on the beach, and with them the bodies of his colonists. Something he was used to. So, what would he do, Edward Warner, the pragmatist? He would turn with patient resignation, and rebuild his colony. Only that way lay ultimate success. Would he spare a thought for his wife? A thought, certainly; she was sure of that. But nothing more. She was gone, and he must expect her to be dead, long before he could ever regain her, even if such a dream were remotely possible. But he had already spelled out his philosophy in that regard, on the beach when confronted with O'Reilly's Irishmen. She was but a single life, and must be set against the chance, no, the certainty, of losing many other lives. To chase behind her was not the act of a sensible man, of a colonial governor with responsibility for so many people, and above all, that was not the act of a Warner.

Wapisiane had moved away, and the fingers were back, dragging her to her feet, beside Yarico and Leaming.

"Oh Christ," Leaming muttered. "Oh, Christ. Why, mistress Yarico? Why us?"

"Bad," Yarico agreed. "For eat."

"Oh, Christ," Leaming said. "Oh, Christ. I could not stand it. I could not . . ."

A push between the shoulderblades with the blunt end of a spear sent him staggering forward. Yarico followed, and Aline came last. She raised her head and looked around her. Alone. She would die alone. There would be no companionship to be found from either Leaming or Yarico. They counted themselves already dead, and no doubt were wise to do so. But she . . . to contemplate what might be happening to her within the hour would be to go mad. She must live for the moment, for every second as it passed. She must believe in her own survival, up to the moment the knife sliced through her buttock. For that was how it began. How often had they terrified themselves like silly children around their safe campfires with tales of Carib custom and cruelty.

She gazed at the mountains and the forest, in a profusion she would not have supposed possible. The sun was now starting to top the peaks themselves, and stream across the empty sea behind them. The mountains rose in front of her and on either side of her, for although they had left the beach only minutes ago, they were already climbing. And these peaks would clearly dwarf even Mount Misery. Yet they were green. And damp in a way St. Kitts and Antigua had never been damp. There was water everywhere, gathering on leaf and rushing down in a series of rivulets toward the sea. Here was a unique land, in the context of those islands. A land where white men dared not come, where the Indian held sway.

They climbed, up and then down. The water did little to alleviate the heat, and they steamed; perspiration gathered on their foreheads and trickled out from their hair, rolled down their legs to meet the water which had already accumulated on their calves and ankles. Her gown and her petticoat—she thanked God she wore only a single undergarment, like most of the colonists' women—had become a soaked mass, clinging to her flesh. But she could also thank God for the hardening process she had undergone in the forest of St. Kitts during the Spanish campaign, for here was a country of a hardness and unevenness she had never experienced. There seemed no end. Whenever they topped a rise there was another peak rising in front of them, and between it and them there was always a deep, stone valley into which they must descend, slipping and sliding, urged onward by their cat-footed captors.

Until, without warning, after they had walked perhaps five miles, their breaths were swept away in an appalling stench which rose from out of the earth before them. They were descending from another hilltop, crawling over fallen tree trunks and pushing damp branches and leaves from their faces, but now they checked, to look down at the valley beneath them, where the trees and the bushes ended, to leave nothing but a wide, long swath of bare rock and stunted scrub, punctuated by steaming pools of water and even a rushing stream, also sending vapor into the air, while on the far side of the valley a much greater mass of steam could be seen exploding into the morning.

"By Christ," Leaming muttered, his terror momentarily forgotten. " 'Tis sulfur. We are on the lip of a volcano."

"Valley of dead," Yarico said.

A spear butt thudded between Aline's shoulderblades, and she stumbled forward. They descended the hillside and into the desolated valley, marching between the streams, careful to avoid the boiling water. The heat was intense, unlike anything she had ever experienced before, and she could almost feel her flesh beginning to blister, while breathing was ever more difficult. But the valley was, after all, no more than half a mile long, and soon enough they emerged into the thick forest on the far side, and within minutes after this, reached the clearing of the Carib village.

And here, whatever terrors, whatever discomforts, they might have experienced earlier, were very rapidly forgotten in the horror of their present. The tribe had anticipated their coming, and now surged around them with shouts and peals of wild laughter, tearing at their clothes, prodding and pinching at their bodies, stroking their faces and pulling their hair. A woman brought a gourd of water, and Aline reached for it with relief, but this was not the Carib way. Her arms and shoulders were seized, and she was forced to her knees, while her hair was pulled, to drag her head backward, and the water was emptied onto her face, to the accompaniment of more peals of wild laughter. It clogged her eyes and nostrils, and only a little got down her parched throat. She shook her head to clear her breathing, and gazed at Hal Leaming, stripped naked, and secured to a stake not fifty feet from where she knelt, the rope pressed around his wrists and neck as she had so often heard described, his body held upright, his feet free and able to move, and they did as he twisted to and fro, and she watched his mouth opening and closing, but it was impossible to hear what he was saying because of the din around her. She closed her eyes, and kept them closed, and heard a scream, and then another, and forced her lids ever tighter together, and breathed, and gasped, and was then jerked to her feet again by hands on her shoulders, with such force that her eyes flopped open.

But Leaming was dead, his body a tattered skeleton, coming closer as she was thrust forward. Oh, God, she thought. But it can only have lasted a few seconds. Less than that. Oh, God, she thought, give me courage for those few seconds. I do not wish to scream and beg. Oh, God.

There was another stake, set only a few feet from the first, and to this she was marched. Her arms were held wide while her clothes were torn from her body, cut free with sharp knives wherever knot or pad would have restricted the tugging fingers. But to be thus humiliated and manhandled seemed irrelevant at this moment. She was aware of some relief at losing the sweat-sodden garments, and even of a momentary feeling of coolness before the heat of the sun and the naked bodies pressing close had her panting again. Then her arms were dragged behind her back and secured, and her shoulders touched the stake. Another cord was being passed around her throat, and dragged tighter than she had expected, so that she had to stand on tiptoe to prevent herself from being strangled. And now, without warning, there was a puff of breeze, which blew her hair in a cloud across her face, and left it there for a few precious seconds, shutting out all the horror around her, before dying to allow the strands to drift back onto her shoulders.

Now, if ever, was the time to close her eyes. But now she could not. She gazed at the men surrounding her, shouting and screaming, waving knives and shells, and gourds, to catch her blood. They surged right up to her, pulled the hair on her head and the hair on her body, squeezed her belly and her breasts; she tensed her muscles against the coming cut which would be the signal for her destruction, and stared at them with as much resolution as she could manage, and discovered that she was still alive. Yet still they danced around her, driving thought from her brain with their maddening cacophony. And still the terrifying cadaver that had been Hal Leaming hung to the stake only a few feet away. Were they trying to make her scream, as they had made him scream? Were they, after all, only children?

Edward had told her, often enough, about the Caribs. "They are not cannibals," he had said, "for the love of human flesh. It is almost a religious act with them. They eat the flesh of a conquered enemy to obtain his strength, his speed, his brain, perhaps. For instance, you will never hear of a woman being eaten. Why should they, when they would expect to obtain nothing of value from her?"

She sucked air into her lungs. She had been so wrapped up in her own terror that she had forgotten those words. She raised her head and looked through the throng, and found Wapisiane, standing by himself beyond the immediate crowd, arms folded across his chest, staring at her. He sought only to terrify her. Warner's woman must be made to grovel for her life. Whatever fate he intended for her afterward, this was a necessary first stage. Aline stared at him for several seconds, summoning all her resolution. Then she threw back her head and laughed.

"You'll find the place has changed," Robert Anderson said as he put the tiller over and brought the lugger around on the starboard tack. The wind was off the shore, and now they were moving into the shelter of the Christ Child.

"I'd not expected less," Edward said, and shaded his eyes. "Changed" was hardly a reasonable description. He saw first of all the French trading vessels anchored in a cluster in Great Road, and beyond, a series of docks and jetties protruding from the beach, and only then the houses of Basseterre. Here were dainty balconies and sloping roofs, a clock tower and what appeared to be a cathedral, all in white wood, gleaming in the afternoon sunlight. But already Brimstone Hill was looming into sight, and even this was different from his memory of it. In place of a bare rock with two cannon peering over its lip he looked at crenellated battlements sheltering a broadside, and behind the roof of a barracks, while above the fortress the cross of St. George fluttered lazily in the wind. Soon they were off Sandy Point, scarcely inferior to Basseterre, although the houses were perhaps less imposing, and the streets more haphazard. Streets, where there had been but one? But now the town stretched in every direction, quite overlying the old tobacco field, while the forest itself had been cleared back to the very foothills of old Misery, and replanted entirely in the slow-waving, graceful canestalks.

A sloop was standing out of the roadstead, and now she hove to and hailed them. "*Dandy,* of St. Kitts. What ship is that?"

Anderson glanced at his governor.

"You'd best tell him, and warn him," Edward said.

Anderson cupped his hands. "*Susannah*, of Antigua. You'll keep a watch for Caribs."

"Caribs, you say?" queried the captain of the *Dandy*.

"Aye. They attacked us yesterday, destroyed the settlement, and took prisoner the governor's wife."

Edward walked away from the tiller. There was sensation: the governor's wife. He looked down into the waist of the lugger, where the men and women clustered to stare at the shore. They were crawling back, with their tails between their legs. And as yet no one in St. Kitts was even aware of their plight. What sort of a welcome would they find? What sort of a welcome would *he* find? Home the prodigal, the beaten man, who wanted only blood. But where would he find those willing to spill their blood for Edward Warner?

The sloop was gone, and the lugger's draft was shallow enough to allow her alongside the largest of the jetties. Edward scooped Joan into his arms—she had wailed the night, a mixture of hunger and alarm, no doubt, and only recently fallen into an exhausted sleep—took little Tom by the hand, and stepped ashore to be stopped by the armed guard on the dock.

"You'll be from Antigua. Your business, if you please."

"My name is Edward Warner," Edward said. "And I'd be obliged if you'd stand out of my way. And out of the way of my people."

The man scratched his head. But he stood aside. Edward handed Joan to Tom and walked up the dock to the sand, to gaze in amazement at the series of buildings which dominated the foreshore some distance to his right. The first stood close to the edge of the nearest canefield, separated from it by a stream of water, clearly manmade, for he recollected no stream there in the past, but which now came tumbling down the sloping fields, perhaps laid out from the very spring where Yarico had first taken him swimming when they had been children. Now its purpose was less to irrigate than to drive, for the rushing water forced a huge wheel into constant rotation, and this in turn drove three massive rollers, around and around, placed so close to each other that the stalks of cane being fed into the first by the attentive slaves were ground into straw; while the juice dripped through the slatted floor into a wooden duct which ran off for a distance of some twenty yards to the next shed, where it entered a huge copper vat, beneath which was an immense fire, constantly being fed, as Father had prophesied, by the crushed cane stalks, while the boiling juice was stirred and skimmed by another group of black men. At the far end another duct took the by now thickened liquid into cooling pans, where it slowly solidified, and waiting here and there were several more slaves to cart off each filled pan to the third shed, where more of their compatriots were waiting to put it through a final purifying process, separating the molasses from the crystals, these last being placed in casks, over the top of which a clay paste was set in place, to keep the sugar fine until it was ready for shipment.

The whole scene was one of such bustle and endeavor on the part of the blacks, and such evident discomfort too, for the heat was intense, the fires adding their efforts to that of the sun, and naturally the aroma as well as the presence of so much sweetness seemed to attract every insect from the entire forest, that Edward almost forgot his own misery.

"Edward? Edward? By God, but what brings you to St. Kitts?"

Philip, wearing a white shirt over loose white breeches, and brown boots, and carrying no weapon save a whip. His hat was a broad-brimmed straw.

Edward squeezed his hand. "I was but admiring the industry." He glanced at the whip. "Are they lazy, then?"

"As lazy a pack of devils as you'll ever have encountered. But they respect the lash." He peered at his brother. "But what ails you, man?" He stared at the Antigua people, already surrounded by a crowd of women from the town. "And all your people? There has been trouble?"

"I would speak with Father."

"I shall send for him on the instant. Meanwhile . . ." He waved his hand. "Mother will be pleased to care for you."

Mother. She too had adapted herself to the climate and her circumstances. She wore the pale blue which was her favorite color, in linen, with certainly nothing more than a single shift beneath; the sunlight silhouetted her legs through her skirt. No gloves, but a wide-brimmed hat, to which was added a parasol carried by an attentive Negress. And of course, all the perfume she had ever enjoyed.

"Edward." She extended her hand, and he bent his head to kiss it. "How good to see you, and after all these years. How is Aline? And the children?"

Edward turned; little Tom staggered up the road behind him, carrying Joan.

"But . . ." Anne Warner's mouth opened into a round O, and she laughed. "You use the lad as a nursemaid? Capital."

"He saved her life," Edward said.

Anne's smile faded as quickly as it had come, and she frowned as she glanced from him to the boy, and then to the jabbering crowd by the waterfront. "There has been some catastrophe here."

"If I could speak with my father . . ."

"I am here, boy." Tom Warner came bustling down from

the canefields; he was dressed very much as his younger son, except that he carried a gold-headed cane rather than a whip, and his face wore too deep a flush for health. But he moved with all the vigorous haste Edward remembered from the past. "Edward. 'Tis good to see you. But there has been trouble?"

"A Carib raid, Father."

"By God. You suffered losses?"

"We have buried fifteen women, seven children, and three men, Father."

"Fifteen . . . By Christ. You were defeated?"

"Outwitted, Father. They made a feint attack on St. John's, and we marched across to repel them, and in the absence of our main force they landed at English Harbor. There were only four men left to defend the settlement."

"By God," Tom said. "Strategy, from savages. They took prisoners?"

"There are three people unaccounted for," Edward said, speaking very slowly. "Hal Leaming, who was in command in my absence, Yarico, and Aline."

"Oh, my God," Anne Warner whispered.

"By God," Tom said, and stared at little Tom and Joan. "Your son . . ."

"Is dead."

"You'll take some wine," Anne said. "Come, Edward, dear Edward." She grasped his arm. "Tom . . ."

" 'Tis not the Carib custom to take female prisoners."

"These are not usual circumstances, Father."

Tom frowned. "There is some mystery here. You had dealings with them in Antigua?"

"I have neither seen nor spoken with an Indian for two years, saving Yarico. But this business goes back farther than that. It is the work of Wapisiane."

"Wapisiane? Wapisiane? Was that not the name of Tegramond's heir?"

"You never found his body among the dead at Blood River."

"I had assumed he had been . . ." Tom glanced at his wife and flushed. "You mean you think he escaped?"

"I know he escaped, Father, because I assisted him. I could not send him to his death. We met in the forest at the moment the assault started, and I persuaded him to leave. We had been friends."

"By God," Tom said.

"And yet he swore vengeance against everything Warner."

"And now he has claimed that vengeance," Anne Warner said. "Oh, poor, poor Edward."

"By God," Tom said. "We'll call a council. Aye, we'll call a council."

Harry Judge took off his hat and wiped sweat from his forehead. "They're assembled, Tom," he said. "And I've sent messengers to Nevis and Montserrat, by fast sloop, to see how they feel down there, and also to be sure that the Caribs have gone south."

"They will have gone south," Edward said. He had drunk three glasses of wine, but refused food. He could not permit a single morsel to pass his lips without risking the breakdown of the cocoon in which he had wrapped himself. He dared not risk thought, or imagination, or worst of all, memory. He could remember too much about the Caribs.

"Well, it'd be best to make sure. I've also doubled the sentries in the fort, Tom, and alerted the guard on windward."

"And the French?"

"Monsieur de Poincy is outside now."

"You'd best meet him, Edward," Tom said, rising from the table. "He's a good man. No Belain there. Come in, monsieur, come in."

De Poincy was as tall as Edward, thin, with a pointed beard and a curiously arrogant toss to his head whenever he spoke. But his voice was soft and his manner entirely courteous. He bowed to Anne Warner, and then held out his hand. "Mr. Warner. I have heard a great deal about you, and about your beautiful wife. It grieves me that our first meeting must take place in circumstances of such gravity."

"I am honored by your grief, monsieur."

De Poincy gazed into his eyes for a moment, and then nodded. "I have brought my principal officers with me, but you must speak with them later. We are very eager to discover what action you intend, what aid you seek, from us in St. Kitts."

There was a moment's silence, as the Warners exchanged glances. This question had been carefully avoided during the hours since Edward's arrival.

"Why, sir," he said, "it is my intention to regain possession of my wife."

They stared at him. "From the Caribs?" Philip asked at last.

"You must know that is impossible," Judge said. "The Caribs do not take prisoners, except . . ." He hesitated.

"To eat them at the stake," Edward said. "Believe me, sir, I know the Caribs a deal better than yourself. And I grieve for poor Hal Leaming. But they do not eat women, sir. They can perceive no advantage in it to themselves. Nor, as you say, do they take them prisoner. Their rule is to commit whatever mayhem they may choose upon their victims on the spot, and then murder them on the spot."

"And the only two taken were Aline and Yarico," Tom Warner mused.

"The one because she is my wife, and the other because she betrayed her people."

"I must confess," De Poincy said, "that I do not follow this conversation."

"My son is convinced that this is no mere raid, monsieur," Tom explained. "But the result of a long-standing feud between our people, and yours, and a certain Carib by name of Wapisiane. He is the sole survivor of his people here on St. Kitts following their destruction by myself and the Sieur Belain."

"Mon Dieu," De Poincy said. "I was not aware that there was any survivor, other than the Princess Yarico."

"Neither was I, up to this moment," Tom said. "But it appears that there was, through some misguided generosity on the part of my son. And it would seem that events have confirmed his fears."

"But this changes matters entirely. I had supposed that your son had come to warn us of the opening shots in perhaps an Indian war, in which my people and I would be willing to play the fullest part. But if indeed this affair is the result of a feud, concerning an event with which no Frenchman now in these islands has the slightest connection, why, then, sir, I do not see how I can ask my people to risk their lives."

"Can you not see that their lives are already at risk?" Edward shouted. "Wapisiane makes no distinction between those who were here when Tegramond was killed and those who were not."

"Yet is he also a man of some ability and common sense," De Poincy observed. "Judging by the way he outmaneuvered your people on Antigua. And as such, believe me, sir, he will always have more sense than to attack a colony as heavily populated and as well defended as St. Kitts."

"That is true, in my estimation," Judge agreed. "I have observed this when I was with the dons, that the Indians would never risk an attack upon any force they were not sure they could overcome."

"Monsieur, one of the women Wapisiane took was a French girl, my wife, the daughter of Captain Joachim Galante. Can you condemn her to—"

"I condemn her to nothing, Mr. Warner. You may rest assured that she is already dead. Of this I have no doubt at all. I grieve for you, young man, believe me, but you *are* young, and your heart and your spirit will recover. And, no doubt, you will know better than ever to show generosity to a Carib again."

"But she is *not* dead," Edward insisted. "I am sure of it. What more terrible punishment could Wapisiane have inflicted on me other than to spread eagle my wife upon the sand as he did all those other women, if only to kill her? His only possible reason for taking her was to make his revenge more complete."

De Poincy half-bowed toward Anne Warner. "You will excuse my bluntness, madame, but if that is the case, then she is more than ever dead, to European eyes. What, would you risk dozens, perhaps scores of lives to regain possession of a woman who has been bedded by a savage? What would you do with her? Chop off her head?"

Edward gaped at him in impotent despair.

"Monsieur de Poincy is right, Edward," Anne Warner said gently. "This is a terrible, horrible, ghastly event, but it is not one which can be altered, now it has happened. We can only be more determined to make sure that it never happens again. Antigua is clearly in need of strengthening. Believe me, we all understand your desire to make the colony a success on your own, but now that has failed, why, you must accept help from your father. He will send you fresh people, in sufficient numbers to make the colony impregnable against further attacks. You must build again. God knows you have done that often enough in the past. As for Joan, you may leave her with me for the time being. It will be my pleasure to care for her, and to secure for her a wet nurse."

"I intend to regain possession of my wife and Yarico," Edward said, speaking very slowly and clearly. "Alive, if they are yet alive, and I am sure they are. If not, their bodies. I could not live knowing I had condemned them to a living death. Nor am I acting entirely selfishly in this matter. Wapisiane may regard his success of yesterday as vindication of his revenge. The Indians who accompanied him will see it only as a great victory over the white man. Their thoughts will already be turning toward the accomplishment of other triumphs. Unless we show them, and show them quickly, that the white man is not to be trifled with, that he will hit back, twice as hard as he was hit."

"Could we show them that," Philip said. "But how is it to be done? We assume these savages came from Dominica. Why not St. Vincent? Or St. Lucia? There are Carib tribes there."

"Tell them, Tom," Edward commanded.

The boy had been silent throughout the meal, watching and listening to the talk. Now he licked his lips. "People of smoke come to Antigua."

"People of smoke?" Anne Warner asked.

"Major Judge will have heard of them," Edward said.

"That I have," Judge agreed. "They are from Dominica, to be sure, and inhabit the crater of a still-active volcano, 'tis said. But how can this boy know that?"

"Because he speaks their language," Edward said. "Does that also answer your question, Philip?"

"So we know they came from Dominica. Is that not an island every bit as large as St. Kitts, if not larger, and entirely covered with forest and mountain? Did not you and I, Edward, with a score of men, successfully resist over a thousand Spaniards here in St. Kitts? How can you consider leading a force which will necessarily be much smaller into the forests of Dominica?"

"Because I know the forest and I know the Carib," Edward said. "I know how to fight him, and I know how much he wants to fight me."

"It will involve meaningless bloodshed," Judge said. "On military grounds, Edward, I would have to say that your plan has small chance of success."

"Believe us, Edward," Anne said. "We honor and respect your desire to go after Aline, but you must see that it is impossible."

Edward looked at his father.

Tom Warner pulled his beard. "It is indeed a terrible position in which to find oneself," he said. "Supposing you were governor of St. Kitts, Edward. What would you do?"

"I'd call for volunteers."

Tom nodded thoughtfully. "Then you have my permission to do so."

"Sir Thomas," Anne exclaimed. "Surely—"

"Hush, woman. These are men's affairs."

"I thank you, sir," Edward said. "And your own part? For this will be important."

Tom sighed. "You and I have seldom followed the same path, Edward, saving on that first and most important occasion, when we set sail for these islands. And no matter what trials have come upon us in the years between, I have never regretted that momentous step. Nor can I convince myself that I have always been right and you wrong. I know now that the massacre at Blood River was a mistake. In allowing Wapisiane to live, you attempted to assuage your conscience, and I cannot blame you for that. Nor can I ever do less than honor to your spirit, which has preserved this colony for me. The day you set foot upon Dominica, be sure that I shall be at your side."

"Father." Edward thrust out his hand.

Philip chewed his lip. " 'Tis certain suicide."

Tom did not look at him. "You shall not accompany us, Philip, no matter how hard you beg. I cannot risk the destruction of my entire family at one blow. You will stay here and care for your stepmother and your stepbrother and your niece. And care for them well. And you, Harry. I must leave an experienced soldier behind."

"Oh, what rubbish you men do talk," Anne Warner cried angrily. "What, will the pair of you storm Wapisiane's stronghold? You'll not get a man to follow you. They have more sense. God curse the day you were born, Edward Warner. You have ever been nothing more than a troublemaker. Go on, then, call for your volunteers, and let us have this mad scheme buried within the hour."

"Aye," Tom said. "The people are waiting." He stepped outside, onto the raised porch of the new Government House, from whence he commanded a view down the main street, which began in the square immediately beneath him. Here the entire populace of Sandy Point seemed to have gathered, milling about, jostling, and babbling into the still evening air. Tom clapped his hands, and again, and then seized a stick and struck the gong which stood close to the steps. The reverberations echoed across the rooftops, and the crowd slowly grew silent.

"You'll all know why we are assembled here," Tom

shouted. "Our neighboring colony of Antigua has been attacked by the Carib Indians, and English Harbor destroyed. Women were slaughtered there, as well as children and men. But what is worse, two of the women were carried off by the savages. Mrs. Warner, wife of the deputy governor of the colony and my daughter-in-law, and the Princess Yarico. God alone knows, and I hesitate to suppose, what terrible sufferings have already been inflicted upon these two unfortunate ladies, but our knowledge of the Carib leads us to suppose they may still be alive. As Christian men we cannot remain here in that knowledge, without making some attempt to rescue them."

He paused, and the crowd stared at him, although immediately there were whisperings, mostly by the women.

Tom licked his lips and held up his hands. "However, this responsibility we have is of small account when set beside the responsibility we have to our own women and children. Were this expedition to be purely punitive, it would not have my backing for an instant. But it must be more than that. As of yesterday we must consider ourselves at war with the Indians. No doubt this is a tragedy some of us long foresaw. We must not shrink from it now. The Indians in Dominica must be made to know that we will not permit them to attack English colonies, no matter how small and isolated, with impunity. That we will visit them with twice the destruction every time they dare take the field against us. Believe me, my friends, this is a necessary act, or you may well awake one day to see Sandy Point itself in flames. It has happened before."

Again the anxious pause, and again the whisperings.

"It will be dangerous," Tom shouted. "Make no mistake about that. But we have the advantage of being led by the foremost Indian fighter in these islands, Captain Edward Warner. I do not have to tell you, lads, that Captain Warner defended this island against the entire might of Spain, with but twenty men at his back, and those unarmed when the campaign started. We can rely upon him. He has lived among the Indians, can think like them, anticipate their every move. He will lead us to victory."

"And it is his wife we are going to regain," someone shouted.

Tom scanned their faces. "Why, yes," he agreed. "It is his wife. Now, lads, you came here to plant sugar and grow rich. By the terms of the agreements you signed with me, you are duty-bound to take up your arms in defense of St. Kitts when

I call upon you to do so. Nothing more. But I would ask you to volunteer to accompany my son and myself to Dominica, resting sure in your minds that this is the surest way of defending this island that we have, and that any other course were to invite the Indians to descend upon us at will. Now, then, who'll be first to volunteer?"

He stopped and wiped his brow, and the crowd stared back at him.

"If Captain Warner is so big an Indian fighter," someone called, "how come he got beat in Antigua?"

"We were attacked in two places at once," Edward replied. "I lacked the men."

"And will you not lack the men on this occasion, no matter how many go with you?" asked someone else.

"This time we will be attacking, not defending," Edward said. "The Indians will not anticipate such an action on our part. No white people save the Spaniards, and then only on occasion, have assaulted the Caribs themselves."

"Because it is too difficult," called a voice. "And for those of us who are taken, 'tis the stake. Long odds, Captain Warner."

"We are not here to argue," Tom bellowed. "Who'll volunteer? What about you Antigua people? Your wives were killed by those savages. Will you not seek to avenge them? Who'll volunteer?"

"To save a French whore and a savage?" someone muttered.

"By God, sir, I'll have your tongue," shouted one of the French officers who had accompanied De Poincy.

"Save your anger, monsieur," Tom called. "For the Caribs. Will you volunteer?"

"To save a French lady, sir? Why, that I will. And my friend here."

"Two blades. There's a start," Tom muttered. "Now, come, my friends. Who'll join our force?"

"Force?" someone shouted. "Four madmen? You brought us this distance to grow cane, Sir Thomas. Not to be eaten by savages. 'Twas that one certain fate you promised would never be mine."

"Aye," someone else agreed. " 'Tis best we all go home to our beds."

The crowd was already breaking up, talking and laughing among themselves, while Edward and Tom stared at them in impotent fury.

"Hold, there," shouted a familiar voice. "Ye'll not lack for support from us, Ted, lad."

"Brian Connor," Edward yelled in delight.

"The same, your Honor. I came as soon as I heard the sad news. 'Tis sorry I am to bring so few, but I could not leave my people without defense." Connor forced his way up the street, clad in helmet and breastplate, and followed by five of the Irishmen.

"Six men?" Tom asked.

"Good men," Edward said, and ran down from the porch. "Brian." He clasped his friend's hand. "By God, but it is good to see you. You know our purpose?"

"To rescue your lady wife, and the princess. Aye. We'll have a share in that, Ted, even if the lass did put an arrow in my thigh, and through poor Paddy O'Reilly. By Christ, it'll be good to get back to campaigning."

"With ten men you'll storm Dominica?" Anne Warner asked contemptuously.

Edward hesitated, glancing from her to the men. "We'll make our plans in the morning, Brian. And I'll be pleased if you two gentlemen will attend us then as well. For this night you are our guests. But once again, I thank you."

He walked back under the sweep of the roof. De Poincy waited. "A sad business, Mr. Warner. But you can expect no more from these people. They are colonists who will, we trust, make good militiamen when the time comes. Not soldiers playing at colonists."

"You'll take a glass with us, monsieur," Tom said.

"The slaves," Edward said. "Would they not fight, if given weapons and promised their freedom?"

"*Mon Dieu,*" De Poincy said. "But the young man has gone mad."

"Indeed, it sounds so," Philip agreed. "Arm the slaves? Promise them their freedom? Where would our lives and indeed our profit be in that event?"

"The people would not stand for it, Edward," Tom said. "And to say truth, I do not think it would be possible. Our slaves are not yet reconciled to their fate here, and it would be idle to pretend they would fight for us."

"So, then, admit that you are defeated and abandon this wild scheme," Anne Warner said. "Surely you can see it is an impossibility now, Edward. More, it is a dereliction of duty. While you stand here dreaming, Antigua lies deserted and undefended. Who can say what forces are already descending upon it? And what of those who survived, and who have abandoned their homes? Should you not be preparing to lead them back, suitably reinforced? I have no doubt that you will find volunteers for *that* purpose. You have been appointed governor. You must accept the responsibilities of that honor."

There was a short silence, broken only by the gurgle of the liquid as Tom Warner poured the wine.

"Your stepmother is right, sir," De Poincy observed. "Chivalry is an admirable concept, but as De Camoens has so admirably illustrated, the age is dead, and our gallantry must now be tempered with that due sense of responsibility to others of which Lady Warner spoke."

Edward drained his glass and went to the window. By Christ, what do they know? he thought. What do they know of love? What did I know of love, up to yesterday morning? So will she be worth loving, when she is regained? She will have been spared nothing by Wapisiane. And no doubt not by Wapisiane alone. She will have been humiliated a dozen, a hundred times, her body made the receptacle for every insult the Indians can think of. Yet will she still be alive, and living, she will prevent herself from going mad by a single thought, a single hope, that of rescue by her husband, by the one man in all the Caribee Isles, perhaps, capable of accomplishing so much. "I have built my life upon the rock which is your determination." That hope, that dream, that belief, would maintain at once her sanity and her life. To fail such a responsibility would surely be to damn himself forever.

Tom Warner stood at his shoulder, a full glass in either hand. "I'm afraid they are right, boy. We have done all we could. Now it is time to cease being husbands and fathers, and become what we are also, governors and leaders, men of responsibility. I know, and you know, that the task of leading involves some painful decisions. Can we truthfully balance two lives against the probable cost of regaining them? Have we the slightest justification for so doing? Have we—?"

He checked as the rumble of the explosion came rolling up the shallow hill, and even as they stared through the window into the darkness, they saw the next flash and heard the next roar.

"Cannon, by God," Philip cried. "We are assailed."

"With blank shot?" Edward demanded. "That is an empty charge."

"But who in the name of God . . . ?" Tom led them outside, but the first boats were already ashore, and running up the street came a dozen seamen, led by a short, thickset man with a heavy moustache. "John Painton."

"None other, Tom Warner," Painton shouted. "And right glad am I to see you still here, old friend. Edward, is that you? By God, boy, I am truly grieved to hear of your trouble."

"But how . . . ?" Edward squeezed the proffered hand.

"I spoke with the *Dandy* sloop but this morning, while running south, and put all sail on to get here, before your expedition left."

"Expedition?"

Painton frowned. "You are going after those savages, are you not?"

"Why, such is my intention, certainly," Edward said. "If it can be done. I will confess I am experiencing some difficulty in recruiting an army."

"You have one, Ned. And a ship. The *Plymouth Belle* is yours, and its crew. Why, man, I have seventy fighting men there, who only want to sharpen their cutlasses on some red devil's hide. We'll sail in the morning."

"By God," Tom said. "You are the answer to a prayer, John."

"A prayer," Edward whispered. He had not thought to pray. But perhaps Aline had been doing that.

"The answer to a prayer," Anne Warner said in disgust. "To a death wish, you mean. You go, Tom Warner. Go and spend your life uselessly. Go and die in some fever-ridden swamp. God curse you, Edward Warner, for bringing your troubles down on our shoulders. God curse you."

The *Plymouth Belle* weighed anchor at dawn. She carried eighty men, every one armed and equipped to the best standards the Warners could manage, and twelve dogs. Her guns were loaded, and spare balls were piled on her decks beside each piece. The sky was clear and the breeze was light and from the northeast as she slipped out of Great Road and directed herself to the passage between the islands.

Almost every inhabitant of the two towns turned out to watch her go, and give her a cheer, even if no doubt the majority of those who stayed behind had little faith in the success of the expedition. Yet eighty men was no mean force. Edward stood on the poop and watched the green land slipping astern, watched the waving flags, the cross of St. George and the fleur-de-lis, flapping in the breeze, the skirts of the women and the waving arms of the men.

His father was beside him. "Well, boy, do you remember the first morning we stood upon this poop and watched Guyana dropping below the horizon?"

"Aye," Edward said. "What a long and uneven road lay ahead of us."

"You have regrets?"

Edward glanced at him. "No. I have no regrets, Father. I've done a deal with my life. Not so much as you, perhaps, but then, I am somewhat younger."

Tom Warner pulled his beard. "Ned, you and I have not had many opportunities of speaking, as men. But these next few days will be a time for manhood, if ever it was needed."

"Do you doubt our success?"

"In the field? Rather do I fear it. You are acting here from an a obligation. 'Tis your heritage, your very manhood, drives you on. Not your heart."

"My heart is scarcely a relevant matter at this moment, Father."

"But if our expedition is to be truly successful, it will be most relevant at the end." He sighed and pulled his beard some more. "It is too easy to give advice. To admonish. I would but say this, and then I am done. This is a mighty undertaking, and although, believe me, I do not doubt its success for one instant, yet am I too aware that it must cost lives, and perhaps make the attainment of peace between ourselves and the Caribs forever impossible. None of these things daunt me in the least where the wife of my son is concerned. Yet are they of great importance, not only to us, but to our grandchildren. They can only be tossed away to the accomplishment of some even more important end. That end is the prosperity of you and your family, and through you, your colonists. However Aline comes back to you, Edward, she is the reason for our venture, and your love for her, no less than hers for you, will be the cause of the deaths that will occur. There can be no quibbling with that point. And I will say this in conclusion: *However* she comes back to you, if you loved her when you married her three years ago, and when, no doubt, you first made love to her even before that, she will be the same woman now, beneath whatever scars Wapisiane may have inflicted upon her. To forget that for an instant were to make a mockery of this entire expedition. Now I have done."

He stumped for the ladder, and Edward turned back to lean on the rail and watch St. Kitts dwindle. Now he could see Antigua as well, green on the eastern horizon, just as by looking to the ship's head he could see the peaks of the other islands unfolding, and perhaps, already, even, the greenest of all, the mountains of Dominica. The Caribee Isles. Thomas Warner's grant. This was their dream, to spread over all these green and fertile islets, to make the Carib ocean into an English lake, to succeed, where the dons had failed, because the dons had sought only to wring the wealth from the land and then return to Seville and Madrid, where the Warners and their people sought new homes. There was the future, and it depended, as his father had so truly said, on the quality of the families, on the love of man for woman, of parents for children, on their determination to succeed no matter what the odds opposed to them. Only that way could they found a nation.

And as Tom Warner's eldest son, as heir to all this, it was above all his responsibility to lead the way down that domestic path. How much of that knowledge had driven him from the beginning? How much of the certainty that Englishmen and Frenchmen must be rivals for this paradise had caused him to select before all others a French girl as his wife? There was nonsense, sound reasoning after the event. It took no account of flowing mahogany-brown hair, of swelling breasts and thin white legs, of that echoing laugh, of the spirit which had created such a rapport with life itself. But to consider those things now must be to consider them as they were now, spread-eagled before Wapisiane. Would he need four of his men to hold her down? Or would he first beat her into submission? Or would he need to do either? Christ, what a thought. So, when she came back, would there be bruises on her body? There would be bruises inside her body, where his weapon had gone questing. These would not be for the seeing, but his own weapon would know they were there, whenever it sought comfort. And what of the mind? Would he ever know whether she had wept or sighed as Wapisiane had forced her from her knees to her belly to chewing the dust? Would she ever admit that? Or worse yet, suppose, with her habitual candor, she admitted it freely? What then? Where do honor and manhood end, and hatred begin?

He remained by the rail all night, doing no more than drink a glass of wine. Not even his father came near him. They could appreciate his feelings even if, no doubt, they could not exactly share them. But his was a position in which any one of them could find themselves, should they not complete this task with dreadful certainty.

In the hour before dawn he dozed, his knees buckling so that he knelt on the deck by the gunwale, to be awakened with a cry of "Sail ho" from the masthead, to struggle to his feet, muscles cramped and head swinging, and watch the three-masted ship bearing down from the northeast.

Tom Warner hurried on deck, accompanied by John Painton and the French officers. "A Spaniard, you think?"

Painton leveled his glass. "No. Why, by God . . ." He frowned into the eyepiece. "The *Caribee Queen*. Tony Hilton."

Edward snatched the telescope. "Tony? By God . . ." He did not recognize the ship. But there was no doubt about its strength. Fifteen cannon bristled at him from each broadside. She could have blown the *Plymouth Belle* clear out of the water. "You'll shorten sail, John, and speak with her?"

"I shall, Ned. But I doubt we need to, as she is catching us in any event. My bottom is too foul for speed."

They lined the rail and watched the privateer approach. Even at a mile distance they could see the tall figure in the rigging. "Ned Warner, by God," Hilton shouted.

"What brings you south?" Edward called, his whole body throbbing with hope.

"The *Dandy* sloop put into Tortuga yesterday afternoon," Hilton bellowed. "We heard there was work to be done."

"By God," Tom muttered. "He must have close on a hundred men in that ship. With his force . . ."

Painton slapped him on the back. "We'll knock a few Indians on the head, for sure, Tom. Aye, we're back where we started, by God. Wapisiane will not stand before us." He pointed forward, to the massive deep green slopes of Dominica. "There's our enemy."

There were no natural harbors in Dominica. As the breeze held in the northeast, the two ships stood on for the southwestern corner, and there dropped their anchors close to an open beach, and disembarked their men.

"Mon Dieu," muttered Jean Solange, one of the Frenchmen. "But this is sand?"

The beach was black.

Edward was first ashore. "Volcanic ash. This island is

hardly more than a large volcano, 'tis said. As are St. Lucia and St. Vincent and Martinique, to the south."

Solange stared at the tree-clad slopes rising above them, and crossed himself.

"I hope there is no chance of an eruption during *our* stay," remarked his companion, Lafitte.

"It'd be rumbling and smoking already," Painton pointed out. "Come on, lads, let's get those weapons ashore."

Edward walked down the beach to greet Hilton as he landed. "Tony. I could hardly believe my eyes. But this is not your fight."

"Any Warner fight is Tony Hilton's fight as well, Ned. You kept Susan safe for me. I'll do no less to get Aline back safe for you. If it is possible."

His face was solemn. Edward nodded. "I am prepared for the worst. And Susan?"

"Is queen of the largest community of cutthroats ever assembled in one place." Hilton's face split into that enormous grin. "And beloved by all, so that she enjoys every minute of it."

"And she was safely delivered?"

"And again. Both sons. We called the eldest Edward."

And what color hair has he got? Edward wanted to ask. "I, too, had a son. The Indians dashed out his brains."

Hilton's fingers ate into his shoulder. "You will have others, Ned, when there are no more Indians to trouble you. Why, Brian Connor, you old devil. Back to the fighting, eh?"

"And proud to serve under Captain Warner again, Mr. Hilton, seeing as how ye're at his side."

"That goes for all of us. Well, Ned, your father is looking anxious."

They joined the other officers, who were peering upward at the forested mountains, glowing in the midday sun; but already there were heavy clouds ringing the horizon, promising rain before night.

"You've a plan of campaign, I have no doubt," Tom suggested.

"It is dictated for us," Edward said. "We cannot use the forest as do the Caribs, so we must persuade them to attack us, and rely upon our superior strength at close quarters. You may be sure they know we have landed, and are at this moment watching us. Nor will they permit us a free passage through the forest, you may also be certain. So through the forest we shall go. We rely on the dogs for a while, and then,

I have no doubt, our nostrils will guide us to the sulfur. We'll leave adequate crews for both vessels, but no one on the beach. John, will you take charge here?"

"I had hoped to be in at the death."

"You may well be yet. I'd have you keep your cannon loaded, and should we return in haste, which could well happen, your fire will cover our embarkation. How many men will you need?"

"Give me thirty to each ship, and I'll fight them, and sail them home, too, if need be."

"Then our numbers are settled at four score for the expedition. Brian, your Irish will form the advance guard, with myself. Father, I'd be pleased if you'd command the main battle in the center, with the people from John's ship. Tony, will your buccaneers bring up the rear, with yourself?"

"Willingly, if that is how you wish it."

"Now, there are things we must remember. First and foremost, we must keep up. We can afford no stragglers. Secondly, at the first alarm, drop to the ground and fire your pieces from there. The Indians' weapons have no long range, and should an arrow strike any one of us, be sure that our muskets, if fired soon enough, will send a ball twice as far as the archer. And there are enough of us to make the forest hum. The third point is a melancholy one, but is the most important of all. No man of us must be taken alive. Should anyone be too badly wounded to continue on the march, he must be prepared to end his own life on the instant. Believe me, the alternative is far more terrible."

"But by the same token, we take no prisoners either," Hilton growled.

"We are about a war, not a parade," Edward agreed. "Well, then, shall we fall to?"

Without giving time for further argument, or further fearful glances at the forest, he commanded the dogs to be loosed, and followed them on the path leading upward through the trees. Brian Connor immediately took his place at his shoulder, bearing the standard with the cross of St. George, and the other five Irishmen were close behind.

" 'Tis strange how the wheel turns a full circle, Ted," Brian muttered. "Now we could be the dons, armor and all."

"Saving that we shall fall for no shallow devices. And that we must be certain there is a Carib village at the end of our march, and our dogs will find it."

He spoke more confidently than he felt. And yet, was there

not cause for confidence? The dogs ran in front of him, maintaining a steady baying as they cast from side to side of the path, and yet always scurrying upward. Enough there to terrify the Indians, apart from the armored mass coming behind. Yet surely Wapisiane would have anticipated nothing less than this, and would have made his preparations.

First of which, undoubtedly, was this forest. There was nothing like it in the more northerly islands. Here was a combination of the wet, clinging, Guyanese jungle with the unending, wearisome slopes of Mount Misery, only these hills did not even go uniformly upward, but rather rose and then fell, sending the column up and down, undulating like a steel-clad snake, while swords and pikes and muskets clanked against armor, and men cursed, and above the column there rose a cloud of steam as sweat dribbled down their faces and bodies and rose into the still air. After no more than an hour he was forced to call a halt and permit the men to drink from the gourds of water they carried, and to rest for ten minutes, or he had no doubt they would be far too weary to carry out any command competently. So then, he decided, there can be little chance of deciding the issue this night.

"An empty forest," Tom said. "They will be waiting behind some easily defensible position, farther on."

"I doubt that, Father," Edward said. "The dogs show too much interest in the forest on either side of this path."

"No doubt because the forest is full of game." Hilton had removed his helmet and emptied water over his head. " 'Tis certain to me that our severest casualties will be caused by heat stroke."

"Aye." Tom mopped his brow. "This is not a march I'd consider for longer than a day."

Edward went back to the Irish, who were already on their feet.

"Ye'd think the varmints would have hit us by now," Connor grumbled. "We're well away from any support the ships can give us."

Edward stared at the empty tree wall. Suppose Wapisiane did not mean to fight at all, but just to have them march forever, until they dropped from exhaustion and lack of food and water? But surely that was utterly unlike the Indian? The Carib fought wherever he could, but also whenever conditions were most suited to his style of fighting. So then, what conditions could be better than this concealing forest? Unless . . . He discovered that the sun had disappeared, although it was yet only the middle of the afternoon. But the entire sky had become blotted out by the heavy black clouds. It was not the hurricane season, so the Indians could hardly be expecting more than a little rain. A little rain, by Christ, he thought, and hurried back down the column.

"You'll keep your powder dry, should it rain," he told the musketeers.

They gazed at him, and panted, and sweated. He must bring them to action soon, or what discipline they possessed would very rapidly disintegrate.

"We'll move on," he told his father and Hilton, and took his place once again at the head of the column. The dogs were released, and went baying up the path. Now it was cooler, and yet not sufficiently so for true relief. And now the clouds were something to fear, as they stumbled forward.

"By Christ," Connor said. "But what is that?"

The dogs had smelled it too, and checked their baying, although they continued to cast around, as the dreadful, dead stench of the sulfur began to drift toward them.

"The people of the smoke," Edward said. "Why, we are at their volcano."

Tom had hurried forward, his face crimson, his breath coming in great pants. "And it wants yet two hours to dark. You'll command a general assault, Ned."

"I suspect it is farther off than we hope or think," Edward said. "The smell will get stronger. But at least we know we are on the right path."

Something struck him on the helmet with such force that he thought he had been hit by an arrow. He half-turned, and looked up, and was hit another stinging blow on the face.

"Rain, by God," he shouted. "Halt. Halt the march. Stay close. Guard your powder." But already he doubted his words were being heard, as the entire afternoon seemed to dissolve.

He had known rain like this, in Guyana. But only his father and Hilton were similarly experienced. For as in Guyana, there was no wind. Just the solid sheets of water which came pouring down, thudding on their helmets to shut out even the possibility of thought, much less conversation, crashing onto breastplates, driving into necks and thighs, trickling down boots, filling scabbards, and turning the earth beneath their feet into a swamp as they crouched beneath the trees. Even the dogs had come scurrying back to their masters, and sat with hanging heads, bays exchanged for mournful wails. Again as in Guyana, time became irrelevant. They might have sat in the forest for an eternity, for days or months, or merely for a few minutes. The noise was incessant, seeming to raise a curtain around them, shutting out the rest of the island just as the teeming water shut out the heavens and most of the daylight. There was no hope of powder staying dry in this heavenly waterfall, and little hope of it drying for some hours afterward, either. As the Indians would have known.

As the Indians would have known. The rain was slackening. It was possible to raise his head and look into the steaming green forest. So, had they ignored the march of the white men for this day, because they had known the rain would come? Or had they but postponed their attack?

He stood up. "Loose those dogs, Brian. Send word back down the column to resume the march."

" 'Tis still raining, Ted, lad," Connor protested. "Should we not wait awhile longer?"

"That's what Wapisiane will be hoping," Edward said. "His bow strings will also have to be dried. We'll march, now. Loose those dogs." He hurried back down the column himself, roused men to their feet with slaps and curses.

Even Tom Warner was slow to react. "You'll press on now?" he demanded. "We've no useful powder."

"And Wapisiane will know that, Father. He will be using the rain as a weapon. We must march."

He got them all on their feet at last, and hurried back up to the head of the column, panting, and each breath now searing his lungs as a slight breeze had arisen to chase away the last of the clouds, but at the same time to blow gusts of pure sulfur across the forest.

The dogs remained unhappy, no longer baying with the confidence of an hour before, but staying closer together, and casting from side to side of the path almost fearfully.

"People, you think?" Connor wanted to know.

"Could be just the sulfur. With the smell this strong, we cannot be far away."

Edward had not finished his sentence before he heard the hiss of the first arrow, and one of the Irishmen gave a cry. "Down," he yelled. "Down. Pass the word back. Down."

He threw himself full length on the sodden earth, jarring his shoulder against his cuirass, and watching an arrow thud into the bole of the tree before which he had just been standing. From farther back along the column there came shouts and curses, but whether they were caused by actual wounds or the discomforts of the earth he could not be sure.

"You'll get those dogs back, Brian," he said.

"Aye." Connor commenced whistling, and the dogs came back through the bushes, but now there were only ten of them.

"Who was it hurt?" Brian demanded.

" 'Tis me, your Honor. Gerald Murphy."

"Is it bad?" Edward asked.

"Sticking up out of me shoulder, your Honor, and hurting like the devil."

"We'll have it out in a moment. Keep down."

But the arrows had stopped. Wapisiane was also waiting.

One of the sailors came crawling up the path, his knees making huge sucking noises every time they left the mud, his clothes and armor covered with the glutinous brown. "Sir Thomas sends his compliments, Captain Warner," he said. "He wishes to know why we do not clear these savages from the bushes, if indeed they are as close as you suggested."

"Because that is what Wapisiane hopes we will attempt," Edward said. "The arrows will do us little harm, but should we enter the forest in small groups, we would become easy victims. Tell Sir Thomas to spare no effort to dry his powder."

"If such a thing is possible," Connor grunted. "Now, then, Gerry me boy, it's coming out."

Murphy uttered a thin wail. "D'ye think it's poisoned, your Honor? I have heard tell . . ."

"Spread about by the dons, Gerald," Edward reassured him. "You'll survive, provided we stop that bleeding. Spare a piece of your shirt, Brian."

"Oh, aye, my shirt, to be sure."

They at least had suffered no diminution in morale. And neither, basically, had the dogs, who seemed glad of the rest, and lay on the wet earth panting and licking themselves. And now the arrows came again, whispering through the trees, striking branches, and falling to the earth with gentle thuds.

Hilton came crackling through the bushes, also on his hands and knees. "What sorry business is this, Ned?" he demanded. "Are we to lie here, skulking, before a pack of naked savages? That were no way to win a campaign."

"It is the only way to win this one, Tony," Edward said. "Patience. And ours is already proving the superior. Else why should Wapisiane waste his arrows on the empty air? We'll move on, the moment it gets dark."

"You'd go through this forest at night? Why, man, that is suicide."

"For whom? Do you imagine the Indians have some supernatural power which enables them to see in the dark?"

"They will certainly hear us."

"I am counting on it. Can you not understand? They will hear the tramp of armored men, the baying of the dogs, coming ever closer, and yet have no certain knowledge of where we are. And we will be guided both by the dogs and by our own nostrils. Remember, they are fighting for their homes, against a force they count at least equal but more likely superior to their own. You must instill this into your people, Tony. *We* have no cause to fear them and their puny sticks and arrows. But *they* know they have every cause to fear our steel and our lead and our dogs."

"By God," Hilton said. " 'Tis a point I had not considered. You are general here, Ned, and right glad am I that it should be so."

The arrows continued to whisper through the trees for more than an hour, and several men were wounded, but only slightly. They grumbled, and fingered their weapons, and stared into the forest, but they obeyed their commanders and lay still, while the afternoon grew cool and the light began to fade. And always the heavy smell of the sulfur lay across the day to remind them of how close they were to their goal. Edward wondered what thoughts were dunning through Wapisiane's mind. The Indian had no means of knowing how many of the white men had been hurt in his attack; would it not be a temptation to launch an assault through the trees? There would be a rapid and certain conclusion to the campaign; Edward had no doubt at all of the outcome, could he but oppose his steel to the Caribs' wood and flesh.

But the forest remained silent, and in time even the steam ceased to rise from the ground and the arrows to strike the trees with their gentle thuds. And now the sun was gone, settled at last behind the mountains over which they had come, plummeting downward toward the quiet sea. He almost smiled. Here he was fighting a battle on his very own terms, at sundown rather than at sunup.

He crawled into the midst of the Irishmen, sprawled on the wet ground, each man holding two of the dogs' leashes.

"You'll give me those, Brian," he said. "And make your way down the column to tell them to prepare to move on. Now, mark me well. It will be dark in a few minutes. Each one of us must keep close to the man in front. More than ever, there must be no straggling. Tell Mr. Hilton."

"I'll do that, Ted," Connor agreed. "We'll be ending it soon, then?"

"God willing."

"Aye. He will be, if He's on our side. I tell ye straight, Ted, I'd not like to spend a night in this dismal, foul-smelling place."

He crawled down the column, and Edward took the leashes. The movement had alerted the dogs, and they were straining and whining. But Edward waited for Connor to return before giving the order to advance. Wearily the men rose to their feet, stretching their cramped muscles, adjusting their breastplates, replacing their helmets. The column gave out a gigantic whisper of sound, which surely penetrated far into the forest, and Edward had the command once again ready on his lips, but the trees on either side remained silent. The Indians had withdrawn. Yet this too was an important pointer to the coming night; Wapisiane had his people as much in hand as Edward had his. There was no easy path here.

He gave the command and loosed the dogs. They bounded forward, and then slowed again, their nostrils clogged by the ever-increasing stench of sulfur. But their task of scenting was finished; they were approaching their role of destroyers.

Now once again the path led upward, as uncertain and as broken as ever, with shattered tree trunks lying across it and sudden soft pits into which the men stumbled with curses. It was a miracle that no one had as yet broken a leg; judging by the comments, it seemed certain there were a few sprains. But the principal obstacle to speed was the air, which grew more difficult to breathe with every step.

The dogs stopped, clustered at the top of the rise. Edward hurried forward to reach them at the same time as the Irishmen. It was now quite dark, and the moon had not yet risen, yet he could tell he was at the edge of a shallow precipice, and he could tell too that he looked down on no forest, but on an empty area filled with clouds of slowly floating vapor. Yet the path had led here, and clearly they were meant to scramble down the steep slope in front of them.

"By Christ," Connor muttered. "But this place grows more miserable with every yard. What do we do now, Ted?"

"Halt the column, for a start," Edward commanded. "And ask Sir Thomas and Mr. Hilton to join me here."

They came forward a moment later, accompanied by the French officers. "By God, what a dismal place," Hilton remarked. "Do we cross that?"

"It would seem there is no other way."

"Mon Dieu," Solange said. "But that is the crater of a volcano."

"And it smokes," Lafitte pointed out.

"It rather steams," Edward argued. "At the least there is no movement of the earth, which must surely accompany a potential eruption. But I would not risk the entire force in such a venture. I will lead a reconnaissance, and see if I can find a suitable way across this valley, and indeed, see if we can find what lies beyond, before returning to you."

"That is madness," Tom declared. "Is it not just what the Caribs will be hoping for, that we will detach small scouting parties which they can destroy?"

"In any event," Hilton objected, "you are our general. If you are determined upon such a course, certain it is you cannot lead it yourself."

Edward chewed his lip. There was solid sense in both their arguments, but he could send no one else, with any promise of success, and the alternative was to admit his plan had been faulty, and wait here for daylight. Worse, it would mean that Wapisiane had once again outwitted him.

"You must know," Yarico said, "how bad you want for come to Wapisiane."

They turned in confusion, reaching for swords and pistols. Not even the dogs had heard her approach—it was asking too much of them to have smelled her amidst the stench of the sulfur—but there she was, a wisp of a figure in the darkness, wearing nothing more than her apron, and unarmed.

"Yarico?" Edward whispered. "Are you not a spirit?"

She tossed her head.

"But how come you here, girl?" Tom demanded.

"Wapisiane send," she said.

"Now, that you'll have to explain," Hilton said. "We had supposed you his captive."

She shrugged. "He beat. He treat like dog. But Yarico not

cry. Yarico got for live. So he say, Yarico live, Yarico princess again, if Yarico help."

"Help?" Tom asked.

Oh, Christ, Edward thought, why cannot they be quiet? Why cannot we let her speak, so that she will tell us the one thing we must know, but dare not ask.

"Wapisiane say, why white men not stop? Indian not fight by night. I say, War-nah never stop. So Wapisiane say, then War-nah come more quick. Path through forest. Round dead valley. I lead War-nah and few men, say for surprise attack on village."

"By God," Hilton said. "There's a cunning devil."

"And he will be waiting to overwhelm the few men," Tom said. "But supposing the entire force takes that way?"

Again the contemptuous shrug. "Then you see nobody. Empty village."

"I begin to get his drift. And supposing we wait for daylight, and make a frontal assault across the valley? I'm assuming the village is on the farther side."

"Village there," she said. "But valley bad. Hot stream, no air. Wapisiane wait on far side, fire arrow, run into forest."

"I begin to wonder if this scoundrel is a savage after all," Tom remarked. " 'Tis certain he has the makings of a general. Well, Edward? What is your decision?"

Edward licked his lips. "Wapisiane sent you to us, Yarico. You betrayed him once. Did he not expect you to betray him again?"

Yarico's eyes gloomed at him in the darkness. "He for care? War-nah come, War-nah die. War-nah leave, Wapisiane big man. But he know War-nah come for A-line."

"And she is there?" he shouted. "By Christ, tell me she is there."

Yarico nodded.

"And well?"

"A-line tie to stake," Yarico said. "And then she laugh."

"She laughed? By God."

"There is a woman," Hilton said. "Now is my last doubt dispelled."

"And what then?" Edward asked.

Yarico gazed at him. "War-nah woman is bitch-dog," she said.

"Oh, Christ," he muttered.

"We shall have their blood," Solange vowed.

"Or they will have ours," Hilton said. "It seems that this

Wapisiane has circumstances very much under his own control."

"Well, boy?" Tom asked.

Edward pulled his beard. "How many men does Wapisiane command?"

She shrugged. "Many people."

"More than we have here?"

Yarico looked over such of the column as she could see. "Perhaps."

"But not many, I swear," Edward said. "Or he'd not be so anxious to get at us piecemeal. Well, then, he is dictating events, at this moment. We must attempt to weaken his control, and we can only accomplish that by surprise. He is expecting you to return sometime this night, with perhaps a dozen of us. Am I right, Yarico?"

She nodded.

"And no doubt he is watching this secret path of yours?"

"Men watch," she agreed.

"And there is no other way to the village, save across the valley below us?"

She shook her head.

"And that too is overlooked?"

"Nobody cross valley in dark," she asserted.

"Because of the boiling water? But surely there *is* a way."

"Boiling stream cross valley," she said. "But not possible in dark. Then spirits of dead rise up in steam. Nobody go in valley at night."

There is no doubt that she believed what she was saying, and thus that the other Indians also believed it. Edward pulled his beard some more. "Where exactly is the village, Yarico? On the far side of the valley?"

"Over there, yes. Village beyond Boiling Lake, where air is clean."

"You have a plan in mind?" Hilton asked.

"I need first of all twelve volunteers to accompany Yarico," Edward said. "Led by you, Tony. This is a most dangerous assignment I give you, because if the rest of my plan does not succeed, you will be cut off."

"While you lead the rest of us across the valley?" Tom demanded. "You have heard that is impossible."

"I fear no Indian ghosts, Father."

"Neither do I. But seventy men, will they not hear us?"

"Probably, should the entire force attempt to cross. I will need another ten volunteers who will brave the valley in the dark, with the certainty of an assault on the Indian village beyond."

"You'd pit twenty-two men against close on a hundred savages?"

"For a start. Our purpose is to make Wapisiane commit his people, and prevent their withdrawal into the forest until we have regained Aline. The advantage of surprise in this will be ours. How long will it take to traverse this path of yours, Yarico?"

"Not long," she said.

"But it must take a long time, the first time. Someone must fall, and seem to hurt himself. Tony, I leave this in your care."

"Aye. We shall take a long time."

"And then," Edward said, "the moment there can be no doubt as to Tony's party finding the village, Yarico, I wish you to slip away into the forest and return here with all speed, and bring on the remainder of the force, with the dogs. By then we shall have forced Wapisiane to give battle, and there will be no disappearing into the forest."

Yarico nodded thoughtfully.

"You will be in command of the main force, Father," Edward said. "And once Yarico returns, you will make all haste to the scene of action, allowing the dogs as much noise as they wish; the sound of your approach cannot help but be discouraging to the savages. But all depends upon my leading my party across the valley before Tony is engaged. We will start immediately."

"On the contrary," Solange observed. "All depends on the Princess Yarico here."

The men gazed at him.

"She was carried off by this Wapisiane," Solange said. "To suffer his revenge, you say, because she betrayed his people. Yet she lives, and does not appear unduly harmed. Now she has come at his bidding, to command us to divide our forces, and to make sure we understand that there is no other course open to us. What proof have you that she has not made her peace with her people? What proof have you that she did not invite them into English Harbor in the first instance, in the full knowledge that Captain Warner and most of his men were on the far side of the island? And now, it seems to me, our entire operation depends upon her fidelity. There will be twelve of us in the Indian village, and another ten approaching from the valley, if they are able, and our fate will be certain, should Sir Thomas not be able to bring up the main body." He paused, glancing from one to the other.

"You must reply, Yarico," Edward said. "Why is Wapisiane trusting you?"

"Wapisiane, pouf," she said. "He not know who cause Blood River. He think War-nah take me like other women. And now, he know you will come, Ed-ward. Because A-line there. You come with few men, he say, or she die, and Indian go in forest."

"And he thinks it is not possible to cross the valley of the dead at night?"

"Not possible," she said. "Much spirit there. You go, you die."

"Aye. Well, Brian, will your boys follow me?"

"Through that graveyard?" Connor shrugged. "We've followed you into worse places."

"I need men I can rely on. What of you, Monsieur Solange?"

The Frenchman hesitated, looking from Yarico to the white men, and then shrugged himself. "I came here to rescue your wife, Captain Warner. It makes little sense to suffer a faint heart now. Lafitte?"

"I will come."

"And three more," Edward said. "I will find them. We will carry swords and pistols, nothing more. Tony, you had best recruit from among your own men, as they know you. But be sure you carry only such powder as has dried."

"I like it not," Tom muttered. "The one thing we decided was that to divide our forces would be fatal."

"There is no other way to force Wapisiane to fight, Father," Edward insisted. "And I believe our surprise will carry the day."

"There is still the matter of timing," Hilton said.

"On arrival at the village, you will fire your pistol, Tony. Be sure that we shall hear the sound. As will my father."

"Valley of dead not possible in dark," Yarico said. "You go, you die, Ed-ward." Her face was solemn.

Edward smiled at her. "Then I'll say farewell, sweetheart. Be sure you play your part."

Carefully he crawled out from the trees and onto the slope leading down to the valley. By now his nostrils were almost accustomed to the endless stench, but it seemed that the heat grew ever more intense as he left the tree screen. And the darkness also. His feet slipped and he went sliding down the rough rock face, cutting his hands. But it was not so far as he had supposed, and a moment later he found himself at the foot of the slope, breathless and bleeding, but not seriously hurt.

"Are ye all right, Captain?" Connor whispered.

"Aye. But you'd best watch your step, Brian. It is a matter of sliding."

"By Christ," Connor said. "By Christ . . ." A moment later he landed beside Edward. But at least he had shown the others the way, and soon they were all gathered at the foot of the slope.

"Now," Edward said. "There must be no more sound."

"As if they'd hear us," Solange pointed out. And it was true that they had to speak quite loudly to make themselves heard over the constant hissing that arose from around them.

"We must first locate the stream," Edward said. "As it is to be our guide. We'll spread out, but keep within arm's reach of each other."

He went forward in the middle, Connor on one side of him and Solange on the other. They crept across what might have been a stony plain, except for the clouds of sulfurous gas which kept slashing at their nostrils.

"By Christ," Connor said. " 'Tis easy to believe this place belongs to the dead, Ted. Should we lose ourselves . . ."

"We'll not," Edward assured him. "What's that?"

There was a sound, half a cry and half a moan, from the right. They hurried in the direction, and found one of the Irishmen sitting down next to the rushing stream.

"By God," he said. "I stepped in it. It came right through me boot. By God, I can feel the flesh boiling."

"You'll walk," Edward commanded. "And quickly. We can afford no stragglers. Now, come, lads. Here's our guide. But there will be other pools, so tread carefully."

He made his way along the side of the seething rivulet; the heat rose from it as if he were walking on the edge of a caldron of boiling water, as indeed he was. The very ground was hot; he could feel it burning through his boots. His breastplate seemed to contain a lake of sweating flesh which was his chest and shirt, and perspiration ran out from beneath his helmet in a constant stream. His very hands were sodden, and he wondered if he would be able to grasp his sword. And soon enough the hissing commenced to his left as well, and he found himself on the edge of a bubbling pool rising out of the ground.

"Be careful," he told his men, and made his way along the narrow pathway between the two springs.

"Christ, I have slipped," Lafitte howled. "Oh, *mon Dieu,* how it burns. I can go no further. I am in agony. I . . ."

"On your feet, monsieur," Edward snapped. "You'll assist him, if you please, Monsieur Solange. Rise or die, monsieur."

Lafitte struggled to his feet, groaning and muttering curses.

"It cannot be much farther," Edward said. "Listen."

From ahead of them even the hissing of the water was lost in a steady, rumbling gurgle.

"By God, it will be exploding next," Connor muttered, and crossed himself.

"That is the Boiling Lake," Edward said. "As Yarico told us, it does nothing but boil and bubble, day in and day out. Yet it marks the inward extremity of this valley. We are close to the village."

He led them forward, and after only a few more yards the ground started to slope upward. Now the lake was close to their left hand; the noise was tremendous, and the heat seemed to have redoubled, if that were possible. But a sudden puff of breeze, coming down from the windward slopes ahead of them, actually cleared the sulfur for a moment and allowed them to inhale clean air.

"We have arrived," he whispered. "Quiet now."

He climbed the slope, the lake ever growling on his left, and found himself crawling past a green bush, while the next puff of wind came hard behind the first. "Here," he said. "Here we wait."

They crouched beside him, gasping, taking off their helmets to wipe their heads, drawing their swords and laying them on the ground.

"How long, do you think?" Solange asked.

"We made good time. If Yarico did indeed delay, then we shall at the least have time to catch our breaths."

"And if she did not delay, it is because she intends to betray us, so a breath here or there will make no difference. Eh, Captain?"

"As you say, monsieur. But she saved my life on more than one occasion in the past. It would not be in her now to wish to take it."

"Supposing there can be such a thing as constancy in a savage. Hark."

The sound of a pistol shot drifted faintly through the air.

"Our signal, by God. Prime your pistols, lads. Quickly now. Remember that at this moment Tony Hilton is fighting for his life."

He scrambled to his feet. Christ, how his heart pounded. Not at the prospect of the desperate encounter which lay only seconds in front of him. He had no fears of that. He intended to conquer this day or die, and he worried little which outcome came about. But the conquering, or the dying, involved seeing Aline again. Seeing what Wapisiane had made of her. And through her, what he would have made of her husband.

"We'll make as much noise as possible," he said. He pointed his sword up the hill and shouted, "Attack, my friends. Attack."

He led them forward at a jog trot, up the slope and into the clear night air. Now they heard the rumble of the volley fired by Hilton's men, away to the left, a ripple of deadly sound. But it would be the only one; Wapisiane would hardly give them time to reload. And now too they saw the glow of the fire in the center of the Carib village, burning low but nonetheless ready to be rekindled with daylight, and by its faint light they could also make out the first of the huts.

Three Indians emerged from the bushes near the village, where they had clearly been placed as a guard, but from where they had sadly neglected their duties. Now they stood in front of the white men, brandishing their wooden spears and shouting, uncertain whether they were facing men or spirits. Edward swung the first thrust of the spear to one side with his sword, and bringing the blade back, felt it crunch on bone even as the man fell at his feet. Then he was through and running into the village without stopping to look at what had happened to the others.

He could hear the shouting of the savages from in front of him now, and the cheers of Tony's men. But in seconds they would have to be overwhelmed. "To me," he shouted at the full extent of his lungs. "To me. Warner."

His men joined him by the fire. The huts appeared to be empty. The Indians had prudently sent their noncombatants into the forest until the outcome of the battle could be decided.

"Over there," Connor gasped, pointing to the trees, where a mass of people could be seen in the darkness, and the cries of the English party could be distinguished.

"We'll burn them back." Edward seized a glowing brand from the fire, thrust it into the palm roof of the nearest hut, and watched the smoke rise, even if it was slow to catch. He ran for the next, the ember now flaming in his hand, and saw Aline.

Beyond the glowing fire, only now visible as his eyes became accustomed to the light, there were two stakes, driven into the ground, dreadfully reminiscent of the Carib village in St. Kitts on that unforgettable day so many years ago. And to the nearest there still clung a tattered skeleton, such flesh as remained hanging from bone and skull already rotted into nothing by the heat. Beyond, Aline crouched at the foot of hers. She was naked, and secured by the wrists to the foot of the stake, so that no matter what happened she could not stand upright, nor indeed do more than crawl. In the gloom it was impossible to see what, if anything, had happened to her; she was a white blur with a mass of mahogany-brown hair, but she was still capable of movement, and indeed had risen to her knees, shoulder pressed against the stake, as she tried to discover what was happening.

"By God." Edward dropped to his knees beside her. "Aline? By Christ, Aline?" He held his breath against the stench which rose from her, so indicative of all that she had suffered during the past three days.

She gazed at him, her brows knitted. Her face was bruised and swollen, and her lips were puffy. Her eyes were dull, but there was recognition and excitement coming into them. "Edward?" she whispered. "Oh, God, Edward."

"They are for us, Ted," Connor shouted.

"But a moment," Edward promised, and rose to his feet. His men had, without bidding, ranged themselves in front of the stake, and now the Indians, discovering themselves assailed in the rear, were coming back through the trees.

"Present," Edward yelled. "Take your aim, now. Fire."

The pistols rippled flame and explosion and black smoke, and several of the Indians fell. The rest checked for an instant.

"Stay close," Edward shouted. "Tony. Tony Hilton. Now, man, now is the time."

There came a whoop from the forest beyond the massed Indians, and one or two looked over their shoulder. The others advanced, checking at a distance of some twenty feet to hurl spears, and one of the Irish fell with a growl of pain.

"We'll charge those men," Solange shouted.

"No," Edward bellowed. "Stay close. They seek my wife."

The Indians came on, a shrieking mass in the semi-darkness. Spears thrust and clanged on breastplate and helmet. Swords swung and men cursed and screamed, and women too, for Edward realized with a thrill of horror that the Caribs were fighting as a nation. Blood flew, and splattered across his face. He thrust and cut, careless of any individual in front of him, aware only that Brian Connor stood on his left hand and the Frenchman Lafitte on his right, aware only that he must kill and kill and kill until he dropped himself from exhaustion, and aware too that this was all he wished to do, to die, while killing, to take as many of the savages to hell with him as he could.

But Hilton had rallied his men, and these too were close, charging the rear of the Indians, forcing them to fight at their backs as well, turning the conflict into an indistinguishable melee. For all their armor and their superior weapons, the white men were outnumbered, and the issue might well have gone against them, had there not now come through the night, echoing above even the screams and the curses, the unmistakable baying of the hounds. Here was the decisive factor. Where there had been a mass of seething naked brown bodies and flailing wooden spears, on a sudden there were only exhausted armor-clad white men, resting on their swords, sinking to their knees, tearing their helmets from their heads and throwing them away, begging for water and help for their wounds.

Edward ignored them as he knelt beside Aline. Trampled on in the fighting, she had shrunk closer to her stake, her cheek pressed against the bloodstained wood. He tore at the ties of his breastplate, released it, and pulled his shirt free. His knife slashed through the thongs holding her wrists, and then he wrapped his shirt around her sun- and dirt- and whip-roughened shoulders, and pulled her upward. She came easily enough, and remained standing against him, hardly breathing, her head resting on his chest.

Now he could properly draw breath and look around him. The village was at last beginning to burn at his back, and send flames upward to illuminate the night, accompanied by dense clouds of smoke and intermittent showers of sparks. The dogs had reached them, casting around, baying, sniffing at the dead bodies, their cacophony the paean of victory. The dead were being dragged into rows, and six of them wore breastplates.

Several others were wounded, but the price for this triumph had been cheap enough, he supposed; not less than a score of the Indians lay dead.

"A famous victory, Ted," Brian Connor shouted. "And is the lady all right?"

"She will be. Now . . ."

"But look here, Monsieur Warner." Solange pointed with his sword, to where two of Hilton's men had an Indian on the ground. "We have a dozen of these, too sore wounded to run away. What do you suppose we should do with them? But this fellow speaks your name."

Edward watched Wapisiane writhe on the ground in a combination of pain and self-hatred, that he should have been so reduced. His leg was shattered by a pistol ball; the bone protruded and his blood drained onto the ground. And now a sailor standing over him kicked him on the shattered bone to bring a moan of agony from his lips. Yet his eyes never wavered, and his gaze never left Edward's face. He expected no mercy, was perhaps not even concerned with the way he would be made to die, but only with his own manner and his own courage at the decisive moment.

"There he lies," Tony Hilton said. "I had thought to have forgotten this face, these eyes. By God, but he'll look good, dangling at the end of a rope. It must be hoisted slow."

Aline turned in his arms, her face pressed against his naked chest. Edward chewed his lip. He had given this man life once before, and it had turned out to be a dreadful mistake. And now he had reason to be harsh. His mind and his body at once called out for revenge. Only his heart suggested different. The Caribs had only defended their land, their islands, after their own fashion. The white men remained the intruders, the aggressors. Nor had they even proved themselves superior, save in the possession of their arms and armor, and their willingness to take advantage of an Indian superstition.

Or was this but the emotion of a tired victor, which would very rapidly pass?

"You leave it to us, Ned," Hilton said. "My sailors will soon enough fashion ropes from the vines that grow around here."

"They are prisoners of war," Edward said. "And as such are subject to the jurisdiction of the governor of the Caribee Isles. I'll speak with my father." He stared into the thronging mass of white men, for the main body had now come up. The main body, but no Father, and no Yarico?

"Where is Sir Thomas?" he demanded. "Where is the governor?"

They scratched their heads. "He was with us, Captain Warner," they assured him. "When we began the assault."

"Brian," Edward said. "You'll hold Mistress Warner. Do not let her go for an instant. Give her some water to drink, and see to her. Do not fail me in this."

"I'll not, Ted. I have too much respect for the little lady. Come ye here, lass. We'll soon have ye safe home again."

Edward hurried away from the glare and the noise and the stench, of blood and sweat and fear, and reached the edge of the forest, and Yarico. She knelt on the ground, next to Tom Warner.

"What in the name of God . . . ?" Edward also dropped to his knees.

Tom sighed, and tried to smile. "I am too old to run through forests, boy. I am afraid I have sorely disappointed the name of Warner." His voice was faint, his breathing uneven.

"What nonsense," Edward declared, but he looked across the gasping man to Yarico, and her eyes were solemn. "We have gained a victory."

"I never doubted that. You hold the reins of greatness, of unending success, in your hands, Ned. Would you but believe that, and dismiss forever the fears and uncertainties which haunt you, you need envy no man on earth. And now it is more than ever necessary that you do so. Yarico. Find me Tony Hilton. And Monsieur Solange. And some other men of probity. Hurry, girl."

Yarico rose, gazed at Edward for a moment, and then ran into the night.

"By God, but this breastplate weighs as much as a cannon," Tom grumbled. "I swear I am being pressed to death like any stubborn rogue."

"Let me untie it for you, Father."

"Leave it be. I'm a soldier, Edward, and if I could not even see action in my final battle, at least let me die dressed like one."

"For God's sake, Father, what nonsense you do talk. You, die? Why . . ."

But now every word was interspersed with a gasp. "Where is that girl? By God, but they are a feeble sex, to be sure. Edward. Is your wife safe?"

"Aye."

"But distressed? That is natural. Edward, remember our conversation on the ship. Men have died here this day. I command you, as your governor and your father, do not make their deaths vain. Hilton. Tony, lad, kneel here and give me your hand."

"By God, Tom," Tony said. "Here is a sorry sight. You are hurt?"

"Aye. But you will not find a wound. Now, listen to me. And you, Solange, because you will testify to this later on. I confirm Edward Warner in his appointment as governor of Antigua, and I remove all jurisdiction of the governor of St. Kitts over him. Mark these words well, gentlemen. You are my witnesses."

"Then write it out when we regain the ship," Hilton said. "And we will append our signatures."

"You'll bear witness to my words, Tony Hilton, and God damn you for an interfering whippersnapper. You'll acknowledge naught but the authority of his Majesty and his commissioners, Edward, but be sure you remember *that* authority at all times. My son Philip Warner will be governor of St. Kitts. You'll see to Yarico and little Tom, Edward. As you have always done."

"You may be sure of that, Father."

"There is a weight from my mind. And you'll endeavor not to find fault with your stepmother, lad. She is ambitious, and now she will have no children to support her hopes. Be gentle with her. And you'll plant cane, Edward. There is my last command. Philip will supply you with slaves. Cane, Edward. 'Tis the crop of the future. Promise me that."

"You have my word. Now, you have talked too well, Father. You must rest, and Tony will have his men prepare a litter to carry you back through the forest. It were best we start soon, for with daylight the Caribs may regain some of their courage, or even attract support from their neighbors."

"But before we go, there is the matter of our prisoners," Hilton said. "Including the devil himself. Wapisiane. Should we not hoist them high, Tom, as a warning to these people?"

Tom Warner gazed at him.

"I would give my vote to that, Sir Thomas," Solange said. "As you have yourself said, these people understand only force, and we would do best by leaving a reminder of our victory, and of our power to repeat it."

Tom Warner gazed at him.

"He dead," Yarico said very softly.

"Dead?" Edward leaned forward, over the short, heavy body, the bluff features, the gray-black beard, the staring eyes. "By God."

A hand rested for a moment on his shoulder, and then was withdrawn. He would not look at them. He knelt beside his father, hardly hearing the noise which came from behind him, the cries of the wounded and the triumphant whoops of the victors. He was aware of Yarico, but it was some minutes before he could raise his head.

"I love him too," she said.

"I think we all did that, even when we went against him," Edward said. "We must leave this place, Yarico. He will be buried in St. Kitts. It will be what he wished."

She remained crouching by the body. Edward walked back toward the village, checked in dismay. As Hilton had said, his men were sailors, used to creating ropes out of string; the jungle vines had provided them with an easy task. Now the twelve Indians dangled from the branches of trees; three of them were women. They had been stripped of even the scanty clothing they wore into battle, and their wounds had not been tended—most still dripped blood, which ran down their legs and hung from their toes. And they had been hoisted slowly. Several still kicked feebly, and strained their weakening muscles against the thongs which bound their wrists.

"You have done the future of our colonies in the Caribee no good here, Tony," Edward said.

Hilton grinned. "I'd argue that point, Ned, seeing that we've ended the lives of a dozen more of these red devils. Your colony, and mine, will only be secure when the last redskin is rotted. You'd do well to bear that in mind. As to any feelings you may have that we owed them some debt because of Blood River, you'd best ask your wife about that."

Edward turned to Aline, who had once again sunk to the ground. She knelt, his shirt pulled into a ball on her lap by her clutching fingers, staring at the fluttering men and women. Her face was hard, but it was too dark to read the expression in her eyes.

The *Plymouth Belle* beat north, the *Caribee Queen* wide on her beam. Each ship flew all the flags and pennants she possessed, and most of the crews remained on deck to shout congratulations at each other and to be sure they were among the first to give the great news to the people of St.

Kitts. On deck, too, were the seven white men, wrapped in canvas but exposed to every possible gust of wind, for the weather was warm, and the journey north had already taken a whole night. Tom Warner lay by himself.

This, then, was the end of a man, who dreamed, and who had made so many of his dreams come true. He had been a soldier, and so had died, on a campaign. He had been surrounded, not by his wife and children and his grandchildren, but by his comrades, and that must have been comforting enough. And he had died in the moment of victory, and with a great many other victories to look back upon. He could have had no doubts about the future of St. Kitts, Edward thought. Now it but remained necessary to make sure that Antigua was protected from the possibility of another Carib raid. Not the possibility, the certainty. They had, indeed, fired the first shots of an Indian war. But had not Tom Warner himself done that, ten years before? They could but carry on his dream, and be prepared to resist the occasional nightmare.

He could but do that, and carry on his father's instructions and admonitions, as well. If he were man enough.

He left the poop and went down the ladder and through the companion doorway into the great cabin. For so short a journey it had been cleared of all gear, and all occupants as well, save two. Aline lay on the starboard bunk, covered by a blanket. Yarico had washed her, and brushed her hair, and now sat by her, watching her, looking up anxiously as Edward entered.

"She ask for you."

"And I am here. Leave us for a spell."

Yarico got up, and hesitated. "Ed-ward . . ."

"I'll not be preached at, Yarico."

She closed the door behind her softly.

Edward sat down, and Aline's head turned. For a few moments they looked at each other. "You must be very tired," she said.

"I have gone three nights without sleep."

"It must have been a horrible experience for you."

"And for you?" he asked.

"It is worse for those who wait, and imagine."

"That is not true," he said. "It must be worse to suffer. I would know, Aline. I must know. Listen, I will tell you first. You know that Joachim is dead?"

Her chin moved slowly, up and down. Her eyes were filled with tears.

"But Joan survived."

Her head turned sharply.

"I do not lie to you," Edward said. "Little Tom saved her life."

"Joan," she whispered. "Oh, God, there is a miracle."

"Hardly less than your own survival."

"He wanted *me*," she said. "He conceived that there could be no greater revenge than that."

"And having got you?"

"I do not know," she said. "I do not *know*. I think perhaps he did mean to kill me, no doubt slowly and with as much unpleasantness as he could devise. I was tied to a stake, within feet of poor Hal Leaming."

"And you laughed at him," Edward said.

She sucked air into her lungs.

"Yarico told me. A proud deed."

"I wanted to defy them. I wanted to defy Wapisiane." Her tongue circled her lips. "My laughter saved my life, Edward. But yet was I his captive, and yet did he mean to have his revenge."

His throat was dry, and his stomach was light. "He alone?"

Her head shook slowly, to and fro.

"How many?" he whispered.

"I do not know." Her hand came out from beneath the blanket, gripped his. "I closed my eyes and tried to close my mind. Or I would have gone mad." She stared at him. "Or would you have preferred that, Edward?"

"The Indian way?"

"Every way," she said. "And other things. There is nothing man can do to woman they omitted. And yet they were careful not to hurt me."

"Not to hurt you," he said. He got up, walked to the stern window, and gazed at the broad, bubbling white wake which spread behind the ship.

"Edward. They could not reach my mind."

He turned. She was sitting up, the blanket forgotten. Her shoulders were roughened with sunburn and bruises, and her breasts were pink. The most beautiful breasts he had ever known, breasts made to fill a man's hand, and how many men's hands had they filled, these past few days?

She seemed able to read his mind. She had always been able to do that. She flushed, and pulled the blanket back to her throat, and lay down. "Had I not laughed," she said, "I think they would have killed me at the stake. They were very aroused. I think they would have torn me to pieces. No doubt that would have been best, Mr. Warner. I am sorry. Then I wished to survive. Then I never doubted that I could survive, and return to you." She watched him cross the cabin and stand over her. "Then I not only loved, Mr. Warner, I thought I was loved, and I thought that our love required survival, demanded survival, for its continuance. I shall not laugh again, Mr. Warner."

How beautiful she was. Almost he stooped toward her. And then he saw the brown hands, stained with mud and filth, clawing at her body, twisting in her hair, and instead he nearly retched. But how valuable she was, in her courage and her constancy. Yet how tarnished, as every white man, every white woman, and every white child in the Caribee Isles, no, in the entire Western Hemisphere, in time, in the entire world, would know. No one would ever look at her again without seeing her stretched on her face in the dust, her legs spread wide. No one.

He ran for the doorway, and the fresh breeze coming in from the north.

"He was a great man," declared the Reverend Sweeting, and raised his head as if daring anyone in the assembly to challenge his statement.

There was no risk of that. The colonists of St. Kitts, men and women, and their children, stood in a huge mass on the slopes of the hill beneath the grave. Only the men on duty on Brimstone Hill were not present; even the slaves had been lined up below their masters and mistresses. There could be no less than four thousand people present, Edward estimated. Some distance from the four nervous men and the excited boy who had landed on these beaches a dozen years before.

And it had, undoubtedly, been Tom Warner's doing. Even the skies, brilliantly blue and cloudless, and the breeze, drifting gently down from the peak of old Misery, and the sea, sparkling blue beneath the glowing sun, seemed to be paying their tribute to the man who had dreamed, and acted, and accomplished.

"He followed his star," Mr. Sweeting said. "And earned himself a fortune and a fame which will endure so long as there is an English-speaking nation left upon this earth. But more than that, my friends. He never forgot who and what he was, and where his duty lay. He was an English gentleman, and he sought always to act as an English gentleman. He was a loving husband and father, and he sought always to act as a loving husband and father. And he was a true Christian, who was ever animated by the spirit of our Lord Jesus Christ, and whose dreams and actions were given power through his desire to propagate the Christian faith."

He was a great man, Edward thought. By any standards. Why stain his memory with hypocrisy? Can greatness, in a worldly sense, ever be separated from harshness and cruelty, from faithlessness and lust? Greatness depends upon success, and success depends upon the possession of all those vices.

But no one present was inclined to dispute even these specious words. The Sieur de Poincy stood on the left of the grave, with his principal officers, among them the two heroes Lafitte and Solange, veterans of the Indian campaign, immediately promoted to commands in the French militia. The Warners were gathered on the other side. A surprisingly small group, for the family and friends of such a man. Lady Warner, her face shrouded beneath a black veil which hung from her broad-brimmed hat, the back of her gown darkening with sweat, for this day she was dressed as she would for court, from gloves to heeled shoes, and no doubt even a corset to hold her straight. Philip Warner stood close, ready to provide her with comfort and support, if need be. His face was solemn. Harry Judge was at his side. Yarico had donned a gown for the occasion, and stood a few feet away, little Tom clutching her hand and gazing into the grave where lay his father. With them was the tall figure of Tony Hilton, in full armor, for he possessed no other clothing, and beside him Brian Connor, short and also very military, together with John Painton.

Edward Warner was by himself, the sun beating down on his bare head, his hands clasped in front. He wore no sword, and his clothes were the homespun of the farmer. The breeze ruffled his hair and plucked at his beard. He knew how many were surreptitiously watching him.

For there remained two other Warners, also standing by themselves. Aline, in a borrowed gown and a borrowed hat, both supplied by her stepmother-in-law, clutching Joan in her arms. Joan had not left her arms since her return.

"And so he died," Mr. Sweeting said. "As a gentleman and a Christian, but more, as the man he was, governor of the Caribee Isles. He perceived his duty, and he went about it without a moment's hesitation, whatever his age, whatever the calls upon his nature to remain in comfort and security. By doing so he put many of us here to shame. And in doing so he died. Yet were even his last moments crowned with success. Can there ever have been a more successful venture than the expedition to Dominica? Have we not now settled accounts with the Caribs once and for all? Is not this island, and all of these islands, now safe for us and our children, aye, and our children's children, to live in? Shall we not build a new nation here, in these tiny paradises? For this must be our charge, my friends, to realize Tom Warner's dream, to watch it unfold, to make it come true. This was the duty he left us, and this is the duty we must perform."

Tom could have spoken those words himself. He might even have written them, for his own epitaph. Because he had spoken them before, many years ago, and watched them turn sour. As these would turn sour. These people had taken no part in the fight against the Caribs, yet they would suffer. Edward had no doubts about that. The Indians were defeated, but they were far from beaten. They had tasted blood against the white men, and now they had a deal to avenge. And were they the only menaces of the Caribee colonies? Were not the Spaniards still the dominating power in this beautiful sea, but waiting their moment to liquidate all intruders? Was there really any possibility of French and English sharing an island as small as St. Kitts for any length of time without again coming to blows? Was there any possibility of the English settlers, even if left strictly to themselves, living in complete harmony, where factions and rivalries sprang up overnight almost like magic?

And supposing all those things were possible, had not Tom himself planted a canker in the very center of the colony, a canker which at present gazed up the hill at the white people solemnly burying their leader, and like the Caribs, watched and listened, and remembered. And prepared to grow.

And yet, foreseeing all these insuperable problems, he must tread the path delineated for him by his father, and count himself fortunate. For Mr. Sweeting was finished, and the grave was being filled, and the people were waiting for him to begin.

"Mr. Sweeting has done my father no more than justice," he said. "He was a great man, and we shall surely miss his leadership and his inspiration. Yet shall we not fail him. St. Kitts has already grown to the proportions of a nation, and I know that it will continue to prosper under the sure governorship of my brother here. My father's dying words were to charge me with the restoration of the Antigua colony. This I mean to do, and immediately. But I will need volunteers, men and women who will be prepared to start their lives afresh, and look for new prosperity."

"We're with you, Captain Warner," Robert Anderson shouted. "We'll be back to St. John's as soon as it can be managed."

"Aye, and you may count on me, Captain Warner," Tom Doughty shouted.

They would not follow him to Dominica, but now the crisis was over they were his men again. And more. There were endless cries of support. He was the hero now. He had fought and won. Time and again. And time and again?

He held up his hands. "I thank you. Mr. Anderson, you'll be in charge of recruiting. I'd ask you to set up a table on the beach. I shall join you within the hour."

"You are to be congratulated, Ned," Tony Hilton said. "Susan will be proud of you."

"And you?"

"I must be back to my rock. We shall never grow rich from the soil, like the Warners, but we pluck a living from the sea."

"And it is more to your taste."

Hilton's mouth split in that tremendous grin. "It was ever so. But you can be sure that if you ever need a stout right arm, and many more besides, you have but to send a sloop north to Tortuga."

"And you will count on me in a similar vein, old friend."

"I never doubted that, Ned. Godspeed."

"And I also must take my leave, Ted." Connor took off his hat. "But I'll pay ye a visit when ye've set yourself up again."

"And meanwhile, Montserrat prospers. We've come a long way from that empty beach, Brian."

"Now, there's a true word. 'Tis a shame poor Paddy O'Reilly never lived to see the day. But he's watching us, ye may be sure. I'll wish ye fortune."

"I, at the least, need say only a temporary farewell," Painton said, "as my next cargo will be bound for Antigua. This was your father's wish."

"And I shall honor his desire, of course," Edward said. "I but wish I could convince myself that what we do is not condemned by God, and does not carry within itself the seeds of our destruction."

Painton laughed, and slapped him on the shoulder. "What, would He condemn us for increasing His congregation? Be sure that all those blacks down there have already been baptized. Believe me, Ned, this is but a necessity, to which you will soon become accustomed. I shall be back in six months."

Edward watched him walking down the hill, behind the slowly dispersing crowd.

"Your day of triumph," Anne Warner said softly. "Well, perhaps you have earned it, Edward. If Hilton and the others are to be believed, and I am prepared to believe them, it was Sir Thomas' last wish that you plant cane in Antigua, and that we supply you with whatever finance is necessary to accomplish that. This also I am prepared to do. But there is an end to the matter. You have chosen to oppose me in every possible way since I came to these islands, and I hold you and your lust after glory and bloodshed as directly responsible for the death of my husband and your father. Take what you wish and go, Edward. We have no wish to see you in St. Kitts again."

Edward bowed. "I would rather hear such a message from the governor, if I may, Lady Warner."

Philip licked his lips. "I endorse Lady Warner's words, Edward. God knows, I have fought with you and for you oft enough, and I have tried to see the world with your eyes. But we are different people, you and I, and you seem to attract at once the support and the anger of the Fates. We would prefer a more settled life here in St. Kitts. And if, as you claim, you possess the finest harbor in the Caribee Isles, then you should not suffer by conducting your own trade with England."

Edward nodded. "Be sure that the Antigua colony will prosper. Nor will I again call on you for assistance, Philip. Yet I am proud to have been associated with you during our battles with the dons. Here is my hand."

Philip hesitated, and then held out his own, and their fingers locked for an instant.

"Now we should be obliged," Anne Warner said, "if you would leave us with our grief. And take your chattels with you."

Their grief. He had not taken half a dozen steps before their heads were close together, discussing the treasures which had fallen into their outstretched hands. Well, let them plot and even prosper. They were behind him now.

And his chattels?

"We go home?" Yarico asked.

"And where would you call home?" he asked.

She gave a shriek of delightful laughter. "Yarico home is War-nah home. And War-nah home is Antigua."

She had even managed to bring a smile back to his face. "Aye, sweetheart. So we will go home. Take the boy, and I will join you on the beach."

Yarico nodded and looked past him. She seemed about to speak, and then thought better of it, grasped little Tom's hand, and went down the hillside.

Edward turned. From these south-facing slopes it was possible to look at Nevis and Montserrat, and the islands beyond. It was even possible to look across the brow of the hillside and catch just a glimpse of Antigua. It should have been possible, had there not been a fluttering skirt in the way. The skirt alone had moved in the past hour, except once, when Joan had cried, and been immediately rocked back to sleep. She had stood this silently while her fate had been decided, the night Tom Warner had returned from England for the last time, and she had waited with equal patience, alone in the forest, until she could seek him, when her people had evacuated the island. Her strength was passive, but it was the greater for that. It was not a strength that word or rumor could tarnish.

And had not Father himself reminded him that he was no less invulnerable, could he but trust himself?

He climbed, and wiped sweat from his brow. But then, it was an uncommonly hot day.

"You must be the most patient woman I have ever known," he said.

"For which I thank God, Captain Warner."

"No doubt we have much to thank Him for, you and I. I'll take the child for the walk. Your arms must be weary."

She hesitated.

"She is my daughter as well," he said gently.

She held out the babe, and her arms fell back to her sides.

"Are you coming?" he asked.

"I would know where, sir."

"My name is Edward, and you are my wife."

"Yet am I walking in as much darkness as the night I first trod this hill."

"Aye," he said. "It can have been the lot of very few women to have been so mistreated twice in their lives, and survived."

"And you condemn me for that?"

He shook his head. "No. I honor you." He held Joan against his shoulder and pointed with his free hand. "These islands, this very sea, are Warner's. And I am of that blessed name, and will hold what we have taken, as will my children. And you are Warner's woman, Aline. Nor can I conceive of any other, living or dead, who could sustain that burden, and that glory, and yet stand erect at the end of it." He held out his hand. "You'll walk with me to the ship, Mrs. Warner."